Dear Readers,

Hooray! I've always wanted these two books to come out in one volume. *Stormy Vows* and *Tempest at Sea* were the first two stories I wrote and they reflected all my hopes and romantic dreams of that period of my life. There's always something special about beginnings—the curiosity, the passion, the excitement. These were also the first of many books to come that had continuing characters. It wasn't intentional, just as it wasn't intentional in my later books. They just became too interesting for me to walk away from them. I hope you find the same joy in reading these stories as I did writing them.

Happy reading!

Iris

Iris

IRIS JOHANSEN

Stormy Vows

Tempest at Sea

BANTAM BOOKS

STORMY VOWS/TEMPEST AT SEA

A Bantam Book / August 2007

Published by Bantam Dell
A Division of Random House, Inc.
New York, New York

These are works of fiction. Names, characters, places, and incidents
either are the product of the author's imagination or are used fictitiously.
Any resemblance to actual persons, living or dead, events, or locales
is entirely coincidental.

Bantam Books and the rooster colophon
are registered trademarks of Random House, Inc.

ISBN 978-0-553-38521-2

These titles were originally published individually by Bantam Books.

Printed in the United States of America
Published simultaneously in Canada

www.bantamdell.com

10 9 8 7 6 5 4 3 2 1
OPM

Stormy Vows

one

BRENNA SLOAN TURNED SLOWLY IN FRONT of the mirror appraising her reflection with critical eyes. A frown creased her forehead and she chewed her lower lip. The simple black wool skirt and white silk blouse had seemed an understated yet chic ensemble when she had chosen it twenty minutes ago, but now she was having second thoughts. Was it perhaps too understated? She definitely wanted to make an impression in what might be the most important interview of her career.

She shrugged and turned away with a sigh. It would just have to do. Her wardrobe wasn't that extensive anyway. She quickly gathered her suede jacket and purse and hurried into the living room.

A chubby golden-haired two-year-old cherub looked up at her from the center of a fiberglass playpen and smiled amiably. He pulled himself up on sturdy legs, looking absurdly adorable in his blue corduroy pants and a T-shirt with LOS ANGELES DODGERS emblazoned across the front.

"We go, Mama?" he asked contentedly. Randy always wanted to go, Brenna thought wryly. For him, every trip was a pleasant adventure, and he certainly had enough of them.

She swung him out of the playpen, planting a kiss on his satin cheek and gathering him close for a quick hug.

"We go," she affirmed. She put him down on the floor while she folded the collapsible playpen, then picked up a canvas bag of toys that was always kept handy. He watched her serenely, familiar with the ritual that was repeated sometimes twice or three times a day.

Tucking the playpen under her arm, she gathered her jacket, purse, and the toy carryall and headed for the door. Randy toddled beside her happily as they left the apartment and crossed to the elevator.

"Mama carry?" he asked. That, too, was part of the ritual. He really didn't expect it, but he tried every time just the same, Brenna thought tenderly.

"No, Randy must walk," Brenna said firmly, as the door to the self-service elevator opened and they entered the small shabby cubicle. The apartment building was only two stories and an elevator was not really necessary, but she blessed it fervently each time she took Randy out. Loaded like a pack horse, as she usually was, she never would have made it without a major catastrophe if she had had to help Randy down the stairs. Besides, Randy loved elevators. It was another magic adventure for him—not as intriguing as the fascinating escalators in the department stores, but interesting all the same.

The elevator door opened, and she shepherded Randy out and down the hall to the manager's apartment. Randy knew the way well and nodded with satisfaction as they paused before the door.

"Auntie Viv," he said placidly, knowing that behind the door was another disciple who provided toys, cookies, and caresses.

"Yes, sweetheart," Brenna said. "She's going to watch you while mama goes out." She rang the bell.

"Come in, Brenna," Vivian Barlow called, and when Brenna and Randy entered, she waved a freshly manicured hand from where she was sitting on an early American couch, applying a coat of clear gloss to her nails. "Sorry, love," she said with an absent smile. "I know you're in a bit of a hurry, but would you mind getting Randy settled before you leave. I have a photography session later on this afternoon, and my polish isn't dry yet."

"Another dishwashing detergent commercial?" Brenna asked, as she unfolded the collapsible playpen and set it up swiftly.

Vivian Barlow nodded her sleekly coiffed gray head. "Yep," she drawled with eyebrows raised wryly. "One of those comparison jobs, where the granddaughter loses to grandma in the beautiful hands sweepstakes." She simpered coyly. "And all because I've washed my china all my born days with antiscum."

"Antiscum!" Brenna laughed.

"Well, it's something like that," Vivian said vaguely. She got briskly to her feet, strolled over to where Randy was sitting on the floor, and kissed him on the top of his head. "How are you, slugger?" she asked fondly. She was an ardent baseball fan, and it was she who had gifted Randy with the Dodger T-shirt. In her early sixties, Vivian Barlow was attractive, well dressed, and beautifully preserved. She also had the warmest smile and the most humorous gray eyes Brenna had ever seen.

A short time after she had become friends with her ultramodern landlady, Brenna had learned that Vivian had been divorced twice and widowed once. In a moment of confidence Vivian had confessed wistfully, "I've always been afraid of missing something along the way, so I reach out and grab." She'd made a face. "I've made some pretty dumb grabs in my time." Vivian had been an actress all her adult life, playing bit parts and walk-ons in hundreds of films and stage productions. When husband number three died and left her a small apartment complex and an adequate income, she had retired, only to find herself completely bored. It wasn't long before she discovered the perfect outlet for her energy in the world of television commercials. She was much in demand these days in the role of the modern older woman who was the antithesis of the crochety granny figures of the past.

"I still think you'd be perfect for shampoo and soap commercials," Vivian said critically. "You have a certain dryad look. It's as though you grew up in some forest glade."

She looked appraisingly at Brenna who was putting Randy's favorite toys in the playpen before lifting him into the center of the mat. Brenna straightened and a grin lit up her face with breathtaking poignancy.

"The John Harris Memorial Home was not precisely a sylvan glade," she said dryly. On the contrary, the orphanage where she had grown up had no time for such foolishness as nymphs and dryads, she thought wistfully.

Vivian looked up sharply, but made no comment.

"You're quite dressed up today," she said.

Brenna didn't look at her as she gathered up her jacket and purse. "I have an audition," she said, almost beneath her breath.

"An audition? Why didn't you tell me?" Vivian asked delightedly. "Where is it? Tell me all about it."

"There isn't much to tell," Brenna said with feigned casualness. "Charles arranged for me to try out for a part in a picture a former pupil of his is producing. It probably won't come to anything."

"I didn't know that Charles had any contacts in films," Vivian said speculatively. "Who is it?"

Brenna drew a deep breath and turned to look at her friend, revealing the tenseness in her face. "Michael Donovan."

Vivian's brows shot up, and she gave a low soundless whistle. "Michael Donovan! What a break for you."

Everyone in films knew of Michael Donovan. Only in his late thirties, he was already a legend. He had shot across the Hollywood firmament like a fiery comet. He was a writer-director without equal, and had recently turned to producing his own films with similar success. He had directed three of the biggest money-making films of all time, and as he had put up the money for two of them, he had become a multimillionaire from the proceeds. He had invested a portion of that wealth in his own film colony in southern Oregon, where he had gathered the best talents in film-making. His image had grown to such proportions that even his name gave off a Midas-like glitter.

Brenna shrugged. "It's only an audition. I'm to read for the casting director, Josh Hernandez." Her composure cracked, and she closed her eyes and took a deep breath. "Oh, Vivian, I'm so nervous."

Vivian patted her on the shoulder. "You'll do just fine," she said bracingly. "You're good, Brenna, really good."

"There are hundreds of talented actresses in this town," Brenna said gloomily. "And most of them are out of work."

Vivian nodded sympathetically. "It's a competitive business," she said. "I doubt you would even make it past the first receptionist at Donovan's casting office without a personal introduction. I had no idea Charles knew Michael Donovan."

"Neither did I," Brenna replied. "I don't think he wanted to trade on the association. That's why it's so important that I do well at the reading. I can't let him down after he went to the trouble of asking for a special favor from Mr. Donovan."

She moistened her lips nervously, and then straightened her shoulders. "Well, they can only turn me down," she said with bravado. She flashed a quick smile at the older woman. "Wish me luck?"

"Break a leg, Brenna," Vivian said.

Giving a quick kiss on the top of Randy's silky head, Brenna left.

It was only as she was maneuvering her ancient gray Honda out of the apartment complex parking lot that she allowed her thoughts to turn back to the interview ahead.

When Charles had told her what he had arranged for her and handed her the script for *Wild Heritage*, she had been stunned. Never in her wildest dreams had she imagined a chance to audition for Donovan. Charles had been almost childishly pleased at her surprise. He explained gruffly that Donovan had been a student of his quite some years before and they still kept in casual contact.

"When I read that Michael had bought the book *Wild Heritage*, I knew you'd be perfect for Angie," he said simply. He patted her on the shoulder awkwardly. "Do me proud, Brenna."

Wild Heritage centered around the character of Angie Linden, a complex young woman struggling to overcome her promiscuous past. It had everything: pathos, humor, and an underlying hint of tragedy. Any actress would give her eyeteeth for the role, and Brenna was frankly skeptical of such a plum being awarded to an unknown. If Charles Wilkes had not been so insistent, she wouldn't have even consented to go for the reading. But she could not disappoint him after all he had done for her.

The address Charles had given her was in downtown Los Angeles, and when she located it, she was surprised to find it was a modest two-story brick building with a discreet plaque reading DONOVAN ENTERPRISES LTD. Rather an unimposing establishment for a man of Donovan's reputed flamboyance, she thought, as she parked in front of the building. After putting coins in the meter, she entered the swinging glass doors. A smiling receptionist directed her to Studio B on the second floor.

Studio B was actually a small theater with a raised stage and several rows of padded velvet seats. Two seats near the door were occupied by a short, dark-haired man in his thirties and a casually dressed red-haired woman of about her own age. The man rose to his feet as she entered, picking up a clipboard from the seat next to him.

"Miss Sloan?" His smile was quick, charging his thin, clever face with warmth. "Josh Hernandez, and this is my assistant, Billie Perkins." The red-haired woman smiled in acknowledgment of Brenna's nod. "It's a pleasure to meet you."

Brenna relaxed slightly, and drew a deep breath of relief. Perhaps it wouldn't be so bad after all. Josh Hernandez was far from the cigar-smoking, beady-eyed executive of her nervous imagination.

A smile lit her face, and Josh Hernandez caught his breath involuntarily. God, he hadn't seen a smile like that since Audrey Hepburn.

"I'm very happy to meet you, Mr. Hernandez," she said shyly. Then looking around the tiny theater, "This isn't at all what I expected."

He grinned and shrugged. "If you get through this intact, you still have to take a screen test. But Mr. Donovan prefers that the first audition take place here. He thinks the stage highlights the actor, and lets us better appraise the body movements."

"Mr. Donovan appears to be a man of original ideas," Brenna said lightly.

"He is indeed, Miss Sloan," Josh Hernandez said ruefully. "He is indeed." He looked down at the clipboard and detached a form. "If you will fill this out, we'll get on with the actual audition."

The audition form was quite short, and in a few minutes she had completed it and returned it to Hernandez.

He gestured to the stage casually. "When you're ready," he said easily.

Brenna mounted the four steps at the side of the stage, and moved to center stage. Drawing a deep breath to still the quivering butterflies, she asked quietly. "Where do you want me to begin?"

"Start with Angie's monologue on page three, scene two," Hernandez said. "Billie will read Joe."

Brenna began to read, and, as usual, once she became involved with the character, she forgot everything else. All nervous apprehension vanished in her absorption with Angie Linden. She actually began to enjoy herself, and was almost disappointed when Hernandez called a halt to the reading. She knew with a confident thrill that it had been a good audition. She had done well.

Hernandez came up the stairs two at a time, a broad grin on his dark face. "A really great job, Miss Sloan!"

She looked up at him hopefully, her face glowing. "You like it?" she asked breathlessly. Hernandez stared down into her face bemusedly. "Damn, if you photograph well, you'll be a natural." Then he added quickly, "The final decision isn't mine, of course. But if I have anything to say about it, you have the role."

"Hold it, Josh!"

They both looked with startled eyes toward the door.

The red-haired man leaning indolently against the doorjamb was dressed casually in faded jeans and a cream-colored shirt with sleeves rolled to the elbow. Despite the casualness of his dress, there was no mistaking his identity. Though Michael Donovan was militantly vigilant of his privacy, he was excellent copy, and newspaper photos of him appeared on occasion. Once seen, he couldn't be forgotten.

Brenna's breath caught in her throat at the explosive impact of the man. He was not at all handsome, she thought dazedly, and then was amazed that she had noticed because Michael Donovan made conventional observations unimportant. His blunt, rough-hewn features carried a power all their own, and the piercing blue of his eyes cut through what wasn't essential with the force of a lightning bolt. The air around him seemed to crackle with the strength and vitality of his personality. The ma-hogany hair and eyebrows, and the tall muscular body were dwarfed by the sheer overpowering virility that emanated from the man.

He moved with lithe swiftness past a dazzled Billie Perkins, to mount the steps and cross to stand before Brenna and Hernandez.

At close range, he was even more intimidating, and Brenna stepped back instinctively, a fact that Donovan noted with narrowed eyes. His mouth twisted cynically as he turned to Hernandez. "I believe you're slipping, Josh," he said smoothly. "It's not like you to make even a tentative commitment without consulting me. Isn't your usual policy, Don't call us, we'll call you?" His eyes traveled intimately from the top of Brenna's glossy head to the delicate bones of her ankles. "It would take something pretty world-shaking to budge you from your standard procedure."

Hernandez was looking at Donovan with dark, puzzled eyes. "There was no commitment, Mr. Donovan," he said quietly. "I do plead guilty to enthusiasm. She gave a damn good reading."

Donovan nodded casually. "She was good, I caught the last half."

Brenna's eyes brightened as they flew to Donovan's face. His gaze had never left her expressive face, and he caught the look of eager expectancy radiating from her. He said briskly, "There's no use raising your hopes, Miss Sloan. You won't do for the role."

The soft doe eyes widened with shock at the cruel bluntness of his statement. "But why?" she asked in bewilderment. "You said I was good."

Donovan had taken the clipboard from Hernandez and was swiftly perusing the information on the personnel sheet. "You were good," he said coolly. "That doesn't mean you are suited for the role of Angie. Any number of actresses could have given an equally convincing reading."

Hernandez opened his mouth as if to protest, but, at a lightning glance from Donovan, he subsided with a shrug.

Donovan continued, "What we need for Angie is someone with more experience."

"Professional experience?" Brenna asked, thinking she understood. Though Donovan didn't have the reputation of playing it safe by hiring box office draws, it was logical that he would not want to gamble a multimillion-dollar movie on an unknown.

But Donovan was shaking his head. "I don't give a damn about professional experience," he said swiftly. "I'm talking about personal experience. You gave a nice surface reading, but I want more than that for Angie. I want the actress who plays the part to reach down and bring up real gut feelings." He gestured toward the clipboard in his hand. "You're only twenty, and you've had no formal theatrical training, so perhaps you're unfamiliar with Stanislavski and sense memory?"

"Stanislavski? Method acting?" she asked dazedly.

"Precisely. I forgot for a moment that you are a protégée of Wilkes'. You're aware that method acting endorses using your own emotions and experiences as the basis for your performance. Angie Linden is a woman who has lived life to the fullest, despite her youth. She's had lovers by the score, and has suffered disillusionment and cruelty." His eyes lingered on her face. "You look as if you still have the morning dew on you, Miss Sloan," he said. "Angie Linden is definitely midnight lace and French perfume."

Brenna could feel a slow anger beginning to build. "Let me understand you, Mr. Donovan," she said carefully. "It's not because I'm not a good enough actress to play the part. You're refusing to give me the role because I don't have a torrid past to draw on for Angie's character?"

His vivid blue eyes were curiously watchful. "That's quite right," he said silkily. "I'm sure you would do very well in ingenue or Juliet roles, Miss Sloan."

"That's the most ridiculous thing I've ever heard in my life," she said flatly, ignoring Hernandez' hastily drawn breath at her insolence. Her anger had leaped to full blaze, and the usual limpid brown eyes were sparkling with feeling. In just a few minutes, she had been moved from hope to bewilderment to disappointment by this arrogant dictator, and now he was denying her a chance that might mean her whole future . . . and denying it on the flimsiest pretext imaginable!

"You think so?" Donovan asked idly, his eyes still observing her as if she were an interesting new specimen at the zoo. "I take it you don't agree with Stanislavski, Miss Sloan?"

"An actress can work with any number of tools that help her perfect a characterization. Theories, like method acting and sense memory, are just that—tools. But they are far from the only tools, if you're to be any good at all. A creative imagination, sensitivity, and just plain hard work are much more important. To subscribe so fanatically to one aspect of a complex whole is utterly absurd." She tossed her hair back from her face, and said emphatically, "To deny me the part because you think I lack sex appeal is totally and completely asinine."

Donovan's eyes were amused as they moved over her lazily, causing a flood of heat to envelope her body. "I never said you lacked sex appeal. Merely experience." Blue devils gleamed in his eyes as he continued softly. "A lack that I would be more than happy to supply."

She could feel the blood rush to her face in a burning blush that was due as much to anger as embarrassment. The knowledge that he was toying with her increased her rage. Donovan's affairs were legion. He was reputedly as sexually active as a tomcat, and with some of the most sophisticated and beautiful women in the world, if the gossip columns were correct. The possibility that he would find a twenty-year-old "ingenue-type" attractive was ludicrous. No, he was merely revenging himself for the insults she had hurled at him by teasing her as a cat would a mouse.

"I don't deserve that," she said quietly, lifting her chin defiantly. "I know you're annoyed with me, but don't descend to that sexist casting couch routine to put me in my place, Mr. Donovan. I have a valid argument and I'm sorry you're too blind and pigheaded to appreciate it." She turned and stalked majestically off the stage, leaving the two men staring after her. She paused at the door, and turned to meet Donovan's narrowed eyes. "You're wrong, Michael Donovan," she said with serene conviction. "I could have made something very special out of Angie Linden." Her mouth twisted wryly. "And if my memory serves, Juliet was a very sexy lady," she said softly. "So you're wrong there, too." She strode from the theater.

two

A WHITE CORE OF ANGER BURNED LIKE A
piece of molten steel in Brenna as she went through the motions
of driving home, picking up Randy from Vivian's, and taking
him back to their apartment. Once home, Brenna put Randy
down for his afternoon nap. She scrupulously removed all the
toys from his bed, knowing that if there was even one distrac-
tion, Randy would find it and refuse to go to sleep. She ignored
his pleading eyes, turned him over on his stomach, tucked his
blanket around him and, patted his round bottom. "Sleep," she
said firmly, and closed the door decisively behind her.

She leaned wearily against the door, feeling as if the violent
emotions of the morning had savaged her and left her weak and
drained. She moved slowly to the couch, and curled up in the
corner, leaning her head on the arm. Unexpectedly a drop of
moisture coursed down her cheek, and she brushed it aside angrily. Tears? No, dammit, she wouldn't cry. She wouldn't give
Michael Donovan the satisfaction of upsetting her that much.
She was tougher than that. Hadn't Janine said that, she thought
suddenly, her throat tightening. She could remember her sister
kneeling beside her bed, her ash-blond hair wild around her
white face, tears streaming down her cheeks. "You're strong,

Brenna," Janine had gasped. "You've always been stronger than me, even though I'm older. Help me, Brenna. Help me!"

Brenna shook her head, her eyes filling helplessly at the poignant memory. "Damn you, Michael Donovan," she whispered huskily, her hands balling into fists. Usually she could keep the memories at bay with her customary determination, blocking out the still raw emotions that had torn her apart and left her defenseless in their aftermath. Now they came flooding back, tumbling over each other in a chaotic eruption brought on by her distressing experience with Donovan.

Janine had been right: Brenna had always been tougher than her older sister, though heaven knows how much was integral, and how much a result of her upbringing in the orphanage that had been the only home they had known since Brenna was four and Janine eight. Their father had deserted their mother shortly after Brenna was born, and, as their mother had had to work long hours to support the three of them, she had not had the time to give her younger child the love and attention she had lavished on Janine. Consequently, when their mother died of pneumonia shortly after Brenna's fourth birthday, Brenna was not as devastated as she might have been. Janine, on the other hand, had been struck down by the second catastrophic blow of her young life, and she never quite recovered. They had been sent to the John Harris Memorial Home when an investigation by the welfare department had uncovered no relatives. Brenna had adjusted quickly to her new circumstances, but Janine had retreated behind a wall of shyness, developing a finely balanced sensitivity that shut away the present, letting in only the familiar figures of the past. Always an imaginative child, she lived in a world of her own making, and clung to Brenna with an almost fanatic need and devotion.

When she had been released from the home at seventeen, Janine had obtained a secretarial position at Chadeaux Wineries in Los Angeles. She had worked hard, and soon had been promoted to the executive offices. When she rented her own apartment, she persuaded the home to release fifteen-year-old Brenna in her custody. Brenna had been as happy as Janine at the move. Though not dependent on her sister for affection, she loved the fragile Janine with a deep, fierce protectiveness that was a result of fighting a hundred battles in her defense with the other children at the home.

That first year had been full of contentment and independence, with Brenna continuing her education at a local high school and becoming increasingly involved in drama classes and high school plays. Absorbed with her first taste of the exhilarating art of acting, she had not noticed, at first, Janine's own infatuation with Paul Chadeaux, the heir apparent to the Chadeaux Wineries. She had met the sleek blond young man when he had picked up Janine for dates, but he had not really registered other than causing her to wonder absently what on earth Janine saw in him. Then, with a knowledge beyond her years, Brenna realized he had an assurance that would inevitably attract an insecure girl like Janine. His aura could be obtained only from growing up with money, the right schools, and a solid family background.

Janine continued to see Paul Chadeaux, and Brenna noted the transformation that manifested itself in her delicate sister. Janine glowed with an almost incandescent radiance, hopelessly infatuated with the man. When that realization came home to her, Brenna began to watch Chadeaux with critical eyes and what she saw filled her with alarm. Paul Chadeaux treated her sister with a selfish unconcern that made Brenna react with fierce indignation. He broke dates without notice, and often spoke to Janine with such impatient cruelty that Brenna wanted to wring his neck. She knew better than to speak to Janine. Paul could do no wrong in her eyes. So she watched helplessly while Janine continued blindly on her path to destruction.

Janine was almost three months pregnant when she confided

in Brenna. She had been childishly happy, as she prepared to go out that night with Chadeaux. Brenna's face had whitened with shock when Janine confessed quite simply that she was pregnant with Chadeaux's child. Brenna had been doing her homework on one of the twin beds, idly watching as Janine put on her makeup at the vanity. Janine had dropped the information into the conversation almost casually.

"Does he know?" Brenna asked numbly.

A secret smile curved Janine's mouth as she brushed her hair slowly. "Not yet," she said dreamily. "I've just found out for sure today. But he'll be glad. I know he will. It'll just mean we'll be married sooner than we expected."

"He's asked you to marry him?" Brenna asked with relief. Perhaps Chadeaux wasn't the swine she suspected.

"Of course he has," Janine said serenely. "There are just some minor problems with his family. Paul's just been waiting for the right time to tell them."

"How long have you been engaged?" Brenna asked grimly.

"About four months," Janine said vaguely, her eyes taking on a glow that lit up her delicate features. "A baby, Brenna!" she said breathlessly. "I've always wanted someone of my very own, and now I'm going to have a husband and a baby. It seems too good to be true."

It seemed too good to be true to Brenna, also, but she couldn't puncture the lovely dream world that her sister was living in. "That's wonderful, Janine," she said gently.

"I'm going to tell Paul tonight," Janine said eagerly. "I can hardly wait."

Brenna watched her leave that night with the feeling of helplessness that had plagued her sharpened to a positive dread.

Janine had awakened her in the early hours of the morning, her face a mask of suffering, almost hysterical with grief, pleading with Brenna to help her.

"I was wrong, Brenna," Janine had sobbed. "He doesn't care

anything about me." Her eyes were wide, as if she were in shock. "He wants to kill my baby. He wants me to get an abortion."

Brenna had cradled Janine's slender body, and rocked her in an agony of sympathy. "It'll be all right, honey," she had whispered huskily.

"He doesn't want to see me anymore," Janine had cried, her eyes wild. "He said I was a stupid fool not to protect myself. He said if I caused any trouble; he'd say the baby wasn't his . . . that I should get rid of 'the little bastard.' " She shuddered convulsively.

Brenna felt a rage so terrible, that if Chadeaux had been in the room she would have killed him. "Forget him, Janine," she'd said fiercely. "He's not worth another thought."

"He's so evil," Janine had said with childlike wonder, "I've never known anyone so evil. He wants to kill my baby. I can't let him do that, Brenna."

"No, I know you can't, honey," she'd said slowly, a chill running through her at the pathetic expression on Janine's face. Always balanced on the thin edge of reality, had this blow been too much for her? "We'll work something out. I promise you. Why don't you go to bed now?"

Janine rose obediently to her feet. "You're so strong, Brenna. You'll help me keep my baby."

In the following months, the thought of the child growing inside her seemed to be the only thing that kept Janine from a complete breakdown. It would have been impossible for her to continue at Chadeaux Wineries, so Brenna insisted that Janine quit her job, and let Brenna assume the burden of responsibility for both of them. Janine obeyed with the docility of a child, and didn't even object when Brenna dropped out of school, and took a job in a neighborhood pharmacy. Brenna had some clerical skills that probably would have paid better, but it would have meant searching further afield for a job and leaving Janine alone too long.

Janine's obsession that Paul would harm her child continued. No amount of gentle persuasion on Brenna's part could convince her that Chadeaux would not suddenly appear and take the child away from her.

It was only after receiving a bill from the prenatal clinic in Janine's eighth month of pregnancy that Brenna realized the full extent of her sister's fear. The bill was for services to Brenna Sloan *not* Janine Sloan. When confronted with the bill, Janine had smiled tranquilly. "I had to do it, Brenna," she'd said calmly. "It's the only way to protect my baby. I've thought it all out. I've been very clever."

"What have you done, Janine?" Brenna had asked tiredly. "Why is my name on this bill?"

Janine had leaned forward and whispered confidentially, "Don't you see, we're going to pretend the baby is yours. Then Paul will have no legal right to the baby. It'll be your name on the birth certificate as the mother, not mine."

"Janine, it won't work," Brenna had said hopelessly, knowing her protests would do no good.

"Of course it will," Janine had insisted serenely. "You'll see, Brenna. Everyone will think the baby's yours." Her eyes clouded. "But the baby will really be mine, you know," she had said jealously. "It's just pretend, like when we were children. You won't try to take my child away from me too?"

Tears had closed her throat as Brenna leaned forward to stroke her sister's thin cheek. "No, it will be just pretend, Love," she'd said huskily.

Janine had never lived to enjoy her baby. Three days after giving birth to Randy, she had died of complications.

An indignant yell caused Brenna to sit bolt upright on the couch, dabbing quickly at her eyes. She was on her feet and into the other room with lithe swiftness. Randy broke off a yell and stretched out his arms invitingly. "Mama carry?" he wheedled, smiling angelically.

"Some nap, young man," Brenna said sternly. She lifted him from the bed and held him close for a brief moment. He felt so good.

"Too tight, Mama," he protested, wriggling vigorously.

In the two years since Janine's death she had never tried to deny the natural assumption that she was Randy's mother. Somehow she had felt that she owed it to Janine that Randy have a real mother of his own, not just a loving aunt. The only people she cared about, Vivian Barlow and Charles Wilkes, had tactfully avoided probing her relationship with Randy. As for the others, she couldn't care less what they thought. It had not taken her long to find that the suggestion that she was an unwed mother still carried a stigma even in these "liberal" times. Brenna's mouth curved bitterly. After two years of being looked upon as a fallen woman, it was ironic that she should lose her greatest career opportunity to date because Donovan had judged her to be too innocent.

Charles Wilkes was getting out of his Volkswagon Rabbit when she pulled into the parking lot at the rear of the theater that evening. He smiled broadly and waved, as she parked in the spot next to him and turned off the ignition.

In his late fifties, Wilkes looked older than his years. His snow-white hair, gray-white beard, and rotund figure made him look like an intellectual Santa Claus. This look was augmented by the gray tweed suit and horn-rimmed glasses perched on his nose.

He was beside her in a moment, and took the sleeping Randy from her as she opened the door of the Honda. He handled the baby with practiced ease, wrapping the blanket more tightly around the small body.

He stood there, his face as eager as a child's.

"How did it go?" he whispered over Randy's head.

She made a face, as she opened the rear door and pulled out Randy's playpen. "It was a complete disaster," she said gloomily. "The *Titanic* was a success story in comparison."

Profound disappointment flooded Wilkes' face. "Hernandez didn't like your reading?" he asked, as they walked toward the stage door.

"Mr. Hernandez liked it," Brenna said caustically. "It was your old pupil that found me wanting."

"Michael was there?" Charles asked incredulously, a pleased smile on his face. "It was kind of him to give the audition his personal attention."

"I assure you I would have been a thousand times more fortunate if he hadn't been so 'kind.'" Brenna bit her lip, then confessed miserably, "I'm sorry, Charles. I let you down. I not only fouled up my chance of a part, but I lost my temper with Mr. Donovan."

A grin creased his face, making him look more cherubic than ever. "Don't worry, Brenna," he said genially. "I imagine it was an interesting experience for Michael. He's so used to being kowtowed to these days, it must have been quite refreshing to have someone stand up to him."

"I'm glad you think so," Brenna said dryly. "Somehow I don't think he felt the same way."

They had reached the backstage door and Charles deftly balanced Randy on one arm while he held the heavy metal door open for Brenna.

The Rialto was actually an old renovated movie house, one of many small neighborhood theaters that had closed after the advent of television. It had remained a boarded-up derelict until Wilkes joyously discovered it among the property listings of a small real estate company. With boundless enthusiasm, he had enlisted the aid of the students of his classes at the university to make the theater a habitable home for his own community theater. Brenna had learned later that Charles had been amazingly fortunate in his find. Los Angeles was the possessor of innumerable amateur theater groups looking for a showcase for their talents in the optimistic hope that one magic night a talent scout or agent would discover them. Shabby and antiquated as the Rialto was, it had become dearly familiar to Brenna in the last two years.

The play they were rehearsing now was an original work of one of Charles' more talented students. Brenna's role was small but important to the production. After playing the lead in the last play, she was enjoying the lighter responsibility that was hers in this charming romantic comedy.

That is, she would have enjoyed it, but for the scene she was forced to do with Blake Conroy. The scene would have been a relatively simple one if she had not had to contend with Conroy's sophomoric shenanigans. In her less irritable moments she could see why Charles had chosen Conroy for the romantic lead. He was an adequate actor, and he certainly looked the part. His bronze curly hair and tall muscular body, together with a rather dashing moustache, made him look as if he had just stepped out of a cigarette commercial. In all truth, he had done just that. He had been a popular and well-paid model before an enterprising theatrical agent convinced him that he was wasted in magazines, and his true métier was stage and screen. He must have been extremely easy to persuade for Brenna found him to be the most egotistical and smugly self-satisfied man she had ever met. Added to that, he was convinced that he was God's gift to women, and spent a good portion of every romantic scene attempting to fondle any available portion of her anatomy that came under his rather moist, fumbling hands.

Tonight was no exception, and when she had unobtrusively moved his hand from her buttocks to her waist for the third time, she was tempted to dig her nails into his well-manicured hand. With some difficulty, she managed to finish the scene and walked into the wings followed closely by Conroy.

When she was far enough from the stage to avoid disturbing the action, she whirled and faced Conroy. Her blazing eyes caused his smug smile to fade. "I've warned you before, Blake," she said tightly. "I won't be handled by you. You either keep your hands to yourself or I'll put some marks on that pretty face of yours." She curved her hand into a claw to demonstrate her sincerity.

A flicker of unease passed over Conroy's face, before his inherent conceit discounted her threat. "I like a girl with spirit," he said smugly, reaching out a hand to cup her shoulder.

A line straight out of a John Wayne movie, she thought with exasperation, slapping his hand aside. "You'll see a violent demonstration of my 'spirit' if you don't listen to me, Blake," she said grimly. "I mean what I say."

"You don't have to pretend with me, Brenna," he said confidently, taking a step closer. "I know what a hot little number like you needs. Why don't I drive you home after rehearsal? You live alone, don't you?"

"No, I don't live alone," she said through her teeth. "I live with my son."

"Oh, the kid." Conroy shrugged. "We'll just tuck him into bed." An intimate smile curved his mouth. "And then I'll tuck you into bed."

"I'm afraid Miss Sloan will be too busy to accommodate you tonight, Conroy."

Brenna froze with shock as she turned to see Michael Donovan strolling casually toward them. He was dressed in a navy blue shirt and slacks and should not have been impressive, but to Brenna's annoyance, he seemed to make his surroundings shrink, as if he were draining their identity from them. Certainly, Blake Conroy became insipid in comparison.

"What are you doing here, Mr. Donovan?" she asked bitterly. "Slumming?"

"We didn't finish our chat this morning, Miss Sloan," Donovan said coolly. "I dislike leaving loose ends."

"I thought we both made our positions quite clear," Brenna replied. "I know I did."

Conroy was listening to the exchange with increasing irritation. He never liked losing the limelight, particularly when he was smugly certain he was making headway. "Can't you see the lady isn't interested?" he drawled. "Why don't you go away?"

Donovan gave him a razor sharp glance that appraised and then dismissed him as though he didn't exist.

"Where can we go to talk?" he asked Brenna tersely. "Charles said you were through for the night. Why don't I take you out for a drink?"

"Now, see here," Conroy protested, moving a step closer to Brenna and taking her arm. "Brenna and I were about to leave."

"I heard," Donovan said shortly. "Something about tucking her into bed, wasn't it?" He smiled mirthlessly. "Forget it, Conroy. In fact, it might be a good idea if you forget about Miss Sloan entirely. She won't have time for you anymore."

"She'll be too busy with you, I suppose," Conroy said sarcastically.

"Right." Donovan nodded, his eyes amused. "You might say, I intend to fully occupy Miss Sloan from now on."

Even Conroy wasn't too dense to catch the double-entendre in Donovan's statement. An ugly sneer twisted his face as he glanced at Brenna's scarlet cheeks. "That's up to the lady, isn't it? Brenna doesn't seem too eager to take you up on your offer." His hand caressed her arm. "How about it, beautiful?"

Brenna gritted her teeth in exasperation. She was tempted to use Conroy as a bulwark against the domineering tactics of Michael Donovan. Yet she knew if she offered any encouragement to Blake, he would make himself more obnoxious than ever.

"Oh, go away, Blake!" she said wearily, running her fingers through her hair.

Donovan chuckled. Reaching out, he took Conroy's hand from Brenna's arm and pulled her closer to his side. She shot him a glance of acute dislike that he ignored urbanely. "Yes, do go away, Blake," he repeated mildly.

Conroy gave a smothered curse, and his look at Brenna was positively lethal. He stalked off, every line of his body expressing his outrage.

"That's the best acting he's done tonight," Donovan said idly.

"You were watching?" Brenna asked, surprised.

Donovan nodded. "I wanted to talk to Charles," he said. "And I wanted to see you perform again. Two birds with one stone, so to speak."

Brenna looked at him skeptically. "You came to see me?" she questioned doubtfully. "That's rather hard to believe."

"I'm a busy man, Miss Sloan," he said curtly. "I don't have time to play games. Now, how about that drink?"

She shook her head wearily. "It's been a long day, Mr. Donovan, and I'm tired." She met his eyes steadily, and for a brief moment lost the thread of what she wanted to say as she was caught up by the sheer magnetism of the man. She took a deep breath and forced herself to look away. "You see, I'm afraid I don't believe you," she said defiantly. "I think you do enjoy playing games. We both know you gave Blake Conroy a completely wrong impression for some reason of your own. You couldn't possibly be interested in me. I'm not your type."

Donovan cocked one eyebrow, his blue eyes narrowed. "Please go on, Miss Sloan," he drawled softly. "I'd be delighted to discover what you judge to be my type of woman."

She shrugged. "Everyone knows that your little playmates are always sophisticated women of the world. I'm sure a 'Juliet type' like me would bore you to tears in no time," she said sarcastically.

Donovan smiled sensually, and, reaching out, ran his hand caressingly along the curve of her cheek. She gasped at the sensation that brought her body to tingling life. A gleam of triumph lit his eyes, as though her reaction gave him a tigerish pleasure.

"Perhaps I'm bored with my usual women," he suggested silkily. "It was you who said Juliet was a sexy lady. Perhaps I would find it interesting to explore that premise more thoroughly."

She stepped back hurriedly, and he let her go, his hand leaving her face reluctantly. Even when he was no longer touching her she could still feel the tug of his overpowering virility. She was tempted to move closer to him, so that she might again feel that tingling aliveness she had never known before.

She forced her voice to coolness. "I don't find that very likely. I think you came here tonight to soothe Charles' feelings for rejecting his protégée, but when you saw me again, you couldn't resist the opportunity to try to get a little of your own back for the insults I tossed at you this afternoon."

There was a flicker of anger behind the blue eyes, and his mouth tightened fractionally. "So young to be so cynical," he said dryly. "Is it only me, or do you hate all men?"

"I don't hate men," Brenna said quietly. "I just don't find them fair or trustworthy where women are concerned."

"Interesting," Donovan said briefly, his eyes keen. She had the odd impression that those calculating eyes had observed, analyzed, and stored up for future use every facet of her physical and mental faculties.

"In this case, you're wrong," he said casually, reaching into a back pocket to draw out a folded, wrinkled manuscript. He held it out to her. "I came to give you this."

She took the script curiously. Printed in large letters on the title page was *Forgotten Moment*. She looked up, startled.

"I want you for the role of Mary Durney," Donovan said quietly. "Charles said you were a quick study."

Brenna nodded dazedly, looking down at the script.

"You'll have to be," Donovan said grimly. "I want you ready for filming in three days."

She looked at him. "I don't understand," she said in confusion. "The trade papers said production started on *Forgotten Moment* two months ago. Mary Durney was being played by some Broadway actress."

"She's not working out. I'm replacing her," Donovan said.

Brenna shivered at the ruthlessness in his voice. "Just like that?" she asked faintly.

"Just like that," he said implacably. He went on, "Mary Durney is a supporting role, but I think you'll find her worthwhile. Played right, she could steal the film."

"Why me?" Brenna asked bluntly.

"Because you're right for her," Donovan said simply. "When Charles asked me to audition you for Angie, he said you had a quality that grabbed a person by the throat and didn't let go."

"You make me sound like a boa constrictor," Brenna said wryly.

"I have a hunch you can be just as lethal to a man," he said lightly, before his tone became coolly businesslike again. "He was right: You have a quality I want. But not for Angie. For Mary Durney."

"For such a devoted mother, you're being shockingly neglectful, Brenna," Blake Conroy said nastily. She had been so involved with Michael Donovan's astounding proposal that she hadn't noticed Conroy's approach. Conroy sauntered over to her, holding a tousled and drowsy Randy, who looked as if he had been snatched up from a deep sleep. He probably had, Brenna thought furiously. She brought Randy to almost all the rehearsals. He played or slept in his playpen in the wings. The cast had adopted him; Conroy was the one person who never had time for Randy. He was obviously hoping to use the baby now in some ploy to get back at her for her rejection this evening. She snatched Randy from him, cuddling the warm, sturdy body protectively.

Conroy surveyed her with sly satisfaction before turning to Donovan, who had gone strangely still. "Touching isn't it?" he drawled caustically. "I thought you'd better realize what you're letting yourself in for before committing yourself. It's a package deal with Brenna, you know. She's quite boringly obsessed with that kid of hers." With a mocking salute, he strolled away, eminently well satisfied with himself.

Michael Donovan's face was expressionless as he asked slowly. "The child is yours?"

"My name's on his birth certificate," Brenna said flippantly. She felt strangely vulnerable before those penetrating eyes. She hugged Randy closer, until he gave a sleepy little grunt.

"And who else's name is on that birth certificate, Brenna?" Donovan asked softly, his blue eyes gleaming fiercely. "Who is the father?"

She could see that, for some reason, he was in a white hot rage. She wondered briefly if he objected to his actresses having family commitments.

"There's no other name on Randy's birth certificate," she said coolly. "It's not required when the child's parents aren't married."

"How old is he?" Donovan asked hoarsely.

"Two," Brenna answered.

"My God, you started young, didn't you?" he asked bitterly. "You must have been barely eighteen when you gave birth to him."

Brenna lifted her head defiantly. "Perhaps you should have given me the role of Angie after all," she said sweetly. "You can see we have a lot in common."

"Yes, I can see that," Donovan said tightly, the flame in the electric blue eyes scorching her.

"Perhaps you would like to retract your offer," Brenna said scornfully. "It might not be very good publicity to have an unwed mother in your precious picture."

"To hell with the publicity," Donovan said roughly. "No one tells me who to cast in my pictures. You're going to be Mary Durney, Brenna."

His arrogant declaration only aggravated the antagonism that his very presence generated in her.

"If I choose to be," she said firmly.

His mocking glance ran over her faded jeans and simple white tailored shirt.

"Oh, you'll choose to be," he said coolly. "I gather your lover isn't offering you and the baby support. You'd be a fool to turn down financial security for you and your child."

Brenna's face flushed at this humiliating reference to her obvious poverty. "Money isn't everything, Mr. Donovan," she said tersely. "Randy is a very happy, contented child. We don't need your money."

"Don't you, Brenna?" he asked lazily. "Think about it. My private number is on the script. Read it tonight, and let me know." He turned to go, and then wheeled back, his gaze sharp as a surgeon's scalpel. "One thing, Brenna," he said tautly. "If your baby's father is still hanging around, get rid of him. Once you're working for me, I don't want him near you!"

He walked quickly away, leaving her to stare after him, her lips parted in amazement.

---

three

THREE HOURS LATER BRENNA THREW THE
script down in frustration, realizing that Donovan was right
again. She must play this role, no matter how she felt about the
arrogant Michael Donovan.

Why couldn't Mary Durney have been a sickly sweet character or a self-pitying martyr, so that she could have tossed the role
back into Donovan's face, Brenna wondered gloomily. Mary
Durney was innocent but no prim miss. She had humor, strength,
and warmth. Brenna was convinced that she could make Mary
Durney live, and she desperately wanted the chance to do just
that. Damn Michael Donovan!

She reached for the phone on the table, and flipped the
script back to the title page on which Donovan had scrawled his
number in bold black numerals. Not allowing herself to think,
she rapidly dialed the number. What if it was almost two in the
morning? she thought maliciously. He had told her to call him
when she had read it, hadn't he? The idea of rousing Donovan
from a sound sleep gave her a degree of satisfaction that surprised her. She had never been a spiteful girl. What was it about
this man that made her want to strike out at him in any way she
could?

The phone was answered on the second ring, and Donovan sounded disappointingly wide awake. When she had identified herself, he said impatiently, "I didn't expect it to be anyone else, Brenna."

"Well." She drew a deep breath. "I want to do it," she said rapidly.

There was a long silence on the other end and then a low chuckle. "I assume you mean the part," he drawled mockingly.

Color flooded her face at the innuendo, and she silently cursed both her inept tongue and the taunting redheaded devil on the other end of the line.

"You know I mean the part," she said angrily.

"Yes, unfortunately I do," he said lightly. She could almost see the amused grin on his face. Then his voice became cool and businesslike. "I trust you can be ready to leave by two this afternoon. You can fly up with me in the Lear jet. We're filming at Twin Pines, you know."

She hadn't known. It hadn't occurred to her that she would have to leave Los Angeles. It should have, of course. Nearly all of Donovan's pictures were shot at Twin Pines now, when not on location. Her mind moved frantically. She'd have to notify the clerical agency, and Randy's nursery school, and Vivian, of course. She knew Charles would be glad to replace her in the play.

"I can leave today," she said slowly. "But you needn't bother yourself about arrangements. I prefer to drive."

"Don't be ridiculous," Donovan said impatiently. "I want you there this evening."

"Then I'll start early," she said stubbornly. There was no way she was going to see more of Michael Donovan than was absolutely necessary. He had a most unsettling effect on her. "Traveling with a baby can be very cumbersome, Mr. Donovan. I prefer to travel by car."

"You're taking the child?" he asked, his tone flat.

"Of course," Brenna said coolly. "Do you have any objections?"

"None at all," he said absently. "I should have expected it, I suppose. I'll work something out."

Brenna wondered what he had to work out. "Then I'll see you this evening," she said firmly. "Good night, Mr. Donovan." She replaced the phone without giving him a chance to object, and leaned back against the cushions of the couch, her head in a whirl. She wondered dazedly how she was going to get everything done, and still leave in the early morning to keep her promise to be at Twin Pines by early evening.

Well, first things first. She must get a few hours' sleep if she was to drive all day. She turned out the light and walked briskly into the bedroom. She set the alarm for six, shrugged out of her navy robe, and settled down to try to sleep.

The alarm came too soon. Brenna felt as tired as when she went to sleep. She took a cold shower, standing under the spray until she at least felt alive again. She brushed her hair and dressed hurriedly in rust-colored high waisted pants and a buttercup-yellow shirt that made her hair gleam in a glossy contrast. No time for makeup, she decided. She made herself a cup of instant coffee, added milk and sugar and carried it to the bedroom to sip as she packed. There was more to pack for Randy than for herself. Her own wardrobe was meager to say the least, but a two-year-old had to have a minimun of at least three changes a day. In the middle of her packing Randy awoke and she had to stop and dress him. After depositing him in his playpen in the living room, she hurried back to resume her packing, ignoring his loud protests. Randy always got up in the morning with a voracious appetite and wanted to eat first thing. She knew she couldn't put off his breakfast for very long, but she wanted to finish packing this suitcase before she stopped again. She had just put the last items in and closed the lid, when the doorbell rang. Who in the world could be at the door at seven in the morning, she wondered.

"Just a minute," she called frantically, trying to fasten the bulging suitcase. She succeeded, only to have it spring open again. "Damn!" she muttered impatiently, giving up temporarily.

On her way to the door, she stopped to pick up a teddy bear that Randy had tossed out of the playpen, and gave it back to that howling individual resignedly. "I know, love," she said with a quick kiss on his silky head. Her sympathy was met by another bellow. She restrained herself forcibly from picking up the mournful little figure and comforting him. She'd never get out of here if she gave in to Randy's pleadings.

The doorbell rang again, and she tore herself from Randy's clinging arms with some difficulty. Randy renewed his heartbroken wailing, and she ran her fingers through her hair in exasperation.

She marched to the door and threw it open, her brow creased in a frown. "What is it?" she asked crossly of the man in jeans and sweatshirt, who stood appraising her coolly.

"You shouldn't open your door without first checking to see who's on the other side, you know," the man said disapprovingly. "I'm Monty Walters. Michael Donovan sent me."

She should have known, Brenna thought with irritation, glaring balefully at the man standing before her. Did Donovan infect all the people around him with his own arrogant bossiness?

"May I come in?" Walters asked politely, stepping forward so that she was forced to give way or be trampled underfoot. A little over middle height, he was in his late twenties, with crisp dark curly hair that framed a face that was surprisingly boyish. The dark eyes, however, were completely adult and just a little cynical.

After the night and morning she had gone through, Brenna

was not about to be intimidated by one of Donovan's underlings.

"I'm sorry, Mr. Walters, but I haven't the time to talk to you right now," she said shortly. "Any last minute instructions Mr. Donovan has for me will have to wait until I arrive at Twin Pines."

There was a flicker of surprise in the dark eyes, and Walters looked at her with new interest. "That's why I'm here," he said coolly. "Mr. Donovan didn't care for the idea of your driving yourself. I'm to personally escort you and the child to the complex."

"That won't be necessary. I can drive myself perfectly well," Brenna said between her teeth.

Walters closed the door behind him firmly. "It may not be necessary for you, Miss Sloan," he said dryly. "But it's of the utmost necessity to me, if I want to keep my job." He looked around appraisingly. "Now I suggest that we get moving. If you'll supply me with the names and telephone numbers of people you want to advise of your departure, I'll attend to that, while you look after your child." He flinched as Randy emitted another piercing howl.

"He's hungry," Brenna said defensively, as she moved toward the playpen.

"Then I suggest you feed him," Monty Walters said bluntly. "But first give me those phone numbers."

Without knowing quite why she was giving in to this aggressive young man, Brenna found herself meekly supplying him with the necessary information. Then she picked up Randy and headed for the tiny kitchenette, where she prepared his usual oatmeal, bacon, and orange juice. Once fed, he regained his sunny disposition, and permitted her to put him back in his playpen with a toy. She swiftly washed and dried the dishes and tidied up the kitchen, then went back to the bedroom to resume her packing.

When she came out of the bedroom, Walters had already

disassembled the portable playpen and high chair and set them neatly by the door, and Randy was sitting on the couch playing with a chain of fascinating colored keys. Monty Walters was standing before the window, his eyes narrowed appraisingly.

"Stained glass," he said, admiring the rich violet and blue of the floral design. "Quite lovely and unexpected. Your work?"

Brenna nodded, thawing a bit at his admiration. She was very proud of that window. "It seemed appropriate," she said, making a face. "You've probably noticed this neighborhood is not high on aesthetic views."

"So you made your own," he observed, looking around the room with new interest. Cream walls provided a classic frame for the window. The furniture was in neutral shades and far from new, and the glowing beauty of the hardwood floor was accented by several brightly colored throw rugs.

"You've done a lot with it," he said thoughtfully, his eyes returning to the window, which was the focal point of the room. "An unusual hobby," he commented.

"It's becoming increasingly popular," she said quietly. "I learned it at school." The children's home had been convinced that idle hands bred mischief and the children had been offered arts and crafts classes of all descriptions.

"I've always thought a person's home reflected a great deal of their personality," Walters said quietly, turning his gaze to regard Brenna soberly. "I like your home, Miss Sloan. I have a hunch you're not just another pretty face."

"If that's a compliment, I thank you, kind sir," she said lightly. "I'm sure you're not just a pretty face, either."

He smiled ruefully. "Did I sound chauvinistic?" he said, shaking his head. "I haven't made a very good impression on you, have I? I guess my pride was a bit hurt at being used as a glorified chauffeur, and I took it out on you." His smile widened appealingly. "Shall we start over?"

Brenna answered his smile with a warm one of her own. "I

think we'd better. It's a long way to the Oregon border." She made a face. "No one would have voted me Miss Congeniality this morning either."

"You're right there," he said impudently, dark eyes twinkling. "Now shall we hit the road, before I manage to alienate you completely?"

Together they packed the Lincoln Continental to its spacious limits. When Brenna had objected to leaving her own car in Los Angeles, Monty had countered that the trip would be much more comfortable in the Lincoln, and Donovan had already arranged for her car to be picked up in a few days. There could be no argument about the drive being more comfortable, she admitted to herself, when they were on their way. The car was the height of luxury. She stroked the wine velvet upholstery of the seat with almost sensual pleasure.

"It's a lovely car," she commented. "Does it belong to Mr. Donovan?"

Monty Walters shook his head with a grin, as he maneuvered the big silver car onto the freeway. "It's mine," he admitted. "I have a vulgar passion for ostentatious cars, but I haven't dared to indulge it until recently."

"Money?" Brenna asked. This car must have cost a small fortune. Though Michael Donovan was reputed to pay his employees very well, she found it unlikely that even the most generous salary would provide a luxury of this magnitude.

"In a manner of speaking." He gave her a sheepish grin. "You see I'm stinking rich."

Her mouth quirked at the boyish awkwardness of this revelation. "I'm afraid I don't see your problem," she said solemnly. "Why couldn't you have a car like this, if you could afford it?"

"I didn't want to remind Donovan that I was wealthy, so I've been driving a '75 Volkswagon for the past two years," he said simply. "It's only lately that I've felt confident enough to risk the Lincoln."

Brenna stared at him in amazement. "Do you mean Michael Donovan would have objected to you buying the car of your choice with your own money?" she asked indignantly. That an aggressive, confident man like Monty could be so intimidated was truly incredible.

"Hell, no!" he said explosively. "But after working like the devil to get this job, I thought I'd better play it low key. He knew my background when he hired me and he was dubious, to say the least, about my willingness to stick to the kind of work schedule he demanded of his employees." His mouth twisted wryly. "I soon understood why. Simon Legree has nothing on Michael Donovan."

"Yet, you're still with him," Brenna observed.

"I guess I'm just a masochist," Walters said lightly. Reaching out he touched a button, and taped music flooded the car with the mellow strains of a Barry Manilow hit. Brenna leaned back and relaxed on the plush velvet seats, letting the strain of the last few hours flow out of her.

In the next several hours Brenna found Monty Walters to be amazingly companionable. He was quick-witted and energetic, with a wry sense of humor that was almost puckish. By the time they had shared lunch, dinner, and almost eight hours of desultory conversation, she felt as if they were old friends.

It was nearing twilight when they crossed the Oregon border, and a brief twenty minutes later they reached Twin Pines.

She didn't know what she had expected of Donovan's Twin Pines complex. Perhaps in the back of her mind had been the idea that it would be the usual movie studio lot like Paramount or Universal. She should have known better.

Twin Pines was as unique as the man who had created it. Located at the edge of a small Oregon lumber town, it looked more like a country club than a movie studio, with low modernistic buildings in redwood and glass, wide streets, and several tree-shaded park areas furnished with picnic tables and benches.

"Impressed?" Walters asked, arching his eyebrows quizzically, as she turned back to him from her eager perusal of the passing scene.

"Who wouldn't be?" she asked dryly. "It's perfectly charming, but not exactly what you'd expect of Michael Donovan."

"On the contrary, it's exactly what you'd expect of him," Walters said briskly. "He's gathered the most gifted and skilled people in the industry here at Twin Pines. People that usually work freelance have been formed into a sort of repertory group. When they're working, he drives them unmercifully. It's just good sense to provide them with the most pleasant surroundings possible to enjoy in their free time."

"You admire him very much, don't you?" Brenna asked curiously.

"You're damn right I do," he replied unequivocally. "There are a few men in every generation who combine creative genius with irresistible drive. When you find one, if you're smart, you grab hold of his coattails and let him carry you to the top."

"I wouldn't have thought you'd be interested in a free ride," Brenna said thoughtfully.

Walters snorted derisively. "There's nothing free about it. Donovan extracts the last ounce of effort from the people around him. You give until you have nothing else to give. Then, somehow, you find he has expanded your limits, so that there is a whole new reservoir for him to tap." His dark eyes were reflective. "He's a complete workaholic, a nit-picking perfectionist, and a totally ruthless exploiter of the talents of his employees," he continued, almost beneath his breath. "But, by God, it's worth it!"

"You don't paint a very comforting picture of my new boss," Brenna said wryly.

"I didn't mean to," Walters said bluntly. "If you need a security blanket, you have no business around Donovan. He'll tear you to pieces."

"I can believe that," she said with a shrug, remembering

Donovan's steamroller tactics in her own case. "Well, I can always leave if I find him too impossible," she said lightly.

He shot her an appraising glance. "I wouldn't count on that," he said coolly. "I have an idea that Donovan has plans for you. And Donovan always gets what he wants."

"Plans?" Brenna asked blankly. She shook her head. "I have a small supporting role in one of his pictures. I'm not important in his scheme of things. What plans could he possibly have for me?"

"Who knows?" Monty said, with a shrug. "Maybe he sees you as the next Sarah Bernhardt." He grinned boyishly. "Whatever it is, you're being given very special treatment, Brenna Sloan. I'll have you know, I'm a very important cog in Donovan's organization," he said with mock conceit. "It's not an ordinary occurrence for me to be ordered to act as chauffeur to an unknown actress. I must admit that my ego was very badly dented when he gave me my instructions."

She smiled in amusement. "I hate to disillusion you, but I'm afraid your original supposition was correct."

He slanted her an oblique smile. "We'll see," he said composedly.

He pulled into a circular driveway that led to a long two-story building, which, like the other buildings in the complex, was constructed of redwood, stone, and glass.

"Employee's quarters," Monty said briskly, in answer to her inquiring look. "You'll find your accommodations are part of your fringe benefits. You're provided with a small apartment at Donovan's expense. The units also supply maid service at your own expense. There's a cafeteria in each residence hall that is open twenty-four hours a day." He grimaced. "They have to be. There are times when we work around the clock to meet the demands of our lord and master."

He pulled to a smooth stop before the front entrance, jumped out, and came around the car with the characteristic energy she was beginning to associate with him.

A husky, sandy-haired teenager in a plaid shirt and jeans came hurrying out the front entrance, and opened the passenger door quickly.

"Good to see you back, Mr. Walters," he said respectfully.

"Thanks, Johnny," Walters said easily, as he helped Brenna from the car.

"This is Johnny Smith, Brenna. He's a sort of jack-of-all-trades. If you need something, ask Johnny."

Brenna smiled warmly at the boy and he smiled back. "You bet," he said cheerfully. "I'll take good care of you, miss."

"Thank you, Johnny," she said quietly.

Monty Walters opened the rear door, and lifted a sleeping Randy out with the utmost care to avoid waking him. He tossed the trunk keys to the boy. "Bring in Miss Sloan's luggage, will you, Johnny?"

Walters escorted her into the bright, cheerful lobby, and paused before the reception desk. A pert, dark-haired girl looked up with a smile that took on a flattering obsequiousness as soon as she recognized Walters.

"Paula Drummond, Brenna," Walters said briskly. "This is Brenna Sloan, Paula. I understand Mr. Donovan's secretary was to contact you with regard to the arrangements."

The dark-haired girl shook her head. "Mr. Donovan called himself," she said solemnly. "It's a pleasure to meet you, Miss Sloan. We have everything arranged just as Mr. Donovan instructed." She picked up the phone and punched several buttons rapidly. "Doris, Miss Sloan is here. Would you come down right away?" She turned to Brenna and Walters, a bright smile on her face. "We've given you one of the guest cottages. I hope you'll be very comfortable there. If there's anything else you need, just call me."

"Thank you. I'm sure everything will be fine," Brenna said awkwardly, a little uneasy over the effusiveness of the receptionist.

"A guest cottage?" Monty asked thoughtfully, with a low whistle. "That's really royal treatment, Brenna. Cottages are reserved for stars and visiting VIPs."

"Then there must be a mistake," Brenna said firmly. "We both know that I'm neither."

"There's no mistake, Miss Sloan," Paula Drummond spoke up quickly. "Mr. Donovan's instructions were very explicit." She looked beyond Brenna to smile at the young woman who had just gotten off the elevator and was crossing the lobby toward them. "This is Doris Charles, Miss Sloan."

Doris Charles was a woman in her middle twenties with short curly red hair and rather plain features that were illuminated by a warm smile. She held out a strong square hand and shook Brenna's hand vigorously. "I'm very happy to meet you, Miss Sloan." She turned immediately toward Walters, who was still holding Randy, and said briskly. "I'll take him." She held out her arms, and Walters obediently put the child into them. Brenna stared in bewilderment as the red-haired woman cuddled the child expertly, her face softening as she looked down at him. "What a little darling he is," she said softly. "His name's Randy, I believe?"

"That's right," Brenna said, confused. "But who are you?"

Doris Charles looked up at her, a small frown creasing her forehead. "I'm your son's nurse. Mr. Donovan flew me up from Los Angeles to care for Randy." she said calmly. "I believe you'll find I have the highest qualifications."

"I'm sure you have," Brenna said tiredly, her head whirling. "But I don't need a nurse, Miss Charles. I take care of Randy myself."

Johnny Smith came into the lobby laden with suitcases that he put down in front of the desk.

"Don't be too hasty, Brenna," Walters said easily. "You'll need someone to care for Randy while you're working. Miss Charles is well qualified to do just that."

Brenna nodded slowly at the logic of Monty's reasoning. "You're right, Monty," she admitted, and smiled at Doris Charles. The red-haired woman seemed to be loving as well as efficient. "I'll be glad to have your help with Randy, Miss Charles," she said warmly.

"Doris," the nurse said briefly, grinning back at her. "I'll take the greatest care of your son, Miss Sloan," she promised.

Paula Drummond cleared her throat gently, and said tentatively. "Now, if you'll tell me which of these bags are your personal possessions, Miss Sloan, I'll have Johnny take them to the cottage. He can come back and take the baby's things to Miss Charles' apartment later."

"What are you talking about?" Brenna asked blankly. "Everything goes to the cottage. Randy is staying with me."

Paula Drummond shook her head. "No, ma'm," she said, "Mr. Donovan was quite definite on that point. Only you are to occupy the cottage. The baby is to remain at the residence hall with Miss Charles."

"I don't care how definite Mr. Donovan was on the subject," Brenna said between her teeth. "I am not being separated from my baby." The nerve of the man, she fumed. Casually disposing of her child like an unwanted parcel. "I don't care where you put me," she went on grimly. "I don't need any fancy cottage, anywhere will do. But wherever it is, I want my child with me."

There was a shocked look on the receptionist's face. "But you don't understand, Miss Sloan," she stammered. "I can't go against Mr. Donovan's orders."

"I'm not going anywhere without Randy," Brenna said flatly. "So you are going to have to, aren't you?"

"It's just not possible," Paula Drummond said, almost in tears. "Please be reasonable, Miss Sloan. Mr. Donovan will be most displeased."

Brenna had opened her mouth to tell the girl what Michael Donovan could do with his displeasure, when Walters interjected smoothly. "You can't do anything about it tonight, Brenna. Paula is only obeying orders, and you'll only get her in trouble. Why don't you go along with the arrangements right now. When you see Mr. Donovan, you can speak to him about making any necessary changes."

The voice of reason again, Brenna thought impatiently, wishing she could fault the argument. She was beginning to understand why Monty had risen so quickly at Donovan Enterprises Ltd. He was a very persuasive gentleman.

"Okay. I'll do as you suggest for the present," Brenna said reluctantly. "But I want to speak to Mr. Donovan right away, Monty."

Monty Walters nodded, ignoring Paula Drummond's outraged gasp. He understood the receptionist's incredulity. One didn't demand an audience with Michael Donovan in his own kingdom of Twin Pines. Such an act was unprecedented, but then so were all Donovan's actions in regard to Brenna Sloan. Perhaps Donovan's reception of her request would be in accordance with this exceptional behavior.

"Mr. Donovan asked me to call him when we arrived," he said quietly. "I'll ask him to get in touch with you." He touched Brenna's cheek lightly. "It's been a long day. Why don't you try to take a nap? You look exhausted."

Brenna nodded ruefully. She probably looked a wreck. With only four hours' sleep last night and the long drive today, she felt achingly tired. "I will," she promised, smiling. "Thank you for everything, Monty."

"My pleasure, Brenna," he said lightly. "I'll see you soon, no doubt." With a casual wave, he turned and walked out the door.

"Well, now that we're all in agreement, we'll get you settled, Miss Sloan," Paula Drummond said brightly. "Which are your bags?"

As she silently pointed out her personal luggage, Brenna was tempted to tell the girl that they were not all in agreement.

There was no way that Michael Donovan was going to get away with this high-handed interference in her personal life. As she gave Doris Charles a few quiet instructions as to Randy's likes and dislikes as to food and his general schedule, she already felt a sense of loss. She and Randy had never spent even one night apart, and she was feeling distinctly shaky at the idea of the parting. He had become the center of her life since Janine died.

"I'll take good care of him," Doris Charles said kindly. "It's only a five-minute walk to the cottage. You can come and see him as often as you wish."

Brenna felt an absurd desire to say thank you. Thank you for telling me I can come and see my own child. She already felt he had been taken away from her. "I know you will," she said huskily, "and it's only for tonight." She brushed the top of Randy's head with a light kiss, and turned away quickly before she changed her mind. She followed Johnny Smith out the far door and down the paved path toward the small, elegant redwood cottage.

four

JOHNNY SMITH UNLOCKED THE FRONT DOOR and touched the wall switch, flooding the interior with light. He preceded her into the room, saying cheerfully, "I'll just carry these on through to the bedroom, Miss Sloan." Taking her silence as assent, he crossed the deeply carpeted living room to a door on the left, leaving Brenna to gaze in amazed admiration at the interior of the cottage.

The living room area was carpeted in pearl gray with matching drapes at the casement windows. The modern furniture was in shades of violet and purple with cream pillows thrown in luxurious profusion on the lavender couch. Clear glass occasional tables gave a tranquil, pristine quality to the living room. In the dining area, a silver bowl with a multitude of floating violets was the colorful centerpiece on a magnificent glass dining table. There appeared to be a small kitchenette leading off the dining area, but she decided not to explore further, and followed Johnny into the bedroom.

Brenna found that the boy had pulled open the drapes and was coming out of the adjoining bathroom. "Plenty of towels," he said briskly. "Sometimes the maids forget."

The bedroom, too, was carpeted in pearl gray with the same violet accents, she noticed. The queen-sized bed was covered with a royal purple taffeta spread, coordinating with the matching drapes at the long French windows.

Johnny pointed to the cream princess phone on the side table. "You dial nine to get an outside line, dial six to get the main hall switchboard." His bright, brown eyes were eager. "Would you like for me to bring you something from the cafeteria, Miss Sloan? It wouldn't be any trouble."

Brenna shook her head, smiling. "No, thank you, Johnny," she said. "Mr. Walters and I stopped for dinner earlier." She realized with a little shock of surprise that this teenager was only a little younger than herself, yet she felt a million years removed from his youthful enthusiasm.

Johnny nodded, and walked briskly to the front door. "The kitchen is well stocked if you feel like a bite later," he said, and then grinned engagingly. "I'm a great one for midnight snacks, myself."

"Me, too," Brenna confided solemnly, from where she stood in the bedroom doorway.

"Be sure and tell the desk if you need me," he said, and with a final grin he quietly closed the door.

Brenna stood there for a moment, feeling a great sense of aloneness sweep over her as the door shut on that cheerful presence. Looking around the exquisite apartment, she wondered dazedly what she was doing in all this luxury. She didn't belong here. She belonged in that small apartment in Los Angeles with Randy. Then she squared her shoulders determinedly. She was just tired and dispirited over the separation from Randy. This was a great opportunity. She would be an idiot to let herself become intimidated by these rich surroundings. She was the same Brenna Sloan here as in her own apartment in Los Angeles. All she had to do was to hold to that truth with both hands, and she'd be all right.

She considered making herself a cup of hot chocolate, but decided not to bother. She was suddenly unutterably weary.

Opening a suitcase, she pulled out a white jersey tailored robe and shower cap, and drifted into the bathroom. She noticed, without surprise, the lavender tub and gray and crystal accessories.

She made the shower a brief but thorough one, wanting only to sample the softness of the queen-sized bed. After toweling off on the huge fluffy towel on the heated rack, she slipped on her robe and gave her hair a lick and a promise with the brush she found on the built-in glass vanity. Then with a sigh of contentment she lay down on the bed, not even bothering to remove the spread. She'd get up and unpack soon, she thought drowsily as her lids closed. And she wanted to be sure to talk to Donovan about Randy tonight. She tried to force her weighted lids open again, knowing she should try to call Donovan before she gave in to this delicious sleepiness. That was the last thought that surfaced before she fell soundly asleep.

It seemed only a moment before she was awakened by a thundering cacophony of sound. She moaned and rolled over, trying to ignore it, but it continued interminably until she realized it was someone at the front door. She sat up, and slowly rose to her feet. Catching sight of the clock on the bedside table, she realized groggily that it was almost ten. She had slept for almost two hours! It wasn't enough she realized, as she stumbled bleary-eyed out of the bedroom, across the living room to the front door, and fumbled with the lock.

She wasn't even surprised to see an extremely angry Michael Donovan on the doorstep. Leaning her head against the door, she peered at him owlishly, observing that he looked as vital and alive as ever in figure-hugging black cords and a black turtleneck sweater, his hair a dark flame above the sombre garments. She wondered sleepily if there was such a thing as an energy vampire. Just the sight of his electric-charged vitality made her feel tired—more tired, she corrected herself drowsily.

"Hello, Mr. Donovan," she said, yawning.

"Good evening, Miss Sloan," he said sarcastically. "I hope I didn't disturb you." He pushed the door open, and brushed by her, closing the door behind him with a resounding slam. She flinched at the sound, as well as at the obvious untruth. It was quite evident that Donovan was not at all sorry to have awakened her. He strode into the center of the living room, and turned to regard her impatiently, looking outrageously out of place in the delicate grays and violets of the room. Like a pirate at a royal garden party, she thought dimly.

"I understand you wanted to see me," he said sarcastically. "I tried to phone you, and it rang off the hook, so I came over."

"You phoned me?" she asked sleepily, trailing behind him into the living room. "You must have called the wrong number," she said tiredly, gravitating toward the lavender couch, and curling up in the corner. "I would have heard it."

"I did *not* call a wrong number," he said between clenched teeth. He moved with pantherish grace to the gray extension phone on the glass end table, and checked the phone quickly. "You have the volume turned off," he said disgustedly, adjusting the dial. "It's hardly courteous to ask me to get in touch with you, and then turn the telephone off, Miss Sloan," he said curtly, his blue eyes blazing.

She felt the stirrings of indignation at the unfair accusation, but she was still too sluggish to take umbrage. "I didn't turn down the volume," she said lifelessly. "It must have been the previous occupant of the cottage."

Donovan's eyes narrowed as they raked over her. "What the hell is the matter with you?" he demanded roughly. "Are you on something?"

"On something?" she asked vaguely. Then realizing what he meant, she woke up with a vengeance. She sat up straight on the couch, swift color pinking her cheeks.

"I do not take drugs, Mr. Donovan!" she said angrily. "I'm merely very sleepy."

He shrugged. "It's an understandable assumption. Your generation seems partial to crutches."

"And yours wasn't?" she inquired sarcastically. "I believe yours was known as the protest generation. You started the whole drug culture."

"Touché," he said ruefully. "Not me personally, I assure you." His gaze ran over her lingeringly. "Are you always so slow to wake up?" he asked abruptly.

"Not everyone wakes up all in one piece," she said resentfully. "Though I'm sure you're one of those who switch on like an electric light."

"Yes, I am," he said absently, his eyes thoughtful. "One of us will have to change," he said obscurely.

She stared at him in confusion, but before she could voice a question he continued curtly. "Monty said there was some problem with your living arrangements. What is so important that it couldn't wait until tomorrow?" he demanded, looking around the richly furnished room casually. "Everything seems to be in order."

"Everything is not in order!" she said hotly, rising to her feet and facing him belligerently. "Randy isn't here with me."

The keen blue eyes became suddenly watchful. "The child?" he asked carefully. "I made adequate provisions for him. Doris Charles has excellent references, and her apartment has been furnished with everything a child could possibly want."

"Everything but his mother," Brenna grated, her hands clenching into fists. "I want him with me!"

Donovan strolled over to the small portable bar in the corner, and poured himself a Scotch and water, before turning to face her.

"That won't be possible," he said coolly. "I prefer that the child be cared for in the residence hall. You'll need all your concentration for the next week or so. I don't want you distracted by maternal worries."

"That's ridiculous," she said angrily. "I've always taken care of Randy myself, and I assure you that my schedule has been more demanding than you can imagine."

"But not as taxing as the one I'll ask of you," he said bluntly. "There are a number of scenes that have to be reshot, as well as the rest of the picture to finish, and I fully intend to bring the picture in on schedule, Brenna," he said forcefully.

"I've agreed to accept Miss Charles' assistance," Brenna said in exasperation. "What difference could it possibly make if she and Randy move in here?"

He took a long swallow of his drink before he answered. "It makes a difference to me. In case you haven't noticed, I run things here."

"So I've been told," she said bitterly, her brown eyes suddenly bright with unshed tears as she gazed pleadingly at him. "Why should you object to me having my son here?" she asked huskily. "Won't you change your mind?"

His eyes were brooding as he met hers across the room. "No, I won't change my mind," he said harshly. "I don't want him here, Brenna."

"But why?" she asked distractedly. "You can't just arbitrarily refuse without giving me a reason."

His eyes narrowed to steely slits, and she knew she had angered him. He carefully put his unfinished drink on the bar, and said coolly. "You want to know my reason, Brenna? Then you shall have it." He crossed the space between them in three swift strides. "You're pushing me, Brenna. I hoped to have more time," he said softly.

"What do you mean?" she faltered, breathless at his sudden proximity.

He shrugged, the black knit of his sweater straining over powerful shoulders. "You're not ready for this yet," he said calmly, "but I'm tired of playing games." He looked directly into her eyes, and said deliberately, "I don't want your child here, because it drives me crazy to see you with him."

Brenna couldn't understand this incredible statement, and she looked up at him in total bewilderment. His two hands reached up to cup her face. "You see, I've discovered you were abysmally wrong about the type of woman that turns me on," he said huskily. "I want you, Brenna."

She felt as if she were being hypnotized by those piercing eyes that held her in a magnetic thrall. He was so close that she could feel the vibrant warmth emanating from him, the smell, the clean scent of soap and the indescribable essence of the male animal. "No," she cried, her eyes clinging to his. "It's crazy!"

"Do you think I don't know that?" he asked savagely. "Do you think I go around seducing twenty-year-old girls as a matter of course? I don't like this one iota." He drew a ragged breath, and spoke more calmly. "All that I know is that when I saw you at the audition yesterday afternoon, it was as if someone had punched me in the stomach. I wanted you more than I have ever wanted any woman in my life. I've got to have you, or go totally insane."

"You're already insane," she whispered. "Things just don't happen like that."

"I didn't think so either," he said harshly. "I seemed to have become completely obsessed by you. I never cared a damn about chastity in a woman before, but the thought of another man having had you before me, makes me want to strangle you."

His eyes gleamed with such savagery that a flicker of fear shot through her, and she took an involuntary step backward. His hands fell away from her, and his mouth twisted cynically. "Don't worry, I haven't reached that stage of barbarism yet," he said hoarsely. "Though I just may, if I ever catch you with any other man. I can't even bear to see you with the child, knowing that another man fathered him."

"Why are you telling me all this?" she said dazedly. "First, you tell me you want some sort of affair with me, and then that you can't bear to have me around my own son." Her voice rose hysterically. "What am I supposed to do? Drown him? You're completely mad!"

He shrugged. "I knew it was too soon," he said. "I was going to wait a little longer, until you got to know me better. I know it's a shock to you." His mouth twisted wryly. "As for the child, I'll just have to learn to tolerate him, won't I?"

"Tolerate?" The word added fuel to her growing anger. That anyone would have to "tolerate" the adorable, sunny imp that was Randy was unbelievable.

"I shouldn't bother," she said coldly. "Neither of us need your tolerance, Mr. Donovan."

"The outraged lioness in defense of her cub," he murmured mockingly. "Tell me, now that I've invited you into my bed, don't you think that we're on personal enough terms for you to call me Michael?"

"As our acquaintance will be ending right here and now, I hardly think it necessary," she said coolly, turning toward the bedroom door.

His hand caught her arm as she walked past him, and he whirled her around to face him. "You're not walking out, Brenna," he said grimly. "You've got a job to do."

"As your mistress?" she asked sarcastically, lifting her chin.

"Eventually," Donovan said coolly. "But at present I have a film to make, and you agreed to take the role of Mary Durney."

"Impossible," she said shortly. "I couldn't do it now."

"You'll do it," he said grimly. "The two things have nothing to do with each other. If you think I gave you the role to apply some sort of sexual harassment, you're wrong. I'll get you into my bed because you want to occupy it, and not for any other reason."

"Then you're going to be very disappointed," she said

defiantly. "I'll never want you or any other man like that, Michael Donovan."

"I think you will," he said with narrowed eyes. "I have no small amount of experience with women, and I'd judge you to be highly combustible material indeed, Brenna Sloan."

"Then you'd be wrong," she said hotly, her denial all the more adamant for the furtive memory of that momentary weakness in the wings of the Rialto.

He shook his head, his face mocking. "I don't think so. It's natural that you should be bitter and afraid of initiating any new relationships. You've obviously been hurt by your affair with Randy's father. Seventeen is an extremely sensitive age for something as traumatic as that to happen to a young girl. It's no wonder you've been rejecting other men since then."

"How did you know I've been rejecting men?" Brenna asked. Then her eyes widened incredulously. "My God, you've had me investigated!" she whispered.

"Nothing so dramatic," he scoffed lightly. "I sent a man around to ask a few questions of the right people, that's all. I knew after I spoke to you at the theater last night that you had some sort of grudge against men. It's my experience that a thorough knowledge of one's adversary is the only basis for success."

"And what did you learn about me?" she asked proudly. "Was it worth your employee's time?"

"Not much," he said laconically. "You grew up in a children's home. You have a secretarial job with Edwards Temporary Agency. You're a devoted mother, pay your bills promptly, and are distinctly cool to any amorous young men who try to approach you."

"Doesn't that discourage you?" she asked caustically.

"Not in the least," he said calmly. "It gives me a good deal of satisfaction to know that you haven't been involved with any other man since Randy's father let you down. I told you I was very possessive about you, and I know damn well I can melt that ice around you, Brenna."

"You wouldn't say you're the least bit egotistical?" she asked sardonically.

"I believe in myself," he said simply. "I wouldn't have gotten as far as I have in life, if I didn't." His sensual lips curved mischievously. "I also believe in chemistry, and we have an abundance of that, believe me."

"So you expect me to go on with the picture as if this interview had never happened?" she asked wonderingly.

"Why not?" he asked coolly. "Now that everything is out in the open, we go back to square one. You need the work and I need an actress. The fact that I also need you as a woman shouldn't concern you unduly. After all, before we had this conversation, I was prepared to wait until you said you wanted me. I still am. I won't promise not to do my damnedest to make you want me, but I'm not about to drag you, kicking and screaming, into the nearest cave."

"Do I have your promise on that?" Brenna asked skeptically.

Donovan's mouth tightened with anger, and his blue eyes flashed. "I'm not accustomed to having my word questioned." He drew a deep breath, and his tension eased fractionally. "What a suspicious little girl you are, Brenna," he said mockingly. "You have my promise that I won't pounce until the picture is finished. After that, if I haven't persuaded you to my way of thinking, all promises are null and void. I'll get you any way I can."

She shivered at the implacable ruthlessness in the lean face. "Can't you see it's no use?" she asked pleadingly.

"No, I can't," he said with determination. "And before I leave here tonight, I'm going to make you realize just what we could have together."

Her gaze flew to his, her brown eyes reflecting the panic of a startled doe. "No," she protested breathlessly, struggling to free herself from his restraining hands gripping her arms. "You promised!"

His hands tightened relentlessly, drawing her inexorably closer, quelling her frantic struggles with effortless strength. "Stop fighting me, Brenna!" He groaned huskily. "Don't you know I have to have something to keep me from going crazy in the next few weeks?" Then she was in his arms, pressed against his muscular body and experiencing the burning heat of his male hardness through the thin jersey of her robe. It was almost as if she were totally naked and completely vulnerable in his arms.

"Let me go," she gasped, twisting desperately to escape the tormenting closeness that was branding her as his possession.

It was as if he didn't hear her. His face held only a glazed absorption. He closed his eyes, drawing in his breath raggedly. "God, I want you!"

His mouth covered hers with such a savage need that she felt that she was being absorbed into him, as if she were becoming a mere extension of the desire that consumed him. His lips covered her face and throat with hot kisses before returning to ravish her parted lips with a dizzying penetration. She groaned helplessly at the sheer sensual pleasure his teasing tongue produced. His hands moved in an agony of frustration, feverishly caressing her back and bottom, cupping and exploring the silken skin through the flimsy material of the robe.

She was swept up in a cyclone of sensation, her body feeling as weak as melted butter as she leaned helplessly against him. He gave a triumphant chuckle as he raised his head to stare down at her with barbaric satisfaction, the electric blue eyes blazing. With deliberate slowness, his eyes holding hers almost hypnotically, his hands loosened the tie at her waist and parted the robe. He stared in glazed anticipation at her silken curves. Brenna could feel a tide of emotion electrify her body at the intensity of emotion on his face. He wasn't even touching her, yet she could feel her breasts firming, their rosy peaks hardening as if he were caressing them. "Damn, you're lovely," he said hoarsely. "You're mine, aren't you? Tell me you belong to me."

Then without waiting for a reply, he lowered his mouth to those teasing peaks that were entreating his caress. His tongue toyed tormentingly with each luscious mound until she was shaking with the erotic reaction that he was arousing in her. She remembered how earlier in the evening she had mentally compared him to a vampire. She realized now, with a swift rush of panic, how correct the simile had been. He was using his overpowering sensual magnetism to drain the resistance from her, leaving her a chattel to an aching need that she had never known could exist.

He raised his head and then slowly closed the robe, tying the belt deftly. He gazed broodingly at her flushed face and soft bruised mouth. Then he caught his breath sharply as he encountered wide brown eyes that were shining with helpless wonder.

"God, don't look at me like that, sweetheart," he groaned huskily, burying his face in her silky brown hair. He carefully withheld his taut body from her pliant curves. "I'm within an inch of picking you up and carrying you into that bedroom and raping you." His teeth nibbled at her ear, causing delicious shivers to run through her body. "And it would be rape, because as willing as I can make that gorgeous body of yours, your mind is still rejecting me."

He rubbed his lower body against hers sensuously. "I don't want only a one night stand with you, love. We're going to be together a long, long time. I want your body, your mind, and your soul. I'm going to own you, Brenna Sloan."

For one mad moment she accepted that arrogant assertion of dominance with blind submission, willing to yield everything to regain the throbbing pleasure he had made her feel. Then the independence of a lifetime asserted itself with a rush of scalding shame. My God, what was she doing, she thought with a sick feeling in the pit of her stomach. Where was her pride and self-respect that she could be vanquished so easily by this man's sexual expertise? Was she to be like her mother and Janine, used by men for their own gratification, and then tossed aside like a piece of refuse?

His grip had automatically loosened at the signs of her surrender, and with one lithe twist she was free of him. She moved quickly to the other side of the room before turning to face him. Her face was pale and taut, and she hugged her arms close to her body as if to form a physical barrier between them.

"Is the demonstration over?" she asked defiantly, lifting her chin proudly. "If it is, I wish you'd leave."

There was disappointment and a reluctant admiration in Donovan's face as he watched her with narrowed eyes. "I almost had you, sweetheart," he said thoughtfully. "I wonder where I went wrong."

"Your mistake was forgetting that I am my own person," she said coolly. "Not some sort of slave for your amusement. You won't get another chance."

His smile was mocking, and his eyes flashed recklessly. "Bad move, darling," he said gently. "Haven't you heard I can't resist a challenge?" Then as she stiffened defensively, he shook his head. "Not tonight. I think I've made enough progress for one night, don't you?"

A scarlet flush dyed her cheeks at the memory of how easily Donovan had brushed aside her defenses as if they didn't exist, leaving her so humiliatingly subservient to his passion and her own.

"Don't worry, Brenna, my promise still stands," he said, shaking his head ruefully. "Though I imagine I'll be taking a hell of a lot of cold showers in the near future." He grimaced. "It wouldn't be at all a bad idea right now."

He strolled back to the bar and picked up his half empty glass and finished the drink in one swallow. When he turned back to her, his demeanor was coolly impersonal.

"Tomorrow morning you'll be free to go over your lines. I'll have Monty pick you up at noon to take you to Sound Stage B. You'll need to be fitted for costumes and meet the director, Jake Dominic."

She should have been relieved at his return to a businesslike attitude, but she was conscious of an illogical resentment that he could so easily turn off his emotions when she was still a mass of quivering butterflies inside. With no little effort she succeeded in masking her discomposure.

"I'll be ready," she said icily, then the last part of his sentence struck home. "Jake Dominic is directing?"

Donovan nodded, his mouth twisting cynically. "I'm surprised you didn't know," he said dryly. "I thought everyone in the business kept up with Jake's activities. In bed and out."

That was a patent understatement, Brenna thought wryly. The entire world displayed an interest in the antics of filmdom's bad boy. Jake Dominic was totally brilliant, and the most sought after director in Hollywood. His success had closely paralleled the meteoric rise of Michael Donovan, and the two men were known to be good friends. His personal life was as attention getting as his career image. Fabulously wealthy in his own right, film success and his satanic good looks proved irresistible to women. Even in an industry where morals were notoriously loose, Dominic's reputation was scandalous. Though Donovan's affairs were legion, he guarded his privacy closely. Dominic, on the other hand, had a reckless disregard for publicity, and was constantly in the gossip columns.

"Jake Dominic," she repeated musingly. She wondered idly if she had fallen from the frying pan into the fire. Surely one rake of Donovan's calibre was enough to contend with.

Donovan's eyes narrowed dangerously. "He interests you?" he asked silkily. "I'm afraid you'll have to forget any aspirations in that direction. I've already told Jake that you're off limits."

She flushed with indignation at the thought of Donovan discussing his strictly dishonorable intentions toward her with his equally dissolute cohort. How dare he stake her out as if she were some kind of property! There was no way that she would admit that her interest in Dominic was less anticipatory than wary.

"From what I understand, Mr. Dominic doesn't take kindly to restrictions of any kind," she said coolly. "So we'll just have to wait and see, won't we?"

Donovan's eyes flickered. "Don't make the mistake of trying to score off me through Jake," he warned tightly. "He might be my best friend, but I'm not about to share you with him."

Brenna shrugged insolently, and opened her mouth to tell him just what she thought of his arrogant statement, when there was a brisk knock on the door.

Donovan's eyes flew to her face. "Are you expecting someone?" he asked sharply.

"Who would I be expecting?" she asked caustically. "I'm the new girl in town, remember?"

With a muttered curse he strode swiftly to the door and threw it open. He surveyed the man who stood there with extreme displeasure.

"What the hell are you doing here, Jake?" he growled sourly. "I thought I had made myself clear."

The deep masculine voice of their visitor was mocking. "You always make yourself clear, Michael. I'm not here to poach on your preserves. I'm here purely on business."

Donovan moved aside reluctantly. "It better be damn pure," he said bluntly, as the other man strolled into the room. "You haven't had a platonic thought about a woman since you were in kindergarten." He turned to Brenna and said shortly, "This is Jake Dominic, Brenna."

Dominic glided forward, lithely graceful as a panther in pursuit of it's prey, to take her hand in his. He was almost sinfully handsome, she thought, with his dark eyes, dark hair, and the face of a fallen angel. If the eyes had the jaded cynicism of one who had done everything, seen everything, and found the world now a trifle boring, it only added to the wicked attraction of the man.

"You're always so gracious, Michael," he said over his shoulder, black eyes gleaming with amusement. Then he turned his attention to Brenna. His glance ran over her with lazy impudence. "Delightful, quite delightful!" he drawled softly. "It's really completely unfair of my barbaric friend here to try to keep such a prize to himself. I'm very happy to meet you, Miss Sloan."

"Cut it out, Jake," Donovan ordered bluntly. "What are you doing here? I told you this morning that I'd have Monty bring Brenna by the set tomorrow afternoon."

"I have to fly to Nevada in the morning to reshoot some scenes on location," Dominic said smoothly. "As you're so determined to have the picture finished on schedule, I thought I'd drop by and have my discussion with Miss Sloan tonight."

"At this time of night?" Donovan asked skeptically.

Dominic checked his watch casually. "It's barely eleven," he challenged. "Since when have you cared about keeping conventional hours where a picture is concerned?"

Donovan muttered a curse under his breath, and gave in abruptly. Turning to Brenna, his glance ran over her flimsily clad body critically. "Get dressed, Brenna," he ordered harshly.

An irrepressible chuckle escaped from Dominic, as the swift color came to Brenna's cheeks. With her head held high, she turned on her heel and strode furiously into the bedroom, slamming the door behind her.

As she quickly discarded the robe and donned panties and bra and a pair of faded blue jeans and a scarlet sweatshirt, she muttered stormy imprecations beneath her breath at the arrogance and chauvinism of men in general, and Donovan and Dominic in particular. Then putting her feet into a pair of scuffed loafers, she marched back into the living room. It did not improve her temper to see the two men apparently on the best of terms, drinks in their hands, talking in a desultory fashion about outtakes.

They both turned at her entrance, and a mischievous smile appeared on Dominic's face as he took in her less than elegant garb. "Ah, the young maid cometh," he said teasingly. "Tell me, Michael, do you think that outfit will sufficiently discourage my lustful nature?"

"Shut up, Jake," Donovan growled sourly.

Dominic cocked an eyebrow, dark eyes gleaming devilishly. "You know what a satyr I am," he said silkily. "I wonder if we should send over to wardrobe for a suit of armor."

"Jake!" Donovan said warningly.

"Or perhaps we could order a chastity belt," Dominic suggested irrepressibly."

"Very funny," Donovan said disgustedly.

"I thought so," Dominic said easily. "Now don't you think we've made Miss Sloan uncomfortable enough with our remarks? It's about time to get down to business. Run along, Michael, we have work to do."

A scowl darkened Michael's face. "I'm going to stay," he said belligerently.

Dominic raised his head, and suddenly the rakish playboy image was gone entirely. "No, you will not," he said sharply, dark eyes commanding. "We have a scene to go over. I have instructions to give, and a rapport to establish with an actress I'm directing in a film. I will not have you standing over us glowering like a jealous lover, and interfering with my work. You know damn well if you were directing, there's no way you would permit it. Well, neither will I!" He turned to Brenna and said in exasperation. "Will you kindly tell our mutual friend here that you're not afraid of the big bad wolf, and that he may leave with your sanction?"

Brenna was stunned at the amazing metamorphosis that had taken place before her eyes. Jake Dominic was obviously a very complex and powerful personality indeed to challenge a man of Donovan's calibre. "I'm not at all frightened of you, Mr. Dominic," she said slowly. "And Mr. Donovan knows very well that I don't want him here."

There was an incoherent exclamation from Donovan as he slammed his drink down on the glass end table and strode angrily toward the door. Jerking it open, he turned to regard them grimly. "The only reason I'm leaving is because you're right, Jake. I'd react the same way to any interference while I was trying to do my job," he said harshly. "But you'd better be damn sure you stick to business!" The door slammed behind him with a resounding bang.

five

DOMINIC FLINCHED AS HE GAZED AT THE still vibrating door. "I wonder just how close I was to being totally mangled," he mused.

"You didn't seem overly apprehensive," Brenna remarked dryly.

His expression was grim. "Don't kid yourself," he said bluntly. "One doesn't tease a grizzly bear without being fully conscious of the possible repercussions. You just have to weigh the values to be gained against the risks involved."

Brenna fastened on the simile. "A grizzly bear?" she asked curiously.

"Strong, powerful, 'the lord of the forest,'" he said, his gaze resting thoughtfully on her face. "How do you see him, Miss Sloan?"

She made a face. "If we're speaking of animals, I think you're completely mistaken; I see him as a cougar." She looked into Jake Dominic's eyes, and finished deliberately. "And you as a black panther."

His lips quirked. "While you, without doubt, are a gazelle. Graceful, fragile, and the natural prey of either of us."

She continued to look at him steadily. "You forget that the

gazelle is also very swift, Mr. Dominic. Given warning, I have no doubt I could elude destruction."

"The big cats give no warning, Miss Sloan," he replied softly. "Which is why you should realize you're wrong about Michael." His appraisal was coolly analytical.

"I would judge that in his usual blunt, bold fashion my red-haired friend has laid all his cards on the table. Michael has no use for subtleties."

Brenna blushed and lowered her eyes. "I've noticed that," she said ruefully.

Dominic looked down at his drink, a slight smile on his face. "I gather the gazelle is in full flight," he said lightly. "That's an unusual circumstance for Michael. It's no wonder he's in such a temper. He's definitely not used to being frustrated."

"Then he'll have to grow accustomed to it," Brenna said calmly.

There was a glimmer of admiration in Dominic's eyes as he looked up. "You know, it wasn't entirely business that prompted me to come here tonight," he said slowly. "After I spoke to Michael this morning, I must admit to being intrigued. In all the years I've known Michael, he's never once warned me off a woman. I felt a certain curiosity to see the woman who had him in such turmoil. Now that I've seen you, I'm beginning to understand his predicament. You could be a very unsettling influence on a man, Miss Sloan."

"Does that mean you're going to ignore Donovan's warning, Mr. Dominic?" she asked challengingly.

His face was surprisingly serious as he shook his head. "Despite Michael's suspicious nature, I'm not about to set off in pursuit of you, charming though you may be," he said coolly. "I may be a thorough scoundrel and totally without scruples where women are concerned, but I place a great value on Michael's friendship." His eyes were half closed, as he continued almost beneath his breath, "I have no problem getting mistresses, but I doubt if I could replace Michael."

For a moment there was a curiously lonely and vulnerable look to his face, but it was quickly masked by cynicism. "So you see, you are in no danger where I'm concerned," he went on lightly. "I'm such a bastard that I can't afford to throw away lightly the few friends I have."

Brenna found herself suddenly liking this difficult, complex man. "I think you would make a very good friend," she said gently.

Dominic's brows shot up in surprise. "I don't believe a woman has ever told me that before," he said.

"I suppose they all just want you for your body?" Brenna said solemnly, her eyes twinkling.

"But of course," he said mournfully. "The heartless creatures persist in ignoring my brilliant mind and tortured soul." He pulled a face, and said melodramatically, "I'm only a sex object to them!"

Brenna chuckled, and they exchanged a glance that was suddenly free of tension. It was no wonder that he was such a heartbreaker, she thought in amusement. He moved from mood to mood with quicksilver rapidity, leaving one constantly off guard.

His black eyes were twinkling as he continued. "I'm really a closet virgin," he confided outrageously. "Please be gentle with me."

She shook her head, a slow smile curving her lips. "You're not at all what I expected, Mr. Dominic."

"Jake," he urged casually. "We're all on a first-name basis here." He put his glass on the table, and taking off his dark blue sports jacket, dropped it carelessly on the couch. "You're not what I expected either, Brenna," he said briskly. "Now, suppose you run along and get your script, and we'll get to work."

She found Dominic meant just that. For the next two hours

there was no vestige of the personal in his demeanor. His manner was quick and incisive as they went over the role. With lightning verbal strokes he filled in the background she would need to fully understand the character: motivation, Mary's interaction and relationships with the other characters, and her own role as a catalyst in the story line.

After the preliminary discussions were over, he had her read through the script, stopping her frequently to explain a point or correct her interpretation of a line. Then he had her go through it again without interruption, watching her with a quiet intensity that she found to be both soothing and stimulating.

When she had finished, he leaned back lazily on the couch and regarded her thoughtfully through half-closed lids.

"You have a quick, intelligent mind, Brenna," he said quietly. "I rather think you're one of those people who never makes the same mistake twice."

Brenna knew a swift rush of pleasure at his obvious approval. She could see why Jake was considered so exceptional. It was incredible that in such a short time he had accomplished so much. She not only felt she understood the character in depth, but he had mysteriously instilled in her both enthusiasm and confidence.

"Thank you, Jake," she said sincerely. "You've made it very easy for me."

"My pleasure, believe me," he said with a grin. "Though Michael doesn't usually let his personal feelings influence his judgment, I confess that I was afraid you might be the horrible exception. I had visions of trying to mold an actress out of some stagestruck ingenue." His face darkened. "God knows, we have had enough problems with this picture."

"Mary Durney was supposed to be played by Tammy Silvers, wasn't she?" Brenna asked curiously. "I read that she won a Tony Award last year for *Little Sins*."

Dominic nodded, his lips thin. "She had excellent creden-
tials, and she looked the part," he said shortly. "But she began to
believe her own press clippings."

Seeing Brenna's still-puzzled face, he continued briefly,
"Temperament on the set, skipped wardrobe fittings, tardiness.
She was a real bitch."

"She had a contract, didn't she?" Brenna asked. "How did
you get around that?"

He smiled with feral satisfaction. "Donovan insists on a
clause in all performer's contracts that permits dismissal if the
actor proves unsatisfactory at any time."

Brenna's eyes widened. "Isn't that rather unusual?" she asked,
startled.

"The option is very seldom exercised," he said coolly.
"Donovan may create stars, but he won't tolerate a performer
behaving like one." His mouth twisted wryly. "He has no need
to. Unknowns and stars alike stand in line to be in a Donovan
Ltd. film."

Brenna nodded slowly, knowing this was true.

For the next twenty minutes they discussed the difference
between stage and film work, Dominic outlining clearly the
techniques and skills the medium would demand of her.

When he finally rose to go, her head was whirling with information that he had fed her with computer-like efficiency.
Shrugging into his jacket, he smoothed his rumpled black hair
quickly, and turned back to Brenna with an easy smile. "I think
we've covered everything," he said slowly. "I'll be back late tomorrow evening, so we won't begin work until day after tomorrow. Report to makeup at 6 A.M."

As she rose and accompanied him to the door, his eyes
took in the confusion on her face with a compassionate understanding that she would never have believed he possessed two
hours ago.

"It will all come together," he said quietly, as he opened the door. "Trust me. I promise that you will be a great Mary Durney." He continued teasingly, "How could you help it with such a brilliant director?"

She smiled. "You're right, how could I help it?" she echoed valiantly. "Good night, Jake. You've been super. How can I ever thank you?"

His dark eyes twinkled wickedly. "If I wasn't on my best be-havior, I'd tell you explicitly," he said with a wide grin. "But as I am walking the path of virtue, I can only beg you not to let it get around that I spent two hours alone with you without making a single pass. It would ruin my reputation!"

"It'll be our secret," Brenna assured him gravely.

As the door closed behind him with a soft click, she leaned against it for a moment, smiling softly. The past two hours had instilled in her a buoyant confidence in her abilities that she had never known before. She was suddenly blissfully certain that everything was going to work out to her complete satisfac-tion.

The panicky urge to bolt and run that had possessed her af-ter the passionate interlude with Donovan had gradually faded as the evening progressed. Why should she give up an opportu-nity that could mean financial security for Randy, and a fantastic start in her chosen profession just because Michael Donovan had decided she was to be his next mistress? The decision was not solely his, she thought defiantly, as she flicked off the lights on the way to the bedroom. She had fended off the most intricate of passes from men who thought she was easy game. She would handle Donovan with the same cool aloofness. Hadn't he prom-ised there would be no confrontation till the picture was fin-ished? It should be a simple matter to see that she was safely out of his reach when the time came.

As for his intention to wear down her resistance before then, she doubted that he would have the opportunity from what Jake Dominic had told her about her proposed schedule. It was going to be nonstop work from now until the final scene was shot. And if Donovan valued his precious timetable as much as he appeared to, he would have to leave her alone to get on with it.

Brenna was determined that he would find her much less compliant at their next encounter. It must have been surprise, coupled with Donovan's undoubted sexual expertise, that had reduced her to such a state of almost abject desire, she thought firmly. Now that she was on guard, she would see that no break in her armor would allow him a similar advantage.

With this firm resolution in mind, she quickly unpacked her bags, and put away her clothes. They filled only one bureau drawer and not even a quarter of the closet space. It was obvious that the residents of these luxurious cottages were expected to possess a far more extensive wardrobe than she did, she thought ruefully. She shrugged philosophically. She had not come here to model clothes but to act, and after Jake Dominic's encouragement this evening, she had every confidence that she could perform that function with a large degree of success.

After brushing her teeth, setting her alarm, and donning her very utilitarian cotton pajamas, she slipped between the cream satin sheets, feeling very much the plain brown wren in this lush Sybarite nest. Weary as she was, it was still a long time before her adrenaline-charged mind gave in to the demands of her exhausted body. Her thoughts were a wildly confused kaleidoscope that whirled in erratic circles over the feverish events of the last two days. It seemed impossible that a person's life could change with such speed. Not only her physical surroundings, but the inhabitants of her new world were strange and exotic, and she felt suddenly very unsure and alone.

But she wasn't alone, she assured herself steadily. She still had Randy, even though he wasn't in her immediate vicinity. She had not given up her determination to change that status as soon as possible. She would find a way to circumvent Donovan's ridiculous orders at the first opportunity. In the meantime, she would focus her thoughts on Randy, the only dear, familiar object in this frightening world. Gradually, as she did this, she was filled with the accustomed warm serenity, and she became drowsy and relaxed.

Yet it wasn't Randy's golden hair and puckish smile that was her last vision before she dropped off to sleep, but the blunt, rugged features and dark red hair of Michael Donovan.

Even though the following day was jam-packed with activity, Brenna was to look on it later as being positively leisurely. The morning was spent memorizing her lines, with special emphasis on the scenes Dominic had indicated he wanted her to concentrate on for the following day. She blessed the fact that she was the quick study that Wilkes had bragged about. By noon she had the scenes learned to her satisfaction, though she knew she would have to refresh her memory each day before going to the set. One of the advantages of work in films was obviously going to be the convenience of focusing one's efforts on one or two scenes a day and not to have to worry about the production as a whole. Whether this would prove an asset in the long run was debatable, she thought skeptically. She knew she was one of those performers who could lose herself in the role when involved in the continuity of an actual play. Whether this magic could occur when she was faced with doing one isolated scene after another in disjointed sequence, she had no way of knowing.

At lunchtime she hurried to Doris Charles' apartment to check on Randy. Donovan had not exaggerated, she discovered when she let herself in at Doris Charles' shouted invitation. Randy had every possible necessity and amusement to keep the most pampered child in ecstasy. He greeted her with his usual cheerful ebullience and then ignored her and went back to painstakingly linking a caboose to the cars of a brightly painted wooden train.

Doris, dressed in jeans and a plaid shirt, was sitting cross-legged on the floor beside him. She looked up with a wide grin as Brenna entered.

"Hi," she said cheerfully. "This young man of yours is on his way to becoming a railroad tycoon. Before we're done, we may stretch from coast to coast. Care to join us?"

Brenna shook her head, her gaze lingering on the chubby romper-clad figure. "I only have a minute," she said wistfully. "I just stopped to make sure that he was all right. Did he sleep well?"

"Like a top," the nurse said serenely. "And he ate a breakfast this morning that would do justice to a lumberjack. I haven't been able to pry him away from all these toys, but as soon as he loses interest, I'll take him down to the pool to get some sun."

"He'll love that," Brenna said smiling. "He's a real water baby."

"I noticed that last night when I gave him his bath," Doris said wryly. "He nearly drowned me!"

Brenna chuckled understandingly. "I've often been tempted to change into a bikini before tackling that particular job," she admitted.

"Hey! I may just try that," the nurse said, eyes twinkling. "Provided I survive our dip in the pool this afternoon." Her gray eyes were kind as she went on gently. "It's always difficult when a mother is separated from her child for the first time. I want you to know that I'm taking the very best care of Randy, and he's adjusting very well."

There was a suspicious moisture in Brenna's eyes and she blinked rapidly. "I'm sure he's doing a good deal better than I am," she said huskily. "He's had considerable experience."

"He's a perfect angel," Doris said enthusiastically. "I'm going to miss him like crazy when this job is finished." She cocked a sandy eyebrow quizzically. "You wouldn't need a permanent nanny by any chance?"

Brenna shook her head. "I'm afraid I couldn't afford you. I'm only just getting started. It will be some time before I can think about employing someone with your qualifications."

The nurse shrugged. "You never can tell," she said easily. "Keep me in mind, if your ship comes in."

Brenna nodded. "I'll do that," she replied lightly. She kissed Randy quickly, and then said reluctantly, "I have to leave now. Someone is waiting for me. I'll try to get back this evening in time for his dinner."

"Fine," Doris said cheerfully. "Whenever you have a little extra time, just call, and I'll bring Randy down to the cottage. I'll always advise reception where we are, if we leave the apartment."

Brenna felt a little pang at the nurse's attitude, as if it were the most common thing in the world for a mother to make an appointment to see her own son. She smothered the illogical feeling at once. It didn't make sense to harbor such envy against Doris. She was a warm, competent person, and evidently got along famously with Randy. She was making the situation as easy as possible under the circumstances.

This didn't prevent Brenna from feeling a trifle dejected as she went to the cafeteria. She joined Monty, who poured her a cup of coffee from the carafe on the table. He watched silently as she absently took a sip, grimaced, and then reached for the cream.

"Something wrong?" he asked with a frown.

Brenna shook her head. "Not really. I'm just suffering withdrawal pains," she said with forced cheerfulness. "Randy is having himself a ball."

There was frank relief in Walters' face, as he said heartily, "That's great! Mr. Donovan told me this morning before he left that I was to make sure you weren't worrying about the kid."

"Mr. Donovan has gone?" Brenna asked slowly, wondering why the news didn't bring the expected relief. After keying herself up in anticipation of an encounter with the man, she felt a real letdown when she realized her efforts had been totally unnecessary.

"He flew to London this morning," Walters said casually. "There's some special effects genius he wants to recruit for the science fiction picture he's planning for next spring."

"When will he be back?" Brenna asked, looking down at her coffee, her lashes veiling the interest in her eyes.

Walters shrugged. "Who knows? He has interests all over the world besides Donovan Ltd." He glanced at his watch hurriedly. "I hate to rush you, Brenna, but you have an appointment with Simon Burke, Donovan's attorney, to sign your contract in fifteen minutes."

Brenna pushed her cup away, and rose to her feet. "Then let's go," she said cheerfully.

The rest of the day passed with the flickering acceleration of an old silent movie. After the contract was signed, Monty escorted her to wardrobe, where she was fitted for the outfits she was to wear in the scenes the following day. From there she was whirled to publicity where she gave a brief synopsis of her background, and was assigned an appointment to have still photographs taken for the publicity releases.

"I'll keep in touch," Monty promised, as he let Brenna out at her cottage that evening. "Let me know if there's anything you need," he said cheerfully. "And don't let Dominic work you too hard. He has the reputation of being something of a slave driver."

In the weeks to come she was to look back with grim amusement at that warning from Walters. She soon discovered that she had as much chance of following that advice as to change the path of a hurricane. Jake Dominic trampled over obstacles as if they did not exist. In his ruthless drive for perfection, he spared neither himself, his crew, nor the cast. Brenna found herself on an exhausting merry-go-round from six in the morning till eight in the evening, and sometimes even later.

Then she would hurry home and spend a few precious moments with Randy, before settling down to work on her lines and blocking for the next day's shooting. If the pace had not been so killing, she would have enjoyed the filming itself. All the members of the cast and the crew had a friendly professionalism that made them a pleasure to work with. And if Dominic was demanding, he was also both stimulating and inspirational. There was no limit to the help and time he was willing to extend to get the results he wanted. Her admiration for his ingenuity and directorial genius grew with every passing day, as the pressure mounted and Dominic labored to bring the film in on schedule.

Because most of the scenes still to be completed were those that had to be reshot with Brenna replacing Tammy Silvers, Dominic's demands were focused almost exclusively on Brenna. When she arrived back at the cottage, she was too weary to do anything but go over her lines and then fall into bed in total exhaustion. She was often too tired to bother to eat, and, always slim and fragile looking, her appearance soon became positively ethereal.

It was this fact that caused Dominic's tightly leashed temper to explode one morning with all the accompanying fireworks, just two days before production was due to be completed.

They had barely begun shooting that morning when he called a strident "cut." He strode angrily toward Brenna, his face darkening ominously. "Wardrobe!" he bellowed furiously. "Dammit, get me someone from wardrobe! What the hell are they trying to do to me?"

Brenna stared at him in confusion as he took her by the

shoulders and spun her around swiftly, cursing steadily beneath his breath. "My God! They've made you into a damn caricature!"

Sandra Stafford, the dark, plump wardrobe mistress, scurried hurriedly onto the set, her eyes anxiously fixed on Dominic's angry face. "Mrs. Stafford," Dominic said sarcastically, "perhaps you weren't aware that Miss Sloan is not supposed to be a holocaust survivor from a concentration camp, but a cosseted daughter of an affluent family." His hand tugged angrily at a loose fold of material. "In short, Mrs. Stafford, her gowns are supposed to fit!"

The wardrobe mistress stared in horror at Brenna's green gown. Though Dominic's condemnation had been exaggerated, the gown was undoubtedly ill-fitting and cumbersome looking.

She cast a frightened look at Dominic's forbidding countenance and said nervously, "I'm terribly sorry, Mr. Dominic. We'll correct it right away."

"In the interim the entire cast and crew sit around cooling their heels," he said caustically.

A flush of anger tinted Sandra Stafford's cheeks pink, as she answered defensively. "I said I was sorry, Mr. Dominic, but it's not really wardrobe's fault. That gown was a perfect fit when we made the final alterations four days ago. Miss Sloan must have lost weight."

"She's right, Jake," Brenna put in quickly. "The dress did fit on Tuesday."

Dominic's displeasure was immediately directed toward Brenna. Turning his back on the relieved wardrobe mistress, his dark eyes went over Brenna critically. "For God's sake, Brenna, you must have lost ten pounds in the last three weeks," he said explosively, his black eyes flaming. "How irresponsible can you get! Didn't it occur to you that your appearance can't change from scene to scene?"

Brenna could feel the humiliating color rise in her face at

this public denunciation. She raised her chin defiantly. "I didn't do it on purpose," she defended herself. "It just happened."

"A stroke of fate, perhaps," Jake said with intimidating softness. "Mother nature waves her magic wand, and you lose ten pounds."

"I may have missed a few meals," Brenna stammered uncomfortably.

"She skipped a few meals," he said sarcastically. "May we inquire how many?"

"I don't remember," Brenna said defensively, becoming angry in her turn. Surely this castigation wasn't necessary. "I told you I didn't do it deliberately."

"Leave her alone, Jake," Michael Donovan said lazily.

They both turned in surprise, squinting against the glare of the lights to see Donovan's familiar figure leaning indolently against a pillar in the far corner of the sound stage. Donovan's red hair burned like a dark flame in the dimness of the shadows as he straightened, and strolled causally forward. He was dressed informally, as usual, in a cinnamon brown shirt and fitted khaki slacks that explicitly molded the strong lines of his thighs.

"Well, well," Dominic drawled sardonically, "the wanderer returns. When did you get home?"

"Last night," Donovan said laconically.

She had forgotten how piercing those blue eyes were, Brenna thought with a shiver, as his mocking gaze examined her face with a familiar intimacy.

"Hello, Brenna." he said softly.

"Good morning, Mr. Donovan," she said with a composure she didn't really feel. It was only the surprise of seeing him so unexpectedly that caused that tingling warmth in her veins, she told herself stubbornly.

Donovan raised an eyebrow quizzically at her formality, and turned to Dominic. "You're in a foul mood, Jake," he drawled. "I can't see that Brenna's done anything to deserve that serpent's tongue of yours. You've obviously been working the girl to a shadow. You're going to have more problems than a few pounds weight loss if you don't let up. She looks almost breakable."

"I'm quite well, Mr. Donovan," Brenna said coolly.

To her annoyance both men blatantly ignored the interruption. "My God, Michael!" Dominic said harshly. "I have a picture to finish. What do you want me to do, set up banker's hours for the girl? You're the one who gave me the deadline for this film. Now it's my job to try and meet it."

"You're quite right, I did set the deadline," Donovan said coolly. "And I'm the one who can change it. Brenna needs a rest. Schedule her out of the shooting today."

Brenna's eyes widened with shock, and she opened her mouth to protest, but Dominic was before her.

"Schedule her out of..." he repeated dumbfounded, then continued explosively, "And what do you suggest we do while Miss Sloan 'rests'?"

Donovan shrugged. "Shoot around her, or give everyone a day's rest. You decide, Jake," he said carelessly. "But make up your mind that whatever you do today, it's not going to involve Brenna."

With a firm hand on her elbow he half led, half pushed Brenna ahead of him off the set, past the gaping crew, toward the door that led to the parking lot.

"What are you doing?" she hissed furiously. "There's absolutely nothing wrong with me, and I have no intention of going anywhere with you!"

"Be quiet, sweetheart," Donovan said serenely. "You're going to do exactly what you're told, for once."

"For once?" Brenna sputtered indignantly. "You've done nothing but order me around since the moment we met, Michael Donovan, and I have yet to get my own way."

Donovan's blue eyes gleamed mischievously. "But then, neither have I, love," he drawled meaningfully.

Brenna blushed fiercely, and tried futilely to wrest her arm from Donovan's iron grip, as they reached the door. "You can't come in here and just whisk me away, without so much as a by your leave to anyone," she protested. "And just look at me. I've got to return this gown to wardrobe!"

He pushed her through the door, and strode quickly toward a sleek gray Mercedes, dragging Brenna along behind him.

"I can do anything I want to do," he said coolly. "I own the place, remember? As for the gown, we'll stop at your cottage and you can change. I'll send someone over to pick it up after we leave."

"Leave? Where are we going?" Brenna squeaked. "Wasn't the entire purpose of this abduction so that I could get some rest?"

"Certainly," Donovan agreed blandly. "And I fully intend that you do just that. Which doesn't necessarily mean that I'm ordering you to bed—" he grinned innocently, "—at the moment." He opened the passenger door and seated her carefully before closing the door and running around to slip behind the wheel. "I'm taking you away from all this, brown eyes," he grated, in a passable Bogart imitation.

"And what if I don't want to be taken away?" Brenna asked archly, trying to smother the fugitive amusement that this new, lighthearted Donovan produced. How many facets were there to Donovan's complicated personality, she wondered helplessly. Each encounter with this human dynamo left her struggling helplessly out of her depth.

He started the motor, but did not put the car into gear. He turned to face her, his expression serious. "You need a break, Brenna," he said quietly, his fingers lightly tracing the faint shadows beneath her eyes that even makeup had not been able to cover entirely. "Jake may be a cinematic genius, but he'll ride roughshod over anything that gets in his way. I'd forgotten you were so vulnerable, or I wouldn't have stayed away so long." His tone was infinitely gentle, his eyes enfolding her in a flowering warmth that could be tenderness.

Brenna caught her breath, and forced herself to look away before that gaze completely dissolved any resistance she could muster to Donovan's powerful charisma. "I'm really quite all right," she insisted shakily. "I'm much tougher than I look."

His hand reached out to encircle one fragile wrist, and she jumped involuntarily at the sensation that passed through her at his casual touch.

"I have no doubt you have the heart of a lion," he said lightly. "But it's obvious that your physical stamina doesn't match up. A puff of wind could blow you away." His eyes darkened angrily. "What the hell could Jake have been thinking of to let you get in this shape?"

A sudden poignant warmth shot through Brenna, melting any remaining resistance. It had been so long since she had had anyone to worry about her physical well-being, she thought mistily. Not since Janine had died, had anyone expressed any personal concern for her. Even with Janine it had been she and not her older sister who was the caretaker. Thinking back, Brenna couldn't remember anyone who had given her this wonderful, comforting feeling of being treasured. She felt a sudden urge to surrender, to throw off the burden of independence and responsibility that seemed too heavy to bear, to lean on Donovan's vibrant strength that she knew would so effortlessly shield her. She knew this mood wouldn't last; soon her independence would reassert itself, and she would once again be ready to do battle in the arena. But not now. She was so tired. Surely it wouldn't hurt to lay aside her armor for just a little while and be young and carefree.

She turned once again to meet his eyes and asked quietly, "So what do you suggest?"

"I have a cottage on a tiny island just off the coast," he said, his narrowed eyes on her face, weighing her every reaction. "We can be there by helicopter in an hour. It's quite beautiful and very peaceful. No telephone, no television, and no Jake Dominic to intrude on your rest. I promise to have you back in your own chaste little cottage before sunset."

"You make it sound very appealing," Brenna said slowly. It sounded like paradise, she thought longingly.

Donovan's rapier eyes read the wistfulness in her face, and he moved in with swift aggression. "I'm not about to rape you, if that's what you're worried about," he said bluntly. "I would hardly incur the expense of a full day of lost production, just to get you into bed. That would make you very expensive, indeed. I don't promise not to try to make love to you, but it will be you that sets the pace. All you have to do is say 'no.'"

"I'll go," she said recklessly.

An almost boyish smile lit Donovan's rugged features. "Great," he said tersely, and putting the car in gear, he backed out of the parking space and drove rapidly out of the lot.

six

THE WHIR OF THE SCARLET HELICOPTER'S rotors died to a whisper, and Donovan reached across to unsnap Brenna's seat belt with swift economical movements. "Stay where you are," he ordered briskly. "I'll come around and help you down."

Brenna nodded absently, as she peered eagerly through the window at the small clearing surrounded by towering pines. They had landed on a square concrete landing pad, and she watched impatiently as Donovan attached lines to the helicopter from steel links embedded in the concrete. He paused to look speculatively at the darkening sky to the west, before coming around to the door and opening it.

"Looks like we're going to get a bit of a storm," he said, as he reached up and, placing his two hands firmly on her waist, swung her easily to the ground. "I was hoping the weather would be good, so that we could go out in the boat," he said frowning. "Are you a sailor, Brenna?"

"I have no idea," she said simply. "I've never been on a boat."

She had said the same thing about flying, when they had arrived at the private landing strip on the outskirts of Twin Pines a little over an hour ago.

Shutting the helicopter door, Donovan took her hand in his and set off up the pebbled path that led across the clearing, into the dense stand of trees.

"I have an idea a man could become addicted to providing you with new experiences, Brenna Sloan," he said thoughtfully. "It would give him a never-ending source of pleasure."

She made a face, as she gave a half skip to keep up with his lengthy stride. "Where were you ten years ago?" she asked lightly. "Orphanage brats lead notoriously dull lives."

His hand tightened protectively around hers. He didn't look at her as he asked quietly, "Was it very bad, Brenna?"

"The children's home?" She shook her head. "No, not really bad," she said matter of factly. "Lonely, sometimes."

They had reached the glade now, and Brenna cocked an eyebrow inquiringly. "Would it be too much to ask where we're going?"

"The cabin is about a quarter of a mile from here," he said. "I thought we'd stop there first to take some steaks out of the freezer, before we take a hike around the island." His eyes appraised the horizon critically. "It looks like the storm may hold off for a while. It's moving slowly."

After that, they moved in companionable silence through the woods. Brenna breathed in the pine-scented, pungent air with warm contentment. For a city bred person like herself this simple walk through the woods had all the attraction of the exotic. She was as lighthearted and happy as a child at this moment, and a great part of it was due to this man, who was holding her hand with such casual camaraderie.

From the moment she had agreed to come to Donovan's island, he had been everything one could have wished in a companion. He had carefully kept any sign of sexual awareness from his attitude during the time he had driven her to the cottage, and waited while she quickly changed into white shorts, sneakers, and a yellow sun top. She had washed the heavy makeup off and hadn't bothered to replace it, relying on the glowing perfection of her healthy skin. She had hurriedly brushed out the elaborate hairdo, letting her hair fall in its usual gleaming curtain down her back. Then they had hurried like two eager schoolchildren to the airstrip to board the helicopter. Somehow it did not surprise her at all that Donovan could pilot the helicopter himself, and was also licensed to fly the Lear jet that was hangared at the field. A man as dominant as Donovan would want to be fully in command, wherever he was.

They had been walking for about five minutes and Brenna could see the outline of the redwood chalet in a distant clearing. She asked curiously, "Don't you find such a totally isolated hideaway inconvenient? I should think you would at least want a telephone to keep in contact with your business interests."

Donovan shook his head decisively. "No way!" he said curtly. "I bought the island two years ago for the express purpose of having a place to go when I wanted to do some writing. I wouldn't get anything accomplished if I could be reached by phone. If anything urgent comes up, Monty can always hire a helicopter or a launch to bring him over."

They had reached the clearing now, and Brenna saw the A-frame chalet. The cabin, while charming, was really quite small. When she commented on this, Donovan smiled, his blue eyes dancing.

"It was quite large enough for the original owner's purpose," he said dryly. "I bought it from one of Dominic's playboy buddies, who had it built to his own specifications.

Suspecting that she knew the answer already, she asked, "And that purpose was?"

"A love nest," he said succinctly.

"I see," Brenna said thoughtfully, her eyes gleaming curiously, a question trembling on her lips.

"And, no, I have never used the cabin for that reason." He anticipated her question with a grin. "I come here to work."

Donovan unlocked the door and, with a mocking gesture, indicated that she should precede him, then followed her closely so that he could see her reaction. He wasn't disappointed.

Brenna gazed around as wide-eyed as a child. A love nest, indeed, she thought faintly. The chalet had a floor plan that provided no privacy whatever. The living room area flowed into the tiny kitchenette with only the free-style cabinets to divide the room. A spiral staircase led to a half-loft that was occupied by a king-sized bed and two bedside tables. The decor was contemporary, with the accent on comfort, and sang with glowing reds and orange. A huge stone fireplace dominated one wall, with a long, scarlet couch and a white fur rug placed cozily before it. There was an almost overpoweringly intimate atmosphere about the chalet, and she was filled with a strange tension under Donovan's mocking stare.

"What, no communal bathing?" Brenna asked jokingly, her eyes not meeting his.

"Now that you mention it," he said lazily, and sauntering over to the far wall, he slid a decorative panel aside to reveal an enormous emerald green sunken tub, surrounded by several white potted ferns.

"The poor fellow was painfully obvious, wasn't he?" Donovan commented casually. "One hopes his little playmates came here with the same aim in view. One look at this setup would send any shrinking violet running for the hills screaming bloody murder."

He slid the screen closed, and, ignoring Brenna's scarlet face, strode quickly to the tiny kitchen. Rummaging in the compact freezer, he triumphantly extracted two paper-wrapped packages and put them in the portable microwave, pushing the button to defrost.

"All set," he announced crisply, coming around the counter into the living room area. "Shall we go?"

Brenna nodded quickly, and hurried out the door and down

the steps, conscious all the time of Donovan's amusement. Once outside, she breathed a covert sigh of relief, and, turning to Donovan, asked eagerly, "Where shall we go?"

He smiled indulgently at the glowing eagerness on her face. "I thought we'd climb the hill and watch the storm approach. It can be quite an experience. Would you like that?"

"I'd love it," Brenna said enthusiastically, her brown eyes shining.

"You're easily pleased," Donovan said dryly, as he took her hand once more, and they set off toward the hill he had indicated. "The last time I saw that much enthusiasm on a woman's face, she'd just been gifted with a diamond bracelet."

"By you, no doubt," Brenna said lightly, ignoring the twinge she experienced at the intimacy implied in Donovan's comment. She was determined to let nothing spoil this day. "How cynical you and Jake are about women. There are a few women in the world who aren't for sale, you know."

Donovan's hand tightened painfully on hers, but his voice was even as he said carefully, "You appear to have a fairly intimate knowledge of Jake's attitudes. Could it be that Jake has been up to his usual shenanigans?"

For a moment she was tempted to lie, to see if she could break the tight control on Donovan's face, but then she discarded the impulse. She wanted no tension to destroy the harmony of the moment. She shook her head. "Nope," she said matter-of-factly, making a face. "The only interest your charming friend has in me is purely analytical. He wants to see how hard he can push me before I collapse."

Donovan's grip relaxed fractionally. "And I'll lay odds he'll probably be there with open arms to catch you when you do," he said dryly.

Brenna giggled helplessly, as she suddenly had a mental picture of a villainous Dominic, complete with moustache and flowing cape, clutching her in a Valentino-style embrace.

A smile tugged at the corners of Donovan's lips at the contagious quality of her mirth.

"I'm glad you find the idea so amusing," he said lightly. "I assure you that is not the usual feminine reaction to Jake."

She tossed her head, tilting her nose saucily. "I've come to the conclusion that you both take yourselves far too seriously," she said sweetly, as they started up the twisted dirt path that led to the top of the hill. "It's about time someone took you down a peg."

Donovan cocked an eyebrow. "You're feeling brave today, aren't you, sweetheart?" he murmured softly. "That wouldn't be in the nature of a dare, would it?"

She backed down hurriedly, at the dangerous glint in his blue eyes. "You and Jake have been friends for a long time, haven't you?" she asked quickly, hoping to distract him.

There was a short silence before Donovan accused softly, "Chicken! I'll let you escape this time, but don't issue challenges unless you're prepared to follow through, Brenna." He watched with amusement as color flooded her cheeks, before he took pity on her. "In answer to your question, Jake and I have been friends since college. We both attended UCLA." He grimaced wryly. "Not that we moved in the same circles. I was a slum kid working my way through by doing construction work on the side, and Jake was heir to Dominic's Shipping—the original golden boy." The look in Donovan's eyes was far away as he murmured, "We were a mismatched pair. God knows why we didn't hate each other. I was a defensive young tough with a king-sized chip on my shoulder, and Jake was a hell-raising bastard who didn't give a damn about anyone. We were at each other's throats constantly, until we found we had one thing in common that made all our differences minute in comparison. We both felt that film-making was the ultimate art form, and we were both determined to make the best damn pictures in the history of the business."

"You had one other thing in common," Brenna said teasingly. "What about your overwhelming modesty?"

Donovan grinned in acknowledgment of the gentle thrust. "Neither of us was ever bothered with an excess of that virtue," he admitted simply. "We always knew what we could do."

Yes, there would never be any doubt in Donovan's mind about his own abilities, she thought, as she stared with new eyes at the powerful body and bold features of the man. Before this she had looked upon him as some sort of super being, sprung fully grown, with the faculty to mold and disrupt her life.

He had unbuttoned his cotton shirt to the waist as they had started their climb, and her eyes were drawn in fascination to the strong shoulders and chest muscles with the dark red patch of wiry hair that narrowed to a fine line as it approached the waistband of his slacks. Those muscles had been formed by hard physical labor on innumerable construction sites, as a young boy struggled desperately to overcome his background and get a decent education. If he was arrogant and cynical, wasn't it a natural by-product of the struggle to survive and reach the dizzy heights which he was innately conscious were his destiny?

"Do you have a family?" she asked, suddenly wanting to know more of the past that had created Michael Donovan.

He shrugged, his face closed. "My mother died when I was twelve. I guess I still have a father wandering around someplace. I really wouldn't know. I ran away from home when I was fourteen."

They crested the hill suddenly, and Brenna drew in her breath sharply at the sight that almost physically assaulted her senses. Gone was the gentle terrain with a dramatic abruptness that was overpowering in its impact. The summit fell away to the sea far below in a sheer drop, and there was nothing before them but an endless stretch of sea and sky. At first glance it seemed that the two were one vast seething entity. The storm was moving swiftly now. The churning cobalt of the waves mirrored the ominous force of the clouds, as the quickening wind strived to bind the dichotomy into a tumultuous whole.

"It's magnificent!" Brenna breathed, awestruck, as she moved irresistibly closer to the edge of the cliff in an unconscious desire to become part of the raw, elemental savagery that was swiftly surrounding them.

"It will be on us in a few moments," Donovan observed. "If you don't want to get half drowned, we should start back right away."

She shook off his restraining hand and stepped closer to the edge. "I've never seen anything like this," she murmured ecstatically. The temperature had dropped at least ten degrees in the last few minutes, and the wind that stung her face and caused her hair to billow out behind her in a wild banner was almost cold.

Donovan let her go, his eyes narrowed and watchful, but not interfering with the emotional response that the storm had stirred in her.

Suddenly they were enveloped in the mysterious golden twilight that preceded the unleashing of the storm. Donovan felt compelled to issue a final warning, which he already knew would be futile by the rapt fascination on Brenna's face.

He was right. She didn't even look at him as she replied absently, "You go on ahead. I'll be along later."

His mouth twisted in amused resignation, and leaning casually against a boulder a little distance away from the figure on the headland, he crossed his arms and prepared to wait.

He didn't have to wait long. The golden twilight faded to violet dimness and the distant growling of the thunder became a savage roar as the heavens exploded, and sheets of rain whipped at them with savage fury.

The exultant oneness with nature that Brenna was feeling was magnified rather than diminished by the pouring rain that completely drenched them in a matter of moments. A cold wind tore at her hair and clothes like a ravening animal. She opened her mouth to let the drops caress her lips, and stretched out her arms in supplication and embrace. She was conscious of the smallness and fragility of each separate limb and muscle of her body, and at the same time she felt as strong and powerful as a goddess from Olympus.

She laughed exultantly, glancing at Donovan's watchful face as she tossed back her sodden hair from her face, still holding her arms before her like a high priestess invoking the fury of the storm. "I'm going to live forever, Donovan!" she shouted triumphantly. "Do you hear me? I'm going to live forever!"

There was a tolerant smile on Donovan's face as he levered himself away from the boulder, and lazily crossed to stand beside her. He, too, was soaked, his shirt and trousers plastered to his muscular body like a second skin, his hair rain-darkened to almost black.

He took her elbow and propelled her firmly away from the edge of the cliff. "You're not even going to live till next week, if you catch a chill from this drenching, you crazy woman," he said roughly. "Your skin is as cold as ice."

"I'm not cold. I feel wonderful. I feel terrific," she said giddily. "I've never felt so alive in my life."

"Yes, I know. You're going to live forever," he said dryly. "But right now you're going to jog back to the cabin to get your circulation working."

With a hand on her elbow, he set the pace and they were soon half running, half sliding down the hill. The dirt path was now a muddy quagmire, and it was almost impossible to keep one's footing. Several times Brenna found herself sitting ingloriously in the mud, the rain pouring over her in buckets while she collapsed in helpless laughter. In this crazy exultant mood, she could take nothing seriously. It was a moment out of time, to be enjoyed and savored to the hilt.

Each time she fell, Donovan picked her up patiently, shaking his head ruefully at her giddiness and urging her on with quiet determination. Once they reached the bottom of the hill, the going was easier, and it was only a matter of minutes before they were running up the steps to the chalet. They were both breathing hard from the run, but as Brenna leaned back against the door, she felt no weariness, only happiness and a bubbling confidence in herself and the world around her. After the countless days of pressure, she was drunk on the sheer exhilaration of being joyfully alive.

She looked blithely around the chalet. It no longer intimidated, but merely amused her. Donovan himself was a far from intimidating figure, sopping wet and woefully mud splattered.

"What would everyone say if they could see the big movie tycoon now?" she giggled irrepressibly.

"They'd say he looked a great deal better than a certain fledgling actress," he said coolly, shaking his head. Brenna's shorts and top were wet and clinging to her slim body, her long, wet hair hanging in ropy strands around her glowing face. "And you're still cold," he went on briskly, as he touched her throat lightly. With swift strides he crossed the room to the portable bar at one side of the stone fireplace, and poured something dark and potent looking into a glass. He returned to offer it to her commandingly.

"Drink it all," he ordered curtly. "It will warm you."

She started to protest that she didn't need warming, but one look at his determined face convinced her that it would be useless. She drained the glass in one swallow and collapsed against the door, gasping, her face a bright scarlet.

"For God's sake, that was straight whiskey," Donovan said impatiently. "You're supposed to sip it, not gulp it."

"How was I supposed to know that?" she wheezed, her eyes tearing. "I've never had whiskey before."

"Another famous first," he said ironically. "Sit down while I see if I can scare up something for you to change into." Not waiting for her reply, he took the spiral steps to the sleeping area two at a time.

She obediently headed toward the scarlet velvet couch, but looking ruefully down at her dripping form, she moved instead to lean against the fireplace. Now that the first violent effects of the whiskey were over, she found that the liquor did make her feel warmer, and what was more, it increased the delicious euphoria that she was experiencing. She was delighted that the whiskey seemed to have no other effect on her, and she impulsively moved to the liquor cabinet and poured herself another. This time she did sip it more cautiously, but found that it still gave her that all-pervading sensation of well-being. She was just about to refill her glass again, when Donovan returned with an armful of clothes and two fluffy white towels. He arched his brows inquiringly, as he looked pointedly at the glass in her hand.

"I've decided I like it," she announced cheerfully, smiling at him. "I must have a good head for liquor. It has practically no effect on me at all."

"Amazing," he drawled mockingly, as he firmly took the glass from her, and set it on the bar. He placed the clothes and towels in her arms, and, strolling over to the ornamental screen, drew it aside and turned on the faucets full force in the sunken tub.

"Get undressed, and into that tub," he ordered briskly. "I'll light a fire, and then put on the steaks."

She stared at him wild-eyed, clutching the clothes to her chest protectively. Surely he didn't expect her to bathe with her privacy ensured only by that flimsy screen?

He had turned away as if he had no doubt of her obeying his injunctions, but as she stood hesitating, he barked impatiently, "Get moving!"

She found herself moving automatically toward the screened enclosure. Once behind the barricade, she found she had more privacy than she had thought. Well, she must bathe off all this mud. She could hurry and be in and out of that sinfully luxurious tub in mere minutes. She sprinkled lavender bubble bath lavishly from a crystal container that she found near the faucets. She ripped off the muddy shorts, top, and the bra and panties beneath, and stepped into the sunken bath with a feeling of utmost luxury.

She quickly scrubbed away the mud and grass stains. Then she rested her head on the ledge at the far end of the enormous tub, stretching full length, and letting the warm silky water flow over her. She closed her eyes and it seemed that the action tuned her other senses to a keener intensity. She was conscious of the sound of running water, and the movements of Donovan as he built the fire in the fireplace across the room. There was the scent of the bubble bath, and the pungent odor of burning pine cones. How deliciously sensual and relaxing it all was, she thought drowsily . . . so relaxing.

"Brenna!"

She opened her heavy lids to stare into blue eyes that were deep and still as mountain pools. Donovan's eyes.

"Hello," she said drowsily. Somehow it seemed supremely natural to open her eyes and have Donovan there, looking at her with that quiet intensity. He was no more than a breath away, sitting on the edge of the tub and leaning close to cup her head in his hands, as he murmured huskily.

"Hello, sweetheart." His lips touched hers in a kiss as gentle as the drift of apple blossoms and sweet as honey. When his lips moved away reluctantly, she gave a little sigh of disappointment, and tilted her head in a little searching movement of frustration.

"You left the bath water running," he said hoarsely. "I called, but you didn't answer." Then his lips were there again, offering quick tender kisses to her yearning lips, her cheeks, the lobes of her ears. She turned her face up to his like a flower to the sun, her expression blindly sensual. He caught his breath raggedly, his eyes darkening with passion and his mouth covered hers, no longer gentle but burning with hunger. A demand that she met with a matching appetite. Her lips parted and his tongue stroked hers in a sensual frenzy, as he groaned low in his throat. Her hands reached up and curved around his neck to bring him closer, her fingers playing in the thick crispness of the hair at the nape of his neck, before running exploringly over the brawny muscles of his back and shoulders. "You're still wet," she whispered vaguely. Breathing heavily, he wrenched his mouth away to bury his face in her throat. She could feel the rapid tattoo of the pulse in his temple. Or was it her own feverish heartbeat, she wondered. He gave a low chuckle, "I'm about to get a lot wetter," he said huskily. "Help me with my shirt, love." He drew back and pulled his shirt from the waistband of his slacks, and then was still. "Help me," he said urgently. "I want your hands on me."

She wanted them on him, too. She obeyed the irresistible urge to touch the spring mahogany hair on his muscular chest, and then growing bolder, ran her hands up his shoulders in a slow, explorative caress. He tensed, and a shudder shook his body. He caught and held both of her hands to his chest for a brief moment before he released them with a rueful sigh. "Perhaps I'd better not have your help after all, love. I'm about to go up like all the fireworks on the Fourth of July." He stripped off the shirt, and threw it to one side, his hands swiftly going to his belt.

It was then that Brenna began to feel the first stirrings of alarm. She suddenly became conscious of the distinctly irregular situation she had become involved in. With scarlet cheeks, she looked down at herself and noticed with relief that the great quantities of bubbles cloaked everything but her shoulders in a snowy mountain of froth.

"Wait," she said shakily, her eyes on the belt Donovan had removed and was about to toss after the shirt. "What are you doing?"

Donovan's quick appraisal took in her pink cheeks and her air of distress. He moved with lightning swiftness to reassure her in a way that had her breath coming in quick gasps, and a melting ache beginning in her loins. When he finally let her go, she was clinging helplessly to him, and barely heard him when he answered between quick, hot kisses, "I want to touch you. I want to touch every inch of you. I want your hands on my body. Don't fight me, sweetheart. I won't do anything you don't want me to. I'll stop the minute you say the word."

This was poor comfort, she thought in confusion, when she wasn't at all sure she would want to say that word when the time came. At the moment she wanted nothing less than he did, and when he broke away to remove the rest of his clothing, she found she didn't even have the modesty to close her eyes. She watched with frank enjoyment as he quickly stripped, then joined her in the bath. How tough and virile he was, she thought dreamily. Those massive shoulders had an almost bull-like strength in comparison to the slim hips and strong muscular legs. "Enjoying yourself?" he asked with a grin. She nodded and smiled shyly.

As he lowered himself into the water beside her, he said, chuckling, "I feel cheated." He touched the foamy covering with one finger. "You wouldn't care to stand up and take a bow, would you?"

She shook her head with a bright blush, and he sighed. "I didn't think so. Well, as I am to be deprived of one sensual pleasure, I'll just have to make do with the others." He stretched out beside her, their bodies facing each other but not touching. "Now let me see," he said thoughtfully. "First, there's scent."

He took a strand of her hair in one hand, raised it to his nose and sniffed delicately. "You smell of fresh rainwater and the sea." He rubbed his nose against the satin skin of her temple. "Lavender," he announced hoarsely. "And woman." He drew a deep breath and murmured, "You also have a fragrance that's just you,

Brenna." He closed his eyes, and said carefully, "I missed you during these past few weeks. I've been sheer hell to work with, and I didn't even know what was wrong with me. I'd never missed anyone before." He opened his eyes, and the intensity of his gaze came as a fresh shock. "I'm never going away without you again."

She knew a moment of panic at the implacable sureness of the statement. Suddenly she felt as if she were caught, caged by the sure determination of this man, who held her transfixed without even touching her.

He must have seen the flash of fear in her eyes because his intensity was instantly masked and he smiled gently. "Where were we?" he said lightly. "Oh, yes, I was about to go on to taste." His mouth touched hers gently, his tongue probing her mouth in a long dizzying exploration that left her shuddering with desire. "Honey and a dash of spice." Donovan, too, was shaking, and she could see that the muscles of his body were taut with tension. "Though your voice is music to my ears, I think we'll skip sound," he said with an effort. "I'd much prefer you silent when we go on to the next and most important step. I've got to touch you, love."

With a boldness that caused her to flinch away, she felt his hand first cradle her waist beneath the water, then draw her slowly into his arms, branding her soft nude body with his iron-hard frame.

"No," she whispered weakly, even as she felt herself melt against him, the tips of her nipples hard and sensitive as they were pressed against the rough hair of his chest. The erotic contact was sending burning messages to every nerve in her body, bidding her to respond in the ancient, primitive way of woman.

"Yes," he groaned, as his mouth took hers in savage hunger. "God! I want you. Let me love you, sweetheart."

His hands were everywhere. Stroking, probing, pressing the

secret silky curves, lifting and cupping her swollen breasts to his eager mouth. She made a sound, part gasp, part moan as he nibbled and sucked at the rosy tips. He raised his head, his eyes dark and glazed. "Do you like that, love? I'll remember."

He rolled her over with one swift movement, so that he was on his back entirely supporting her slight weight, one muscular leg parting her thighs, his hands still cupping her breasts lovingly. She was now intimately conscious of his shocking arousal, as his lower body began a rhythmic thrusting motion.

She was shaking and trembling like a leaf, as he played upon her body as a master musician would on his beloved instrument. Every nerve was exquisitely sensitized to the touch of his body, and she knew that she was wildly desperate for the completion he could give her.

"I'm going to take you now, love." He breathed against her breast. "Tell me you want me to take you!"

The passionate injunction sent a spiraling shock through her, that did much to revive the thinking process which had been suspended at the command of her aching body. She knew he would keep his word and let her go, if she insisted. But, God, how could she insist, when he had tuned her body to this feverish pitch of need? Yet she knew she must refuse him, if she was to salvage any portion of her independence. Donovan was still almost a stranger to her. He had never mentioned love, only desire, and even if she did feel the same desire, it was still not enough.

"Brenna!" Donovan's voice was roughly impatient, as he waited for the acquiescence that he fully expected.

It was the hardest thing she ever did to look into Donovan's eyes and say huskily, "Let me go, Michael."

His face echoed his shocked disbelief, and his hands tightened on her possessively. Then his eyes flamed with anger. "You don't mean that," he said roughly. "You want it as much as I do."

She shook her head stubbornly. "I want you to let me go," she said shakily. "I want you to keep your promise, Michael Donovan."

His eyes narrowed and there was a ruthless curve to his mouth as he said coolly, "You know I could force you to say yes."

She said honestly, "Yes, you probably could. I seem to have little resistance where you're concerned." She looked fearlessly into his eyes. "But I don't think you will. You value your integrity, and that wouldn't really be keeping your word, would it?"

There was a flash of anger in the hot blue eyes as he pushed her away with a violent shove.

"Damn you!" he said harshly. With rapid, jerky movements, he was out of the tub, wrapping one of the towels around his waist. As he looked down at her, there was a fierce savagery about his tautly held body that caused her to shrink back against the side of the tub.

"Get out of there and get dressed. I'll give you exactly three minutes!"

He strode from the enclosure, pushing aside the screen with a violence that threatened to topple it. She heard the soft thud of his bare feet on the spiral staircase, before she scrambled out of the tub and dried hurriedly. He hadn't said what would happen in three minutes, but if his expression was any harbinger, she didn't want to find out. She grabbed frantically at the clothes on the floor at the edge of the tub and donned a pair of green swimming trunks that came almost to her knees and a white short-sleeved shirt that was equally voluminous. Looking down at herself ruefully, she knew she looked a complete sketch. If any outfit was designed to turn a man off, this one was. She refused to ask herself why she felt a niggling sense of dissatisfaction with her appearance. After all, that was what she wanted, wasn't it? Even a Marilyn Monroe would have been safe in a costume like this.

She stepped hesitantly from behind the screen just as Donovan came down the stairs. Dressed in faded jeans and a pale blue workman's shirt he looked devastatingly virile and attractive. He finished rolling up the sleeves as he came toward her. His face was expressionless, but there was an undeniable tenseness about him that made her look away involuntarily. A caustic smile curving his mouth, he walked past her to the bar and poured himself a drink.

"You'll find a comb and brush upstairs on the bedside table," he said coolly. "I'll put the steaks on."

Her eyes widened. "We aren't leaving?"

"It's still raining," he pointed out. "You'd be drenched again before we got halfway to the 'copter."

"I wouldn't mind," she said hesitantly.

"Well, I would," he said decisively. "We have two more days of shooting before the picture is finished. I can't afford to have you ill." He took a long swallow of his drink.

"I see," she said shakily, her doe eyes wide with pain.

"Damn!" Donovan slammed his glass down on the bar. "What do you expect of me, Brenna? You tease me until I'm almost insane with wanting you, then turn me off cool as a cucumber. And when I display a little bad temper, you look at me as if I'd slapped you!"

"I never meant to tease you," she whispered huskily, tears brimming.

"No, I don't think you did," he said moodily. "That's why we're having this discussion down here, instead of upstairs on that king-sized bed." He ran a hand through his hair. "I can't figure you out."

She shrugged wearily. "I'm not very complicated, Michael."

"The hell you're not," he said bluntly. "You want me, I know you do. Yet you're behaving like a frightened virgin instead of the experienced woman you are. I don't know what kind of bastard it was who messed you up like this, but if I ever meet this ex-lover of yours, I'll probably kill him."

She almost smiled at how close he had come to the truth. She was indeed a frightened virgin. But she wasn't frightened of sex, as he surmised. She would have welcomed her first experience with delight, if she could have been assured that the joy would not turn to ashes after the first flames faded.

Donovan picked up his drink and drained it. He looked directly into her eyes, and said quietly, "Someday you're going to belong to me in all the ways there are, Brenna, and you're going to enjoy it completely!" He put the glass down on the bar and looked down at it thoughtfully. "I've been very patient for me, but I've reached the end of the road." He looked up, and said coolly, "What I'm saying is, that after I take you home today, the gloves are off."

She smiled uncertainly. "You pounce!" she said jokingly.

"I pounce," he affirmed softly. He turned away, his long strides carrying him to the kitchen. "As for now, you can enjoy your temporary reprieve. The steaks should be done in about ten minutes."

She was too tense to obey this injunction in the hours that followed. Donovan was the perfect host. He conducted an urbane and noncommital conversation that was designed to put her at ease, but only succeeded in increasing her nervousness. Despite his self-control, there was an undercurrent of restrained violence about him that was reminiscent of the rumble that preceded the eruption of a volcano.

After they had eaten the really excellent steak and salad Donovan had prepared, they had coffee before the fire. Even the glowing intimacy induced by these cozy surroundings brought no change in Donovan's demeanor, and Brenna began to relax. She should have known that Donovan always meant exactly what he said. She was safe for today.

The rain stopped late in the afternoon, and Donovan made immediate preparations to leave, indicating that he was just as eager as she to end this strained situation.

They arrived back at the residence hall well before sunset. As Donovan drew the Mercedes to a halt at the front entrance, she turned to face him, her hand on the door handle. "You don't have to come with me," she said quickly. "I have to stop at reception to make sure Randy's all right."

His mouth tightened. "I'll come with you," he said decisively. "I promised to deliver you back to the cottage, and I'm going to do just that," he added bitterly. "We both know how I value my promises."

As she got out of the car, she realized what a ludicrous sight she must present in Donovan's outsized clothes, her long hair in two thick braids down her back. She must look about ten years old, she thought wryly.

There was no censure on the receptionist's face, as they entered the lobby. Paula Drummond's manner was almost obsequiously servile, when she noticed Donovan following closely behind Brenna.

When Brenna asked if there had been any messages from Doris Charles, the girl checked her box, and then said brightly. "She left word that they will be at the pool till seven. The shower this afternoon prevented Randy from having his afternoon swim, so she brought him down about half an hour ago."

Brenna nodded. "Then I'll go down to the cottage and change," she said. "Will you tell Doris that I'll be up to see Randy before he goes to bed?"

Paula nodded, still shooting curious glances at Donovan's expressionless face. "I sure will," she said cheerfully. "Oh! I almost forgot. There was a message for you." She shuffled the cards efficiently. "Mr. Paul Chadeaux," she announced. "He phoned about ten this morning and then again about an hour ago. The last time he called he left a message." She turned the card over. "He wants to see you, and he will call on you about eight tonight."

Brenna turned away from the desk, her face suddenly white.

She moved numbly, her limbs working automatically to carry her out the far door and down the path to the cottage. She was hardly conscious of Donovan following her till she was almost halfway to the cottage. Then he grasped her elbow with an iron hand.

"Who is Paul Chadeaux?" Donovan asked harshly.

Who was Paul Chadeaux? What should she answer, she thought almost hysterically. The man who was responsible for her sister's death. The father of Janine's baby. The devil incarnate. My God, what did he want with her? She hadn't even seen him for almost three years, and he'd never even seemed to notice Janine's kid sister. The answer was heartstoppingly obvious: Randy.

Donovan's hand tightened, and he spun her around to face him. "Answer me, Brenna," Donovan ordered fiercely. "Who is this Chadeaux?" His face was set, his blue eyes narrowed suspiciously. "If he's some boyfriend who has followed you from Los Angeles, you can just get rid of him. I won't have you seeing any other man. Do you hear me?"

She broke away from him, hardly knowing what she was doing, her stride automatically lengthening as she neared the cottage. "I'll have to see him," she murmured. She had to be alone, she thought desperately. She had to think what to do. She had to be prepared when she saw Chadeaux again. Oh, God! It was almost seven!

She could vaguely feel the anger emanating from Donovan, as he silently escorted her to the cottage and waited while she unlocked the door.

"I'm not leaving until you tell me who this man is, Brenna," he said tightly. "He must be damned important to upset you like this."

"You have to go," she said distractedly. She knew she couldn't cope with a jealous Michael Donovan right now.

"Who is he, Brenna?" Donovan asked inexorably.

"He's Randy's father," Brenna answered desperately. "Now will you leave?"

Donovan muttered a curse beneath his breath, before he said harshly, "You don't have to see the bastard. I'll notify security that he's not to get within a mile of you."

"No!" Brenna said sharply. "Don't do that. I have to see what he wants."

"You want to see him?" Donovan's voice had a dangerous softness.

"I *have* to see him," Brenna said wearily. "Now will you please go, Michael?"

There was a muttered imprecation, and then Donovan turned on his heel and strode angrily away.

seven

BRENNA ENTERED THE COTTAGE AND CLOSED the door with a sigh of relief. Until this minute, she hadn't been sure that Donovan would really leave. She felt a trace of surprise that he had left without an argument, and she knew she had not seen the last of him this evening. But he was at least giving her the breathing space she needed badly. There was so little time before she had to meet Chadeaux.

Why did he want to see her after all this time, she wondered frantically. In the first wild bitterness after Janine's tragic death, Brenna had wanted to confront Chadeaux with his guilt, but she had refrained for Janine's sake. Janine had been so fanatically opposed to Randy having anything to do with his father, that Brenna had felt any contact with Chadeaux would be a betrayal of trust.

She cynically discarded the idea that Chadeaux may have discovered paternal feelings at this late date. He had been too eager in his insistence that Janine have an abortion, and too brutal in his rejection of both her and the baby, when he had thought that there might be repercussions from their affair.

Her mind raced wildly in circles, trying to find an answer and finally giving up in despair. She would have to wait for the meeting with Chadeaux. But whatever he wanted, he would not find her as easy to deal with as Janine, she resolved with unaccustomed hardness.

Brenna marched decisively into the bedroom, and threw open the closet door. The first order of business was to convince Chadeaux that he was not dealing with a naïve youngster but a sophisticated adult.

Forty-five minutes later she looked with approval at the reflection in the mirror. The pink, sleeveless *cheongsam* with it's high mandarin collar and the stylish slits on each side of the skirt gave her just the air of worldliness she desired. She had brushed out the childish braids and piled her hair on top of her head, leaving several wispy strands to curl around her face alluringly, and the dashing gold earrings were definitely not for the nursery set. She had used more makeup than usual, and her doe eyes appeared enormous in the perfect oval of her face. She slipped on bone high-heeled sandals, with a hurried look at the clock on the bedside table. It was almost eight, she noticed with panic. Not that time had ever meant anything to Paul Chadeaux. One of the things that had most annoyed her about Chadeaux, when he was dating her sister, was his constant and discourteous tardiness. He clearly had not reformed in that respect, for it was almost eight-fifteen before there was a knock at the door.

When Brenna opened the door, she experienced a small shock. Her hatred and disgust for Paul Chadeaux were such that she had expected the marks of guilt and weakness to be reflected on his face. Instead, he looked the same as on that first day Janine had introduced her to him. The same carefully styled blond hair and rather expressionless gray eyes, the same aristocratic features and full sensual lips curved now in a mocking smile. He had always dressed rather formally, and that, too, had not changed. The steel gray business suit was faultlessly tailored to flatter his tall, lean frame.

His gray eyes roved over her with insulting intimacy. "Well, well," he drawled softly. "Little sister has grown up, and very nicely, too. I'd hardly recognize you as the skinny kid that used to stare at me so antagonistically with those big brown eyes."

Her mouth twisted bitterly. "You'll find I'm still antagonistic, Paul," she said coolly. "And I hardly think you're here to reminisce about old times. Perhaps you'd better come in." She closed the door, and preceded him into the living room. She was amazed that she could present such a composed facade, when inwardly she was shaking with fear and revulsion. She was a better actress than she thought.

Chadeaux gave a low whistle, as he looked around appreciatively at the luxurious appointments of the cottage. "Very nice," he said. "You're obviously doing very well for yourself. So little Brenna is going to be a big movie star."

"Nonsense!" she said sharply. "I have a small supporting role in my first film. How did you know where to find me, Paul?"

He shrugged. "Your landlady was very cooperative when I told her the kid was mine," he said casually. "She seemed to think you were his mother. Maybe she thought I was going to make an honest woman of you at last." He seemed to find the idea very amusing, and Brenna had to clench her fists to keep from slapping the smug smile off his face.

"Why did you want to see me?" she asked bluntly.

"You're not being very hospitable," he complained mockingly. "Aren't you going to offer me a drink?"

She drew an impatient breath, and said quickly, "No, I'm not going to offer you a drink. I don't want you here. Please state your business and get out."

His mouth twisted, and his gray eyes took on an ugly glint. "You always were an uppity bitch." he said sneeringly. "You never did like me, did you, little sister?"

"No, I never did," she said flatly. "I like you even less now. Why are you here?"

He crossed the room and seated himself in the lavender wing chair without asking permission. "I want the kid," he said mockingly. "I've decided it's time I heard the patter of little feet around my lonely bachelor pad."

She stared at him incredulously. "You can't be serious," she said scornfully.

"Oh, but I am," he said, lazily stretching his legs out before him. "I've gone to a great deal of time and trouble to track the kid down. Don't make the mistake of thinking I'm not totally sincere in my devotion."

He took a gold cigarette case out of his jacket pocket, selected a cigarette and lit it leisurely. "I actually started out looking for Janine. Then I found out that she was dead, and that you had the child. Then I had to trace your whereabouts," he said complainingly. "It's all been a complete bore."

"How sorry we are to inconvenience you," Brenna said ironically.

"I should think you would be," he said pettishly, ignoring her sarcasm. "After all, I am willing to take the kid off your hands."

"The 'kid's' name is Randy," she said, between clenched teeth.

"I know. I know," Chadeaux said impatiently. "Your landlady told me that. "Run along and get him, will you? I want to get the night coach back to San Francisco."

Brenna's eyes narrowed suspiciously. "San Francisco? I thought you lived in Los Angeles."

He shrugged, his eyes sliding away from hers. "I thought I'd drop Randy off at the Chadeaux vineyards. He'll be better off with my family."

"You couldn't care less about Randy," Brenna charged bitterly. "Why do you really want him, Paul?"

An unpleasant smile touched his full lips. "I don't really have to answer to you," he said arrogantly. "But I will. Why not?"

He drew on his cigarette lazily. "My grandmother is all hung up on this dynasty thing. She's been nagging me for years to marry and settle down. They want a fitting heir for the Chadeaux

Wineries. One they can mold into the good little boy I never was," he said sneeringly. "The old lady has already told me that unless I provide her with an heir, she'll stop my allowance and cut me out of her will."

"Don't you think she'll object to an illegitimate child?" Brenna said caustically. "I seem to remember that you told my sister that you'd refuse to acknowledge the baby if Janine went to your family."

"Situations change," he said with satisfaction. "The old lady is getting desperate. She'll welcome the kid with open arms. She's even promised to settle up my gambling debts."

"Providing you give her Randy," Brenna said grimly, her face mirroring her rage and disgust.

Her contempt pierced even Chadeaux's thick ego. "Get the kid!" he ordered angrily.

"Go to hell!" Brenna said deliberately. "Randy is mine now, and I'm not giving him up."

Chadeaux's face flushed with anger. "Listen, bitch," he said coldly. "I'm the kid's father. You're just his aunt. I have a right to him."

"You forfeited any rights you had before he was born," Brenna said. "I wouldn't turn a stray dog over to you, much less a small child."

"You may not have a choice. The Chadeaux family have very important connections in California. I think any court in the state will lean toward the natural father over the claim of some little actress."

She smiled sweetly. "But then it's up to you to prove that you're the natural father, isn't it? I think you'll find that a little difficult."

His eyes narrowed warily. "What the hell do you mean? Janine told me I was the father."

"And you rejected her," Brenna said bitterly, her mouth curling. "Is it any wonder that Janine refused to name the father on Randy's birth certificate?"

He shrugged. "I can get around that. There are plenty of witnesses that knew Janine and I were having an affair at the time. I'm the only logical candidate."

Brenna smiled triumphantly. "You would be, if it was Janine Sloan that gave birth to Randy," she said softly. "But according to the birth certificate, she didn't. Brenna Sloan did."

Chadeaux's mouth gaped open. "You're lying," he accused angrily. "That's totally absurd. Why would Janine do a crazy thing like that."

"Perhaps in the end she was a little crazy," Brenna said, her eyes clouded with pain. "Crazy with fear and rejection and loneliness. Crazy to protect the one human being that was to be hers alone. I thought it was insane, too, but now I wonder if she somehow knew that Randy would need to be protected from you."

Chadeaux jumped to his feet, his fists clenched. "You won't get away with this," he snapped. "I need that kid, and I'll find a way of getting him. You're just making it a little more difficult. I'll hire detectives who will punch a million holes in your story. They'll turn up a dozen witnesses who will swear you're not Randy's mother."

Brenna felt a chill at the threat, but she couldn't let him know he'd frightened her. "It will take a long time to do that," she said coolly. "Do you really have that much time? I believe you mentioned something about gambling debts?"

There was a speculative look in the shallow gray eyes as he looked her over critically. "We might come to an agreement," he said slowly. "You want the kid. I need the money. Grandmother wants me settled with a wife and family. What do you say we make everybody happy? Why don't we fly to Vegas and get married?"

Brenna could feel the blood drain from her face in shock. "You must be mad," she whispered. "I can't stand the sight of you."

"I'm not overly fond of you, either," Paul said caustically. "You're too independent. I was going to make the offer to Janine, when I found her. She was much more my type."

Suddenly Brenna couldn't stand any more. She felt sick at the sight of him.

"Get out!" she said harshly. "I don't ever want to see you again."

"Well, that's too bad," he said nastily. "Because you're going to see a hell of a lot of me in the next few months. In court and out, little sister!"

"If you don't leave, I'll call security to force you to go," Brenna said tensely.

"Oh, I'm leaving," Chadeaux said, as he bent to crush out his cigarette in the crystal ashtray on the table. "But don't think I won't be back." He strolled casually over to the door, and turned to look at her as he opened it.

There was such a malevolent viciousness in his expression that she caught her breath in fear. "Good-bye, little sister! See you soon."

As the door closed she flew over to it and locked it hurriedly, as if to lock out the threat that had been evident in Chadeaux's last statement. He meant it. Chadeaux would stop at nothing to get Randy, now that he saw an advantage in it. There was no way she could let the little boy fall into those carelessly cruel hands, she thought frantically. She walked into the living room, pacing agitatedly back and forth, trying to see some solution to the problem. She hadn't a doubt that given time, Chadeaux could produce the witnesses he needed to press his claim. Janine's ploy had been flimsy at best. How could Brenna stop him if he actually took her to court? His arguments had merit. The Chadeaux family had great wealth and power. How could she possibly fight them if it came to a custody battle? She froze, as an even worse thought came to her. What if Chadeaux got an injunction giving him temporary custody of Randy pending the outcome of the trial?

She whirled, and ran into the bedroom. She took two suitcases out of the closet and threw them on the bed before picking up the telephone extension and dialing reception. "Paula, this is Brenna Sloan. I've got to leave at once for Los Angeles. An emergency. Will you contact Doris and have her pack for Randy, and have him ready to leave in twenty minutes? And I'll need Johnny to drive me to Portland to get a flight." Paula Drummond answered with her usual bright efficiency, expressing polite concern before she hung up.

Brenna started to fill the open suitcase, tossing in the clothes with no regard to neatness or order. She was well aware it was panic that spurred her to this rash decision, but what else could she do? Her only chance of keeping Randy from Chadeaux was to disappear with Randy and hide. It was only money that motivated Chadeaux's desire for Randy. If she could remain undercover long enough, Chadeaux would have to find another solution to his money problems. Then, perhaps, he would consider the child the burden and annoyance he had previously.

She had filled one suitcase and was halfway through with the second, when there was a knock on the front door. That would be Johnny. She started to call out for him to come in, when she realized that she had locked the door. "Just a minute, Johnny." She hurriedly crossed to the door to let him in.

Michael Donovan brushed her aside and strode into the cottage. He crossed to the open bedroom door, and, with a raking glance, took in the open suitcases and the hurried preparations for departure. He turned slowly, and Brenna flinched at his furious expression and blazing eyes. In their short acquaintance she had seen him angry many times, but never like this. He looked like a dangerous animal ready to spring.

"Johnny won't be coming," he said softly. "I told Paula I would attend to everything."

Brenna bit her lip to keep it from trembling. "Does Paula always act as a spy for you?" she asked shakily. The sight of him had been a shock that threatened to vanquish the little control she still had over her emotions.

"Not always," Donovan said harshly. "Let's just say, she knew I'd be interested in your little emergency!" His leashed anger broke through it's bonds. "My God! That bastard only had to get you alone for an hour, to make you go running back to him like a bitch in heat. Don't you have any pride or self-respect? The son of a bitch got you pregnant and then deserted you!"

She was stunned. He actually thought she was running to Chadeaux instead of away from him. The ridiculousness of the surmise seemed wildly funny in her desperate state, and she laughed hysterically.

It was a mistake. In two strides he had reached her, his hands gripping her shoulders brutally as he shook her. "Shut up, damn you!" he rasped, his eyes like hot coals in his white face. "Do you think I'm just going to let you walk away from me? You're not going to him. I'll stop you any way I can." His eyes were tormented as they ran over her contemptuously. "Look at you. You couldn't wait to get rid of me, so that you could dress up for him. Did it work? Did he think you were even more beautiful than he remembered? Is that why he asked you to come back to him?"

"No! no! You've got it all wrong. I'd never do that. I couldn't." Tears were running down her cheeks as the last of her fragile control vanished. "I hate him," she said brokenly. Suddenly she collapsed against him, clinging to his rock-like strength with desperation, her body wracked with sobs.

Donovan was frozen with surprise for a long moment, and

then his arms went slowly around her to hold her securely. "Then why are you going back to him?" he asked bluntly. "Does he have some kind of hold on you? For God's sake, tell me what's wrong, Brenna."

"He wants Randy," she said baldly. "He's going to take Randy away from me." She stepped back reluctantly from that magically warming embrace, and immediately felt alone and vulnerable again. "I was trying to run away from him," she said wearily.

"You were also running away from me," Donovan said coolly. "And any chance you might have for a career. Do you think any film-maker in the business would take a chance on you again, once it got around that you'd run out before the picture was finished?"

"No, I guess I didn't think at all," Brenna admitted huskily. "But I still would have done the same thing if I had. I can't let Paul Chadeaux get his hands on Randy." She wiped her eyes childishly with the back of her hand.

"No one is going to take your child away from you," Donovan said with conviction. "I won't let them. If you had come to me instead of flying into a panic, I'd have told you that."

She shook her head ruefully at the sheer royal arrogance of the man. It would not happen, because Donovan did not will it so. Long live Michael Donovan. In spite of herself, she couldn't help being a little reassured by his boundless confidence. Aside from their burgeoning personal relationship, Donovan had a business interest in seeing that Brenna Sloan completed his picture on schedule. He would bend the same ruthless energy to her problem as to any other obstacle that got in his way.

She opened her lips to confess that Randy was not her child but Janine's. She knew he was entitled to know everything, if she was going to solicit his help. Under the circumstances, Janine would surely forgive her for breaking her promise. Suddenly

Brenna was beset by doubts. Would Donovan be as eager to help her if he knew the child wasn't hers? He had no affection for Randy. Wouldn't he, like everyone else, think that she should turn Randy over to his natural father? She couldn't take the chance. Randy was too important to her.

Donovan strolled over to the bar and made himself a drink. Pouring her a small whiskey, he returned to hand it to her.

She accepted it, a small smile curving her lips. "This seems to be your day for plying me with liquor," she said.

"You need it," he said curtly. "Now suppose you tell me why you think Chadeaux has a chance of gaining custody of Randy. Didn't you say the father wasn't named on the birth certificate?"

Not looking at him, Brenna briefly related Chadeaux's threats. She purposely did not mention Janine, leaving Donovan to assume that it was Chadeaux's intention to hire detectives to find witnesses to their affair that had so terrified her.

"That's all?" Donovan asked, his eyes narrowed on her flushed face. "You're sure he wasn't trying to blackmail you? He didn't offer to leave Randy with you for a consideration?"

Brenna shook her head, relieved that he had mistaken her guilt for distress. She made a face. "He made an offer," she admitted dryly. "But I couldn't take marriage with Paul Chadeaux even for Randy."

Donovan looked at his drink. "Marriage," he said thoughtfully. "The bastard must know you very well. In time, when you'd gotten desperate enough, you might have given in to even that. It's obvious you'd do anything for the child." He took a long swallow of his drink. "It makes you very vulnerable, Brenna. I can see that I'm going to have to build a fence around you to keep out the predators."

"A fence?" Brenna asked blankly.

"I'm going to marry you myself," Donovan said coolly.

She felt her heart lurch, and the blood rush dizzily to her

head. "That's not very funny," she said breathlessly, moistening her lips.

"It wasn't intended to be," Donovan said calmly. "I've just offered you a solution to your problem. Marriage to me would safeguard your claim to Randy, and protect you from any further harassment from Chadeaux. I know how to take care of my own."

"He could still locate those witnesses and push his claim to Randy."

His eyes were totally ruthless. "Not if I claim that I'm Randy's father. I don't relish the idea of casting myself as a seducer of a teenage Lolita, but I imagine my word would be taken over Chadeaux's. I pour a lot of money into the state's economy, and I have a few friends in high places."

Brenna's eyes were wide with shock. "No one would believe you," she said. "I didn't even know you three years ago."

Donovan shrugged. "Who's to know that?" he asked sardonically. "For every witness that Chadeaux produces to testify that you were his mistress, I'll have two to swear you were mine. In case you haven't heard, money talks!"

"You'd pay someone to perjure themselves?" Brenna asked, aghast.

"If necessary," Donovan said bluntly. "Would you rather lose Randy? There are no guarantees that you'll get justice just because you're right. Sometimes justice has to be manipulated." He smiled tightly. "However, it may not come to that. Your ex-lover seems to be a little on the shady side. I may be able to put the screws on him in some other way. I'll get my lawyers on it tomorrow." He drained his glass, and set it down on the coffee table. "It would be best if we were married immediately," he said simply. "Shall we say, three days? That will take care of the waiting period, and give you a chance to finish the picture. I'll send the company doctor by the set tomorrow to take care of the blood test."

"Wait!" Brenna protested, holding up her hand distractedly. "I've got to think. It's all going too fast." Donovan was proceeding with his usual steamroller tactics, and she felt she would be swept away in the wake of his single-minded drive like a leaf in a storm if she didn't slow him down.

"What's to think about?" Donovan asked impatiently. "You get your son, your career, and a wealthy husband. What more could you want?"

The bitter cynicism in his face hurt her in some mysterious fashion. "Why are you doing this?" she asked bewilderedly. "Yes, I'm getting all that, but what are you getting out of this marriage?"

The blue eyes were suddenly impenetrable as Donovan considered her question. "What am I getting?" His mouth twisted cynically. "I'm getting Brenna Sloan in my bed until I tire of her. I get a chance to work off this obsession I have for you. Closeness has been known to kill stone dead more than one great passion. Maybe I'll get lucky."

"You expect me to..." Brenna blushed, and then was furious with herself when Donovan raised an eyebrow mockingly.

"You're damn right I do," he said bluntly. "This isn't some storybook. This is real life, Brenna. There's always a price tag on everything. Sometimes it's hidden, but the price is there. In this case, I don't think you'll find it hard to pay."

Brenna shivered. "You make it sound so...business-like," she said unhappily.

"I think I can promise you it won't be at all business-like once we're in bed," he said dryly. "We really turn each other on, remember? I told you once I don't play games. I like all the cards on the table. For saving your son for you, all I want is your word that you won't leave me until I tell you to go."

Brenna's mouth twisted wryly. "Yet you retain the right to toss me aside whenever you get bored with me," she said sadly.

"Jake said you always had an escape clause written into every contract."

There was a flicker of emotion deep in Donovan's eyes before he looked away. "That's right, I do," he said coolly. "Do I have your promise?"

Brenna's throat was tight and aching as she looked at Donovan's hard, expressionless face. She had a fleeting memory of another Donovan walking with her hand in hand through the woods. Why did it hurt so much to realize she might never reach further than the physical with this man?

"Yes, you have my promise," she said wearily.

"Good," Donovan said briskly, as if he had never expected anything else. He dropped a light kiss on her forehead as if she were a small child. "You'd better get to bed. You're exhausted. I'll see you tomorrow."

Her face must have reflected her surprise, for a sardonic smile twisted Donovan's mouth. "You expected me to drag you off to bed once I had your word? You must have had some poor lovers, Brenna. Now that I have a commitment from you, I can wait." He grimaced. "Not long, but I can wait." She was staring after him, still speechless, when the door closed behind him.

eight

BRENNA SIPPED HER CHAMPAGNE, GAZING over the crowded living room with a curious feeling of remoteness. It was almost as if she were a guest and not the central figure at this wedding reception. There was no possibility of her occupying center stage with Michael Donovan in the same scene, she thought wryly. Even the glamour surrounding the bride was eclipsed by a groom with Donovan's dynamic charisma.

Not that she had been neglected. On the contrary, she had been fussed over and toadied to, to such an extent that she was forced to move to this quiet corner to escape. She had no illusions that it was her own charm that had instigated such an effusive display. Two hours ago the little nobody actress had become Mrs. Michael Donovan, and so must be cultivated. She had the ear of the throne.

"A bride for such a short time and left all alone? Michael isn't usually so careless with his possessions." Jake Dominic's mocking voice made her look up quickly. Devastatingly attractive, as usual, in conventional black evening clothes, he was a welcome sight to Brenna, after putting up with the fawning sycophants all evening.

"He appears to be busy," Brenna said calmly, her eyes searching out Donovan's red head in a far corner of the room, as he bent to listen attentively to a distinguished gray-haired man.

"Judge Simon Arthington, State Supreme Court Judge," Jake said thoughtfully. "And before that, I saw him with Senator Atkins. Unusual company to cultivate on one's wedding day, wouldn't you say?"

"Perhaps he's just being a good host," Brenna said evasively. "They are friends of his, aren't they?"

"Oh, they're friends of his," Jake said cynically. "Michael is a very generous contributor to their campaign funds. They're very fond of him." He looked around the room distastefully. "I see several other 'friends' of Michael's here." He shrugged, and turned to smile charmingly at her. "Have I told you how lovely you are tonight? You're something out of Tolstoy."

She smiled back at him, wrinkling her nose saucily. "I should be. I was too busy slaving for you to go shopping, so Michael had wardrobe run me up this little number. I have an idea it was originally meant for a remake of *War and Peace*."

All joking aside, she really loved the gown. It was an exquisitely simple garment in lemon yellow, embroidered with white daisies. The empire cut and low round neck merely hinted gracefully at the smallness of her waist and hips, but boldly accented the swell of her breasts. She wore no jewelry and only a garland of daisies on her head. Her hair had been brushed to a sensuous silken sheen and allowed to fall almost to her waist, to complement the romantic aura of the gown.

"Oh, yes, Michael was in a great hurry for this wedding, wasn't he?" Jake asked casually. "But not too hurried to arrange this elaborate reception for you, Brenna. I suppose you're very fond of parties. Most women are."

Brenna made a face. "I hate them," she said frankly. "This kind, at least. I enjoyed the one on the set yesterday, to celebrate the end of the picture. Michael made all the arrangements for the wedding and reception."

"Curiouser and curiouser," Jake said softly, black eyes gleaming. "I happen to know that Michael is bored to death at parties. He never attends one unless it's absolutely necessary for business reasons. Then, when he's finished, he's usually found in a corner, munching dip and glowering bad-temperedly. Yet on the most private and personal event of his life, he throws an elaborate party, invites people he couldn't care less about, except to use. And he proceeds to ignore his beautiful bride, who he's obviously crazy about, and spends his time cultivating judges and senators!" Jake's expression was as alert and watchful as a pouncing cat as he asked mildly, "You wouldn't know anything about all this, would you, Brenna?"

Brenna looked down at her champagne. "Why should I know anything?" she asked quietly. "Michael always does what he wants to do."

Jake's eyebrows rose cynically. "And if you do, you're not about to satisfy my curiosity," he said knowingly.

Brenna looked up, a smile lifting the corners of her mouth. "Exactly," she said succinctly.

He sighed. "I was afraid of that," he said. "I couldn't get anything out of Michael, either."

"Why should you bother, Jake?" Brenna asked curiously. "Michael knows what he's doing."

"None better," Jake agreed lightly. "I suppose I'm feeling a touch of unaccustomed responsibility. I've never been a best man before."

"You were very convincing," Brenna assured him solemnly. "You and Nora practically stole the show. It was nice of Nora to be my maid of honor, wasn't it?"

"She likes you," Jake said simply. "The whole crew likes you. You're a very popular person, Brenna Sloan. I even like you."

Brenna sketched a mocking curtsy, her brown eyes dancing at such a graceless compliment from a man who was reputed to have one of the smoothest lines in the world. "I am duly hon-ored," she said demurely.

"You should be," he said dryly. "I don't think I've ever told a woman I liked her before. It may be a first for the *Guinness Book of World Records*."

Brenna let out a little bubble of laughter. Dominic cocked his head, a pleased smile on his face, "I do like that laugh of yours. Most women giggle or tinkle. You sort of gurgle like run-ning water. You should do it more often."

"Working under you isn't a matter for laughter, Jake Dominic," Brenna said severely. "You almost killed me."

"You held up better than most actresses would." He shrugged. "You have stamina."

It was a compliment to be treasured from Jake Dominic, and Brenna began to feel as if the heartbreaking, exhausting work may have been worth it after all.

"I saw the final rushes last night," Jake said slowly. "They were good." He took a sip of his champagne. "You were damn good."

Brenna's eyes flew to his face.

He looked at her steadily, taking his time. "You were so good, that everyone in the audience is going to wonder why Dirk jilted you for Nora." He frowned teasingly. "You've endan-gered the credibility of my masterpiece."

"Jake, do you mean . . ." Brenna trailed off breathlessly, afraid to continue.

"I mean that you were great," he said simply. "I mean that Donovan has not only got himself a wife, he's got himself a new star."

"Jake!" Brenna exclaimed exuberantly, launching herself into his arms. Careless of their champagne glasses, and the glances of the amused guests, she hugged him ecstatically.

They were both laughing hilariously, Jake holding her around the waist with one arm, while he rescued the champagne glasses with the other, when Brenna felt a hand on her shoulder.

Donovan plucked her neatly from Jake's embrace, to rest possessively in the curve of his arm. "Mine, I believe," he said coolly to Jake. Then his eyes went to Brenna, and her smile faded as she met the dangerous glint in his. "I'm happy to see you're enjoying yourself, my dear," he said silkily. "It's the most animation I've seen you display today."

"Take it easy, Michael," Jake advised softly. "She was just happy. I told her about the rushes."

Donovan's tension relaxed fractionally, but his tone was still less than cordial when he said, "I've had enough of this charade, Brenna. It's time we left."

Dominic raised his eyebrow and gave Brenna an I-told-you-so glance. "I would slip away quietly if you want to avoid the usual embarrassing remarks and foolishness. My car is parked in front of the residence hall." He handed Donovan the keys. "I wouldn't suggest you use your Mercedes. I heard some of the stunt boys plotting to rig up yours à la James Bond."

A reluctant smile creased Donovan's face, as he shook his head ruefully. "My God! What will they be up to next? Thanks, Jake."

With Dominic urbanely covering their retreat, Donovan and Brenna quietly exited through the kitchen door, and made their way quickly up the path in the direction of the residence hall.

"I've arranged to have Randy and Doris Charles moved from their quarters to my home tomorrow," Donovan said abruptly. "I thought under the circumstances that we would dispense with the usual honeymoon nonsense and just go directly there tonight."

Brenna was aware that Donovan had his own home a short distance away from the main complex of Twin Pines, so this decision came as no surprise to her. Donovan's workload for the next few months would be staggering with both the post-production for *Forgotten Moment* and the start of the filming of *Wild Heritage* on the agenda. Brenna was surprised at the curiously defensive note in Donovan's usually urbane manner. Had he really thought that she would expect the usual romantic trappings despite the conditions of her marriage?

"Yes, of course," she said serenely. "It would be a foolish gesture when you have such a full schedule."

For some reason the sweet reasonableness of this statement seemed to only increase Donovan's irritation and a black scowl clouded his face. "How very sensible of you," he said caustically. "And how lucky I am to have such a pragmatic bride."

Pragmatic? That was hardly the correct word to describe her mood at this moment, she thought. She was married to this redheaded dynamo, who had taken charge of her life, and changed it out of all recognition. This was her wedding night. In a short time, she would give herself to him in the most intimate, physical sense. Why wasn't she frightened, she wondered. She was excited, nervous, and even shy, but not frightened.

Donovan was moodily silent on the short drive to his home, and it was only as they pulled into the curving driveway and halted before an extremely large, two-story house of mellow pink brick, that the silence was broken.

"It's perfectly lovely," Brenna said softly, gazing at the house.

It was lovely. There was an indescribable beauty about the house with it's wide bay windows and climbing ivy. It had a subtle air of welcoming warmth and permanency about it, that was at odds with the rest of the modern style architecture of Twin Pines.

Donovan smiled mockingly. "You're surprised? I thought you would be. When I had the house built, I told the architect I wanted it to look like it had been here for a hundred years and would be here for another hundred. I live a fast life that has constantly changing values. I like the idea of having some semblance of permanence to come home to.

"There are no live-in servants," he went on coolly. "I have a woman from town, a Mrs. Haskins, who comes daily and two girls who come in twice a week. Besides that there is the gardener and all-around handyman, Joe Peters. Oh, yes. I've recently hired a chauffeur for you, Bob Phillips."

She looked at him, startled. "I don't need a driver," she protested. "I wouldn't know what to do with one."

"You're a lady of substance now," he said mockingly. "You'll get used to it."

She doubted that. But looking around the foyer a few minutes later, she knew she would have no problem getting used to this aspect of Donovan's wealth. There was nothing pretentious about the decor. She had half-expected antiques after Donovan's statement in the car, but this was not the case. The house was decorated in no particular period, and with only one general theme: comfort. Every piece of furniture that graced the house had the mellow patina of expert craftsmanship, lovingly executed.

"I think coffee is in order, after all that champagne," Donovan said briskly. "I want to talk." He gestured to the double door in richly glowing mahogany. "If you'd like to go into the library and make yourself comfortable, I'll bring it through."

"Couldn't I go with you?" she asked impulsively.

He arched an eyebrow. "Why not?" he asked with a shrug, and she followed him down the hall to the large bright kitchen done entirely in sunshine yellow and white.

"Sit down," he said casually, waving to the breakfast bar with its high stools upholstered in rich white leather. "I'll be with you in a minute."

As Brenna perched on a high stool and watched him as he

measured coffee into the chrome percolator, she thought what an incongruous sight they must present in their ultra-modern surroundings. She in her romantic finery and Donovan in dark formal evening clothes. He did not wear evening clothes with the same air of being born to them as Jake Dominic, she mused. Despite the faultless tailoring, the smooth material seemed to confine rather than cover the powerful shoulders, and led one to wonder at the untamed body beneath the civilized trappings. She felt a sudden surge of liquid weakness in her every limb at the sheer raw virility of the man as he prowled about the kitchen at his homely tasks.

He looked up suddenly and surprised her looking at him. His hands were arrested for a moment, as he effortlessly read the message that she was scarcely aware she was projecting.

"If you don't stop looking at me like that, I won't be responsible," he said huskily. "And I've got to talk to you."

She flushed, and looked down at her hands loosely folded on the yellow countertop. "I don't know what you mean."

"You do, but I won't argue with you," he said roughly. "I've made a decision that I thought would suit you down to the ground, but it won't work if you keep throwing out signals. I want you too much."

She looked up in bewilderment, her doe eyes wide and asking in their frame of dark lashes.

"I've decided to give you a little more time before you fulfill your part of our little bargain," he said bluntly. "God knows how long I'll last, but I figure I can hold out for a week or so."

A cold sinking lethargy washed over her in a chilly tide that confused and frightened her. Why did she feel this sudden sense of loss?

"I see," she said quietly. "May I ask why you're being so generous?"

His mouth twisted cynically. "Perhaps I'm developing a taste for the joys of self-denial and abstention," he said dryly. "Or perhaps those big brown eyes of yours make me feel like a hunter out of season."

"That's very kind of you," she said lifelessly. "I appreciate your consideration."

"You're damn right it is," he said frowning. "I guess the truth is, I've never had to blackmail a woman to get her into bed with me before. It's leaving a bad taste in my mouth."

He suddenly reminded Brenna, rather endearingly, of a small boy who had been told that Christmas had been canceled this year.

"I thought I'd give you a chance to get to know me," he said gruffly. "Perhaps we could be friends. We seemed to be doing pretty well on the island, before you got into that damn bathtub."

Brenna hid an amused smile at the accusing tone of the statement. She wondered if he had conveniently forgotten that he had ordered her into that bathtub.

"Do you think it will work?" she asked solemnly, her eyes twinkling. She was suddenly feeling wonderfully lighthearted.

"Hell, I don't know!" he growled sourly. "But the alternate is to forget about the coffee, and I take you upstairs and don't let you out of that bedroom for a week."

"I see," she said earnestly. "Well, then perhaps we'd better try." An impish grin curved her lips, and her brown eyes were shining mischievously. "After all, I wouldn't want to take you away from your work."

There was a trace of disgruntled conjecture in the blue eyes, as Donovan took in the demure smile on Brenna's face.

"Don't get too cocky," he said warningly. "It's only a postponement, not a reprieve."

"Who knows what can happen in a week," she said breezily. "You may decide I don't appeal to you. After all, I'm not your regulation sex goddess."

"No, you're not," he agreed, his eyes suddenly dark and intense, as he came slowly forward to stand before her. There was a breathless electricity in the air, as he reached out with one finger and traced the fine contour of her cheekbone. "You're much too thin; a strong wind could blow you away. Your face is lovely, but I've seen lovelier. Except for your eyes, it's not an outstanding face." He cradled her face in his hands with a yearning tenderness. "And then you smile, and all I want to do is pick you up and carry you away somewhere, so that you'll never give that special smile to anyone but me." His lips touched hers gently. "You're much more dangerous to a man than any sex goddess, sweetheart."

She stared up, mesmerized, into his lean, tan face, feeling tears brighten her eyes and her throat constrict painfully. He was doing it again, she thought helplessly. She could fight against his blatant sex appeal, but what defense could she offer against this aching tenderness that left her conscious of an ephemeral something just out of reach.

"I think we'd better forget about the coffee tonight," he said hoarsely, as he turned away abruptly. "I've had your things put in the second bedroom on the right, at the top of the stairs. You'll forgive me if I don't show you to your room." The muscles in his back and shoulders were tense beneath the fine material of his evening jacket, as he walked over to the coffeemaker and pulled the plug from the socket.

He turned back when there was no movement from the breakfast bar, and found Brenna sitting quite still, staring at him with dazed, dreamy eyes. "Brenna, dammit!" he started in exasperation, then broke off as her expression changed not a whit. "Have a heart, love," he said huskily. "I can't take much more."

Brenna shook her head dazedly, as if just coming awake. She slipped from the stool, and with a breathless, "Good night" and a flurry of lemon chiffon, she was gone.

It was only as she was halfway up the stairs, her heart beating with a wild exhilaration and a singing happiness surging in her veins, that she realized what that ephemeral element was that was causing this breathtaking delight. She was in love with Michael Donovan.

Brenna stretched lazily, before adjusting the vinyl lounge chair to the recline position, not forgetting to remove her sunglasses, as she prepared to increase the already golden tan she had acquired in the past two weeks. Michael had teased her unmercifully when she had forgotten to take the glasses off, and it had resulted in her having owl-like rings about her eyes for two days before her tan had evened out again.

She smiled reminiscently, a glow of contentment warming her face as she thought about the last two weeks. It had been a lovely time. Each golden day had been added like charms on a bracelet that she hoped would encircle her for an eternity. She had grown to know Michael Donovan with an intimacy that she had never thought possible. Looking on him now with the eyes of love, she found him both more difficult and simple in nature than she had first imagined.

He had kept his promise about the ultimate intimacy, but she found him to be a compulsively physical person. He was constantly touching her, holding her hand and playing idly with her fingers as he talked, stroking the silky fall of her hair in the evenings while they sat on the couch in the living room and listened to music. There were light sweet kisses and casual embraces in abundance. All were carefully controlled and designed not to upset the delicate balance of their relationship. Even on the evenings they had guests, usually members of the cast or crew of various Donovan projects at the complex, he would absently knead her shoulders as she sat comfortably at his feet by his chair in the library, as they all engaged in one of the informal bull sessions that she soon discovered were a way of life at Donovan's home.

She loved it all. After a childhood deprived of cuddling and embraces, Donovan's casual fondling made her feel warmly treasured.

Donovan did the majority of his work at home, she found. He had both an editing and projection room at the house, and there was a constant flow of people from the complex in and out of the house at all hours of the day and evening. He sometimes spent a few hours in the morning at his executive office at the complex, but most of the time he worked at the house, and his workday seemed to span most of the hours of the day and evening. He was a workaholic, as Walters had told her, and he was passionately in love with the making of films.

To her delight, she discovered that this did not necessarily shut her out of his life. After the first few lonely days, he arbitrarily ordered her into the editing room, much to the amusement of the crew. While they worked and argued and generally ignored her presence, she curled up in a chair in the corner, watching in fascination or leafing idly through a book or script. On occasion, she would look up to find Donovan looking at her with an absent smile, that she met with a blissfully contented one of her own.

In the afternoons, she usually tried to spend time with Randy, or lazily sunbathed by the pool in a bikini, where Donovan joined her on occasion for a brief swim before he returned to work. These were the times she liked the best. When they would talk quietly, exchanging viewpoints and exploring each others minds and personalities, or just sitting in companionable silence, enjoying the warmth of the sun.

She was well aware that she owed a large measure of the mellow serenity of those days to the self-control that Donovan was exercising. Though the fact that Donovan was not used to restraining his sexual urges was painfully clear, and there were times she felt his patience was wearing dangerously thin, Donovan never made her consciously aware of the fires banked low beneath the surface.

The only cloud in this halcyon hiatus was Donovan's persistent rejection of Randy. Though not deliberately unkind to the child, the sight of him seemed to trigger a brooding moodiness in Donovan that almost invariably resulted in Brenna sending for Doris to remove the boy before the atmosphere became definitely strained. She had tentatively tried to broach the subject of his attitude once, only to be met with a steel-like hardness.

"Leave it, Brenna," he had said curtly. "I know all the logical and reasonable arguments. I realize he's an individual, and should be accepted as such. If he belonged to someone else, I'd probably be crazy about him. Hell! I like kids."

"Then why are you so unfair to Randy?" Brenna had asked huskily, her eyes bright with tears. "He's only a baby."

He had given a smothered imprecation, and kissed her gently, his hand stroking her hair with exquisite tenderness. "Because I am not rational and reasonable when it comes to you," he had said simply. "And it drives me crazy when I see him, and know that he's another man's baby and not mine. I'm trying, dammit, but it's just going to take time."

She had been very close in that moment to revealing the truth about Randy and Janine. Now that she was aware of the deep love that she had for Donovan, it was agonizingly painful to let a barrier exist that could be toppled by a few words. Surely they had grown close enough that she could put her trust in Donovan. She did not know what made her hesitate, but in the next moment Donovan was called away to the phone, and the opportunity was lost.

When Brenna first realized she loved Donovan, she went through a period of depression and sheer unadulterated panic. How had it happened, she wondered bewilderedly. Why hadn't her distrust and cynicism toward men protected her against this calamity? And if she had to fall in love with someone, why did it have to be Michael Donovan, with his penchant for noninvolvement and his reputation for being a tomcat extraordinaire?

She gradually accepted the fact that it was too late for questioning. The fact existed. She did love Michael Donovan, and in the past two weeks she had become aware that he was eminently worth loving. Not only was he brilliant and possessed of an electric charisma, but he had an unswerving honesty and directness with his associates. If he was ruthless in his dealings with those who got in his way, he was generous to a fault with his friends.

She had come to terms with her love for him now. She knew without question that though she desperately wanted his love, if that wasn't to be, she would accept what he would give her, for however long it would last. Just the experience of loving him would enrich her as an individual, and make her stronger in spirit than when she had come to him. She would have gone to bed with him gladly. That she had not offered herself was only because each day that passed strengthened their knowledge of each other, and she felt she urgently needed his friendship first if she was ever going to win anything from him but passion.

Brenna rolled over on her stomach and put her head on her folded arm, after shifting the long swatch of hair over one shoulder to expose her back to the rays of the sun. She yawned drowsily and her lids were growing deliciously heavy, when she was rudely awakened by a sharp slap on her rounded bottom.

"You look entirely too comfortable, woman," Donovan drawled. "Turn over and entertain me like a dutiful wife should."

She opened her eyes to see Michael settling in the lounge next to her. Dressed in black trunks, his tan muscular body looked lean yet powerful, the springy dark red hair on his chest lending him a sensual virility that caused a heat to flow through her body that was not from the sun.

"How dare you look so vigorous?" she said sleepily. "You

were up till four this morning working with that writer on the script changes for *Wild Heritage*. And then you had breakfast with me at nine. Don't you ever get tired?"

He arched an eyebrow wickedly. "I'm glad to see you're keeping an eye on my nocturnal habits," he said teasingly. "It bodes well for the future." He shook his head in answer to her question. "I don't need much sleep. Four or five hours is more than enough. I guess it's because of my childhood. When I was working all the hours there were to get out of the slums, I always thought sleeping was a waste of time, if not my actual enemy."

She felt an urge to reach out and touch his arm, not in desire but in sympathy for the boy that was. She knew better than to give in to the impulse. Donovan was proud, and that boy had fought his battles and won them a long time ago.

She sat up and swung her legs over the side of the lounge. She leaned lazily back, bracing her weight on her stiffened arms. "How is the preproduction work going on *Wild Heritage*?" she asked casually.

"Well enough," Donovan answered. "We should be ready to start shooting next week."

"You're not directing *Heritage* are you?" she asked. "Didn't I hear you tell Jake you were giving it to that TV director who had never done a theatrical film?"

"What big ears you have, grandma," he said with a grin. "Tim Butler is a terrific director. He did fantastic things with that David and Bathsheba mini-series, and I have too many irons in the fire right now."

"Speaking of *Wild Heritage*, I have a bone to pick with you," she said severely. "I was talking to Jake about your views on method acting the other evening. When I told him what a fanatic you were on the subject, he nearly fell off the couch laughing. He said you must have been pulling my leg."

Donovan looked down at the two delectable limbs in question and murmured, "What an intriguing idea."

"Michael!" Brenna said warningly. "Why did you give me all that garbage about experience and method acting if you didn't mean it?" As she continued to think about it, her indignation grew. "Why didn't you give me Angie? I was damn good. I know I was!"

"Yes," he said lazily. "You were better than any of the others who tested for it." He leaned back, and tipped his head back like a cat arching lazily in the sun.

"Michael!" she said in exasperation.

He turned and smiled mockingly. "Jake has an exceedingly big mouth," he said calmly. "Now I suppose I'll have to confess. I made up all that tripe about method acting on the spur of the moment to give me an excuse not to hire you for Angie. I knew from the minute I saw you that I couldn't let you have it."

As she opened her mouth to protest, he quickly put his hand over her lips to silence her. "In case you hadn't noticed, there are two sexually explicit bedroom scenes, and in one Angie is nude. It's necessary for the story. There was no way I could tolerate you doing that . . . even then." His tone was grim. "I would have felt like killing someone, before the damn picture was finished."

When he removed his hand, she looked at him solemnly. "I didn't notice," she said in a small voice, a flush pinking her cheeks.

"I didn't think you had," Donovan said with a grin. "I was feeling a bit guilty about taking it away from you, when I realized Mary Durney was available. I could have my cake and eat it, too. It's going to be a hell of a good movie. I'm going to make a bundle on it."

"Egad, what a shockingly commercial mind you have," she exclaimed in mock horror, her eyes twinkling. "What about art for art's sake?"

"I'm just a bloody capitalist," he admitted, with an underlying seriousness beneath the lightness of his tone. "I consider myself an artist, and a very good one. I make the very best films of which I am capable. I'm a storyteller par excellence. In our society, the most revered reward for achievement is money, not critical acclaim, and I'll be damned if I don't wrest the greatest reward possible for my work."

She was silent for a long moment before she asked, "Have you ever not made money on one of your films?"

"Once I came pretty close," he said thoughtfully, his blue eyes reminiscent. "I was just starting out, and it was only my second film. The critics panned it and the public stayed away in droves. Everyone said it was too simple, the imagery not exotic enough."

"What did you do?" she asked curiously.

"I borrowed enough money to get me to Cannes, and entered it in the festival," he said simply. "It won best picture. Then I brought it home, and sent the actors around to every talk show on the circuit. The picture didn't win the Academy Award that year, but it was nominated." He grinned lightly. "And I made a small fortune on it."

"Tribute," Brenna said thoughtfully.

"Tribute," he agreed quietly.

They were silent in a perfect accord that lasted for a few golden moments.

"Come on, lazybones," Donovan said briskly, rising to his feet. "I'll race you to the end of the pool."

She shook her head. "I've just been in. I'll wait for you here."

She watched as he dived cleanly from the side and did three laps in the pool, his arms cleaving the water with power and precision. When he hoisted himself out of the water at the edge of the pool, he wasn't even breathing heavily, she noticed ruefully. She threw him a towel which he caught deftly and proceeded to dry the thick mahogany hair, then his body, before wrapping the towel around his middle, and sauntering back to the chair where she was sitting.

Her eyes narrowed thoughtfully, as she watched him approach.

"You look like a gladiator at the Roman Games," she commented, her lips quirking.

"And you would have been a scandalous vestal virgin," he returned lightly, his eyes surveying her bikini-clad figure with frank enjoyment. "Did you know that the vestals were not released from their bonds of chastity until they had served for thirty years?" He sat down beside her on the lounge, his eyes suddenly intent and still. "I'm beginning to feel a definite kinship with them," he said huskily.

She looked down, her eyes shy. The air about them was crackling with the the intensity of his feelings. Brenna was vividly conscious of her near nudity, the softness and curves and the satin smoothness of her skin that seemed erotically fashioned to be pleasing to the hard, muscular form of this man.

She didn't pretend to misunderstand him. "It's only been two weeks," she said with forced lightness.

He reached out to stroke the silky curve of her shoulder. "It seemed like two years. Why do you think I've been working so hard? I'm not used to celibacy, Brenna."

Her eyes flew to his face, and a blush dyed her cheeks at what she saw there.

"God knows, I've tried to be patient," he went on roughly. "I wanted you to come to me. I didn't want to take you. Every night when I finally did get to bed, I'd lie there aching, knowing that you were just across the hall. I've been going through hell. I can't take it anymore."

He lifted her effortlessly so that she was sitting on his knees. His mouth covered hers with an aching sweetness, and then with a groan, his lips parted hers and his tongue invaded her with a savage need. With a swift movement he rolled her over so that they were lying side by side on the recliner, his mouth open and working erotically on hers, demanding her responses. His leg urgently parted her thighs. His thighs felt rough and masculine, she thought feverishly, the fine hair caressing the smoothness of her limbs with a sensual abrasiveness.

"God, you feel so good," Donovan groaned breathlessly, burying his face in the curve of her shoulder. With shaking hands he worked at the back fastening of her bikini top, and in seconds the flimsy strip of material was removed from between their bodies. His hands reached around to curve over her swollen breasts, kneading the sensitive mounds with a rhythmic urgency that caused her to cry out with the sudden heat that shot through her body. She arched against him convulsively, her hips moving blindly in an attempt to fit herself to his loins.

He shuddered, and tore the towel from around his hips in a frantic attempt for a closer unity, and Brenna drew her breath in sharply, as she felt the taut flesh burning through the cool dampness of his trunks. His mouth was on one taut nipple, his tongue teasing it maddeningly while his thumb flicked its sensitive mate, until she was writhing, her breath coming in little gasps. "Please," she begged. "Michael, please . . ."

One hand traveled from her breast to the tense muscles of her stomach, stroking and rubbing the silken skin caressingly, before slipping down beneath the bikini briefs, his other hand loosening the ties at her hips. He lifted and threw back his head, the cords standing out on his strong throat. "God! I want you! Now!" he said, tormented. He closed his eyes, his hands still moving compulsively on her body.

He drew a deep breath, and a convulsive shudder shook his body. Suddenly he rolled away from her, and was on his feet beside the recliner, his hands clenched into fists. He looked down at her, his chest heaving with the effort he was making for control.

She looked up at him, her bare breasts moving rapidly with the same emotion that was wracking him.

"Cover yourself!" he said thickly. "Or so help me, I'll take you right here and now, and I won't give a damn how public it is."

She sat up slowly and looked around for something to cover herself. The bikini top seemed to have disappeared, and she was looking around for it vaguely, when Donovan gave a smothered imprecation and reached down for the towel he had discarded. He threw it to her impatiently.

She clutched it obediently, tucking it beneath her arms, not realizing how provocative the pose was.

Donovan's face was set in harsh lines, his blue eyes burning with flames not yet subsided. "I've got appointments and meetings set up all day and most of the evening," he said grimly, his gaze drawn compulsively to the high curves of her breasts beneath the towel. "So you have another reprieve. It's your last one, Brenna, and for only twenty-four hours." He lifted his hand as if to ward off her protests and arguments, though, in truth, she was not saying a word, just gazing at him with wide, luminous eyes.

"I can't help it if you're not ready, or if you want more time," he said harshly. "I've waited long enough." He turned on his heel, and strode away toward the house, aggressiveness and belligerence in every step.

Brenna settled back on the recliner, still clutching the towel and gazed after him, a loving amusement in her eyes and the deliciously contented smile of a cat who'd just been given the deed to the dairy.

nine

"I'LL BE BACK BEFORE FIVE," DORIS CHARLES said worriedly. "You're sure you don't mind taking care of him for a few hours? After all, I had a day off just two days ago. I feel a little guilty taking off again so soon."

Brenna grinned. "Remember to whom you're speaking. I'm the Cinderella girl who never even dreamed she'd have a nanny for Randy only a month ago. Besides, a trip to the dentist isn't exactly a wild spree. Haven't you ever heard of sick benefits?"

"Well, if you're sure..." Doris said doubtfully, and Brenna briskly assured her that she was quite sure, and with a little more coaxing, Doris Charles was persuaded to leave.

Brenna shook her head ruefully, as she picked Randy up in preparation for a trip to the sandbox in the corner of the patio. Sometimes she thought Doris was a little too dedicated to Randy. That infected wisdom tooth must have been excruciating, yet she had put off having it pulled for almost a day, because she didn't want to leave Randy with his own mother. She would enjoy having Randy to herself again, Brenna thought happily, and Doris would surely be back in time to take Randy over while she dressed for dinner. The note Michael had left her at breakfast had said he'd join her for dinner at eight.

She had not seen Michael since he had left her at the pool yesterday, but Mrs. Haskins had told her this morning that he had gone to the complex to see Mr. Walters. He would probably be closeted with Monty most of the day, and lucky to be home for dinner, she thought anxiously. Then her frown cleared miraculously as she remembered Donovan's lovemaking by the pool yesterday. She had an idea it would take more than a business meeting to keep him from keeping their appointment tonight.

She put Randy down in the sandbox and handed him his pail and shovel. She settled down in a nearby lounge chair with a script that Michael had given her two days ago with a brief comment that the feminine lead had possibilities. She had only gotten through the third scene, but she could already see what he meant. She was soon absorbed in the snappy dialogue of the romantic comedy.

"What a domestic scene. It really touches my paternal heart." The tone was sarcastic and the voice was that of Paul Chadeaux.

Brenna looked up, shocked, her face paling as she realized it really was Chadeaux standing before her, sartorially perfect in a dark blue lounge suit, his gray eyes ugly.

"What are you doing here? Who let you in?" she asked hoarsely.

Chadeaux sat down on the lounge chair opposite her and answered coolly, "Your housekeeper was very obliging. I explained that I was a friend of yours, and she told me to go right on through to the terrace."

It was an understandable error, Brenna thought numbly. Chadeaux was well dressed and personable, and Mrs. Haskins was accustomed to a constant flow of guests coming and going in this house.

Chadeaux was gazing critically at the golden-haired baby playing contentedly in the sandbox. "He's a good-looking kid," he said impersonally. "He has the Chadeaux coloring."

"Many children are very blond when they are young," Brenna answered coolly. "Their color frequently darkens as they grow older."

He shot her a poisonous glance. "You have all the answers, don't you? You and those smart-alec lawyers your husband turned loose on me. It was pretty clever of you to put a noose around Donovan, and get him to do your dirty work."

Brenna's lips tightened. "We have nothing further to talk about, Paul," she said tersely. "Please leave."

Chadeaux smiled nastily. "You think you've won, don't you, little sister? Well, don't count on it," he said. "Donovan may have enough clout to put a spoke in my wheel, but I'm not about to be beaten by some upstart movie mogul." His face twisted balefully.

"You have no choice in the matter," Brenna said, moistening her lips nervously.

"You're wrong. There's always an angle; you just have to find it." Chadeaux's gray eyes were narrowed and sly. "And I've figured the angle, little sister. It's all very simple." He rose lazily to his feet. "You and I and junior, over there, are going on a little trip. We're going to a nice private place where the two of us can 'negotiate.'"

She stared at him incredulously. "We're not going anywhere with you," she said flatly. "Why should we?"

"Because I'm a desperate man, little sister," he said venomously. "The men to whom I owe money are not very understanding of custody battles and legal delays. If I don't produce their money by next Tuesday, I'm in big trouble."

He reached out and grabbed her wrist brutally, jerking her to her feet. "Get the kid. We're leaving right now!"

She struggled futilely in an attempt to break his hold. "You're crazy," she said furiously. "Do you think you can just drag us out of here? Do you think I won't fight you? All I have to do is call and Mrs. Haskins or one of the servants will be right here."

Chadeaux's grip tightened agonizingly on her wrist, and she cried out in pain. "But you won't call," he said menacingly. "Because you have a certain fondness for that sweet little tyke of mine."

Brenna could feel the blood drain from her face as she stared at him in horror. "What do you mean?" she whispered hoarsely, her eyes wide and frightened.

"Children are very vulnerable," he said softly, and his gaze traveled significantly to the swimming pool a few yards away.

"My God! What kind of monster are you?" she said, fear making her sick. "He's your own child."

"I told you I was desperate," he snarled. "I'm not stupid enough to murder the little brat, but I'm not above making him quite uncomfortable if I have to." He smiled unpleasantly. "But I'm not going to have to do that, am I, Brenna? You couldn't stand knowing that you're to blame for causing the little angel any pain, could you?"

"No, you mustn't hurt him," Brenna said sharply. "I'll go with you. Just don't hurt Randy!"

"I thought you'd be reasonable," he said smugly. "Now, let's get going. My car is parked in the driveway out front. I see there's a path that circles the house. We won't need to go back inside."

"I need to change," she said quickly, "and I'll have to get some things for Randy." If she could see Mrs. Haskins, perhaps she could signal her in some way, she thought desperately.

Chadeaux shook his head. "Do you think I'm stupid?" he asked arrogantly. He casually gazed at her lilac slacks and white sun top. "You're okay as you are, and I can buy anything the kid needs on the way. I'm not about to let you be tempted to make a dumb move, and start shouting for help. Now, get the kid before I lose my temper." He released her arm with a little shove. "Move!"

Brenna backed slowly away from him, rubbing her bruised

wrist and thinking frantically, trying to see a way out of this horror that would pose no danger to Randy. Chadeaux was a weak,
self-indulgent man but in this case he had the desperate viciousness of a cornered rat. She had no doubt that Chadeaux meant
what he said when he threatened Randy. She knew from experience how callously cruel he could be.

"Shall I do it myself?" Chadeaux asked with soft menace. "If
you force me to, I won't be as gentle with him as you will."

"No, please," she said, alarmed. She walked over to the sandbox and lifted the protesting baby, cuddling him protectively.

"Good," Chadeaux said grimly. "Now, keep on being a
smart girl, and we'll get along fine."

His hand beneath her elbow, he propelled her quickly across
the terrace and down the stone walkway that encircled the house.

Brenna searched wildly for some sign of the gardener or Bob,
her driver, but neither were in evidence. When they reached the
red Buick rental car, she was forced to admit to herself that if she
were going to get out of this dangerous predicament, she could
not rely on outside help. She must find some way to save Randy
herself.

They were a few miles out of Twin Pines, approaching the highway when Brenna made an attempt to reason with Chadeaux for
the last time. "You do realize this is kidnapping?" she asked quietly. "You could go to jail for a long time. If you'll just let us go,
I promise I'll forget all about it."

"How generous," Chadeaux jeered scornfully. "As it happens, I won't need your generosity. After I get what I want, I
will let you go and you won't dare go to the police."

They had reached the highway now and, to her surprise, he
didn't turn south toward the California border, but north.

"We're not going to Chadeaux Park?" she asked with some

trepidation. She had been hoping she could appeal to the more reasonable members of the Chadeaux family.

"Randy and I will be going there later," Chadeaux said. "Right now, we're headed toward Portland. I want to be close to the airport, so that I can get a plane immediately." He shot her a mocking glance. "After you prove how cooperative you can be."

Brenna shook her head. "I'll never let you have Randy," she said quietly.

"We'll see, little sister," he said softly. "We'll see."

It was almost twilight, and they had reached the outskirts of Portland, when Chadeaux suddenly pulled off the highway. A blue neon sign blinking on and off announced their arrival at the Pinetree Motel. Chadeaux drew up before the small office with a lighted vacancy sign in the large glass picture window.

It was a singularly unimpressive establishment, Brenna noticed drearily. The U-shaped motel units were constructed of gray brick and cedar. Green shutters framed the windows of each individual unit, and the faded and peeling paint gave the motel a generally seedy air.

"This will have to do," Chadeaux said briefly. He reached for Randy who had been lulled to sleep by the motion of the car. "I'll just take the kid in with me when I register. I don't think you'll have any bright ideas about taking off while I have him."

Chadeaux returned to the car in a short time, and drove to the far end of the court to a unit with a large brass number seven on the door.

"My lucky number," he announced with satisfaction, parking directly in front of the door. "Everything is going to turn out just fine, little sister."

Brenna hugged Randy's body to her nervously as Chadeaux indicated that she should get out of the car.

Chadeaux unlocked the door and pushed her in ahead of him, shutting the door behind him.

Brenna looked around her wearily. The room was small and shabby, with the regulation twin beds and the combination desk-dresser that was common to small-town motels everywhere. At least the room looked fairly clean, Brenna thought tiredly.

She laid Randy down on one of the beds, gently brushing a lock of hair from his forehead.

She turned to Chadeaux, and said, "It's past his dinnertime. He must have something to eat."

"He's asleep," Chadeaux said, with a shrug. "He'll be all right for a while." He removed his jacket and threw it on the bed beside Randy. "In the meantime, we can come to an understanding."

Brenna looked at him steadily. "I don't know what you expect to accomplish, but whatever it is, it's not going to work, Paul."

A flicker of anger flashed in the shallow gray eyes. "It had better work," he said malevolently. "Or you're going to be very, very sorry, little sister."

"Stop calling me that!" Brenna snapped, her nerves raw and quivering from the worry and tension of the past hours.

"I'll call you what I please, bitch," he snarled. "I've had enough of your insolence. Now you're going to do what you're told."

With three strides he was across the room. His hands fastened with brutal ferocity on her slender shoulders, and he watched her face with savage enjoyment as he slowly tightened his grip until the pain was excruciating. She cried out in agony.

"Shall I tell you what you're going to do, little sister?" he said tauntingly. "You're going to sit down at that desk over there, and you're going to write out a complete account of Randy's birth, naming me as the father and Janine as the mother, and confessing all the details of Janine's little plot. You're going to give names, dates, and places, so that it will stand up in any court in the country."

Brenna shook her head, her face twisted in pain from the grip that felt as if it were a medieval torture clamp.

"I won't do it," she gasped, tears running down her face. "I'll never let you have Randy."

"Dammit! You will!" Chadeaux snarled furiously, shaking her back and forth, like a dog with a rag doll. He spun her around, and twisted her arm behind her back as he forced her across the room to the desk. As he pulled the desk chair out, his grip loosened fractionally, and with a lightning movement Brenna jerked free and whirled away from him. She backed away, her breast heaving, her eyes wild with fright.

"Damn you!" Chadeaux swore furiously and charged after her, grabbing her once more by the shoulders and trying futilely to subdue her frantic struggles as desperation lent her additional strength. Their struggles had led them to the edge of the vacant bed near the desk, when Chadeaux saw a way of gaining the advantage.

Using the weight of his body, he overbalanced her and she fell heavily onto the bed, striking her head on the wooden headboard. Blinding pain was followed by a moment of darkness, and she went limp beneath Chadeaux's weight. With a swift, satisfied exclamation he pinned her arms above her head, holding her helpless.

He looked down at her in triumph, breathing hard. Suddenly his expression changed, taking on a lustful malevolence that frightened her more than his anger. His gaze went lingeringly over her tousled hair and the top that was now barely covering the tips of her heaving breasts. He ran his tongue over his full lips and his eyes narrowed into gleaming silver slits.

"Suddenly I'm not in a hurry for that affidavit," he drawled thickly. "I think I'll just see if you're as good as your sister." His mouth pressed down brutally on hers, bruising the soft inner flesh against her teeth, as she frantically moved her head from side to side to escape him.

"Get off her, Chadeaux." The words were said with a soft menace that held all the danger of a bared stiletto.

Chadeaux froze, and Brenna drew a breath of infinite thanks-giving.

Donovan held the key to the room in his hand. Obviously he'd used his influence to get it from the motel office. Now he hurled it furiously to the floor and lunged across the room. He jerked Chadeaux up from the bed, throwing him violently against the wall. He followed, his powerful hands squeezing the collar of Chadeaux's shirt into a stranglehold, causing congested color to mount in Chadeaux's frightened face.

"Wait!" Chadeaux gasped desperately, "Listen to me!"

Donovan's face was a mask of rage, his eyes the flaming blue of the fires of hell. "No, you listen. If you say one more word, I'm going to beat you senseless." Donovan grated, between his teeth. "I may still do it, even if you don't."

Brenna sat up dazedly, her eyes fixed in fascination on Donovan. She didn't blame Chadeaux for his almost abject ter-ror. There was such an aura of rage about Donovan that it was as if he were surrounded by an invisible wall of flame.

Donovan's words came with the soft rapidity of a machine gun. "I'm going to tell you this once, Chadeaux, and never again, so you listen carefully. You're never to see my wife again. You're never to talk to her on the telephone. You're never to write to her. You're most particularly not to lay a finger on her again. If you do, I swear you'll wish you had never been born! Do you understand?"

Chadeaux nodded, his eyes bulging, as he gasped helplessly for air.

Donovan turned to Brenna, and her breath caught. She shrank back against the headboard at the white hot fury in his face.

"Get up, and get out of here," he ordered harshly. "Bob Phillips is waiting outside. Take Randy out to him."

Brenna scrambled off the bed, experiencing a few moments of dizziness that caused her to falter momentarily before rushing around to pick up Randy from the bed and hurry to the open door.

Donovan was waiting there, his face white and set. He hesitated a moment, then, as if unable to resist the impulse, he turned back and strode to where Chadeaux was cringing against the far wall.

"I told you I might do it anyway," he said coolly, and struck him a bruising blow to the chin. Chadeaux grunted once, his eyes glazing over, and then slid slowly down the wall, unconscious.

Without giving him another glance, Donovan turned and walked away, grabbing Brenna by the elbow and sweeping her grimly from the room.

As he had said, Bob Phillips was standing by the Mercedes, a worried frown on his craggy face. He carefully avoided Brenna's eyes as they approached. "Everything okay?" he asked Donovan.

Donovan nodded tersely. Taking the sleeping Randy from Brenna, he handed him to Phillips. "Doris Charles will be at the Portland airport by now. I radioed Monty to have her flown here over an hour ago."

Brenna felt her head whirling in bewilderment, as Phillips put Randy carefully in the front seat of the car. Things had been moving too fast since Donovan had appeared on the scene. She took an automatic step toward the child, and Donovan's hand tightened on her elbow. "No," he clipped harshly. "You come with me."

He led her to an ancient Chevy pickup truck parked a few spaces away. She allowed him to help her into the vehicle with a meek docility that was foreign to her. She felt only a dull curiosity as he put the truck in gear and with much coughing and sputtering eased it onto the highway.

"Where are we going?" she asked remotely. She wished vaguely that the fierce throbbing in her head would stop.

"I landed the 'copter at a private airport about three miles from here," he said shortly. "I rented the truck from a kid who services the airplanes."

Brenna nodded weakly, leaning her head against the back of the seat. She closed her eyes to shut out the brilliance of the oncoming headlights that only increased the stabbing pain behind her eyes. She vaguely realized that there were many questions still unanswered, but she had no energy or strength to ask them at the moment. It was enough, for now, that Randy and she were safe and on their way home to Twin Pines.

Donovan seemed to have a similar disinclination to talk, and the transfer from the pickup to the helicopter was made in virtual silence. It wasn't until they were underway for almost twenty minutes that she realized from the mirrored shifting horizon that they were over water. The shock of the discovery jolted her sharply out of the haze of pain and weariness that had enveloped her since she had first seen Donovan at the motel.

"There's some mistake," Brenna shouted over the noise of the rotors, pointing at the still waters of the Pacific below them.

Donovan's mouth twisted. "No mistake," he said with a coolness that was belied by his taut, chiseled face and burning eyes. "We're going to the island."

Brenna shook her head. "We can't," she protested in confusion. "I have to get back to Randy." Somehow in the bewilderment and exhaustion of that moment, the urgency to be with Randy, and reassure herself that he was blessedly safe and secure was paramount.

Donovan shot her a brief glance that had the force of a blow. "I realize how devoted you are to your son," he said coldly. "He's being flown back to Twin Pines, and will be well taken care of. You, however, are going to the island," he finished inexorably.

She shook her head in dejected bewilderment. She couldn't understand why Donovan was so displeased with her. It was not her fault that she had been forced to go with Chadeaux. Even if

Donovan had been put to a certain amount of trouble on her behalf, he still did not have to be so irascible. Her mouth twisted wryly at the blatant understatement. He was obviously in a white-hot rage. But why were they going to the island, she wondered uneasily.

When she hesitantly ventured the question to the grim stranger beside her, she received no answer other than a contemptuous smile that did nothing to put her mind at rest.

He wasn't any more communicative after they had landed the helicopter on the island, and made their way through the woods, their path lit by the powerful beam of Donovan's flashlight. His pace was fast and relentless, and he made no concession for her smaller stride, merely propelling her ahead of him with a determination that gave her neither breath nor strength for protests or questions.

It was not until they had reached the chalet, and he had shut the door and flashed on the overhead light, that he turned to regard her white face, tousled hair, and rapidly heaving breast with cool appraisal. "You look like you could use a drink," he said impersonally, crossing to the portable bar and pouring her a small brandy. He returned to hand it to her with an expressionless face.

She took a small sip of the amber liquid, and made a face at the obnoxious taste, though it did feel glowingly warm going down. After he had given her the glass, he went back to the stone fireplace and was in the process now of building a fire with swift economical movements. She watched him for a moment, then went over to the scarlet couch and curled up in one corner of it, her legs tucked beneath her like a small child. Indeed, she felt like a child, she thought wearily. One who had been punished unfairly, and who now still had to face the incomprehensible anger of grown-ups.

Donovan had succeeded in bringing a brisk crackling blaze

to life, and he turned from where he was kneeling to regard her once more with that inexplicable air of cold antagonism. "Feeling better?" he asked carelessly, and as she nodded silently, he rose and removed his dark suit jacket and tie, throwing them both carelessly on the velvet arm chair. He rolled up his sleeves baring his powerfully muscled forearms, and, crossing back to the bar, made himself a drink.

He did not join her on the couch, but returned to the fireplace to stand with his back to the flames, his legs spread apart and the orange glow a fiery aureole around him. He looked one with the flames, Brenna thought hazily, the combination of the brandy and shock making her dreamily fanciful. He was Lucifer, springing from his fiery kingdom. The vibrant vitality that was always present in him seemed to be almost a visible and dangerous force tonight. Her tortured nerves, that had begun to relax infinitesimally with the soothing effect of the brandy and warmth of the fire, tightened warily as she met the impenetrable blue eyes of the man opposite her.

She brushed a swatch of hair away from her cheek, and moistened her lips nervously. "How did you know where to find us?" she asked falteringly.

The line of Donovan's lips hardened, and he finished half of his drink in a quick swallow. "I suppose like most women, you're enamored of explanations, and must have everything laid out for you," he said cynically. "I wouldn't probe too deeply into my discovery that you were gone, if I were you. My emotions are still a bit raw, and I'm trying hard to control my less than civilized impulses."

She looked at him bewilderedly. "I don't understand." she said slowly, her brown eyes widening.

"Still playing the innocent?" he asked derisively. "You do it very well, Brenna, but the game is over." He took another swallow of his drink. "However, I'm willing to satisfy your curiosity." He leaned indolently against the side of the fireplace.

"Bob Phillips was in the garage, tinkering with the Mercedes, when he saw you get into the car with Chadeaux. He hadn't been notified that you were going out today, so he called through to my office on the car phone to check." Donovan's mouth twisted bitterly.

"I recognized the description of Chadeaux at once, and told Phillips to follow you and report back to me on the CB radio. I was at the airstrip in ten minutes, and have been in constant contact with Phillips on the ground ever since. When it became evident that you were headed for Portland, I radioed Monty to pick up Doris Charles and get her there on the double."

Brenna rubbed her head wearily, her face still puzzled. "But why would Phillips notify you just because he wasn't told I was going out?"

Donovan shrugged. "It was his job to keep track of you," he said coolly.

Brenna put her glass down very carefully on the end table beside her. "Do you mean that Phillips wasn't a chauffeur at all?" she asked quietly. "That he was some sort of spy with orders to report to you?"

"Not a spy, a bodyguard," Donovan replied incredibly. "When you married me, you automatically became the target of all sorts of undesirables, from kidnappers to cranks who think they have a grudge against me for one reason or another. I was trying to protect you." He smiled mirthlessly. "I trusted you. We had a bargain. You're to be complimented. You were very convincing. I don't often trust a woman's word."

Brenna flinched at the stinging sarcasm of his tone, and the smoldering anger that couldn't be mistaken in his eyes. She began to feel a rising sense of aggravation at Donovan's antagonistic attitude. She had played the victim long enough in this scenario. First with that swine Chadeaux, and now with Donovan and his incomprehensible sniping.

"I'm a bit tired of your sarcasm and innuendos, Michael,"

she said lifting her chin. "I have nothing to be ashamed of, and if you have some complaint, I wish you'd speak up."

"I believe the time for speech is past," Donovan said harshly, as he replaced his glass on the bar. "We have nothing further to discuss, Brenna. It's time for the payment of debts." In two long strides he had reached her, pulling her to her feet and into his arms with an explosive release of the savagery that had smoldered just beneath the surface. His mouth crushed hers with a brutal strength that bruised her lips and robbed her of breath. She grew faint and dizzy as it seemed to continue interminably.

When his lips left hers they were both breathing hard, and she leaned weakly against him, her shaking legs unwilling to support her.

"What was the matter, Brenna?" Donovan said savagely, his blue eyes burning. "When I told you it was time you kept your bargain, did you panic at the thought of giving yourself to anyone but that miserable bastard, who used you and then deserted you? Did you decide you wanted him after all?" His mouth covered hers again as if he were draining the very life force from her. "Did you phone him yesterday after I left you, and tell him to come for you?" he asked harshly, as his hands fastened in her hair and pulled her head back roughly.

"No, it's not true," Brenna whimpered. Never in her wildest imaginings had she thought that Donovan would believe she had gone with Chadeaux willingly. She put her hands against his chest protestingly. "You must believe me, Michael," she said huskily, looking up at him entreatingly. "I didn't go with him of my own accord. He forced me."

"What truly incredible eyes you have," Donovan said mockingly, his face hard. "They have the gentleness and innocence of a young doe. You might even have been able to fool me again, if I hadn't seen you on that bed with Chadeaux." The memory of that scene caused his face to darken with such primitive rage, that Brenna felt the first thrill of real fear course through her. "God! I wish I'd killed him," he said hoarsely.

"I was fighting him," Brenna insisted desperately. "We fell..." He cut her off with a kiss that was even more savage than the ones that had gone on before. When he released her, she knew with a feeling of hopelessness that he had gone beyond reasoning.

"Shut up!" Donovan said huskily, his eyes wild. "He was making love to you. Phillips said you got into the car willingly. You even sent Doris Charles away for the afternoon so that you wouldn't have to make any explanations about taking Randy away."

Brenna closed her eyes. It all fitted together so neatly, she thought wearily, and it formed such a completely erroneous and incriminating picture.

How was she to convince Donovan of the truth, when suddenly she was too tired to think coherently? Her head was aching intolerably, and her knees were shaking and weak with reaction to this final strain on her nerves. She knew she must try to convince Donovan how mistaken he was, but the lassitude that was slowly enveloping her made the effort seem superhuman in scope.

"No more arguments?" Donovan asked grimly. "Good." He shifted his hold and scooped her up in his arms, and headed for the spiral staircase. As he passed the lightswitch, he hit it, plunging the chalet into darkness that was relieved only by the flickering light from the fire.

As Donovan negotiated the stairs, Brenna tried desperately to muster the energy to protest. This was all wrong, she realized dimly. The gossamer fabric of trust and friendship they had woven so painstakingly was now rent and torn, and Donovan's savage jealousy was threatening to destroy the pitiful remnants that remained. He carried her to the king-sized bed and placed her on the silken counterpane, then he straightened and started to undo the buttons of his white shirt.

He looked down at her, a dark anonymous shadow whose grim, taut features were occasionally illuminated by the upward surge of the flickering firelight. "I thought our first night together should be spent here, under the circumstances," he said mockingly, as he stripped off the shirt and threw it aside. "I find it most fitting that the consummation of our marriage should be in surroundings that have witnessed a multitude of similar meaningless and shallow interludes." He was swiftly stripping off the rest of his clothes, the firelight playing across the powerful shoulders and pectoral muscles of his chest.

Vulcan! she thought dimly, from some distant primal memory, as he joined her on the bed. His hands were deft and experienced as he brushed away her protesting hands, and drew the white suntop over her head, loosening the front closing of her bra with cool efficiency.

Knowing that her remonstrances would have no more effect than a flimsy canoe before a tidal wave, she felt she had to try once more. "Please, Michael," she whispered huskily. "Not like this."

"Yes, precisely like this," he said thickly. "If you expected gentleness or courtly passion, forget it. You've forfeited the right to anything but this." His hands had removed the lilac slacks, and dispensed with the minute bikini panties that were the last barrier between them. Brenna felt a flash of shame send a burning blush over her entire body, as his eyes ran over her naked beauty in almost impersonal appraisal.

"I'm going to use you, Brenna," he said hoarsely. "I'm going to use this lovely body of yours in every way I know how, and when I've finished, I'm going to do it all over again. I'm going to drown myself in you to the point of satiation, and when I've rid myself of this crazy obsession I have for you, I'm going to kick that lovely tail right out of my life and hope to God I don't have to look into those lying eyes ever again."

He pulled her close, the touch of his warm vibrant flesh

against her own waking her from the dreamy lassitude that had enfolded her like a warm blanket. She reacted helplessly, as she always did, to the magnetism of his powerful body. Though his words lacerated her spirit, her flesh recognized only that this was Michael, the man she loved, and so there must be a response.

As their bodies touched, Donovan's coolness vanished as if it had never existed. His body hardened against hers, as he buried his head in her shoulder, a convulsive shudder rippling through his large frame. "Damn you!" he groaned brokenly. "Why is it that I only have to touch you, to turn on like a teen-ager with his first woman."

His lips covered hers, his tongue invading her to ravish her mouth as his hands were ravishing her body. He was memorizing every line and curve. His hands caressing and branding at the same time, so that she felt that after tonight there wouldn't be an inch of her that was not known and possessed by him. His mouth was at her swelling breasts, and then on the softness of her belly, before returning to her mouth again in a fever of desire.

She arched against him, no longer caring how this sensual witchery had started. She wanted only completion. The desires they felt had been banked low for too long. She could feel the need for him burn hot in every vein until she was gasping and moving helplessly, her hands running first in compulsive caresses over his smooth, muscular shoulders only to bury themselves in the thick crisp hair at the nape of his neck.

His knee parted her thighs and he knelt above her, his hands filling themselves with her breasts. His hair-roughened chest was heaving and his blue eyes glazed with emotion, as he looked down into her flushed face and glowing eyes.

"I want to devour you," he growled thickly. "I've never wanted a woman like this in my life."

Brenna was one throbbing, pulsing entity as she writhed

beneath his tormenting hands. Dimly she was aware that there was something she should tell him. She tried, "Please," she gasped. "I must tell you . . ."

"Too late," he muttered hoarsely. "Too late for anything but this." And his hips plunged forward ruthlessly.

Brenna gave a muffled scream at the hot piercing jolt of pain that wracked her with shocking suddenness. Her hands, that had been caressing, now tried frantically to repulse the intruding body that was suddenly stiff and still above her.

"My God!" Donovan swore, his eyes stunned and unbelieving as he looked down at her pain-filled eyes.

"Please. Let me go," she whispered, her hands pushing at him futilely.

He closed his eyes, his face taut with the battle he was waging. When his eyes opened, they were glazed and desperate. "I can't," he groaned. "God! I can't do it. I promise I'll make it good for you, sweetheart."

He started to move with exquisite care and patience, and he kept his word. Soon the pain was gone, lost in a rapturous vortex of sensation that seemed to be both the beginning and the end of all sensual pleasure. As she began to respond, meeting thrust for thrust with wild passion, he forgot his caution and, holding her close, he plunged again and again, his voice murmuring hotly in her ear. "God, you're so tight, sweetheart. That's it, move with me, love. Put your hands on me. Touch me, Brenna."

The passionate litany was as much an aphrodisiac as the sweetness of his lips, that moved to caress the curve of her ear and the sensitive cords of her neck. She had never known such spiraling pleasure could build to this unknown dimension that was almost painful in its intensity. It continued to build until she felt lost in rapture, before the spiral shattered in a blinding explosion that left her panting and clinging desperately to Michael, her nails buried in his shoulder, as he collapsed helplessly against her in an agony of satisfaction.

Her arms held his shuddering body firmly and tenderly. She received almost as much pleasure out of the knowledge that the supreme enjoyment of her body had brought the powerful man to this pitch of dependent need, as she had derived out of her own sexual fulfillment.

He moved off her slowly, his breathing still rapid but his heartbeat slowing as he settled on his back, his arm curved possessively around her.

Michael reached down and pulled a white fur throw from the foot of the bed. He tucked it around them, changing his position so that her head was nestled in the curve of his shoulder, her shining brown hair splayed over his chest.

Brenna nestled contentedly closer, feeling as delightfully relaxed and drowsy as a kitten. She yawned, her heavy eyelids closing irresistibly.

"Don't get too comfortable," Michael advised firmly, his deep voice rumbling beneath her ear. "You have quite a few explanations to make."

Her eyes flew open as the realization struck her. She had been so lost in the rapturous euphoria of her first experience with physical love, that she had forgotten everything but the pleasure of giving herself to Michael in this exquisite fashion. But now it was brought home to her that Michael knew!

She stiffened, and would have raised her head to look at him, but his hand instinctively closed on her hair in jealous possession, holding her prisoner in his arms. "Talk," he ordered briskly. "I don't believe I've ever had a virgin before, but the condition is quite unmistakable."

Brenna was glad that her head was still buried in Donovan's shoulder, as the warm color rushed to her face. "I suppose you want to know about Randy?" she mumbled.

"I think I have some cause to be curious," Michael said dryly. "I believe the last recorded case of Immaculate Conception was almost two thousand years ago."

She drew a deep breath, and then said with a rush, "Randy is not my child."

"I guessed that," Donovan said ironically, his hand idly stroking her silky hair. "However, I would like to know the identity of the mother of the child I'm claiming to have fathered."

"My sister Janine," Brenna said quietly.

As briefly as possible she related the circumstances of Randy's birth and her subsequent guardianship, as well as Chadeaux's plan to gain custody of Randy and the details of the abduction today.

Michael's hand on her hair paused in its stroking action, and she felt his body stiffen with anger. "And may I ask why you didn't tell me all this when I suggested our little bargain?" he asked with steely softness. "Surely you realized you'd have to be honest with me when we went to bed. Or did you think you could postpone paying off indefinitely?"

"No," she protested indignantly, wriggling away from him and sitting up. She was unaware in her agitation, that the coverlet had dropped to her waist revealing two enticing pink nipples, peeping out from the tangle of brown satin hair. "I wanted to go to bed with you. It was you who suggested the postponement." She ran her fingers through her hair wearily. "I don't know why I didn't tell you. I was frightened and upset. Randy is all the family I have."

"You didn't trust me," Donovan said sharply. "What the hell did you think I'd do, turn the child over to that bastard?"

"You didn't like Randy," Brenna said reluctantly, not looking at him. "I couldn't take the chance."

Donovan began to swear fluently under his breath. "I never said I had a personal dislike for the child," he said between his teeth. "Of all the muddle, addle-brained, completely asinine bit of reasoning, you take the prize."

Brenna tilted her head defiantly. "He was my responsibility," she said defensively. "How could I be sure what you would do? I hardly knew you."

"You knew me well enough to be willing to jump in bed with me," he said caustically, levering himself up into a sitting position. Even in the dimness of the firelit room, she could see the flicker of anger in his eyes. "But you didn't know me well enough to trust me to protect a helpless child!"

"I wasn't willing to jump into bed with you," Brenna said stung. "You gave me no choice."

Donovan's smile was coolly cynical. "You didn't want a choice," he drawled. "You wanted it as much as I did. I just gave you the excuse you needed." His eyes were strangely brooding, as he smiled mirthlessly, his gaze raking over the tempting beauty of her bared breasts and slim waist. He shrugged as his hands came out to clasp her slender shoulders. "Why should I care if I have your confidence?" he asked bitterly. "I have what I bargained for."

As his hands tightened on her shoulders to pull her into his arms, Brenna flinched and gave a cry of pain.

"What the hell?" Michael ejaculated, startled. He fumbled with the bedside lamp, and suddenly the room was filled with light.

"My God!" he brushed her hair gently away from her shoulders, revealing the livid, purple bruise marks on the satin skin. Michael's face was white and set, his eyes sick, as he asked hoarsely, "Did I do that?"

She looked up at him startled, her eyes wide. "No, of course you didn't," she assured him quickly. "It was Paul Chadeaux," she said ruefully. "He wasn't overly gentle in his attempts to get me to sign that affidavit."

Donovan muttered an obscene imprecation, and reached out to touch a bruise with gentle fingers. "I should have killed him," he said grimly. "What other damage did the bastard do to you?"

Brenna was suddenly frightened by the deadly anger mirrored in Donovan's eyes. "Nothing, really," she said deprecatingly. "I hit my head on the headboard when we fell on the bed, but it only hurt for a moment." She touched the side of her head gingerly.

Donovan brushed her hair aside until he found a sizable lump. She flinched as he touched the swelling, and Michael's mouth tightened ominously. "It must have hurt like hell. You're lucky you don't have a concussion." His electric blue eyes narrowed dangerously. "God! I wish I had him here now."

"It's over now. Let's forget it," Brenna said nervously.

"Yes, you forget it," Donovan said absently, his eyes thoughtful. "You've suffered enough. I'll take care of it."

"Michael, no," she protested firmly. "I'm the one who suffered injury, and if any redress is to be exacted, it would be up to me to do so. This isn't the Middle Ages, dammit. I won't have you rushing around fighting my battles as if I was some idiotic, simpering damsel in distress."

Donovan's lips quirked, and there was a flicker of amusement on his taut face. "Sorry, darling. Women's lib is out in this case," he said mockingly. "I warned you that I take care of my own." His hand slid down her shoulder to cup her breast, his eyes noting her suddenly indrawn breath with a gleam of satisfaction.

"Don't worry, I'm not going to take Chadeaux apart with my bare hands, as much as I'd enjoy it. I'll find another and more permanent way of dealing with him. You can be sure he won't ever bother you again." There was absolute assurance in Donovan's voice and Brenna shivered at the ruthless glint in his eyes.

His expression became moody as he stared into her apprehensive face. "Poor Brenna; you're a frightened lamb in a world of ravening wolves," he said soberly. "We men haven't treated you very well in your young life, have we, love? A father who deserted you. Chadeaux causing the death of your sister, and saddling you with a child to raise." His face clouded. "Even I ended up by practically raping you. How can anyone condemn you for hating the lot of us?"

Brenna looked at him helplessly. How could she tell him it wasn't hate she felt for him, but love. Even in the throes of passion he had never indicated that he felt anything for her but a wild, obsessive desire of the flesh. To confess her own feelings, when she knew he did not share them, would leave her open and vulnerable to the most agonizing of rejections. Perhaps he was right, and she had been hurt too much in the past to put much faith in lady luck handing her the prize of Donovan's love.

Donovan's expression hardened, and his mouth curved cynically. "No answer?" he queried mockingly. "Or is that the silence of assent?"

He shifted his hand and pulled her forcefully into his arms, kissing her with a rough passion that caused the familiar melting sensation to begin in her lower body. When their lips parted, he murmured huskily, "You'll just have to continue hating and distrusting me, Brenna, because I'm not going to let you go. I'm holding you to our bargain till hell freezes over."

"Or until you tell me to go." she said with a catch in her voice, remembering the words of their original bargain.

He bore her down on the bed, his hands and lips beginning their passionate ritual. "Yes, until I tell you to go."

ten

"YOU'RE LATE, BRENNA," MARCIA OWENS SAID with mock severity, her dark eyes twinkling. "That's the second time this week. Better watch it or you'll be getting a pink slip in your pay envelope." Donovan's secretary was an attractive, dark-haired paragon of efficiency. She was in her middle thirties with a wry sense of humor, and this wasn't the first time she'd teased Brenna about her dual position as Donovan's wife and unpaid help in the office.

Brenna made a face at her. "Sorry, Marcia. I wasn't feeling well this morning. I must be coming down with something. I told Michael to go on without me, but I felt better later so I came on in."

She shrugged out of her tailored peach pantsuit jacket, and hung it in the closet, placing her brown handbag on the hook beside it. "I know how much you depend on me," she added teasingly, as she strolled back over to the desk.

They exchanged smiles of complete understanding. They both knew that Brenna's presence was completely superfluous in the executive offices at Twin Pines. Marcia Owens handled Donovan's affairs with the exceptional efficiency that he demanded of all his employees. Brenna's contribution consisted of typing a few letters, occasional filing, and relieving Marcia for her coffee breaks. Nevertheless, Brenna enjoyed her mornings working in the office with Marcia. They had formed a great friendship in the last three weeks, and she had discovered a rapport with the older woman that she had found with few of her contemporaries.

The secretary shook her head ruefully. "You must be a glutton for punishment," she said lightly. "Why don't you stay home and pamper yourself? It isn't as if Mr. Donovan is cracking the whip over *your* head." Marcia Owens studied her boss's wife with envy-free admiration, thinking idly how truly lovely the girl was in the simple cream silk blouse and the peach slacks. It was true that Brenna had been of negligible help since she had volunteered her assistance, but she sincerely liked Brenna Donovan and enjoyed having her quiet, cheerful presence in the office.

It was obvious to her that Donovan felt the same way. Brenna seemed to exert a subtle, soothing influence on her employer on the mornings she was there. Though it was not in any way obvious to anyone that did not know Donovan extremely well, Marcia had worked closely with the man for some six years, and she could read the signs. She remembered how he had come out of his office yesterday, a stack of contracts in his hand. While he explained to her what he wanted done with them, his eyes were drawn, as if by a magnet, to the unobtrusive figure of his wife across the room at the filing cabinet, where she was quietly filing some papers. He had not interrupted his instructions, he had not even spoken to Brenna, but his absent gaze had not left her until he had turned to return to his office.

Brenna shrugged. "I get bored. I'm not used to being a lady of leisure. I spend the afternoons with Randy, but he doesn't really need me now that he's got Doris. And if I didn't have something constructive to do, I'd be climbing the walls."

Marcia Owens smiled sympathetically. "After the premiere of *Forgotten Moment* I don't think you'll have that problem. You'll have more offers than you can handle," she said comfortably. "I hear you're absolutely super in it."

Brenna tapped the desk lightly. "Knock on wood," she returned. "In the meantime, I'm a mere dogsbody. What challenging task do you have for me today?"

As Brenna painstakingly began to file the stack of contracts Marcia had handed her, a wry smile curved her lips at the half-truth with which she had evaded Marcia's question. How could she confess that, after three months of marriage, she was still so besottedly in love with her husband that she couldn't stand to be separated from him for an entire day? It was a phenomenon that even the most understanding modern would look upon with unabashed skepticism. As the premiere date approached, Michael had found it necessary to spend more and more time at the executive office working with publicity and distribution.

After a week of such separations, Brenna had complained of boredom, and asked with careful casualness if she could drive in with him mornings and help in the office. Donovan had accepted just as casually, and she had become a fixture in the past three weeks. It wasn't entirely satisfactory, but at least she was close to him. She could see him, exchange a quiet word, and occasionally go out to lunch if his schedule permitted. It was for this reason she had been outraged by the bout of nausea that had plagued her this morning. There was no way some pesky virus was going to cheat her out of another morning with Michael. She had stayed home two days ago, and hadn't seen Michael until he came home for dinner that night. She had been right to fight it, Brenna thought happily, for she felt quite all right now. Sheer mind over matter, she thought cheerfully. The problem was, she had grown spoiled during the past three months, she admitted sadly to herself. Though she had not had Michael entirely to herself while he continued to work at home, she had seen much more of him than was the case now.

They had spent two heavenly days on the island, and during

that time Brenna had learned a great deal about herself and Michael. She had found that she had a capacity for physical passion that shocked and amazed her. In Donovan's arms, she became a pupil so eager for her lessons, that on occasion Michael would laugh with amusement and triumph, before giving her what she entreated him for. That he was pleased with her passionate nature, she knew for a certainty. He whispered it in her ear in the wild throes of lovemaking. She saw it in his eyes when she moaned with need as he brought her to the final ecstasy. As she had guessed, Donovan was an extraordinarily demanding and sensual lover, who frankly enjoyed the act of making love. He was inventive, surprising, and so skillful that she knew before she'd been in his bed a week that he had so attuned her body and sexual responses to his demands that he could arouse her body from across the room with just a look. Her face grew dreamy, as she remembered a morning last month when he had done just that.

She had been sitting in the editing room, curled up in her favorite chair in the corner of the room, when Donovan had looked up. His eyes had gone dark, as they had wandered intimately over her slim curves, lingering over the high curve of her breasts that suddenly became firm and swollen under the tailored blouse. A hot flush dyed her cheeks, and she could see the pulsebeat in Michael's temple in that moment of almost painful awareness. She never remembered what excuse Donovan had given to the two technicians he had been talking to, nor how they had gotten from the editing room to the upstairs bedroom. It had been a wild rapturous lovemaking that had left them panting and exhausted in each others arms.

Donovan had raised his head from her breast to kiss her lips with infinite tenderness. "Remind me to declare the editing room off limits to you, love," he said huskily. "How do you expect me to get any work done, if you persist in seducing me?" Then he had yelped as she'd bitten his ear in retaliation.

In reality, no seduction was needed to tempt Donovan into her bed. He was a man who needed physical assuagement more frequently than most, and there wasn't a night that he didn't reach for her with a hunger that seemed to grow rather than diminish with the passing of time. It had filled her with relief when she realized that Donovan did not appear to be tiring of her. It had been her most persistent fear in the past months. Inexperienced though she was, she realized that men often grew bored with sexual affairs once the novelty had worn off, and Donovan's reputation for discarding mistresses frequently seemed to indicate that he grew bored more easily than most. What was sheer heaven to her, might become repetitive and dull to a man of his experience. When he had shown no signs of lessening passion, she had breathed a profound sigh of relief. She lived with the sad knowledge that Donovan did not love her, indeed, might never love her, but as long as he wanted her physically, she had a hold on his emotions and that was better than nothing. It was much better than that, Brenna thought wistfully, Donovan might not give her love, but he did give her profound physical ecstasy.

An added bonus of Donovan's knowledge of Janine's tragic story, had been a complete change in his attitude toward Randy. As he had told her, he sincerely liked children, and had a way with them that was fast making Randy his willing slave. He now often joined her in the afternoon to play with Randy and just laze by the pool in an aura of domestic contentment that filled her with a poignant wistfulness. Carefully, she did not let herself linger too long on these bittersweet memories. She must take one day at a time in a relationship such as hers with Michael, and savor each one to the utmost. Who knew how many days she had remaining? Passion without love was a reputedly unstable and ephemeral commodity.

She had finished the filing, and had turned to Marcia to request something else to do when the door to Donovan's office opened, and her husband came out accompanied by a short, gray-haired man in a rumpled brown business suit. Michael was being uncharacteristically charming for a man of his blunt, abrasive personality as he ushered the man to the front door, and Brenna wondered idly who the rather anemic-looking individual could be.

The smooth charm was gone in an instant, when he turned around and spied Brenna standing by the filing cabinet. He did not respond to her smile, as he crossed to stand before her, a frown making his roughhewn features even more intimidating. "What the hell are you doing here?" he asked bluntly. "I told you to stay in bed."

His roughness no longer phased her. "I'm much better now," she said serenely. "It's just a bug."

"I wish you'd called me," he said. "I have a date for lunch that I just can't get out of."

Brenna felt a twinge of disappointment, which she valiantly strove to hide with a smile. "No problem," she said quietly. "I'll find someone else to have lunch with." She made a face at him. "You're not irreplaceable you know, Mr. Donovan."

His eyes took on a strange stillness. "Aren't I?" he asked lightly, with a thread of underlying seriousness. "I'm beginning to think you may be, Mrs. Donovan."

He touched her lightly on the tip of her nose before turning briskly and returning to his office, leaving Brenna with a radiant face and eyes that reflected the sudden hope his light remark had given her. She firmly chastised herself for making too much of the teasing statement. He probably hadn't meant anything by it, but it was the closest he had come to admitting that there might be a future for them beyond the boundaries of a marital affair.

Her dazed eyes met the amused stare of Marcia, and she flushed with embarrassment. "Who was that funny little man with Michael?" she asked quickly, hoping to avert one of Marcia's teasing wisecracks.

Marcia raised a knowing eyebrow at the rather obvious diversion, but she answered obligingly. "Daniel Thomas; he is some sort of genius in the research department of Cinetron films. Mr. Donovan thinks he might be on the right track in developing cinematic videotape. He's been trying to persuade him to quit his job with Cinetron, and come here and concentrate his efforts solely on developing the videotape. He's having a few problems convincing him. Evidently Mr. Thomas is nearing the retirement age and has built up quite a bit of seniority with Cinetron. So far, the large monetary settlement hasn't been the persuasion that your husband thought it might be." She shrugged. "It's only a matter of time. Mr. Donovan always gets what he wants."

Brenna nodded, smiling. "That's for sure!" she said vehemently and then blushed again as Marcia broke into an irrepressible chuckle.

Brenna had no doubt that Michael would find a way to obtain the services of Daniel Thomas. She had become aware that Michael had a violent antipathy for the whole Hollywood system, where more often than not films were initiated purely on their box office potential and not on artistic merit. He, too, believed a brilliant picture deserved an equally brilliant monetary reward. But in his eyes an expertly crafted motion picture was the goal, not the tinkle of the box office cash register. Though he still had to deal with the Hollywood money men occasionally, he was gradually attempting to cut himself and Twin Pines entirely free from the system. Evidently, this little man held one of the keys that Donovan had been searching for.

At present all theatrical films had to be processed by the film laboratories in Hollywood, but Donovan was convinced that it was just a matter of time before theatrical films could be transferred to tape. Time, and research geniuses of the calibre of Daniel Thomas, Brenna corrected herself. Once such a film was developed, it would break one of the major chains that still bound Twin Pines to Hollywood. Donovan most certainly would bend every effort to winning Thomas to this purpose.

The rest of the morning passed fairly quickly, with the usual stream of visitors in and out of Donovan's office, and the light clerical duties that Marcia gave her. She had just finished typing the last page of a contract when she looked up to see Jake Dominic standing before her, looking tan and fit and incredibly handsome in white pants and a navy blue sports shirt.

"Jake!" she said delighted, jumping up and giving him both her hands in greeting. She hadn't seen him since about a week after the picture was completed. Michael had told her that immediately after a picture was finished, Dominic always set sail in his luxurious yacht, *Sea Breeze*, and was gone for an unspecified time, until he was rid of the tension of directing and grew unutterably bored and eager to return to work. That the cruise always included the presence of a beautiful and willing woman went without saying. This time Brenna had heard it rumored that his companion had been the wife of the head of state of a small South American country, and that the State Department had been biting its collective fingernails with fear that, this time, Dominic's affair would cause an international incident.

Yet here he was, looking as casual and arrogant as ever, as he smiled down at her with that wickedly arched eyebrow. "My God, Brenna," he said teasingly. "What other uses is Michael going to find for you? Wife, mistress, actress, and now secretary. I'm going to have to whisk you away on my next cruise, just to see that you get a rest."

"From what I hear, the women you take on your cruises get considerably less rest than I do," Brenna said dryly, her eyes twinkling. "You look in reasonably good health for a man who has been reputedly dodging machetes, or is it *bolos?*"

"Neither," Dominic said lazily. "It was all much ado about nothing. The lady's husband is quite complacent as long as she handles her affairs discreetly."

Brenna giggled at the thought of a cruise with Jake Dominic being considered discreet, and a reluctant smile tugged at his lips. "I missed that laugh of yours," he said softly, and his dark eyes were suddenly tinged with a touch of loneliness. "It was a bore," he said wearily. "More so than usual."

Again Brenna felt that poignant tug of sympathy for this brilliant man who had everything a man could want, and was still jaded and even curiously lonely.

"Perhaps next time you should try a Swede," she said lightly, trying to gently nudge him out of his depression.

It worked. Dominic's mercurial temperament responded, and the black eyes gleamed mischievously. "I've already gone that route," he said with a shudder. "They're much too aggressive. I was totally exhausted by the time I got back to port."

"What about her?" Brenna asked grinning.

"Oh, Helga immediately took off for Switzerland with her ski instructor. I hear he was a candidate for the Olympics before she got her hands on him." He sighed morosely, his eyes twinkling. "He's never been heard of since!"

Brenna chuckled irrepressibly. "What are you doing back in Twin Pines?" she asked. "Michael didn't mention you were doing a picture?"

He shrugged. "I'm ready to go to work. If I have too much time on my hands, I get restless, and *voilà*—trouble."

"It seems I've heard rumors to that effect," Brenna agreed demurely. "Are you the important lunch date my husband can't break to escort his own wife?"

"Not me, sweet, but I'll act as a substitute, if you'll wait until I see that unchivalrous husband of yours," he said. "I want to pick up a script Michael told me about. Some thriller about a nuclear power plant. Michael says it has possibilities."

"Done," Brenna said cheerfully. "I'll be ready to leave when you're finished with Michael."

With a wave of his hand, Dominic entered Donovan's office without knocking, and Brenna went to the closet to get her jacket and purse. When she returned to her desk to extract the contract from her typewriter and hand it to Marcia, she was amazed to see the older woman convulsed in laughter. As Brenna stared at her blankly, the secretary wiped tears from her eyes and gasped penitently. "Sorry, Brenna, I was just eavesdropping, and it struck me as funny."

"What did?" Brenna asked, puzzled.

Marcia's eyes danced. "The calm way you accepted the foremost rake of the western world as a second-best substitute for your husband. No one would believe it."

Brenna grinned. It did seem funny when she looked at it from Marcia's point of view, and if one didn't know that the husband in question was Michael Donovan.

"If you'll forgive me for interrupting your chat, I'd like to see Mr. Donovan." The husky voice was dripping sarcasm, and they both looked up, startled, at the woman who had entered the office unnoticed. Brenna's eyes widened as she recognized the woman standing there. The large violet eyes, wild riotous ash-blond hair, and curvaceous figure were as famous as the throaty voice. Melanie St. James, who had rocketed to stardom in her first picture, a Michael Donovan production. With a pang, Brenna recalled that the gossip columns had also been filled with speculations regarding Donovan's torrid affair with his gorgeous protégée.

Marcia Owens recovered her aplomb swiftly. "Is Mr. Donovan expecting you?"

The pouting lips tightened. "Of course, he's expecting me," she said arrogantly. "We have a luncheon date."

Brenna felt a cold pain somewhere in her midriff, as she heard the woman's words. So this was Donovan's inviolate, unbreakable luncheon date, she thought numbly.

Marcia Owens shrugged, and picked up the phone. "I'll tell him you're here," she said coolly. "At the moment he's with Mr. Dominic."

"Jake Dominic?" Melanie St. James inquired, her eyes taking on an almost greedy glitter. "I've never met him. Is he working with Donovan now?"

"Occasionally," Marcia answered remotely, and spoke into the receiver. "Mr. Donovan will see you now. Miss St. James," she said as she replaced the receiver. "Go right in."

A smile of triumph lit Melanie St. James' face. "I told you he'd see me," she said with smug satisfaction. "After all, he called *me*." She swept by them and into Donovan's office, leaving Marcia Owens in an agony of sympathetic embarrassment as she carefully avoided Brenna's eyes.

Brenna said nothing as she moved toward the restroom like a sleepwalker. Refusing to think of anything at all, keeping her mind carefully blank, she washed her face and put on fresh lipstick. She tidied her hair carefully, taking as much time as possible, so that she wouldn't have to return and be present when her husband swept the voluptuous actress out of the office. She was not consciously thinking, but her instinct for self-preservation prevented her from exposing herself to that degree of torture.

When Brenna returned, Dominic was standing by Marcia Owens' desk and they stopped speaking abruptly when she entered the room. Dominic took one look at her set white face, muttered an imprecation beneath his breath, and crossed to take her by the elbow. "Dammit all, what fools you women are," he said roughly. "Come on, we're going to lunch and I'm going to try to talk some sense into you."

He half led, half propelled her from the room, and any protests she might have made were quelled by the grim stormy look on Dominic's face. This was not the same Dominic she had joked and teased with such a short time ago. She obeyed meekly as he settled her in his black Ferrari and whisked her to a small restaurant on the edge of town. It looked more like a small brick residence than a restaurant, and there was only a small sign quietly advertising quality cuisine in discreet letters.

It was only after they had been seated at a quiet corner table and Dominic had given the order for both of them, that he turned to Brenna with quiet determination in every line of his face.

"All right, now we talk," he said briskly. "Will you please tell me why you're looking like a Christian who has just been thrown to the lions?"

Trust Jake to think in such visual terms, she thought numbly, but she had no intention of confiding in him. The wound was too raw to bear probing by that ruthless intellect. "Perhaps I'm not feeling well," she said evasively. "Marcia will tell you I was a little under the weather this morning."

"Bull!" Jake said succinctly. "We both know the reason you're falling apart at the seams. I hoped to get you to bring it out in the open yourself. But if you won't, I will."

"I don't want to talk about it," Brenna said rigidly, looking down at her folded hands on the white damask tablecloth.

"Too bad!" Jake said coldly. "Michael's my best friend, and I hope you're going to be a close second, Brenna. I'm not about to let some foolish, womanish misconception hurt either of you. Now, let's talk about that promiscuous little sex kitten Michael took out to lunch today."

Brenna flinched. "I don't see any evidence of misconception," she said with an effort. "It seems to be perfectly clear."

"It always does to a woman," Jake said dryly. "Did it ever occur to you that he could have a reason, other than the obvious one, to see the beauteous Miss St. James? They are in the same business, you know."

"She isn't under contract to Donovan any more," Brenna

said miserably. "Everyone knows that she signed with Fox two years ago."

"About the same time she and Donovan called it quits," Jake observed coolly. "If I remember, it was Donovan who tired of her. So why the hell would he want to stir up the ashes of a dead love affair?" He grimaced. "Believe me, there's nothing less appetizing once you're through with a woman."

Dominic's brutal frankness was less than comforting when she realized his ruthless attitude was essentially the same as Donovan's. She shivered uncontrollably with the pain of the thought. Would Donovan some day feel the same distaste for her as he did his past mistresses? Was he, even now, trying to tell her, in this cruel and ruthless fashion that she must not count on any real permanency in their relationship?

"You're a good friend to Michael, Jake," she said huskily, her brown eyes bright with unshed tears. "But I think it's you who isn't reading the situation correctly."

"Hell!" Dominic said roughly, his black eyes worried. He covered one of her hands with his own. "Michael doesn't give a damn about Melanie," he said earnestly. "Take it from one who knows. Before you came along women were just something to use and throw away to Michael. In fifteen years, I've never seen him act the way he does about you. The man's obviously crazy about you, you little fool."

"That's comforting," she said bitterly. "Maybe I'll last a few months longer than Melanie St. James." She ran her hand through her hair wearily. "Jake, I know you're doing what you think is best, but all this discussion is tearing me to pieces." Her lips quivered uncontrollably. "I couldn't possibly eat anything. Would you please take me home?"

Jake sighed, and his face was a picture of dissatisfaction as he took some bills from his wallet and threw them on the table. "I should have known better than to try to argue with a woman where her emotions are concerned," he said gloomily, as he rose. "Come along, little martyr. I'll take you home where you can sulk, and brood, and build up a really horrendous case against Michael by the time he gets home tonight. *Women!*"

Perhaps due to this last harsh condemnation of Jake's, Brenna tried to do exactly the opposite when Dominic had dropped her off. She kept herself feverishly busy all afternoon. Playing vigorously with Randy in the pool, then cleaning out and rearranging dresser drawers in her bedroom. She tried to read a script that Michael had left for her, but this was a lost cause. Her mind refused to take in one word of the dialogue.

Michael called three times that afternoon, but she refused to speak to him, giving a vague excuse each time to the puzzled and upset Mrs. Haskins. When he made his last call, he left a message that he wouldn't be home to dinner, a message that Mrs. Haskins delivered with barely concealed, righteous satisfaction. The housekeeper adored Donovan, and she obviously thought Brenna was mistreating her idol.

Brenna herself refused dinner, and returned to her room to settle down and wait for Donovan's return. She realized at once that this was a mistake as clouds of depression rolled over her horizon, making her as brooding and self-pitying as Dominic's accusation. She jumped up, and hurried to the bathroom, filling the aqua tub with steaming, bubbling water while she bundled her hair on top of her head. She dropped her clothes carelessly on the floor and stepped into the tub, reclining full length, her head resting on the plastic pillow affixed to one end of the tub. The water was warm and soothing and like liquid silk against her flesh. Suddenly she remembered that first day on the island, and Michael beside her in that Sybarite sunken bathtub that was built for lovemaking. She could feel her nipples harden, as her mind helplessly replayed the love scene, the first of many that had gradually bound her to Michael with golden chains. She could feel the silent tears that she had fought all day long run down her cheeks in silent profusion, and she knew the time had finally come for self confrontation.

Jake had not truly realized why she had been so devastated by Michael's luncheon date with Melanie St. James. She was not foolish enough to think that Michael had finished with her yet: He was still too eager to possess her. Their lovemaking was too good for her to make that mistake. It may have been a perfectly innocent interlude as Jake had suggested. What had shaken her world to the foundation was her own reaction to that first agonizing suspicion that Donovan might be growing tired of her. The pain had been breathtaking, blacking out the joy of living as if it no longer existed. She had realized then how she had been deceiving herself.

Since she had first discovered her love for Michael, she had convinced herself that an emotion that beautiful could only enrich her, and make her stronger in the years to come. She had not realized that Michael had painted the canvas of her life with his own bright hues, and without him, all the exuberant vitality would vanish as if it had never been. Her love for him had grown with each passing day. Heaven knows what stage of dependency she would reach if she remained with him any longer. If she left now, it would be like losing a limb but she would survive. If she waited until she was discarded, as Michael had left her with no doubt she eventually would be, she was not at all sure that it wouldn't destroy her. It had been that realization that had so stunned her and left her bereft—the knowledge that she must leave Michael, and that it must be accomplished soon for self-preservation's sake. She must break her word to Michael, because she knew he was not ready to let her go yet.

The tears continued to flow and she brushed them aside impatiently. She had always had to be strong and independent. She would get over this stupid pain and weakness and emerge stronger than ever. She would leave, and never see that strong-willed Irishman again. She would make a life for herself and Randy, and it would be a good life. She closed her eyes and the maddening tears continued to flow. She would do all these things, she assured herself sadly, but first she would take one final night for herself. She would say a last "good-bye" to her love, Michael Donovan.

She got out of the tub, drying quickly, powdering liberally with her lavender-scented talc, before donning her favorite negligee set. It was a wonderfully romantic gown. Its white silk background was sprinkled with minute pink roses. The tiny sleeves, low rounded elasticized neckline, and empire waistline lent a Regency air to the ensemble. The matching peignoir was a loose drift of white chiffon with long loose sleeves. She slipped into a pair of white satin mules, and brushed her hair into a bright shining cape. She looked with bittersweet approval into the long oval mirror on the closet door. Yes, this was the image of her that she wanted Michael to hold in his memory when she was gone. She turned off the bedroom light, and left the room to go downstairs to wait for Michael.

She was curled up in one corner of the couch in the living room, idly leafing through a magazine, a little over an hour later when the front door was thrown open explosively. She could hear Donovan's rapid footsteps in the hall.

He came through the living room door like a small hurricane. He had discarded his suit jacket and was dressed in black slacks and a white shirt opened carelessly at the throat. His hair glowed brilliantly under the overhead light, and, as usual, he seemed to draw all the radiance in the room to himself. His face was taut and angry, as he crossed to the couch and pulled her roughly to her feet. "Dammit! I could beat you," he said furiously. "What the hell do you mean by refusing my phone calls? You know damn well I was tied up with appointments and couldn't come to you. I've gone through hell all afternoon, since Jake called and told me what an asinine snit you'd gotten yourself into. *Women!*" he finished disgustedly.

A little smile curved Brenna's lips. "That's what Jake said," she said, her brown eyes twinkling.

He paid no attention. His jaw was set belligerently as he continued harshly. "You're going to shut up and listen to what I have to say, dammit. I had a damn good reason for taking Melanie to lunch, and if you weren't so stubborn, I would have told you what it was when I called."

"Have you had anything to eat?" she asked quietly, her eyes running lovingly over the blunt, rough features.

"What?" he asked, caught off balance for once, blue eyes surprised.

"Did you have any dinner?" she asked.

"No, I didn't take the time," he said impatiently. "Look, Brenna, we've got to get this straightened out."

"I'll fix you an omelet," she interrupted, smiling. "You can tell me all about it while I'm cooking. The coffee is already prepared."

She wriggled out of his grasp and preceded him down the hall and into the kitchen. He followed her closely, almost as if he suspected her of trying to escape him. She gestured to the breakfast bar. "It won't be a minute," she said serenely. She poured him a cup of coffee, added the small dollop of cream he used, and stirred it briskly. She carried it carefully to the bar and set it before him.

His hand closed on hers as she released the cup, and she looked up to meet eyes that were bright with suspicion. "What game is this you're playing, Brenna?" he asked. "Jake said you were more upset than he'd ever seen you this afternoon. Yet now you're as cool as a cucumber. Don't you want to hear about Melanie?"

She returned his gaze steadily. "If you want to tell me," she said quietly, "but it's not really necessary. Jake was right; I over-reacted."

She could feel the tension gradually leaving Donovan's body. "I'm glad you realize that," he said lightly. "I had visions of having to chase after you and drag you back by your hair."

Brenna's gaze dropped to their interlocked hands. "I'm still here," she said evasively. "Now, if you'll release me, I'll make that omelet."

His grip reluctantly relaxed, and he leaned back on the stool and idly watched her as she bustled around the kitchen, beating the eggs, adding the milk, and heating the omelet pan, before pouring in the mixture. He didn't attempt to speak until she set the savory omelet before him, poured herself a cup of coffee and perched on the stool opposite him.

He took a bite of the omelet and looked up at her. "I needed Melanie to do a favor for me," he said abruptly. His mouth twisted cynically. "Not that Melanie ever did anything for anyone without suitable compensation. This was no exception. I had to write her a very hefty check for her trouble." He was eating steadily, his eyes watching Brenna's serene face alertly for signs of distress or suspicion. "I persuaded her to try to charm someone I want to join my organization. The old man is a great fan of hers, and I thought introducing her to him might conceivably tip the scales my way."

"Daniel Thomas?" Brenna guessed.

Donovan nodded. "That's right. He joined us for lunch today."

"Did it work?" Brenna asked, sipping her coffee slowly, and idly studying the way his thick, crisp hair clung to his head like a molten cap.

Donovan shrugged. "It's too early to tell. If it doesn't, I'll try something else."

He had finished, and he pushed his plate away. He took a swallow of coffee, and his hand reached out once more to clasp hers.

"You scared the hell out of me, you know," he said quietly. "I even called Phillips and told him to report to me if you left the house."

"Poor Bob. What a skittery female he must think me," she said lightly. She returned the pressure of his hand affectionately, and then rose and reached for his plate and utensils. "I'll just rinse these and put them in the drain."

"No, leave them," he said thickly. He drew her gently around the bar, to stand before him, his eyes running over her with a look that was a long embrace. "You grow more beautiful every day, do you know that?" he said hoarsely. He reached beneath the misty robe to pull the elasticized neckline down to bare her shoulders, before putting his lips to the pulse beat in the hollow of her throat. It leapt, as it always did, at the light touch of his tongue. Her breath almost stopped, as his hands closed on her breasts and thumbed the nipples through the light silk of her gown. He, too, was breathing quickly as his lips closed on hers in a long kiss that left them both languid and hot with need.

"You'd better be upstairs and in bed in two minutes," he said raggedly, as their lips parted. "Unless you want to explore how erotic making love in a kitchen can be."

She grinned and kissed him gently. "Some other time," she promised lightly. She turned away quickly, as a swift jolt of pain went through her. There would be no other time after tonight.

She was waiting for him when he came into their bedroom a few minutes later, sitting quietly on the bed, her feet tucked beneath her. She had removed the robe and slippers, and had an air of childlike docility as he approached her.

His eyes were warm and intent on her as he started to unbutton his shirt.

"No!" she reached up and stopped him. She knelt on the

bed, and her fingers replaced him at the task. "Please, I want to do it," she whispered, her doe eyes wide and pleading. "I want to do everything for you tonight. Show me how to make you happy."

She slowly unbuttoned his shirt, and slipped it from his massive shoulders, placing little gentle kisses on his chest and throat as she did so. She had spoken only the truth when she said she wanted to make him happy. Not only did she want to capture a very special memory for herself, but she wanted to give Michael the same joyous gift. Her arms slipped around his strong throat, and she kissed him gently, tenderly, with all the love she possessed for this difficult, exciting man. "Show me," she entreated quietly.

In the hours that followed he did show her what she desired. She memorized every muscle of his body as he had once done to her. She learned with lips and hands how to raise him to the height of desire and satisfaction, and in doing so, reached her own rapture. They came together not once, but many times that night. Donovan was as indefatigable and insatiable as she, as if half comprehending the desperation that drove her to pour forth her love in this the only way Michael would accept. It was shortly before dawn when Donovan fell asleep, his arm still cradling the warmth of her body.

But Brenna remained wide awake, her strained desperate eyes on the gradually lightening sky seen through the bedroom window. She knew, with a wrench that threatened to tear her soul apart, that it was time for her to go.

eleven

IT WAS A LITTLE AFTER NOON WHEN THE
taxi pulled up before the Rialto theater, and the driver politely
came around to open the passenger door. Brenna got out, payed
the amount on the meter, and headed for the stage door with a
hurried stride. It was her last step in her flight from Donovan,
this meeting with Charles Wilkes, and she was anxious to get it
over with.

It seemed incredible that less than eight hours ago she had
been in Michael's arms, and now she was seeking Charles' help
in removing her from his world permanently. The silent, almost
furtive escape from Twin Pines with only an overnight case and a
sleeping Randy, and the long drive to the airport in Portland
seemed years, not hours ago., She had been in luck. After parking the Mercedes, and leaving the keys in an envelope addressed
to Michael at the ticket counter, she had been able to get a flight
down to Los Angeles within thirty minutes. She only had time
to phone a very concerned and puzzled Charles Wilkes, and arrange to meet him at the theater at noon, before the flight was
called.

Brenna was reluctant to ask for Wilkes' help, but she saw no
other alternative. She had frighteningly little money after she

had paid for the plane tickets and the taxi to Vivian Barlow's apartment to drop Randy off. She desperately needed a job and a place to stay, and it could not be in Los Angeles. She had broken her commitment to Michael, and she knew how determined and ruthless he would be in claiming what was due him. Charles had contacts with repertory troupes throughout California, as well as ties with several universities and academic establishments. If anyone could get her to a safe haven, it was her former mentor.

The stage door was open, as she expected, and she stopped a moment to smooth her hair, and tuck the melon silk blouse into her camel slacks. There was no sense in looking more disheveled and desperate than necessary. Charles was going to be concerned enough, when she asked for his help to escape from Michael. He had been almost childishly pleased when he had learned of their marriage.

She walked quickly down the shabby, dimly lit hall to Wilkes' small office. The door was slightly ajar, and she could see a small pool of light from the metallic desk lamp on the ancient pine desk. She pushed open the door.

"Come in, Brenna."

The blood drained from her face, as she stared transfixed at the red-haired man, who rose lazily to his feet at her entrance. Donovan was casually dressed, as always, in rust corduroy jeans and a cream cotton shirt that was left carelessly unbuttoned almost to his waist. He had rolled his sleeves up to the elbow.

"Michael!" Brenna said, stunned. She took an instinctive step backward, as panic urged her to flee.

"Don't even think about it," Donovan said, his voice hard as steel. "I'd catch you before you reached the stage door." His blue eyes were cold and razor sharp. "You're going to come in, and we are going to have a few words before we go on to my apartment. Do you understand?"

Brenna shook her head sadly, as the shock of his appearance dissipated. "No, Michael, I'm not coming back to you," she said quietly.

"You will," he said arrogantly. "I don't know what this is all about, but I intend to get to the bottom of it."

Brenna came a few steps into the room, her brown eyes pleading. "All the discussion in the world won't change my mind. Let me go, Michael."

A muscle twisted in Michael's jaw. "The hell I will."

Brenna sighed tiredly. After all the pain and agony of leaving him, she would have to do it all again. "Where is Charles?" she asked despondently. "Did he call you?"

Donovan shook his head. "I called him about thirty minutes after you did. When I discovered you were gone, I knew you'd run to either him or Vivian Barlow. I told him we'd had a little marital spat, and that I'd meet you in his place." His mouth twisted cynically. "He was delighted to oblige. Charles loves a happy ending."

"I'm sorry you've gone to such trouble," she said, not looking at him. "I'm afraid it was a waste of your time. Good-bye, Michael." She turned to go, but he was around the desk in seconds and grasping her arm in a clasp of steel.

"No way, Brenna," he said silkily. "You're coming with me, and we're going to talk. Because if you walk out of my life, you're going to do it alone. You're not taking Randy with you."

Her eyes flew to him incredulously. "What are you talking about? Randy's mine!"

"Possession is nine tenths of the law," he quoted ruthlessly. "And I have possession. He's on board the Lear jet right now enroute to Twin Pines with Doris Charles. Monty picked him up from Vivian's apartment five minutes after your taxi pulled away from the curb."

Brenna shook her head dazedly. "No," she said desperately. "You're lying. Vivian wouldn't give Randy to a stranger."

"You've forgotten how persuasive Monty can be," he said coolly. "And after all, he was your husband's representative." He reached behind him, and lifting the phone receiver punched a number rapidly. "Speak to her yourself," he said mockingly, offering her the receiver. Two minutes later Brenna handed the receiver back to him, her face white. "It's virtually kidnapping, you know," she said numbly. "You're as bad as Paul Chadeaux."

His face was rigid with anger, and the blue eyes flickered dangerously. "I'll let that pass for now," he said coldly. "But don't push your luck, Brenna. I'm not feeling particularly tame at the moment."

Neither was she. The shock and numbness was melting rapidly under mounting rage and indignation. How dare even Donovan pull something this arrogant and cruel?

"So what's the next move, Michael?" she said bitterly, her brown eyes flashing angrily. "What ransom are you asking to give me back my son?"

"At the moment, only that you accompany me to my apartment," he said. "As I said, we have some talking to do." He gestured to the door. "Shall we go?"

The taxi ride to the high-rise apartment complex was made in complete silence. Brenna's anger rose steadily as she had time to dwell on the sheer audacity of Donovan's move. It was not enough that he had all but wrecked her life and the chance of happiness with any other man, but he had to take from her the only other person she loved as well. By the time they had ridden the elevator up to the penthouse apartment, and Donovan had unlocked the door, she was almost fuming.

She swept angrily into the apartment and stomped down the thickly carpeted stairs to the sunken living room. She threw her purse on the rust modular couch, and looked around distastefully, noting the air of lush affluence. Cream carpet, expensive contemporary furnishings, and a beveled mirrored bar, all bespoke unlimited luxury and power.

"Very impressive!" she said scornfully, whirling to face him. "Rather like a set—'movie mogul's penthouse apartment.'"

"I'll give my decorator your compliments," Donovan said, strolling toward her, narrowed blue eyes on her defiant face. "Those were my instructions exactly. I use this apartment chiefly for business meetings. I find a little healthy intimidation very beneficial."

"Is that why you brought me here?" Brenna asked bitterly. "Am I to be intimidated by the great Michael Donovan?"

Donovan's mouth tightened. "I brought you here so that you can explain why you broke your word to me and ran away. If I have to intimidate you to get an answer, then so be it." His eyes darkened broodingly. "We shared something pretty special last night, and I woke up this morning to find you'd left me, presumably for good. I want to know why? Was it Melanie St. James?"

Brenna shook her head impatiently. Her anger was inexplicably seeping away, replaced by the treacherous yearning that always beset her in Donovan's presence. "No, it wasn't Melanie," she said wearily. "I just couldn't stay any longer. Please try to understand."

Donovan's hands closed on her shoulders, his face white and set. "I *don't* understand, and I *won't* accept it! I know damn well you haven't been unhappy these last few months. Tell me why!"

Suddenly she couldn't stand it any longer. It was sheer torture being so catechized when her emotions were raw and bleeding. "What difference does it make whether it's now or later," she cried. "It was only a matter of time, anyway."

"It was time that I needed," he said grimly. "I think I know what happened. With your background, I realize how difficult it must be for you to trust yourself to a commitment to any man. I thought I was making progress, but this little incident with Melanie blew the whole thing up in my face." His mouth firmed determinedly. "Well, we'll just have to start again."

His words only added to her distress and confusion. "By holding my son hostage for my good behavior? How long do you think you can get away with that?"

His blue eyes met hers with implacable determination. "I can use it today and perhaps tomorrow. The next day I'll find another lever to keep you with me. And the next day I'll find another. I'll keep on until there are no more tomorrows."

"Why?" she whispered, her gaze clinging to his, while an impossible hope stirred to life.

"Because I love you, you stupid woman," he grated between his teeth. "Because I damn well can't live without you."

Her mouth flew open, and her eyes grew round. For a moment she was unable to respond due to the sheer stunning impact of what he had said.

"I know you don't want any permanent relationship with me," he said raggedly, shaking her a little. "But dammit, I know I can make you love me in time, and I'm going to buy that time any way I can!"

She shook her head dazedly. "This doesn't make any sense," she said, bewildered. "You made it very plain that our marriage was only temporary."

"I was afraid I'd scare you off," he said bluntly. "I knew damn well what I wanted from the moment I saw you, but after I found out about your distrust of men, I knew I'd have to play down any hint of commitment." He shrugged, his expression belligerent. "Well, it's too late for that now. I intend that this particular commitment will last the rest of our lives. So get used to it, Brenna!"

Her eyes dropped, as a wave of unbelievable joy rushed through her. *Michael loved her*. Michael Donovan loved and wanted her, not for just the present but forever.

He must have misunderstood her silence for that of despondency, for his hands moved to cradle her face tenderly. "God!

Give me a chance, sweetheart," he pleaded hoarsely. "I can make you happy. Just give me a chance."

Her eyes lifted to his, and all the radiance in the universe was shining from her eyes. "And you call me stupid, Michael Donovan," she said, trembling. "You're the one who is supposed to be experienced with women. Can't you tell when one green girl is mad about you?"

She flowed into his arms, and pulled his face down to hers. Michael's eyes were blank with shock, and his body was stiff and still as he looked down at her. Then her lips touched his, and he crushed her to him in a convulsive embrace that left them both glowing and breathless. Her hands moved down from his shoulders to caress the hair-roughened muscles of his chest as she spread a multitude of joyous little kisses over his jaw and chin. "Oh, Michael, I do love you so much!" she breathed. "I'll love you forever and ever, do you know that?"

A deep chuckle rumbled from the chest under her hands. "If you don't stop that, you're going to be asked to prove it," he said dryly, his blue eyes twinkling. "And as much as I lust after that luscious young body of yours, I still think we need to talk." He drew her down on the couch, and pulled her around so that she was half-sitting, half-lying in his arms. He kissed her lingeringly.

"Do we really have to talk?" Brenna asked yearningly, one finger lazily tracing the well-defined curve of his upper lip. He caught her hand and held it firmly.

"We do," he said with determination, his mouth twisting. "I want everything clear, all cards on the table. We're not going to have any more problems due to misconceptions. We've wasted too much time already."

She sighed deeply, and his gaze was drawn irresistibly to the delicious curve of her breast under the melon silk shirt. His hand reached out, as if to caress those tempting mounds before he stopped with an effort.

"I think we'd better talk very quickly," he said huskily. "Who'd ever have guessed you'd turn out to be such a passionate little witch. You're a constant temptation to me, love."

She smiled, her eyes embracing him with such a dazzling wealth of love that he caught his breath. "Only for you," she whispered. "I only want you, Michael."

"It had better stay that way," he threatened jokingly, his hand tenderly stroking her hair. "I've been wild with jealousy since the moment we met. That actor at the theater, Paul Chadeaux, even Jake."

"Not Jake," she said unbelievingly. "You know Jake would never violate your friendship."

"With my mind, maybe, but my emotions were another matter. I know, better than most, what a rake he can be, and women fall for that devil's face of his like a ton of bricks. You wouldn't be the first to develop a passion for him without Jake even making the effort."

"Yes, he is utterly devastating," Brenna agreed teasingly. "I can't think why I prefer ugly, bad-tempered Irishmen."

"Shall I tell you," he asked mischievously, and bent to whisper in her ear.

A blush crept over her, but she met his eyes challengingly. "Promises, promises," she taunted.

"Exactly," he said succinctly, and she flushed again, her fingers playing with a button on his shirt as she avoided his eyes.

"Did you really know you loved me that first day?" she asked curiously.

He nodded, his face suddenly serious. "It was as if the roof fell in. I didn't know what hit me. At first, I thought it was just lust, but before you left that day I knew it was a hell of a lot more than that." He closed his eyes, and said slowly, "It was tenderness, and passion, and a crazy kind of nostalgia." He opened his eyes, and they were dark with feeling. "A longing for home, and you were that home. I wanted to cherish and protect you till the day you died."

Her eyes were brimming with tears. "Yet when you offered me our bargain, you said it would only last until you grew bored and told me to go," she said.

"That meant forever, because I could never tell you to go," he said quietly.

She swallowed hard over the lump in her throat, and said lightly. "That's all very well, Donovan, but you could let a girl know."

He touched the tip of her nose lightly. "You haven't been exactly communicative yourself, brown eyes. How could I confess eternal love to you, when you didn't even trust me enough to tell me about the baby?"

"Randy?" Brenna asked, puzzled, "but you knew . . ."

"No, our baby." Donovan interrupted impatiently. "Don't you think it's time we talked about it?" He stroked the arch of her brow with a caressing finger. "Did you think there was any chance at all that I wouldn't want *your* baby?"

"*Our baby?*" Brenna asked blankly.

Donovan gazed at her bewildered face, and his brows arched in surprise. He gave a low whistle. "Well, I'll be damned. You didn't know." He chuckled. "Didn't they teach you where babies come from in that orphanage?"

Brenna sat bolt upright, as her mind scrambled to assimilate and correlate the evidence that substantiated Donovan's astounding statement.

"I'm going to have a baby!" she announced incredulously. "But how did you guess?"

"Hardly a guess," he said dryly, his blue eyes dancing. "If you'll recall I've had an intimate and pleasurable knowledge of that lovely body of yours for the past three months." He grinned teasingly. "Unlike you, I was anticipating just such an occurrence. In fact, I was planning on it. It was going to be one of the ties that bound you to me."

"A baby!" she hugged him ecstatically. "When?" and she started counting back mentally.

His arms went around her. "I figure about a month before the Academy Awards," he drawled. "That'll give you time to get back that sylphlike slimness, before you collect your Oscar for best supporting actress."

She ignored his gentle teasing, as she buried her face in his shoulder. "I may decide to give up acting," she said dreamily. "I may not have the time once the baby is born."

His amusement was abruptly stilled, as he pushed her away from him with a stern hand. His face was serious as he said, "Listen, Brenna, I might be a bit of a chauvinist, but I didn't get you pregnant to turn you into just another house frau. I admit my instincts are to lock you up in a harem and throw away the key, but I'm a realist. I want you to be so damn happy that you'll never *want* to leave me. You're an intelligent and gifted actress, and I want that part of you to be just as fulfilled as the wife and mother. So when the baby's born, you go back to work." He kissed her lightly. "We'll arrange things so that you can do both."

"Monty warned me that you were a slave driver," she said, smiling mistily. "He also said that it was worth it."

His hand tilted her head back. "It will be, my love. I promise you. It will be." And his lips closed on hers.

one

IT WAS SHORTLY BEFORE MIDNIGHT WHEN
the yellow Volkswagen drew to a surreptitious halt on the deserted dock. A sudden gust of wind swirled the light fog in gossamer wisps around the small car, and caused the three artificial
daisies fastened to the antenna to bob with jaunty cheerfulness.
The headlights flicked out and the two women occupants peered
cautiously out the windshield at the dimly lit pier that was their
destination.

"I told you it would be all right," Jane Smith said cheerfully,
grinning at the older girl, in the driver's seat. "Les said there
wouldn't be anyone around at this time of night. There's only
one night watchman, and he doesn't make his rounds for another two hours."

Penny Lassiter shook her head in exasperation. "Good Lord,
Jane, this is a private marina. We could be arrested for trespassing. As for what else you're planning, they'd probably lock you
up and throw away the key." She ran her fingers worriedly
through her glossy brown hair, as she made one last attempt to
dissuade her friend from the reckless course she had chosen.

"Nonsense," Jane said sturdily. "It may be technically illegal,
but it's not as if I'm going to do anything really criminal. I'm doing this only to make a statement and gain enough publicity so

that our petition will gain momentum. Besides, Les says that if I'm caught, the court will probably let me off with just a warning. They're always lenient with student demonstrators."

Penny Lassiter arched her eyebrow skeptically. "If it's so safe, why doesn't Les Billings do the job himself instead of letting you take all the risks?"

Jane smothered a little sigh as she gazed at her friend's worried face. She knew that Penny had neither liked nor trusted Les Billings since he had joined their antinuclear society a few months before. Penny had a deep and sincere belief in what they were doing in trying to stop the building of the new nuclear power plant north of Miami, but Les Billings's ideas for accomplishing this aim were too radical and dangerous, in her estimation.

"Les couldn't be the one to do it," Jane explained patiently. "He was the one who went on board with the food delivery to case the ship. If anyone saw him, they might recognize him. It's much less likely that I'd be noticed."

"Case the ship?" Penny echoed incredulously. "My Lord, you even sound like an experienced second-story man." She bit her lip worriedly, her eyes on Jane's determined face. "Oh, damn, why did I have to let you become involved with this group at all? I should have known that you wouldn't be satisfied with marching or collecting signatures on a petition. You don't even know the meaning of halfway measures. You just rush in full speed ahead and think you can set the whole world right." She frowned. "Well, this is a little more serious than the collection of strays and derelicts you're always bringing home to the dorm. This could be big trouble."

"Yes, little mother," Jane said soothingly, "but it won't be, I promise you." She'd become used to Penny's maternal lectures in the year that they'd been roommates at the University of Miami, but she never made the mistake of becoming impatient or undervaluing the affection that provoked them. After losing her parents as a small child and living the gypsy life of an army brat under her grandfather's stern guardianship, she'd learned the hard way that love was a treasure that must never be taken for granted.

But Penny was steadily ignoring Jane's attempts to reassure her in this case. Her gaze was now traveling unhappily over Jane's petite figure, garbed in a black turtleneck sweater and dark jeans. Her small feet were encased in black canvas sneakers. In the black shapeless sweater, she looked nearer fifteen than twenty. "And you're insane if you think you won't be noticed and remembered if you're spotted on that yacht."

"Oh, but I've got that covered," Jane said mischievously, as she began tucking her short mass of curls beneath a black ribbed stocking cap. "Or I will have soon."

"I wasn't referring to your hair, damn it," Penny said in a thoroughly exasperated tone. She shrugged helplessly at Jane's disbelieving expression. It was a long-standing argument between them that Jane persisted in believing herself plain and insignificant, despite Penny's insistence to the contrary. Jane passionately hated the blazing red of her mop of silky hair that refused to do anything but curl riotously around her heart-shaped face, and she contemptuously referred to her strange golden eyes, framed in extravagant dark lashes, as "cat eyes." It was true that Jane's features, except for the huge eyes, were nondescript, but there was a certain tender curve to her lower lip and a mobile vitality to her expression that made them hauntingly memorable. In this case, dangerously so.

She reluctantly relinquished that argument, but immediately attacked from another angle. "You even look like some kind of a cat burglar. Is all this necessary?"

Jane grinned as she admitted sheepishly, "I don't really know, but they always dress like this in the movies. I figured that there must be some reason for it."

"The whole affair makes no sense at all," Penny argued

desperately. "Why pick on Jake Dominic's yacht for your demonstration? He has nothing to do with the building of the nuclear plant."

"Publicity," Jane said tersely. "Jake Dominic's just finished directing a motion picture that has a pronuclear slant. Les chose Dominic because he says that it will attract more attention than if we'd picked an ordinary businessman."

It was a fact that couldn't be disputed, much as Penny would have liked to discredit Billings in any way she could. Jake Dominic was the original golden boy. He had fallen heir to the fabulous Dominic shipping fortune at twenty-five and had promptly delegated authority in the corporation to continue to pursue his passion for directing films. In the past twelve years, Dominic's brilliance and fantastic success in his chosen field had been rivaled only by his scandalous and dissolute personal life. His wild escapades and numerous affairs had made him the sought-after prey of eager journalists in every country in the world.

"Yes, the newspapers will probably plaster the story all over the front page," Penny concurred gloomily. "Together with the account of your arrest and jail sentence."

Jane shook her friend's arm reprovingly. "Stop talking like that," she ordered cheerfully, "I'm not about to get caught. We have it all worked out." She reached in the back seat for her backpack, and as she strapped it on she continued soothingly, "Look, Penny, it will all be over in another hour. All I have to do is to row out to Dominic's yacht and climb the anchor line to get on board. I make my way to Dominic's cabin and write my message on the wall. Then I leave my backpack with the bomb in it in the cabin and row back to the pier." She tightened the strap of her backpack and smiled winningly. "Then you pick me up here and take me out for a well-deserved pizza. Your treat. It's another three days before I get my monthly insurance check."

Penny Lassiter flinched. "I wish you'd forget about that bomb, and just write your blasted statement on the wall," she said unhappily.

Jane shook her head stubbornly. "They might ignore the graffiti. We need to make them angry enough to make a fuss." She shrugged. "After all, it's not as if it were a real explosive. It's just a stink bomb. Les made it himself at the chemistry lab," she continued with satisfaction. "He says that when it goes off, it will cause a positively nauseating odor that will permeate the whole cabin and all the furnishings."

"Well, that should upset them enough to content even Les Billings," Penny said sardonically. "And what, may I ask, is Jake Dominic supposed to be doing while you're redecorating his cabin? No one could sleep through all that."

"No problem," Jane said blithely. "He's still in New York. There was a picture in the morning paper of Dominic and his latest mistress at Club 54." She frowned. "It's really too bad that he's not here. We'd get much more press coverage if he were on the spot."

"And it would also be much more dangerous," Penny said firmly, seeing the speculative gleam in Jane's golden eyes.

"Perhaps you're right," Jane said impishly. "If Dominic were here, I'd have to worry about stumbling over not only him but his latest bedmate. You know that Dominic always takes a woman on his cruises."

"You've been reading the gossip columns again," Penny said absently, her worried eyes on Jane's glowing face. "Jane, don't do this," she urged seriously. "It's not worth the risk."

"Of course it is," Jane said firmly, her golden eyes alight yet serene. "If you believe in something and it has value for you, then any risk is worthwhile." She leaned over and kissed Penny lightly on the cheek. "Relax, Penny. It's going to go off smooth as silk."

Penny shook her head slowly, her brown eyes oddly sad. "They'll probably crucify you," she said quietly. "This cynical old world doesn't have a place for people who care as much as you do, Jane."

"Then, I'll just have to *make* a place for myself, won't I?" she asked tranquilly, as she opened the door and jumped out. "Remember, be back here in one hour," she said, and she slammed the door. With a jaunty wave of her hand, she hurried toward the pier, where the rowboat waited.

Jane Smith cautiously opened the cabin door and slipped noiselessly inside, closing it after her with the utmost care. She leaned against the door in the stygian darkness for a brief moment and tried to still the rapid beating of her heart.

Despite her brave words to Penny, she was finding her first attempt at housebreaking—or was it yacht-breaking—a terrifying experience. She closed her eyes for a second and relived the panicky, helpless feeling she'd known as she had clung like a koala bear to the anchor line while she'd worked her way up . hand over hand, inching toward the deck that had seemed a mile above her, while the threatening darkness of the sea waited for her first mistake.

Once she had reached the deck there was no difficulty in finding Dominic's cabin, thanks to the rough map Les had drawn, which she'd faithfully memorized. Still, it was a bit nerve-racking to be cast in the role of an intruder, even if your cause was just. Well, the sooner she got the job done, the sooner she could get out of here. Her eyes had now become used to the darkness, and she could dimly distinguish the shape of a king-sized bed a yard or so away and various pieces of furniture scattered around the room. On the far side of the cabin, she could discern the outlines of a large porthole. She would have to use the wall opposite the bed, she decided.

Undoing the straps of the backpack, she pulled it off and unfastened the pouch, extracting the can of red spray paint. She silently glided forward, going around the bed. The floor was obviously lavishly carpeted, she noted, as her sneakered feet sank into the cushioned softness without making a sound. Her hands swiftly explored the paneled smoothness for art plaques or paintings. All she needed to do was to destroy one of Dominic's masterpieces, she thought grimly. She'd read that he was as ardent a collector of art as he was of women. The area was clear. She breathed a sigh of relief and backed away, aiming the nozzle of the spray can carefully. She fleetingly considered flipping on the light, but discarded the idea immediately. It would be too risky, and the message just had to be readable, not a thing of beauty.

She pressed her finger on the button and released a stream of paint, her arm moving in sweeping movements over the surface of the wall. It went quite quickly, and in a few minutes she neatly recapped the paint can and dropped it into her pouch. Her hands fumbled momentarily in the bag until she found the timer switch connected to the square metal box. She flipped the switch and then dropped the backpack carelessly on the floor.

Jane moved cautiously toward the door, wishing she could see well enough to hurry. Les had said the timer would give her forty-five minutes to get off the ship and back to the pier, but she didn't like to push it. It had taken her almost fifteen minutes to climb that terrifying anchor line.

"What the hell!"

The exclamation erupted from the king-sized bed, and Jane froze in horror as her eyes flew in the direction of the sound. The voice had been rough and masculine, and she experienced a ghastly sinking sensation as she realized to whom it must belong. She turned to flee, but it was already too late. The shadowy figure launched himself from the center of the bed in a tackle that knocked her neatly from her feet and pinned her to the carpet.

Jane struggled frantically, her fists beating at the wide shoulders, her body writhing and kicking beneath the heavy masculine weight that was holding her helpless.

Suddenly she froze with shock as her touch communicated a frightening fact to her startled brain. My God! The man was nude! Her fists relaxed, and her palms slid tentatively over the hair-roughened chest, then glided exploringly over and around his hips to gingerly touch his hard buttocks. She jerked her hands away as if they'd been burned. It was true!

"Damn!" the man swore harshly, as his hands moved over the revealing softness of her body beneath the masculine attire. He roughly tugged the woolen cap from her silken curls, which smelled faintly of vanilla. "Not another one! This must be some kind of record. Two persistent women in one night!" His hands moved exploringly down her throat to the delicate curve of her shoulders. "Why not?" he drawled. "I'm finding your rather bizarre approach quite tantalizing."

Incredibly, Jane felt his loins lift and then rub with sensual aggression against her own, and she made a sudden movement of protest. He rapped out roughly, "Lie still, damn it!" Then his mouth covered hers.

Jane inhaled sharply in breathless shock as the warm hard lips pressed demandingly on hers, expertly parting them to invade her with savage intimacy. It was a bizarrely exciting sensation to be held helpless under that virile male body while his lips and tongue toyed with her own with ruthless expertise. The swiftness of his physical attack had left her dazed and bewildered, and the passionate onslaught of this nude stranger was suddenly met with a primal reaction from her woman's body. An aching warmth flooded her loins, and the tips of her breasts hardened in response to the stimuli his body was feeding her. Her lips opened yearningly to allow him eager access in his delicious love play.

He gave a deep groan of satisfaction, and his hands closed slowly over her small high breasts.

The intimacy of the caress caused her to stiffen in surprise. Abruptly Jane came to her senses. What was she doing? she wondered wildly. She was deliberately inviting the man to rape her! She resumed her frantic struggles against him with renewed desperation. The man's nude body was hardening in arousal, her movements acting as a provocation rather than a deterrent, she realized helplessly.

His mouth left hers and buried itself in her throat. "Be quiet, woman," he said thickly, his tongue teasing the hollow of her throat. "Give me what I want right now. I'm not in the mood for games tonight."

"No!" Her protest was smothered by his lips once more, and her mind searched frantically for an escape route. He was much too strong for her struggles to be anything but a minor annoyance to him. Her mind arrived at no answer, but her body acted instinctively to protect itself.

Her strong white teeth fastened on his sensual lower lip, and she bit down viciously, holding on like a terrier until he jerked his head away with a roar of rage. His weight was suddenly lifted from her, and she quickly jumped to her feet.

Jane experienced a moment of disorientation as her eyes eagerly searched the darkness for the outline of the cabin door. There it was! She made a swift movement toward the portal, but she had waited too long. The cabin flared into brilliant light.

two

THERE WAS NO QUESTION THAT IT WAS JAKE Dominic who stood at the light switch by the door, Jane thought resignedly. She had no problem recognizing the face from the newspapers. The black frown on his face gave his features a distinctly Mephistophelian cast. High cheekbones, sensual mouth, and dark expressive eyes lent him a satanic charm that was augmented by the black brows, one of which was slightly crooked, giving him a look of perpetual mockery. It was entirely in keeping with the cynical set of Dominic's mouth and jaded weariness in the ebony eyes. His crisp dark hair, worn slightly long, was ruffled from their struggles, and made him appear wild and careless.

Tall, broad-shouldered, slim-hipped, his whipcord body possessed a virile magnetism that was blatantly attractive. Jane's eyes dropped in fascination to the springy dark hair on his bronze chest, which gradually narrowed to a thin line as it reached his flat stomach. Her gaze flew quickly back to his face as her own face flushed scarlet. Dominic stood there as arrogantly unconcerned as if he were fully dressed, but she did not have the same *sang-froid*. She'd never been alone with a naked man, and she felt desperately uncomfortable—though perhaps she had better begin worrying about Dominic's emotional rather than his physical reaction. The man looked absolutely furious, black eyes blazing, nostrils flaring. His lip was bleeding freely where she'd bitten him, the sensitive flesh already starting to swell.

Jake Dominic's stormy gaze had become riveted by the lettering on the wall, and he stared at it incredulously. Jane turned and surveyed her handiwork with dismay. In three-foot cursive letters was the spray-painted slogan NO NUKES, and below it, in even larger letters, NUKES STINK. It was fortunate that it had been dark when she'd used the paint, she thought absently. If she'd seen the loveliness of the rich walnut paneling, she could never have brought herself to desecrate it.

Dominic's gaze returned to Jane, noting the tousled red hair and wide, frightened golden eyes. His eyes lingered for a moment on the swollen pink lips before he leaned indolently against the wall and wiped his hand over his bleeding lip. Though his face was still angry, there was a trace of amusement in his voice as he drawled softly. "Well, I'll be damned. If I haven't caught myself a baby terrorist."

Jane lifted her chin indignantly. "I'm no such thing," she argued defensively; "I'm a protester, not a terrorist." She gestured to the wall. "There's nothing in that to fill anyone with terror."

"It's a question of semantics, is it?" he asked lazily. "Regardless of what you may call it, you will admit that it's blatantly illegal."

She nodded reluctantly. "I suppose it is, technically."

"Technically, hell," he said roundly. "Vandalism, destruction of property, breaking and entering." He touched his lip gingerly. "And assault."

"Assault," she gasped, the angry color pinking her cheeks. "I was defending myself. You were trying to rape me."

"Rape!" Dominic exploded, his eyes sparkling dangerously. "I don't have to rape women. You were more than willing, my little terrorist. Your hands were all over me."

"Only because I couldn't believe that I had a totally nude,

bare-assed pervert on top of me," she shouted, her golden eyes blazing. "Why the hell don't you wear pajamas?"

A look of astonishment wiped the anger from his face. "I haven't worn pajamas since I was ten." His black eyes gleamed strangely. "You'll forgive my insensitivity, I trust. It's not often that I have a baby burglar drop in on me without invitation."

Suddenly her anger was gone, and she drooped disconsolately. What difference did any of it make? She had been caught, and she was frighteningly aware that the consequences could be more serious than she had dreamed before Dominic had reeled off that staggering list of charges.

"If you're through amusing yourself at my expense, I'd appreciate it if you'd just call the police and get it over with," she said dejectedly.

"Oh, yes, the police," Dominic said idly. "I suppose we had better call someone in authority." He reached for the white telephone on the table by the door and punched a number rapidly. After a moment he spoke into the receiver, his eyes still fixed on Jane's pale, weary face. "Hello, Marc. I'm sorry to wake you, but I think you'd better come down to my cabin. It seems we have an intruder." He replaced the receiver gently and turned back to Jane. "Now, while we're waiting, why don't you make yourself useful and clean up this lip? It's beginning to sting damnably."

Jane's eyes darkened with concern as she responded instinctively to the appeal for help. The lip was looking uglier by the minute, she noticed guiltily. It must be very painful. She impetuously moved forward to stand before him, touching the lip tenderly with a finger. "I hurt you," she said huskily, her eyes swimming with tears. "Please forgive me."

Her tone was patently sincere, and even Jake Dominic's cynical appraisal could detect no false note in the heartfelt apology. He smiled curiously, his dark eyes flickering. "I have the glimmering of an idea that you're not a very good terrorist, redhead." He took her hand and pulled her gently toward a door on the far side of the room. "Come along and play Florence Nightingale." He opened the door to reveal a luxurious bathroom, decorated in various shades of blue.

Jane followed him docilely into the small compartment, and while he half sat, half leaned on the cobalt-blue vanity counter, she carefully bathed the lip in cold water. Dominic flinched once, and her eyes clouded in distress. She made a low sound deep in her throat. Her reaction seemed to fascinate him, and for the remainder of the cleaning procedure, he studied her face with curious, narrowed eyes. When she'd finished, he slipped off the counter and, taking the washcloth from her, threw it carelessly into the sink.

"I'm obliged," he drawled casually. "It feels much better now."

Jane smiled in relief. "I'm glad," she said simply. "Now will you do something for me?"

His crooked eyebrow arched quizzically. "What?" he asked warily.

"Put on some clothes!" she said, the annoying color rising in her cheeks again.

He chuckled. "Oh, yes, you do have a hang-up about that. I'd forgotten. Well, as I can't leave my prisoner alone, you'll have to come with me." He strolled lazily out of the bathroom and, going to a built-in paneled closet, he slid back the door and took out a pair of dark trousers and pulled them on easily. He shrugged into a cream sport shirt and thrust his feet into a pair of Gucci loafers.

He turned and raised an eyebrow at Jane. "Satisfied?"

She nodded shyly, not meeting his eyes.

"You should be," he said teasingly. "My ass is no longer bare, and I assure you that I haven't been interested in kinky perversions for a number of years. That was quite unfair."

Then, as the color once more flooded her face, his expression became serious. "Go over there and sit down," he ordered quietly, gesturing to an easy chair covered in charcoal velvet that was situated just a few feet from the graffiti-covered wall. "I have a few questions that I want answered."

"Shouldn't we wait for the police?" she asked despondently, sinking obediently into the chair.

"I think you owe me an explanation," he said. "After all, it's my wall you ruined."

Dismayed, Jane's eyes swiftly flew to the paneling. "Is it really ruined?" she asked. "Isn't there anything we can do to save it? It's such a lovely wood."

Jake Dominic gave an exasperated sigh. "No, you've done too good a job on it. The paneling will have to be replaced."

"Who was the other one?" Jane asked suddenly, her golden eyes wide and inquiring.

"I beg your pardon?" Dominic said blankly as he sat down on a corner of the bed, facing her.

"You said that I was the second persistent woman tonight. Who was the other one?"

"It would hardly be gallant of me to reveal names," Dominic said dryly. "Let's just say that when I arrived on the *Sea Breeze* this evening, I had an unpleasant surprise in the form of a lady whose ego was a good deal keener than her intelligence." His lips twisted cynically. "She evidently thought that seduction could fan the dead embers back to life."

Denise Patterson, the gorgeous blond talk-show hostess, Jane guessed shrewdly. Dominic had evidently grown bored with her and broken off their affair last night. For a moment she felt a fleeting sympathy for the woman who'd thought she could hold Jake Dominic after he had tired of her. According to the gossip columns, Dominic's affairs were becoming even more ephemeral of late, and seldom lasted more than two weeks. Looking into that cynical, restless face, she could well believe it. When a man had seen everything, done everything, and had only to reach out to receive anything he desired, it was no wonder that he had become jaded.

That mocking devil's face was now frowning impatiently. "I'm not here to satisfy your curiosity. I believe that I was about to ask you a few very pointed questions. What's your name, redhead?"

"Jane Smith," she answered absently, thinking how the unbuttoned shirt stretched over the virile chest made him look more sensually naked than when he was totally nude.

Dominic's mouth twisted. "Not very original."

Her eyes flew to his face. "No, it's true," she protested. "Why would I lie? You'd find out anyway."

He shrugged. "Now the important question. Why me?"

"Your new film," Jane said simply. "It's got a pronuclear slant."

Dominic shook his head in disgust. "For God's sake, it's a blasted suspense thriller," he said harshly. "It's not a message film."

Her eyes met his in crystalline honesty. "It was the publicity angle," she said quietly. "We figured an incident with you would hit the front page."

"It might at that." He grimaced. "And who, may I ask, are 'we'?"

Jane's eyes widened in alarm. "No one," she said quickly. "This is all my idea; no one else was involved."

"It will probably go easier on you if you tell the police who else was responsible," he suggested coolly.

Jane shook her head at once. "I couldn't do that," she insisted stubbornly. "There wasn't anyone else."

For some curious reason, her answer seemed to please him. He regarded her with an enigmatic smile. "You know that you're in a great deal of trouble?" he asked as he studied the quivering of her soft pink lips and the raw fear in her golden eyes.

"I know," she said huskily, biting her lip nervously. "But . . . but there wasn't anyone else."

The cabin door was flung open, and three large, intimidating men rushed into the cabin. Jane looked up, startled, as the trio came to a screeching halt just inside the cabin door while they bewilderedly absorbed the scene in the cabin. One uniformed man in his late fifties, with gray-streaked hair and a tough, weathered face, was obviously in command of the other two, younger men, who were dressed in jeans and crew-neck sweaters.

Jake Dominic looked up, his brows lifting in mock surprise. "Hello, Marc. You certainly took your time about it," he said to the older man, lazily rising to his feet.

"I roused a few of the men—I thought we might need help," Marc replied absently, his stunned eyes taking in the crude message on the wall and then wandering back to the fragile-looking girl in the gray armchair.

"I think we can handle her between us," Dominic said, his lips twitching. "Captain Marcus Benjamin, may I present Jane Smith, girl terrorist."

Jane threw him an annoyed glance. "I wish you wouldn't keep calling me that," she complained.

"Sorry, Jane," Dominic said urbanely, his hands buttoning his cream shirt. "I'm still having problems with those semantics."

Benjamin's mouth tightened in irritation as he turned to face the two younger men, who were grinning irrepressibly at their captain's discomfort. "You can go back to bed, men," he said briskly. "Tell Jim to stay on duty on deck in case we need the launch."

The smiles were immediately wiped from the faces of the seamen at Benjamin's whiplike tone. They sketched a respectful salute and exited hurriedly.

Banjamin turned back to Jake Dominic and Jane, his expression grim. Jane shivered at the stern, authoritative figure the large man presented in his dark-blue uniform. "Now, what is this all about?" Benjamin asked, frowning.

"I was trying to determine that, when you and your bully boys burst into the cabin," Dominic said lazily. "It seems that

Miss Smith took umbrage at my latest directorial effort and decided to make her opinions known."

"Very expensive umbrage," Benjamin said gruffly. "You'll have to send to Sweden to replace that panel." His gray eyes narrowed as Jane gasped in alarm. "What do you want done with her? I have a launch standing by to take her ashore. You'll have to go with her if you intend to press charges."

"That's right, I will, won't I?" Dominic observed noncommittally, his eyes on Jane's face. "Are you ready to face the music, Jane?"

Jane moistened her lips nervously, but her chin was set determinedly as she said valiantly, "Yes, Mr. Dominic." She slowly got to her feet. "It probably won't be as bad as all that," she went on bravely. "I hear the police go easy on student protestors."

"Then you've been misinformed," Benjamin said bluntly. "They regard a crime exactly the same, no matter who commits it. You're in big trouble, young lady."

Jake Dominic frowned and said impatiently, "You're frightening the child, Marc."

Benjamin shrugged. "There's no use in her fooling herself, Jake. There's a good chance that she'll go to jail for this night's work."

Jane could feel the last remaining color drain from her face at the captain's grim words. The situation was taking on all the nuances of a nightmare, and she knew a dizzying sense of panic.

"Will you stop intimidating the girl?" Dominic said roughly, "She's just a kid."

"No, it's all right," Jane said quickly, drawing a deep breath to steady the quivering in her stomach. Her hand was shaking as she nervously loosened the collar of her dark sweater. "I knew there would be some risk involved."

"But not this much," Dominic guessed shrewdly.

"I would have done it anyway," she said simply.

"Then you're an idealistic young fool," he said harshly.

Jane's eyes dropped before the scorching fire in his. "Perhaps," she whispered huskily, "but I'd still do it."

"Well, have you made a decision?" Benjamin asked impatiently. "Are you going to press charges, or are you going to let the girl get off scot-free?"

Dominic's eyes gleamed mockingly. "It's quite a difficult decision," he drawled. "It would be a bit of a bother going in to press charges." Jane looked up, her face lighting up with hope. "On the other hand, I wouldn't be a responsible citizen if I encouraged crime in our youth, would I, Marc?"

Benjamin made a sound that was half snort, half cough, and entirely derisive.

Dominic ignored the rude expression, and strolled casually over to Jane. He lifted her chin so that he could look into her eyes. "I rather favor a compromise," he said easily. "I'll not report the incident if you'll agree to come along on the cruise and work to pay off the damage."

Jane knew such a surge of relief that her knees felt as if they would not hold her. "Oh yes, please," she said eagerly. "I'll do anything you say."

"Anything?" Dominic goaded gently. "You're dangerously impulsive, Jane Smith."

The color once again flooded her cheeks at the teasing note in the deep voice, but her eyes were steady. "I'll work very hard, Mr. Dominic," she said earnestly. "It's very generous of you to give me the chance."

"Oh, I can be very generous when it pleases me," he answered coolly.

"And just what duties is Miss Smith to perform to earn that generosity?" Benjamin interrupted caustically.

Jake Dominic's hand released Jane's chin, and he turned away. "You'll find something for her to do, Marc," he said. "I'll leave it up to you."

"Will she be with us for the entire cruise?" Benjamin probed. "You planned to be gone almost two months."

Dominic smiled. "Oh, yes, the entire cruise, I think," he said gently, his black eyes gleaming. "After all, it was a very expensive panel."

Benjamin's eyes narrowed as he detected the restless flickering in the depths of Jake's ebony eyes. "I'll remind you of what you just told me," he said warningly. "She's just a child."

Swift anger darkened Dominic's face. "For heaven's sake, Marc, I'm not bringing her along to warm my bed," he said harshly. "She'll work her way, just as I said."

"And that's all?" Benjamin asked skeptically.

A reluctant smile touched Jake Dominic's lips. "Damn you, Marc," he said in grudging admiration, "you never give up, do you?" He shrugged. "She amuses me," he said simply. "Tonight is the first time in three bloody weeks that I haven't been bored out of my mind."

"So you're going to keep her around as some kind of pet?" Benjamin asked bluntly.

"Not as a pet," Dominic drawled, his brows arching mockingly. "Perhaps as a court jester."

"Hadn't you better ask the young lady if she agrees to your terms?" Benjamin asked dryly. "Perhaps she would have some objection to donning a cap and bells."

"I think she might prefer it to prison stripes," Dominic suggested silkily. "But yes, why don't we ask her?" He turned and gazed down at Jane's bewildered face. "What about it, Jane? Part-time slavery, part-time court jester. Is it a deal?"

There was a nameless challenge in the dark face that struck an answering spark in Jane's own adventurous spirit. After all, what was the man asking of her? She couldn't believe that a man of his sophistication and brilliance would find her entertaining for very long, but she couldn't deny that Jake Dominic exerted a powerful attraction. It shouldn't be an onerous task to spend time in his quicksilver presence. Besides, what choice did she have?

"It's a deal," she said quietly.

"What about her parents?" Benjamin asked. "You can't just shanghai the girl. They'll have you up for kidnapping, not to mention possible charges of corrupting a minor." He gave Jane's diminutive figure a disparaging glance. "She can't be over eighteen."

Jane bristled indignantly. "I'll be twenty-one in six months. And both my parents are dead. I can do as I choose."

"Good!" Dominic said briskly, his mouth quirking. "By the way, do you play chess?"

Jane's face was puzzled as she answered, "Why, yes, I used to play often with my grandfather."

Jake Dominic shot a sly glance at Benjamin. "You see, Marc," he said flippantly, "it's kismet."

"So it would seem," Benjamin said sarcastically. "Well, if you're set on keeping her, I'd better find her a place to sleep."

"Yes, you do that, Marc," Dominic said lightly, "Run along with Marc, Jane."

Jane stood up and obediently moved toward the waiting captain.

"Just a moment," he said, bending to pick up her backpack from the floor. "You forgot this."

Jane turned and held out her hand as he moved toward her.

"It's heavier than it looks," he said, weighing it casually.

"Oh, that's just the bomb," she said absently. Then, as she perceived both men's stunned expressions, she giggled helplessly. "It's just a stink bomb," she assured them, her face alight with amusement. She glanced at her watch. "There must be something wrong with the timer," she commented. "It should have gone off ten minutes ago."

"Let's not take any chances, shall we?" Jake Dominic asked testily, carrying the backpack over to the large porthole. He opened the porthole with one hand and drew back his arm to toss the bomb into the sea. "I have to sleep in here tonight."

Jane grinned and turned to follow Benjamin from the room.

The explosion as the bomb hit the water was deafening, and a shock wave rocked the ship, causing Jane to stumble against Benjamin. The captain instinctively put out his arms to catch her, but she tore away from him to whirl and stare in horror at the fiery glare that still illuminated the darkness beyond the porthole.

"Oh, my God!" she breathed, her eyes wide with shock. "Oh, God, I didn't know." How could Les do such a thing, she thought incredulously? If the bomb had gone off while Jake Dominic lay sleeping, he would surely have been killed, and who knew how many more would have been hurt? The blast had been awesomely powerful. If anyone had been injured, then she, too, would have been responsible. She had brought the bomb aboard. She had even set the timer. "Please, believe me," she pleaded brokenly, tears running silently down her cheeks. "I would never have done this; I didn't know."

Jake Dominic had been thrown against the easy chair by the force of the blast. Now he slowly straightened and looked at her grimly. "Oh, I believe you," he said tersely, his face a shade paler than it had been before. "You wouldn't have perched on top of a live bomb for almost an hour and then forgotten it existed, if you knew what your friends were up to."

Jane drew a quivering breath of relief. "I don't suppose you'll let me work off my debt now," she said uncertainly. "I can understand if you want to turn me over to the police. It was a terrible thing to do."

"You're damn right it was terrible," he said harshly. "It was also stupid, irresponsible, and dangerous. You should have your head examined to have become mixed up with a bunch of idiots who would perpetrate something like this. You obviously need a keeper!"

Benjamin's voice sounded from behind Jane. "Shall I ready the launch?"

Dominic's eyes flared angrily. "Hell, no," he said. "Why should I let a group of crackpots do me out of my personal slave? She goes with us. Now, get her out of here before I change my mind." He turned away and gazed out the porthole, his back taut and angry. "We'd better get underway at once and not wait until tomorrow. Someone's bound to have seen that explosion, and we don't want to answer questions from the Coast Guard."

"Right," Benjamin said laconically. He opened the door and, taking Jane by the arm, pushed the dazed girl ahead of him into the hall. Before he shut the door he spoke dryly to Dominic's expressively furious back. "I'll have to agree with you, Jake. She's certainly not boring."

Jane was pleasantly surprised by the interior of the cabin she was shown to on one of the upper decks. Though small and compact and obviously meant for crew instead of guest occupancy, it contained a narrow single bed covered with a bold gold-and-cream plaid spread, and a built-in Danish-modern night table was beside it. The floor was covered with an attractive beige carpet. There was a small matching chest of drawers to the right of the door, and the walls were paneled in the same rich walnut as the master suite.

Benjamin gestured to the door at the foot of the bed. "Shower," he said briefly. He turned away saying. "You'd better get some sleep. Your work day aboard the *Sea Breeze* will start from tomorrow on at 6:00 A.M."

"Captain?"

He turned back, his gray eyes inquiring.

"Are we really going to leave right away?" Jane asked hesitantly.

Benjamin nodded. "You heard Dominic. I'm not accustomed to disregarding my employer's orders, Miss Smith."

"No, of course you're not," she said absently, her golden eyes clouded with worry. "It's just that if I don't let my roommate know that I'm safe, she'll be absolutely frantic. Would it be possible for you to get a message to her before we set sail?"

"It might be arranged," he replied expressionlessly. "If you'll write down the phone number, I'll see what I can do."

"Thank you. I'd be very grateful," she said, accepting the pen and paper he extracted from his jacket pocket. She wrote Penny's name and their dormitory phone number on the paper, and continued, "It's a phone in the hall at the dormitory. If Penny's not at home, give any of the girls the message."

"And what message is that?" Benjamin asked dryly.

"Just that I had to go out of town for a few months, and that I'll write her as soon as I have the opportunity."

"Very discreet," he observed laconically. "I'll see that she's told, Miss Smith. Good night." The cabin door closed quietly behind him.

Jane looked longingly at the bed before turning away resolutely and striding briskly to the tiny shower cubicle Benjamin had indicated. She felt positively grimy from the perspiration and dirt resulting from the evening's strenuous activities. She would not climb between the sheets of that pristine single bed until she, too, was fresh and clean. Besides, she thought grimly as she stripped off her clothes and stepped beneath the spray of hot water, if she was to be summoned to work in just a few hours, it was quite doubtful that the stern, crisp captain would tolerate being kept waiting while she showered.

The fountain of warm water was deliciously soothing as it poured over her stiff muscles, releasing the coiled tension, which she had not even been aware of. The evening had really tied her in knots—and no wonder, she thought ruefully. In all her life she'd never lived through such a wild, madcap sequence of events.

Not that her life had ever been tame, she acknowledged wryly. Her grandfather had sworn that she attracted trouble like honey attracted bees, and she couldn't deny the charge. She had never tried to cause her grandfather problems, but she knew from the moment she came to live with him that his precise, well-ordered existence had altered irreversibly. It was her impulsiveness that had caused most of the problems, she thought gloomily. No matter how many times her grandfather had told her to think twice before she plunged into action, she could not live with the maxim. Perhaps her grandfather's life would have been more serene if his work as a colonel in the Army Corps of Engineers hadn't taken them to the four corners of the earth. There certainly had been more scope for mischief in the more primitive parts of the world, where she'd spent a good many of her formative years.

It had been even more difficult for her grandfather to understand his volatile young charge because he himself was not a warm or affectionate man, nor the least bit impulsive. Jane shook her head in self-reproach at the familiar pang, remembering the hurt and bewilderment she'd felt as a child when her advances had been met with such chilling formality. All that was in the past now. When her grandfather had died of a stroke eighteen months ago, she'd sworn never to indulge in maudlin self-pity.

She turned off the shower, stepped out of the stall, and reached for the fluffy white bath towel on the rack over the commode. Her grandfather would have been horrified at her present dilemma, she thought ruefully, patting herself dry. But the situation wasn't all that bad, when she thought about it. She would no doubt have to work extremely hard in the next two months, but she was used to that after her years with her grandfather. She would just take one day at a time, and soon her sentence on the *Sea Breeze* would be over.

Jane tossed the towel aside and, picking up the clothes she'd discarded, hung them up neatly in the tiny built-in closet. She was glad the jeans and sweater were sturdy and easily cared for, as were the briefs and bra. There was no telling when she would be able to scrounge a change of clothes on board.

She flipped out the light and slipped between the sheets, shivering as the crisp, cool material touched her bare skin. She plumped the pillow vigorously and nestled her fiery head in its softness with a sigh of content. The last thing she was conscious of was the low throb of the engines as the yacht put out to sea.

---

three

THE NEXT MORNING PROMPTLY AT SIX CAP-
tain Benjamin showed Jane a stretch of deck that appeared to extend into infinity. He then handed her a bucket of water, soap,
and a scrub brush, and said silkily, "I won't waste your time on
needless instructions. I know how eager you must be to get
started on your new duties. Just carry on until you're told to
stop. You did say that you'd be willing to do anything, Miss
Smith."

Jane made a face at his straight, uniformed back as he
strolled briskly away.

Four hours later she wished her defiance had taken a more
tangible form. Very tangible. Like a swift blow with a sledge-
hammer on that distinguished, gray-streaked head. Jane dipped
her scrub brush into the bucket of dirty water, then leaned forward on her hands and knees to vigorously scrub the wooden
deck. She felt as if she must have prayed herself around the entire
circumference of the blasted ship by this time. She brushed a
strand of hair away from her forehead for the hundredth time,
leaving still another smudge on her face. Though the denim material of her jeans was quite tough, it didn't offer sufficient protection for her knees. She was dreaming longingly of a lovely pair
of thick athletic knee pads when a deep voice spoke over her head.

"So you're our big bad terrorist?" it drawled teasingly.

Jane looked up to see two long legs clad in sparkling white polyester standing directly in front of her. She sat back on her heels to regard balefully the vigorous young male torso and handsome face connected to those legs. Her tormentor was in his early twenties, dressed in the pristine freshness of white slacks and the beige waist-length jacket of a steward. His crisp blond hair and tanned features added to the impression of wholesomeness. The original Mr. Clean, Jane thought sourly, brushing a curl away from her perspiring forehead.

He squatted before her and looked with such frank, good-humored curiosity into her face that she was forced to admit grudgingly that there had probably been no malice in the remark. The clear blue eyes and sunny smile reflected only a gentle camaraderie.

Jane rubbed the small of her back wearily. "Aren't you afraid of being contaminated?" she asked dryly. "You're the first crew member except Captain Benjamin who has spoken to me this morning."

"It's not the men's fault," he said defensively, "The old man has passed the word that there's to be no fraternization."

"Then why are you disobeying the orders?" she asked, "Aren't you afraid of the captain, too?"

"Yep." He grinned amiably. "But I figure that I'm safe for the next thirty minutes or so. I just took the captain his lunch." He offered a large brown hand. "I'm Simon Dominic. Did you really plant a bomb in Jake's cabin?"

"Jane Smith." She started to put her small hand in his; then, noticing the dirt and soap on it, she withdrew it hastily. "Sorry," she muttered with a grimace, "I'm not very presentable. Yes, I did plant a bomb in Mr. Dominic's suite, but it was purely accidental."

Simon Dominic whistled soundlessly, his blue eyes twinkling. "How intriguing. I can't wait to hear how you managed to plant a bomb accidentally."

Jane shook her head, smiling reluctantly. "It's a long story."

"And one you're not about to confide," he guessed.

"Not at the moment," she agreed, grinning. "Dominic? Are you related to Jake Dominic?"

"Very distantly," he confessed wryly. "Cousin Jake is about four times removed in blood and about forty million dollars removed in substance. He doesn't object to a bit of nepotism in the company, fortunately. My father is a vice-president of Dominic Shipping, and I'll be allowed to climb the corporate ladder myself as soon as I've put in my training period." He frowned in puzzlement. "Why aren't you using the electric scrubber? I'd think it would be far easier on your knees."

Jane's eyes darkened ominously. "The *Sea Breeze* has an electric scrubber?" she asked carefully.

"Several." Simon Dominic nodded. "Would you like me to get one for you?"

Jane drew a deep breath, trying to control the anger that surged through her. Benjamin had given her the brush and bucket with no mention of the machine that could have made her task a hundred times easier. Damn him!

She was tempted to agree at once to Simon's suggestion. She doubted if Benjamin would push the matter once she'd switched tools. She opened her lips to ask Simon to bring the machine and then closed them again, her eyes thoughtful. According to Benjamin's reasoning, his action in making her work as difficult as possible was entirely justified. Benjamin's code required that she accept her punishment and earn her place as a member of the crew. Jane could understand and respect his philosophy. She had no doubt that her grandfather, given the same circumstances, would have reacted in the same way. It was going to be a long two months, and an aching back and sore knees might be a small price to pay to earn the captain's respect.

"No," she said slowly, "that won't be necessary."

Simon Dominic shrugged. "Whatever you say," he agreed,

rising to his feet. "Tell me, are terrorists permitted lunch, or are you only allowed bread and water?"

Jane smiled as she dipped her brush in the water. "I assume that I'll be eating all my meals with the crew from now on," she answered dryly. "The captain made it quite clear that I'm to have no special privileges."

"In that case, I'll brave his wrath and ask him if I can show you where the mess is located."

"Thanks, I'd appreciate that," Jane said warmly. She was going to like Simon Dominic.

With a blithe salute, the immaculate figure turned and walked back toward the bridge.

True to his word, Simon Dominic returned in an hour, and after accompanying her to her cabin, where she washed hurriedly and ran a comb through her hair, he escorted her to the crew's mess.

The mess was actually a large common room with a number of tables of varying size and a cafeteria-style serving area. The room was obviously used as a recreation area as well, she noted. There was a yellow-and-black dart board fixed on one wall, and one large table with leaves that could be opened to convert it into a Ping-Pong table.

Jane followed Simon through the serving line, conscious of the lull in conversation as she followed him to a small table, unloaded her tray, and sat down opposite him.

"I feel like Lady Godiva," she whispered as she poured dressing on the crisp garden salad.

"We should be so lucky," Simon joked, his blue eyes dancing. "They'll get used to you. We're not used to females on board ship, and you must admit your manner of signing on was a bit unusual."

"I certainly wouldn't recommend it," Jane answered, smiling. She took a bite of her salad and shook her head in amazement. "This dressing is absolutely fantastic. I imagine Captain

Benjamin has no problem keeping his crew if the food is always this terrific."

Simon lifted his brows wryly. "The chow isn't always this good," he admitted. "Jake Dominic brings his own chef on these cruises, and he takes over the meal preparations from Max, our regular cook."

"Simon, could I ask a favor of you?" Jane asked impulsively.

"Anything," he promised lightly, adding, with a grin on his pleasant bronze face, "as long as it's not planting one of your 'accidental' bombs."

"I don't have any clothes," Jane said earnestly. "Do you have any old shirts or sweaters that I might use until I can get my roommate to send me some of my own?"

He looked doubtfully at her tiny figure and then at his own large frame. "You'd be lost in any of my clothes," he told her, shaking his head. "But I'll ask some of the other men and see what we can come up with."

"Thank you, Simon." Jane smiled radiantly. "I could see myself in these same jeans and sweater for the next two months." She gestured distastefully at her soiled jeans and the black sweater, which was now much the worse for wear.

"Well, you'll need something cooler than that sweater where we're going."

"Really? Where are we going?" she asked casually. Then, her eyes dancing: "For that matter, where are we now? I'm afraid I've been too preoccupied to even wonder."

"We're in the Gulf of Mexico," Simon replied. "We'll be cruising along the eastern coast of Mexico to the Yucatan and then possibly around Central America to Venezuela."

"I've never been to Mexico," Jane said dreamily. She grimaced as she came abruptly back to earth. "I'll probably not even get off the ship if Benjamin has anything to say about it."

"Oh, I don't know," Simon said optimistically. "Evidently

he's lifted his nonfraternization rule, or he wouldn't have let me take you to lunch. Perhaps the old man is softening."

"Perhaps," Jane echoed skeptically.

At sundown that day she was no longer skeptical. She was sure that Benjamin had a will of iron and a heart to match. Every muscle and bone in her body ached. Her knees in particular were affected; they were swollen and bruised to a point of agonizing sensitivity. The sun had caught her face, and her nose was red and tender.

Jane gritted her teeth as she leaned over once again to soap the wooden deck. Benjamin had told her to continue scrubbing until he told her to stop, and she'd be damned if she'd quit before that time, even if she had to work through the night. She flinched as she put pressure on the wooden back of the brush and it rubbed against a blister on the palm of her hand. At least it was cooler, now that the sun was going down, she thought tiredly, as a vagrant breeze ruffled her hair, darkened with perspiration to nearly auburn.

For the past two hours she'd been in a haze of exhaustion and pain. Only sheer stubbornness had prevented the tears from flowing. She would rather fall flat on her face than admit defeat to that heartless monster of a captain.

A large shadow fell across the wet deck, but Jane didn't look up until Marcus Benjamin spoke.

"What the hell do you think you're doing?" he growled impatiently. "Do you realize that it's almost eight o'clock?"

She clenched her teeth and continued to move her brush, albeit a trifle slower. "I'm following orders, *sir*," she replied caustically. "I'm scrubbing the bloody deck, *sir*," She dipped the brush in the bucket and then brought it down hard on the deck, noting with satisfaction that a drop or two of the dirty water splashed on Benjamin's highly polished shoes. "If you'll kindly move, I'll finish my work, *sir*."

"Damn it, what do you think this is, a slave labor camp? You'll work a regular eight-hour day just like the rest of the crew," he said grimly.

Jane threw her brush in the bucket. "I thought I was the exception, sir," she said, meeting his eyes defiantly. "I believe I was told to continue my work until I was told to stop, Captain."

"I have other duties besides acting as a warden to you, Miss Smith," he said shortly. "I assumed you'd have the intelligence to stop at the end of a normal work day."

"Are you saying that I may stop for the day?" she demanded. "I want it quite clear, sir."

"Yes, you may stop working," he said between his teeth.

She struggled to her feet, staggering as her knees abruptly gave way. Benjamin instinctively reached out to help her, but she angrily shrugged his hand away. "I'm quite all right," she said, lifting her chin proudly. She bent and picked up her bucket and brushed past him disdainfully, her back ramrod straight, and stalked away, leaving Benjamin to stare after her indomitable figure.

After luxuriating beneath first a hot and then a cold shower, Jane felt almost human. Using some of the emerald-green shampoo she found in the holder by the shower nozzle, she washed her hair until it was squeaky clean. Wrapping the towel around her torso and another around her hair, she left the cubicle and crossed to the bed. She settled cross-legged on the bed and examined her knees. They were definitely swollen, and faintly purple. By tomorrow it would be like kneeling on knives to rest her weight on them, she thought gloomily. Why hadn't she unbent and asked Benjamin to change her duty? She instinctively shook her head at the thought. No, she wouldn't give him the satisfaction of seeing her beg, no matter what the consequence.

A brisk knock sounded at the door, and she called out, "Just a minute." She grabbed the improvised toga she'd fashioned from a bed sheet. Ripping off the towel and slipping on the toga, she padded barefoot to the door.

Simon Dominic stood on the other side, his arms piled high with various articles of clothing. He grinned as he beheld her toga-clad figure and turbaned head. "That's very exotic. I doubt if anything the boys contributed will be as alluring."

"Oh, Simon, thank you," she said gratefully, reaching for the clothes. "Won't you come in?"

He shook his head. "Your cabin is officially out of bounds, per Captain Benjamin," he said. "I just brought these by. I hope some of them will do."

"They'll have to," Jane answered lightly. "Thank everyone who donated to the cause, will you?"

Simon nodded, his blue eyes sympathetic. "I'm afraid that I've got bad news for you." He spoke hesitantly. "Captain Benjamin told me to give you a message when he knew that I was coming down here. You're to report to the lounge in thirty minutes for your secondary duties."

For a moment Jane didn't realize what he meant. Then she understood. Secondary duties. Jake Dominic must have sent for her to play court jester. Well, he was not going to find her very amusing tonight, she thought tiredly. She would probably be back in her cabin in an hour.

Simon's face was grim. "There's absolutely no call for this," he said indignantly.

"These duties will be very light," she assured him soothingly. "Thank you for caring, but it will be all right. Honestly. I'll see you at breakfast tomorrow, Simon."

"Right," Simon said, turning away with a comradely wave of his hand.

When Jane appeared in the lounge some forty-five minutes later, she felt that she fully resembled the buffoon of Jake Dominic's original simile. Her khaki pants were rolled up in thick, bulky cuffs, but there was nothing she could do about the baggy seat or the looseness of the waist. The thin cream sweater that she had teamed with it came almost to her knees, and the long sleeves kept slipping down from her elbows, where she had pushed them. Her hair was still slightly damp, and curled in wild ringlets all over her head. Jane had smiled philosophically when she'd caught sight of herself in the mirror in the cabin. There was no way she could compete with the gorgeous and well-dressed women of Jake Dominic's acquaintance even when she was at her very best. What difference did it make if she looked like something out of a circus?

Jake Dominic was sprawled in an enormous brown leather easy chair, his feet propped on the matching hassock. She noted with some disgruntlement that he looked devastatingly attractive in dark fitted pants and a red crew-neck sweater.

He looked up absently from the script he'd been studying, as she came in the door. His dark eyes widened, and his lips twitched uncontrollably as he leisurely looked her over from her water-stained canvas tennis shoes to the unruly red curls. He tossed the script aside and said mockingly, "I must admit you present an amusing spectacle, but you really shouldn't have gone to all this trouble."

Jane strode forward to stand directly in front of him, her hands planted belligerently on her hips. "Mr. Dominic, I'm very tired. I haven't had any dinner yet, and I have a wretched sunburn that's not improving my disposition. You know very well that I have nothing to wear, and I would appreciate your not making cheap jokes at my expense."

He arched an eyebrow quizzically. Then his eyes narrowed and the laughter was abruptly banished from his face. "I'm a bit tired myself, redhead," he answered softly. "I've been working on this awful script all day trying to draft some cohesion into the greatest hodgepodge of symbolistic tripe it's ever been my misfortune to read. I'm not sunburned for the simple reason that

I've not stuck my head out of this room all day. I will grant, however, that I do have one advantage over you other than my sartorial elegance. I have eaten dinner."

He rose with swift grace and, taking her by the wrist, pulled her behind him as he strode with long steps to a beautifully carved mahogany bar. Pushing her firmly onto a cushioned stool covered in antique-gold velvet, he went behind the bar and said briskly, "We can remedy that if you'll settle for sandwiches and coffee. Will ham do?"

She nodded dazedly. "That . . . that will be fine," she stammered, as she watched him kneel before the copper-toned portable refrigerator under the bar and withdraw an oblong plastic container that opened to reveal pink ham sliced paper-thin. He brought another container from a side cabinet that contained deliciously crisp hard rolls. He built her a sandwich with quick practiced movements, adding tomato, lettuce, and mayonnaise at her request. He poured her a cup of coffee from a thermos jug at the end of the bar and set the lot before her with a little flourish.

"Anything else?" he asked blandly. "I believe there's some caviar and pâté de foie gras in the refrigerator."

"No, thank you," Jane said, making a face. "That sounds perfectly dreadful. I've never understood how anyone could really enjoy caviar."

"Neither have I," he confessed, his dark eyes twinkling. "But my chef is an incurable snob and insists that no self-respecting multimillionaire should have a refrigerator unstocked with caviar."

Dominic poured himself a cup of coffee, and, leaning his elbows on the bar, watched her wolf down the sandwich with every evidence of enjoyment. "You *were* hungry," he commented. "What caused you to miss dinner?"

Jane looked up to meet his eyes before she replied noncommittally, "I was busy." She was not about to complain to Mr. Dominic about her treatment at his captain's hands.

He touched the tip of her sunburnt nose with a light finger. "I see Marc's found you something to do outside," he said casually. "That should be a welcome change after burrowing in college classrooms all winter."

Jane's mouth curved in a wry smile. It was obvious from his remark that Jake Dominic was ignorant of the precise nature of the duties Captain Benjamin had assigned her. Well, why should he be apprised of such pedestrian arrangements? It was the duty of the captain and the crew to see that everything ran with clockwork efficiency on the *Sea Breeze* so that its owner would not suffer a moment of discomfort or displeasure.

"Yes, it's quite a change," she agreed dryly. She took a sip of the excellent coffee. "Why are you working? I thought you were supposed to be on vacation."

"I want to get these script changes out of the way and get it back to the producer," he said, lifting his cup to his lips. "It should only take a few days, and then I'll be free to relax."

Jane looked thoughtfully into the restless dark eyes. Did he ever really relax? she wondered idly. She'd seen no evidence of it in the brief time she had been acquainted with him. He seemed charged with a leashed vitality and a crackling virility that should have been disconcerting to a girl of her limited experience of men. Oddly enough, this was not the case. Perhaps it was the unconventional nature of their first meeting that had dispensed with the usual reservations that would have beset a relationship between two such opposites. At any rate, she felt as completely at ease with this man as if she'd known him from the cradle.

"If you're so busy, I'm surprised you bothered to send for me," she remarked as she finished the last bite of the sandwich and pushed the plate aside.

"All work makes Jake a dull boy," he misquoted audaciously, his black eyes gleaming. "After working all day on that mishmash of a script, I felt the need for the soothing pursuit of pure logic. In short, Jane Smith, you're going to give me a game of chess."

She grimaced ruefully. "If you're looking for a game involving logic, you've made an unfortunate choice for a partner. My grandfather used to nearly tear his hair out in frustration at my game."

"All the better," Jake Dominic said promptly, with a tigerish grin. "It will be a little like destroying that damn screenwriter in effigy."

"What a charming idea," she said with sweet irony. "With my being said effigy, I assume?" A glint of determination shone in the golden eyes as she cradled her cup in her hands and looked him directly in the eyes. "It may not be as easy for you as you believe. I don't give up easily, Mr. Dominic."

"I'd be disappointed if you did. I don't enjoy victory if it's handed to me on a plate." He finished his coffee with one swallow and put his cup on the bar. "Shall we get to it?" he asked politely, gesturing to a game table in the corner.

"Why not?" Jane felt a thrill of anticipation run through her that was far in excess of the challenge involved. What was it about the man that made a simple game take on such excitement and significance?

Setting her empty cup on the bar beside his, Jane slipped off the stool and followed him to the game table, her eyes flitting curiously around the large lounge.

It was a singularly beautiful room. Its focal point was the magnificent Persian carpet that covered the highly polished wooden floor. The conversation center consisted of a long couch crafted in rich, tufted brown leather, and two huge easy chairs with their own matching ottomans. The walls were paneled in the same gorgeous walnut Jane had noted in the other cabins. On the walls were several paintings that were obviously originals.

Jane paused in front of one particularly fine El Greco, admiring, as she always did, the astonishing excitement he could convey in a simple landscape.

Jake Dominic retraced his steps to stand beside her, his eyes on her absorbed face. "You like El Greco?" he asked, his crooked eyebrow arching mockingly. "I should have guessed. He, too, was something of a revolutionary."

Jane ignored the gibe as she continued to gaze enthralled at the painting. "He cared so passionately," she said slowly. "You can see it in every brushstroke. Thank God you didn't have this in your cabin. I had nightmares about spraying one of your masterpieces by accident," she confessed with a shudder.

"If you had, I would have broken your reckless little neck," he told her with grim sincerity.

"I tried to be careful," she said defensively. "I examined the entire area before I sprayed."

"It was so dark you couldn't see a thing," he said tersely. "How could you be sure?"

"The same way I knew you were naked," she said unthinkingly. "I ran my hands over it."

Then, as she realized what she had said, scarlet flooded her face. She avoided the spark of amusement in Dominic's dark eyes and rushed on desperately. "I'm ready to play now."

His lips twitched as he said solemnly, "It's a pity you weren't ready to play then. If you'll recall, I was more than willing."

Jane lifted her chin, swept with regal dignity to the game table, and seated herself sedately. "You know what I mean," she said severely.

He nodded as he seated himself opposite her. "I hope your game is more concise than your words, Jane," he drawled. He opened a drawer in the table and drew out a carved teak box. "You could be in deep trouble in no time at all."

The next few hours proved this comment to be depressingly

true. It took a relatively short time for Jane to determine that she was hopelessly outclassed by Jake Dominic. Her grandfather had been a good, solid methodical player, but this man was clearly in the master class. His strategy was as complex and ruthless as the man himself. She knew herself to be a fairly good player, with flashes of almost intuitive brilliance. Her fatal weakness lay in that streak of impulsiveness that had been the bane of her grandfather's existence. Even so, at the end of two hours of play, when Jake Dominic had inevitably put her in check, she felt that she'd given a reasonably good account of herself.

Jake leaned back in his chair, one long, graceful hand toying idly with her queen. "You know that you could be much better than you are?" he asked quietly. "All you need is a little self-discipline."

"I know," she agreed, making a face. "It was drummed into me often enough by my grandfather. But I can't bring myself to play that way. It would take all the fun out of it."

"Even if it would eventually furnish you with the fruits of victory?" His eyes were curiously searching.

"I'm not that goal-oriented," she said casually. "I'd much rather enjoy myself along the way."

"I'm afraid I can't agree with your philosophy." His mouth curved in that familiar mocking smile. "I always find winning worthwhile. I make a habit of it."

She already knew that. Jake Dominic had devoted the same single-minded effort to his chess game that he would to any more serious project.

Jane smiled happily as she helped him to collect the ivory chess pieces and replace them in their velvet-lined box. "Well, the contrast of viewpoints makes for an interesting game," she commented, and concentrated on putting each piece properly in its indented place in the box.

Dominic's eyes flickered with amusement as they fixed on

the girl's almost childishly intent face, her pink tongue unconsciously protruding from the corner of her mouth as she gravely put the last piece in the box and closed the lid carefully.

"Yes, it makes for an interesting game," he repeated slowly, accepting the box from her and replacing it in the drawer.

Jane smothered a yawn as she pushed back her chair and stood up. Now that the tension of the game had ended she was suddenly overpoweringly sleepy. "Thank you for the game, Mr. Dominic," she said, sounding like a polite little girl. "If you don't mind, I'll say good night now."

"Would you like some more coffee?" he offered lazily, rising to his feet. He looked at his watch. "It's only a little after eleven."

She shook her head firmly. "I must get to bed," she said with a grimace. "I have to get up at six."

"Oh, yes, I'd forgotten," he replied absently, with a trace of annoyance in his voice. "Run along to bed, then," he said curtly. "But be sure you report here at eight sharp tomorrow evening."

"Tomorrow?" she asked, smothering another yawn. "You want me to come again tomorrow evening?"

"I said so, didn't I?" he asked testily, his expression half amused, half annoyed at her obvious lack of appreciation of his desire for her company.

"Okay," she muttered inelegantly, turning to leave.

"Jane!"

She half turned, to gaze at him like a sleepy kitten from those great golden eyes.

"See that you eat dinner tomorrow. I refuse to wait on any woman two nights in a row."

four

THAT FIRST DAY SET THE PATTERN FOR THE ones that were to follow. Jane's second day scrubbing decks was even more uncomfortable than the first. The pain in her bruised knees was agonizing, and seemed to grow in intensity as the day wore on. The only relief from the misery of pain and exhaustion came from the increasingly open display of sympathy and support from the other members of the crew.

Simon had introduced her to a number of the crew at breakfast that morning, and Jane had found them to be a genial and friendly group, altogether different from the rough, tough, blustery image she had always had of men who made their livelihood on the sea. That they all possessed a streak of gallantry she was to learn later in the day.

One by one, with seeming casualness, they wandered by the area where she was working. And always they brought gifts, ranging from a drink from a thermos of coffee, to the presentation of a panama hat to shade her from the sun and a pair of rubber gloves to relieve her chapped and reddened hands. Though the gifts were invaluable in themselves, it was the sympathy behind them that gave her the strength to complete that second agonizing day.

Her time with Jake Dominic in the evenings became a price-less oasis in the desert of those next few days. No matter how ex-cruciatingly tired she was at the end of the day, she had only to open the door of the lounge and see Jake look up with that mocking smile to feel a rush of new vitality. It was inexpressibly soothing to sit over the chessboard and watch the wary flicker-ing behind those ebony eyes as she presented him with an unex-pected challenge, or to listen to his amusing stories of life on the set as they sat over coffee. Jake Dominic continued to treat her with the affectionate indulgence that he might show a preco-cious niece, and this arrangement met with her entire satisfac-tion. She was fully aware that in any other role, he would be a highly dangerous commodity. She doubted her ability to handle any encounter with the much-publicized rake of the tabloids. She much preferred the Jake Dominic who teased her about her cat eyes, trounced her soundly at chess, and let her leave him at the end of the evening with no more than a casual wave of his hand.

But by the fourth day not even the anticipation of the eve-ning to come could dull the sheer agony Jane was experiencing. She'd borrowed two elastic bandages from Simon to bind her knees, which were now swollen twice their normal size and were a livid purple. The bandage provided a little protection, but as the day progressed she began to feel a trifle nauseous from the pain. She did not bother to go to lunch that day. She merely crawled to the rail and sat leaning against it, her eyes shut against the glaring noonday sun. She gently massaged her left kneecap, which for some reason appeared to be in worse condition than the other. She really must eat dinner, she thought wearily. She'd need all the strength she could muster to get through tomorrow.

But by evening it didn't seem to be worth the effort to make her way to the mess. After a quick shower, she rebandaged her knees and lay down on her bunk to nap for the two hours' respite before she had to report to the lounge. Luckily she took the precaution of setting the alarm on her clock, for when she collapsed on the bed she fell into an exhausted sleep.

The alarm woke her with its strident ring, and for a moment Jane was tempted to shut it off and roll over and go back to sleep. Then she sat up and began to dress in the oversized khaki trousers that she had worn that first evening. She grabbed her own black turtleneck sweater, which she'd washed out by hand the night before, and slipped it on. She went into the bathroom to run a comb through her hair, and her reflection in the mirror over the sink sent a shiver of distaste through her. She looked like a sick cat, she thought gloomily. She spent the next few minutes massaging her pale cheeks with the rough terry towel to restore the color to them.

When she opened the door to the lounge ten minutes later, she drew a deep breath and fixed a bright smile on her face before she strolled forward, making a conscious effort not to hobble.

Jake Dominic was sitting at the bar, a glass of bourbon in his hand and an impatient frown on his lean dark face. Tonight he was wearing faded jeans that hung low on his hips and hugged the muscular line of his thighs with loving detail. His navy cotton shirt was left carelessly unbuttoned almost to the waist, and Jane's eyes were drawn in fascination to the triangle of dark wiry hair on his powerfully muscled chest.

Jane had a fleeting memory of the rough virile feel of that hair against her fingertips. She felt a sudden warmth in her cheeks, and she looked away hurriedly.

"You're thirty minutes late," Jake said. "I was about to send someone to get you."

She made a mocking bow. "Forgive me, O honorable master," she said in a singsong, lowering her lashes demurely. "Your lowly servant humbly begs to be excused for this grievous misdemeanor."

A reluctant smile curved his lips. "Impudent scamp," he

charged. "Be careful, redhead. One of these days I'm going to teach you a little respect." He rose to his feet and swallowed the rest of his drink.

"What do you call our chess games?" she asked lightly. "If you ever think of a more severe lesson than you dish out over that chess table, I may not show up at all."

A flicker of annoyance touched Jake's face. "You'll do as you're told," he said coolly. "I own you, remember?"

Perhaps it was her weariness that urged her to prick at that arrogance. "But only for two months," she reminded him sweetly. "Our agreement was just until the end of the cruise."

His face became even darker, and Jane wondered idly what had served to put him in such a savage humor. Surely the fact that she was a little late couldn't have annoyed him to this extent.

An unpleasant smile twisted his lips. "That's right, redhead," he said silkily. "It was just for the duration of the cruise. But I don't believe I specified the exact length of the cruise. Who knows—I may feel the need for an extended rest." His eyes flickered moodily. "How would you like to continue with your duties for the next six months?"

Jane gave him a distinctly skeptical look. "That would be a greater punishment for you than it would be for me," she said serenely. "I'd wager you'd be bored to tears in no time, Mr. Dominic. You're not exactly the playboy type."

"There are a number of people who would disagree with you," he said bitterly. "Don't you read the gossip columns?"

"I'm not saying that you don't try to maintain the pose," Jane said kindly. "But you're much too dynamic to be really successful at it."

Jake Dominic's dark eyes narrowed. "You're very confident of your own powers of judgment," he said softly. "I think you should be aware that I heartily dislike being considered predictable, little one." There was such a wealth of menace in his tone that Jane took an involuntary step backward.

The action brought a glint of satisfaction to his eyes. "If you're through with your amateurish psychoanalysis, I suggest we get on with the game," he said coldly, and he turned and walked away.

The game that night bore no resemblance to the ones that had preceded it. Jake Dominic was out for blood tonight. From the first move it was clear that he meant to vanquish her in the most brutal and humiliating method possible. In a little under an hour he had her in check.

Jane looked across the table into the ebony eyes gleaming in triumph, and said ruefully, "I guess you put me in my place. Remind me not to make you angry again. My self-esteem can't take it."

Some of the ruthlessness faded from his face, to be replaced by an odd watchfulness. He shook his head incredulously. "Don't you know that you're supposed to be ground beneath my heel?" he asked dryly. "What does it take to put you down, Jane?"

Jane shrugged, her smile shaky. "Oh, I'm suitably chastised, I assure you. You can be a very intimidating man, Mr. Dominic."

"Jake, damn it," he said impatiently. "What's the point in addressing me so formally, when you know I get nothing but cheek from you?"

"Jake," she repeated, the name sounding strangely intimate on her lips. She pushed back her chair and rose slowly, her knees stiff from inactivity. "Well, Jake, I believe I'll call it a night. I'm afraid your court jester isn't providing you with the proper degree of amusement this evening. Perhaps another time."

The dark eyes flared with annoyance. "It's early yet. Stay a bit," he ordered arrogantly. "I'll give you another chance."

She shook her head. "Not tonight," she said, turning away.

Jake's hand snaked out to grasp her wrist, obviously meaning only to stop her, but the stiffness of her legs caused her to be momentarily unbalanced, so that her left limb rammed into the table leg. A flash of hot agony shot through it, and a cry of pain broke from her.

Jake's eyes widened in surprise. "What the hell!" he exclaimed, his hand loosening around her wrist. His lightning glance took in the pasty color of Jane's face and the helpless quiver of her lips. "My God, what the hell happened?" he asked roughly. "You look like you're about to pass out."

She shook her head as the wave of nausea gradually subsided. "I hit my leg," she said shakily. "I'll be all right in a minute." She sank back into her chair and closed her eyes, breathing deeply to still the sudden quivering weakness in her stomach.

With a muttered oath Jake was out of his chair and kneeling in front of her, his hands swiftly rolling up the loose leg of her khaki trousers.

She opened her eyes in sudden alarm and reached down to stop him. "No," she said quickly. "I'll be fine. Just give me a moment."

Jake's dark eyes were grim. "You're not going to stop me, Jane, so don't try," he said harshly. "You barely touched that table leg and yet you're almost fainting with pain. I'm going to find out why."

His determined gaze held hers for a long moment before she dropped her eyes. She couldn't fight him right now, she thought wearily. She hadn't the strength.

He had rolled the cuff over her knee, and now his swift, dexterous hands were unrolling the elastic bandage. He unwrapped the last layer of cloth and pulled the bandage away to reveal the ugly purple swelling of her kneecap.

"Good God!" he swore harshly. "What the hell have you done to yourself? That knee must be terribly painful."

Jane wet her lips nervously with her tongue. "It's not that

bad," she said. "It will be fine in a few days." She tried to cover
the discolored bruise with her trouser leg, but he stopped her, an
ominous frown clouding his face. His sharp glance had now
noted the slight thickness beneath the other pant leg, and with a
terse but descriptive obscenity he proceeded to roll it up. His
face was rigidly controlled as he unwrapped the second bandage
and saw the swollen knee.

He sat back on his heels, and his gaze traveled from knee to
knee with incredulous eyes. "You've got to be the most stupid
little bitch on the face of the earth!" he said explosively. "Haven't
you got the sense to know that those bruises need attention? You
shouldn't even be on your feet, for God's sake."

"They'll be all right," she insisted stubbornly. "I'll bathe
them in cold water when I get back to my cabin." She started to
rise, and he pushed her unceremoniously back into the chair.

"Stay where you are," he ordered. "I don't want you on your
feet again until you have my permission. Which probably won't
be for at least a week," he added grimly, as he eyed the abused
knees sourly.

"That's not possible," Jane said stubbornly. "I've got to work
tomorrow."

Jake's lips were taut with anger as he remarked sarcastically,
"Your devotion to duty is praiseworthy, but I run things around
here, if you recall. You'll do what I say and like it. I'll tell Marc
I'm sending you to bed for the next week."

"No!" she cried forcefully, her golden eyes blazing. "I won't
have Captain Benjamin think I came running to you because I
couldn't take it. I'm going back to work tomorrow, and you
can't stop me!"

Jake's eyes narrowed at her words. "What can't you take,
Jane?" he asked with the softness of a stiletto sheathed in velvet.
"Why should Marc think that you'd run to me?"

"I can take anything your precious captain hands out," Jane

said, breathing raggedly, "anything! And neither you nor anyone else is going to keep me from being on that deck in the morning!"

"We'll see about that," he said. "But right now you're going to tell me what you're going to be doing on that deck tomorrow."

"Why, scrubbing it, of course," she said bitterly, suddenly reckless. "Miles and miles of it. How else do you think my knees would get like this?"

Jake Dominic went suddenly still. "You're saying that Benjamin has had you scrubbing decks on your hands and knees for the past four days?"

Jane tossed her head. "Why not? Fresh sea air, sun, healthful exercise," she enumerated caustically. "As you said, quite a change from the classroom."

Anger flared in the dark eyes. "Damned if I don't almost see why Marc did it," he said between his teeth. He rose to his feet and crossed to the phone extension at the bar and dialed rapidly. He spoke into the receiver. "Marc, I want you in the lounge immediately." Without waiting for a reply he replaced the receiver and turned to look at her.

Jane looked infinitely vulnerable lying back in the chair, her cheeks pale, her diminutive body in its oversized garments slight and fragile. The only signs of strength were in the defiance in her eyes and the indomitable set to her soft pink mouth.

"Why didn't you tell me?" he asked curtly.

She lifted her chin. "It wasn't your concern. For that matter, it still isn't. It's entirely between Captain Benjamin and myself."

He gazed at her in incredulous anger. "Damn it," he said harshly. "I own the *Sea Breeze*. I employ every person aboard her, and you say it's not my concern when my captain abuses you?"

"I am not abused," she said crossly. "I wish you'd just stay out of it." She tightened her hands on the arms of the chair and attempted to lever herself into a standing position.

"Damn it, can't you ever obey orders?" he roared. He crossed the room in four strides and swung her up in his arms, ignoring her startled gasp.

She started to speak, but he cut off her words. "Shut up! Just shut up!" He carried her to the brown leather couch in the center of the room and dropped her on it with all the gentleness of one disposing of yesterday's garbage. "Now, stay there!"

Jane pulled herself into an upright position, very affronted by this undignified treatment, and opened her mouth to tell him just what he could do with his orders. This extremely hazardous course of action was interrupted by the arrival of Marc Benjamin.

The captain looked his usual commanding, unruffled self in his dark-blue uniform. His keen gray eyes impersonally noted Jane's presence on the couch, before he turned his attention to Dominic. "You wanted to see me?" he asked composedly.

Jake crossed to the bar and poured himself a brandy. "You could say that," he said tersely. "I hear you've been acting like a virtual Captain Bligh with our reluctant guest here."

"I didn't say that!" Jane protested hotly. "I told you this was none of your business." She turned to the captain and said quickly. "I'll be on deck tomorrow at the usual time, Captain Benjamin."

"You needn't try to protect me, Miss Smith," Benjamin said coolly. "I'm quite capable of making my own explanations."

"Protect you!" Jane sputtered furiously. "I'm not protecting you, my dear Simon Legree. I just want no interference in what is strictly a private battle. I have no intention of winning by default."

Benjamin didn't pretend to misunderstand her. "It seems you've done just that, whether you like it or not," he answered impassively.

"Not on your life," Jane said emphatically, her eyes burning like a flame in her white face.

"I can't believe this." Jake came forward to stand beside the couch. "If you'll stop squabbling like two kindergarten children, I'd like that explanation, Marc."

The captain shrugged. "There's nothing to make a fuss about, Jake," he said calmly. "Miss Smith and I were just having a little battle of wills. I'll change her to another duty tomorrow."

"You'll do no such thing!" Jane cried, struggling to get to her feet.

Jake pushed her back on the couch. "Be still!" he ordered roughly. He turned to Benjamin and asked grimly, "What type of work did you imagine she could do with legs like these?" He reached down and pulled the khaki pants up to reveal her swollen kneecaps.

Benjamin gazed in stunned horror, for once jolted out of his cool aplomb. "Good Lord!" he swore beneath his breath. He looked up at Dominic, his gray eyes stricken. "I didn't know, Jake," he muttered. "I swear I didn't know. Why the hell didn't she tell me?"

"Because she's a stubborn young fool with more courage than sense," Jake said curtly. "I gather she was under the impression that you were trying to break her spirit." He shook his head in disgust. "I'd expect such behavior from a young firebrand like Jane, but what provoked you to go this far?"

Benjamin swallowed hard, looking slightly sick. "She may have been right. I don't know. She was so damned defiant that it got under my skin. Every day I thought she'd give in and ask me to change her duty, and every day she threw her refusal right back in my face." His hands came up to cover his eyes. "God, I feel rotten."

Jane felt her anger begin to drain away as she saw the unhappiness and self-reproach in Benjamin's face. She could grudgingly understand the irritation that had driven him to such lengths. Hadn't she been stirred by the same pride and stubbornness that had goaded the captain? She knew the same treacherous melting that she always experienced at the sight of another's distress or pain.

"I should think you would," Jake said scathingly. "You've acted with the same asinine stupidity that she has."

This remark was met with resentful scowls from both antagonists.

"It wasn't the captain's fault that I bruise easily," Jane said defensively, with an abrupt about-face. "You hired him to run your blasted ship for you. If he thought that I'd be of most value scrubbing decks, then that's what I should do." She scooted to the other end of the couch to evade Jake's reach and rose to her feet. "In fact, that's what I insist on doing!" she added emphatically. She turned and marched toward the door, brushing by the stunned captain with a curt nod. "I'll see you tomorrow morning at the usual time, Captain Benjamin."

The captain was having a predinner drink with Jake in the lounge one evening, shortly after they had sighted the northern coast of Mexico, and was mentally congratulating himself on his diplomatic brilliance. It appeared that his solution to the problem Jane had presented was working very well indeed in the past several days. His self-satisfaction in this respect was suddenly blasted into the stratosphere by a call from his first officer, Jim Davidson.

When he turned away from the phone, he grimaced as he picked up his whiskey. "I should have known that it was too good to last. That was Jim Davidson on the phone. It seems that we have a slight disciplinary problem with the crew. Five of them were caught shooting craps in the storeroom." He looked down gloomily at his drink. "One of them was your problem child, Jane Smith."

Jake Dominic lifted an eyebrow mockingly. "Surely that's

not so reprehensible," he said easily. "You've always allowed the men to gamble on the *Sea Breeze*."

"Not for money," Benjamin said shortly. "Evidently there was quite a bit of cash involved in this particular game."

"I see," Jake replied thoughtfully; then his eyes lit mischievously. "And what discipline are you going to administer to these miscreants? Scrubbing the deck?"

"Lord, no!" Benjamin said with a shudder. "The men are easy enough to deal with. They know that the standard punishment for gambling is to stop their pay for a few days. But how in the hell do I discipline Jane, when she's not even earning a salary?"

Jake rose from the barstool and wandered over to the porthole to stare absently out at the tranquil sea that was just beginning to be stroked by the scarlet rays of the setting sun. "I'll take care of it." He spoke casually, over his shoulder. "As you say, she's my problem."

"I didn't think you'd want to be bothered," Benjamin said slowly. Though Dominic had inquired once or twice about Jane, he'd never once visited his charge in her cabin during the time that she'd been confined.

Jake Dominic turned around to face him, a sardonic smile on his face. "It would hardly have been discreet to display more than a casual interest in our little invalid. You know damn well if I'd paid so much as a courtesy call to Jane's cabin, the entire ship would have assumed that she was my mistress. The next two months are going to be difficult enough for her without that particular problem to deal with."

That Jake had been acting chivalrously to protect Jane had obviously never occurred to Benjamin. "So you haven't grown bored with your court jester yet," Benjamin remarked dryly. "That must be some kind of record for you, Jake."

He shrugged, his dark eyes shuttered. "She's an amusing

child. I enjoy having her around." He smiled. "Even when she raises hell."

"Shall I tell Davidson to send her to you for discipline, then?" Benjamin asked slyly. "It wouldn't do to exempt her from punishment. It would set a bad precedent."

There was a trace of uneasiness in Jake's face. "It really wasn't a very serious offense," he suggested tentatively. Then, as Benjamin continued to stare at him implacably, he said in exasperation, "Oh, damn it to hell! Yes, send her to me. I'll think of something."

Benjamin smothered a smile as he turned away and once again lifted the receiver of the phone to give the order.

Jane arrived in the lounge five minutes later. She wore her own black jeans and a man's yellow sport shirt with the tails knotted under her small high breasts and the sleeves rolled up above the elbow. She also wore an expression of determination and defiance as she strode angrily into the room.

"It's utterly ridiculous for you to punish the men for having a friendly dice game," she cried furiously. She stopped before them, her breasts heaving, her flaming hair seeming to take additional fire from her blazing eyes. "It's absolutely medieval of you to withhold their pay for indulging in an innocent game on their own time!"

The two men exchanged amused glances before Benjamin attempted to assume a stern expression. "A game quite frequently ceases to be friendly when money is involved," he said coolly. "The rule is quite reasonable on shipboard. Men have been known to lose an entire month's salary when faced with their boredom of days at sea. Some of these men have wives and children to support at home. How would you like them to be in need, even hungry, because of a 'friendly' little dice game?"

Jane's eyes were wide and stricken. "I never thought of that," she said in a subdued tone. "You're quite right, of course."

"Of course," Benjamin agreed promptly. "However, we're here not to discuss the men's punishment, but your own, young lady. Not only have you disobeyed my orders about leaving your bed, but you've engaged in an illegal dice game."

Jane made a face. "My knees are almost entirely healed now, so there was no reason to stay in bed. It was driving me absolutely bananas. And I wasn't actually gambling. I didn't have any money, so Simon was just letting me throw out the dice for him."

"Simon?" Jake asked, his dark eyes narrowing.

"Your cousin, Simon." Jane said, surprised; then, as he continued to look puzzled, she quoted impishly: "Four times removed in blood, forty million dollars in substance."

"Oh, yes, Gordon Dominic's boy," Jake said dryly. "I'd forgotten that he was on board."

"You should get to know him better," Jane said with enthusiasm. "Simon is a super person."

"I'm glad you think so," Jake said tersely. "Personally, I don't think much of a man who involves a young girl in illegal gambling."

Benjamin raised his eyebrows at this hypocrisy from a man who had led dozens of women into much more iniquitous indiscretions, but he wisely withheld comment.

"It wasn't Simon's fault," Jane said staunchly. "He wouldn't even have been there himself, if I hadn't told him I had never seen a dice game and asked him to go with me."

"So it was you who lured the all-American boy down the path of wickedness," Jake said lazily, taking a swallow of his drink. "It did seem a little out of character, from what I remember of Simon."

"Couldn't you excuse him from punishment, just this time?" Jane pleaded wistfully. "It hardly seems fair that he should take the blame because I was curious."

"I can't understand your fascination," Jake remarked. "Surely a covert dice game in a deserted storeroom is a little on the sordid side."

"Well, actually it was rather exciting," Jane said with a reminiscent smile. "You see, I'd never seen anyone gamble before. My grandfather was very strict about things like that."

"I can't make an exception in Simon's case," Benjamin said emphatically. "Any more than we can in your own." He turned to Jake. "Have you made a decision as to her punishment?"

A curious smile lit Jake Dominic's dark face as he stared with narrowed eyes into Jane's. "Oh, yes, I think so," he drawled. "Where's the closest gambling casino, Marc?"

Benjamin answered warily, "San Miguel. It's a few miles down the coast." His eyes narrowed as he saw the flickering devilment in the other man's expression.

"Good," Jake said with satisfaction. "I've thought it over, Marc, and what Jane needs isn't discipline, but knowledge. We need to show her the wickedness of these games of chance so that she may satisfy her curiosity and get it out of her system."

"Rather an unusual solution," Benjamin said sardonically. "So you intend to take her to San Miguel tonight." It was a statement, not a question.

Jake nodded, his eyes still on Jane's face, which had suddenly come alive with excitement. "I feel it my duty," he said mockingly. "Care to come along, Marc?"

"I think I'd better," Benjamin said grimly. "San Miguel isn't Monte Carlo, you know. It's little more than a dive. It's certainly not the type of place you'd take a lady."

"Well, we can take care of that easily enough," Jake replied, his eyes running over Jane's slight figure. "Just find her a loose coat and that stocking cap she had on when she burgled my cabin. The lights are bound to be dim in the casino, and she'll have no trouble passing as a boy."

"I'll wear the white sweater Simon lent me," Jane put in eagerly. "I'm lost in it."

"Just the thing," he agreed promptly, his lips twitching.

"Should I bind my breasts?" Jane asked worriedly, looking down at her feminine roundness with profound disapproval.

Jake made a sound between a cough and a gasp. "No, I don't think that will be necessary," he said solemnly, not looking at her. "Why don't you run along and get into your disguise? Meet us on deck in thirty minutes."

"Right," Jane agreed happily, and ran from the lounge.

Jake released the whoop of laughter that he'd been suppressing. He bent over the bar, his shoulders shaking helplessly with mirth.

Captain Benjamin looked on in disapproval. "I'm glad you're so entertained," he said caustically. "You know that this isn't a wise venture, Jake."

Still chuckling, Jake commented, "Sometimes being wise can be abysmally dull, Marc. I can't wait to see her reaction to San Miguel."

Benjamin frowned. "I don't like the idea of exposing a girl to that kind of atmosphere just to furnish you with a few kicks, Jake."

"She'll be safe enough with both of us there to protect her." Jake said carelessly. "Jane's wild to go. You saw her face."

The captain nodded reluctantly. "I can't deny that. But damn it, she doesn't have the best track record for choosing what's good for her!"

"Why, Marc, you sound positively fatherly."

"The girl needs someone to take care of her. And neither of us has the qualifications for the job."

Jake slapped him on the shoulder. "For heaven's sake, Marc," he said impatiently, "we're not adopting the girl; we're only taking her out." He swallowed the rest of his drink and set his glass on the bar. "Now, while I go down and change, why don't you run along and check to make sure Jane's not doing something drastic?"

"Drastic?" Benjamin asked, puzzled.

Jake Dominic's eyes danced. "She seemed very concerned about looking like a boy." He grinned. "What's more girlish than a woman's crowning glory?"

"Crowning glo—you mean her hair?" Benjamin asked, his eyes widening. "You think she'd cut off all her hair?"

"It wouldn't surprise me," Jake said mildly.

"Oh, my God!" Benjamin exclaimed, and he bolted from the room.

five

THE CASINO WAS LOCATED AT THE TOP OF A hill overlooking the dusty, picturesque port town of San Miguel. The trip up the winding dirt road proved only a short ten minutes in the ancient rattling taxi that Jake Dominic had magically produced at the dock, and they were soon pulling into a bumpy, unpaved parking lot.

Jane peered eagerly out the window, her golden eyes blazing with curiosity and excitement. The parking lot was crowded even this early in the evening, she noticed. The large one-story prefab building that housed the casino was painted an astounding flamingo pink, and the name Tropicana was blazoned in nauseating chartreuse over the double doors at the front entrance.

"Disappointed?" Jake asked lazily, when she made no comment.

Jane shook her head. "Oh, no," she said positively. "It's just as I imagined a dive would look." She frowned in puzzlement. "Except for all those lights." Both the front and rear of the casino were lit by several brilliant streetlights that illuminated the area until it was almost as bright as daylight.

He shrugged. "At a place like this it's probably necessary if you don't want to come back to a car with no tires."

Benjamin nodded in agreement. "I've seen thieves completely strip a car inside and out in ten minutes," he said dryly. "And that was in downtown Mexico City!"

Instructing the taxi driver to wait and ensuring his compliance with a sizable monetary exchange, Jake ushered them leisurely from the car, through the double doors, and into the crowded, smoky interior of the casino.

"It's utterly fantastic," Jane breathed ecstatically. "It's like the movie set from *Casablanca*."

Jake flinched. "Please," he protested, with a pained expression. "Rick's Place at least had a certain class. This is more like the cantina scene from *Duel in the Sun*."

The entire far wall of the room was occupied by a long narrow bar. The rest of the large room was furnished with several green baize tables, offering various games of chance. The dimly lit room was crowded and noisy even this early in the evening. The patrons were almost exclusively male, for the most part Mexicans, dressed in dark trousers and the ubiquitous long white shirts and sandals.

The exception to the masculine atmosphere was provided by several voluptuously endowed *señoritas* in low-cut scarlet gowns who were presiding as dealers at the gaming tables. The old-fashioned ceiling fans served only to shift the smoke-laden air rather than freshen it, and the faces of the gamblers were shining with perspiration as they crowded close to the tables as if magnetized by the red-gowned dealers.

"Stay close to either Marc or me," Jake ordered. "And keep that cap pulled down!"

Jane nodded eagerly, jamming her hands in the pockets of the oversized jacket Captain Benjamin had provided, and swaggered after the two men with what she hoped was a boyish gait. Jake and Benjamin's goal was the crowded roulette table where Benjamin elbowed a place for Jane. Marc Benjamin and Jake swiftly purchased chips from a dark-haired beauty, who gave them a dazzling smile, and they proceeded to play for several minutes, with indifferent success.

"Would you like to try your luck?" Jake asked quietly, pushing some chips in front of her.

Jane shook her head. "I'd rather watch." The excitement and tension on the faces of the players was infinitely more interesting to her than winning or losing.

Jake shrugged. "It's really not my game either," he said, looking around restlessly. "I think I'll try to find a blackjack table. Do you want to come with me?"

"No, I'll stay here with Captain Benjamin," Jane said absently, her eyes on an obese man whose good luck was being raucously celebrated by much back-slapping and shouting. She was vaguely aware of Dominic's withdrawal.

For perhaps an hour she continued to watch with undiminished interest the goings-on at the roulette table before she, too, became restless. She looked down the table at Benjamin, hoping that he would also be ready to move on to another table. He looked quite content, however, his eyes fixed intently on the spinning wheel and a large stack of chips in front of him. He was winning heavily and would probably not even notice that she'd gone, she decided. She hadn't received more than a passing glance from any of the clientele of the casino. It should be safe enough for her to drift around by herself for a while.

She faded away from the table and pushed her way through to the sidelines to decide where to go next. She spotted a dice table in the corner of the room and decided to start there. For the next thirty minutes she visited several tables, with gradually dwindling interest. It was with some relief and pleasure that she finally spotted Dominic at a table across the room.

Jane started forward eagerly, only to stop abruptly after a few paces. The game Jake Dominic was playing was not confined to the cards in front of him. The ravishing Mexican dealer was leaning toward him with an unmistakable glint of invitation in her dark eyes as she murmured something to him that brought a cynical smile to his lips and a look of appraisal to his eyes. His eyes wandered leisurely over the woman's generous curves, lingering for a long moment on the cleavage that was blatantly displayed in the low-cut gown, before he gave the woman an answer that made her smile with sultry contentment.

Jane felt a stab of pain so intense that it took her breath away. For a moment she stood there, her emotions raw and confused, before her mind clamped a protective shield over the hurt and started to provide her with a rationalization for that revealing moment of agony.

Of course she had felt something when she'd seen Jake with that woman, she told herself. They had grown so close in the companionable evenings alone together that she knew a certain sense of possession. It was natural that she would feel a trifle bereft when Dominic showed the unmistakable signs of desire for another, even though the relationship he was contemplating with the sexy woman was far different from the casual friendship he had with Jane. She should have known that a virile man of Jake Dominic's reputation would immediately seek out a woman willing to satisfy his desires when the opportunity presented itself. It had been surprise, not pain, that had shaken her in that first moment, she told herself firmly.

She turned away, carefully avoiding looking at the intimacy of the couple at the blackjack table. Jake would not welcome a third party at this stage, she thought unhappily. Abruptly all pleasure was drained from the evening, and the scene that had been fascinating a few minutes before was now merely sordid.

She drifted over to the sidelines again, and leaned against the wall to watch the action in the smoky room with only casual interest. She was conscious now of the heat of the room. Her sweater and the loose coat that enveloped her were stifling, and she could feel a bead of perspiration form at the nape of her neck.

Her gaze ran casually around the room and then stopped abruptly. There was a small, nearly hidden door at the far end of the long, mirrored bar, which she had overlooked in her first glance around the room. It obviously led outside to the rear of the building, and as she looked, a steady stream of gamblers wandered through the door. None ever returned, though she watched carefully for another ten minutes. Her curiosity was irresistibly piqued.

She straightened slowly and moved forward, her gaze fixed in fascination on that mysterious door.

Jake Dominic looked indifferently at the card the Mexican woman had just dealt him, before lifting his eyes to gaze with slightly more appreciation at the generous cleavage revealed by the dealer's low-cut gown. Then his forehead creased in a puzzled frown when his glance passed from those pleasant pastures to drift restlessly about the room. The crowd had thinned now, and he could see Benjamin, still at the roulette table. But where the devil was Jane?

Suddenly there was a loud commotion at the far end of the bar as a short, stocky Mexican came bursting through the door shouting something to the bartender and waving his arms wildly. The bartender grabbed a baseball bat from under the bar and ran out the door, followed closely by the man who had summoned him.

Jake hurriedly threw his cards on the table and crossed the room to the roulette table in seconds.

He grabbed Marc Benjamin by the arm and asked tersely, "Where the hell is Jane?"

"I thought she was with you," Benjamin said, surprised.

Jake had a chill of foreboding as he remembered the brilliant lights that surrounded the casino. The lights in the parking lot were self-explanatory, but what about the lighting in the rear?

He reached across the table and grasped the dealer's arm as she reached out to take in the house's winnings. "That door by the bar," he asked urgently. "Where does it lead?"

The woman shrugged her bare shoulders. "*Pelea de gallos*," she answered indifferently.

"*Pelea de gallos!*" He started for the door at a dead run. "Cock-fight!" he shouted over his shoulder to Benjamin, and heard a violent exclamation. The captain caught up with him as Jake went through the door.

The scene that greeted their eyes was a wild melee of shouting, angry Mexicans who had left their wooden spectator benches and gathered around the pit arena in the center of the clearing. The object of their rage seemed to be the small figure lying on the hard-packed dirt in the center of the arena who was virtually covered by the bodies of several furious men, their fists swinging as they competed with one another in their attempts to do the worst possible damage to the red-haired gringo beneath them.

"My God! It's Jane!" Jake breathed, and without thinking he dashed forward, pushing and shoving through the crowd till he reached the pile of bodies. Lifting and pulling the men off her with frantic strength, he finally uncovered the dust- and blood-covered body of Jane Smith clutching a huge glossy black cock in her arms in a deathlike grip.

"Are you all right?" he shouted as he warded off a punch to his midsection from a burly man who didn't appreciate having his revenge thwarted.

Jane nodded as she got shakily to her knees and then to her feet, while Jake and Marc Benjamin, on either side of her, kept the crowd back by the primitive but effective method of punching whatever vulnerable spot on their antagonists' bodies presented itself.

"Let's get out of here!" Jake shouted, as he saw the bartender with the baseball bat edging closer.

They each grabbed one of Jane's arms and rushed forward,

knocking heads and punching faces indiscriminately as they progressed slowly across the clearing to the side of the building. When they broke clear of the crowd, they ran desperately for the waiting taxi, with a stream of shouting men hard on their heels.

They reached the taxi and piled hurriedly into the back seat. Jake shouted, *"Vamanos!"* in such a commanding voice that the startled taxi driver immediately reversed the car with a screech of tires, almost running over the first vanguard of their pursuers.

This resulted in another burst of threatening curses and fist shaking, as the driver sped out of the parking lot with his foot jammed down on the accelerator and his frightened eyes on the angry mob in his rearview mirror. He continued to drive with breakneck speed down the hill, half muttering prayers for himself and half curses against the crazy gringos who had gotten him into this.

Jake turned to Jane, his expression grim. "My God, you've still got that damn cock," he said disgustedly, looking with disfavor at the beady-eyed bird in Jane's arms. "I gather that revolting creature is the reason for all this?"

Jane nodded, her breathing gradually steadying. "It was terrible." She shuddered, her golden eyes darkening to topaz at the memory. "Those horrible men were making them fight with those hideous spurs on their feet. They were bleeding and hurt and nobody cared. I tried to make them stop, but they wouldn't listen."

"So you grabbed one of the birds in the ring to assure that they would," Benjamin surmised, shaking his head incredulously.

"It was the only thing I could do," she explained simply. "But it made them awfully angry."

"I can imagine," Jake said dryly. "A good bit of money rides on those birds."

"Well, I'm glad I did it," Jane said defiantly. "They were wrong to be so cruel."

"There are thousands of people doing cruel things in this

world." Jake said caustically. "Are you going to try to right all their wrongs?"

Her eyes filled with tears. "I had to do it," she repeated huskily.

"Do you know that you almost got yourself killed back there?" Jake asked through clenched teeth.

"Leave her alone, Jake," Marc said with rough kindness. "She's had enough for one night."

"I could break her neck," Jake said savagely, his gaze taking in her bruised and bleeding lip and her left eye, which was darkening rapidly. "Just look at her, damn it."

Jane shrank back against the solid shoulder of the captain. When she spoke, her lips trembled pitifully. "I'm sorry," she apologized miserably. "I didn't mean to cause any trouble."

"You *are* trouble," Jake said tersely as the taxi pulled up at the dock where the launch waited.

He jumped out of the taxi and half assisted, half jerked Jane out of the car. He reached into his pocket and pulled out several bills, which he handed to the driver with a curt "*Gracias*." The taxi driver's glower turned to a broad smile as he saw the size of the bills. He touched the brim of his wide straw hat in a respectful salute and drove off with a triumphant roar.

Meanwhile, Marc Benjamin had exited from the other door and had lithely jumped down into the launch and started the motor.

As Jake lifted Jane into the boat, the captain asked, above the low throb of the engine. "You're not going to let her take that cock on the *Sea Breeze*, surely?"

"What the hell do you suggest we do with it?" Jake asked bitterly. "Toss it into the sea? Jane would probably dive in after it."

"We could always give it to your chef and see what he could do with it," Marc drawled wryly. "It would certainly be a challenge to his expertise."

"No!" Jane cried, shocked. "You wouldn't." Her arms tightened protectively around the rooster.

"Of course we wouldn't," Jake said disgustedly. "He's joking, for heaven's sake." He turned to Benjamin. "Get us back to the *Sea Breeze*, Marc, or, so help me, I may toss them both into the sea!"

When they arrived back at the yacht, they were assisted aboard by a surprised and curious young seaman who tried not to stare too obviously at the disreputable-looking trio. Both Jake and Marc showed the signs of the violent free-for-all they'd been engaged in. Jake sported a bruise on his cheekbone that was rapidly turning a livid purple, and Benjamin's usually immaculate uniform jacket was torn raggedly from the lapel to the shoulder seam.

Jake carefully took the cock from Jane's arms and handed it to the seaman. "Be careful of the spurs," he cautioned, ignoring the man's dumbfounded expression. "Take him down to the storeroom and give him feed and water."

"I'll do it," Jane offered. "He's my responsibility."

"The hell you will," Jake said annoyedly. "You're coming down to my cabin so that I can have a look at those bruises. Coming, Marc?"

Marc Benjamin shook his head ruefully. "I'd better go to my own cabin and make some repairs. I'll be along later."

Jake nodded briefly and, taking Jane by the elbow, propelled her ahead of him, leaving the seaman to look after them, wondering blankly what the devil one fed a fighting cock.

Jake opened the door of his cabin and pushed her ahead of him into the room, flipping on the lights as he did so. Jane looked around her with interest. The night of her intrusion, she'd had no opportunity to appreciate the beauty of the master cabin. The thick carpet, she noted, was a silver gray, as were the shades on the bedside lamps. The spread that graced the king-sized bed was black velvet. The simple, elegant decor was oddly ascetic, considering its owner's worldliness. The only glaring note in the understated richness of the cabin was her own graffiti scribbled on the wall across from the bed.

Jane winced. "Can't you cover that up until you can have the panel replaced?" she asked.

Jake followed her glance and shrugged. "Marc offered to have his men make some temporary repairs, but I told him to leave it alone. I'm learning to live with it."

He strode into the bathroom, pulling her along with him. Once there, he lifted her onto the vanity counter while he rummaged in the medicine cabinet for unguentine and iodine.

"This isn't really necessary, you know," Jane said gently, watching his lean, taut face. "I'm sure you and Captain Benjamin took more punishment than I did. Those crazy men were hitting one another more than they were hitting me."

"How very comforting," Jake jeered. "So instead of broken bones and internal injuries, you only have severe cuts and bruises." Despite the anger in his voice, his hands were incredibly gentle as he washed the cut on her lip with a cold cloth. "At the rate you're going, you'll be lucky if you live to be twenty-one."

She smiled tremulously. "I promise that I'll be more careful in the future," she said lightly. "At least until the cruise is over. I fully intend to make sure you get your money's worth in labor to pay for that panel."

"Damn the panel!" Jake spoke harshly, his black eyes flaming. "Do you have any idea what would have happened if that mob in the pit tonight had discovered that you were a woman?"

Her golden eyes flew to his face in bewilderment. "You mean . . ." she whispered, and blushed uncontrollably. "But they were so angry. . . ."

"My God, Jane!" Jake said savagely. "Anger can be as much of an aphrodisiac as any other stimulant. Don't you know that?"

She shook her head, her eyes suddenly frightened. "No, I didn't know that," she answered simply.

"It figures," he said shortly. "For a girl who's lived all over the world, you've picked up relatively little common sense. That grandfather of yours must have kept you tied up."

"Everything happened too fast," she replied defensively. "I didn't have time to think and analyze every movement I made. I just knew that I had to stop them before they killed those two birds."

Jake carefully applied iodine to the cut lip before answering. His tone was grim. "I should have chained you to my wrist before I took you into that place."

Jane dropped her eyes. "You would have found that a trifle inconvenient," she said obscurely, remembering the sultry beauty at the blackjack table.

His eyes narrowed. "What's that supposed to mean?" he asked, critically examining her eye. "You're going to have a beaut of a shiner," he commented.

"Nothing," Jane murmured, as he tilted her chin and dabbed gently with the cold cloth at her swollen eye.

"You should never try to lie, redhead," he said dryly. "You're clear as glass. Now, answer me."

"It's just that I saw you with that woman," Jane said awkwardly. "I'm sorry if my getting into trouble interrupted you."

"What woman?" Jake asked, puzzled. Then his eyes gleamed mischievously. "Oh, that woman." He threw the cloth into the sink and uncapped the small jar of unguentine and started smoothing the salve around her eye. "We hadn't reached the point where an interruption would have caused me any really traumatic frustration."

Jane felt a rush of inexplicable relief at the knowledge that he had obviously forgotten the woman existed until she mentioned her.

"She was very beautiful," Jane said tentatively.

"Luscious, quite luscious," he agreed absently. Then he

grinned mockingly. "What are you hinting at, brat? Are you under the same impression as Marc, that I can't survive the cruise without a woman in my bed?"

"Well, you do have that reputation," Jane said demurely, her golden eyes dancing, "but you seem to be holding up very well, for a satyr."

"You know, I'm tempted to make that black eye into a matched set," he said in a conversational tone. "Not only do you deprive me of sexual solace, but you have the supreme insolence to taunt me with it."

She giggled, and he flashed her a smile of such warmth that her heart skipped a beat. "Laugh, will you?" he said with mock ferocity. "I ought to make you take the luscious Consuelo's place in my bed tonight."

She made a face. "You're not that hard up," she said with an impudent grin.

"Well, it would be a bit like taking a prizefighter to bed," he granted dryly. "But you know how we satyrs are—anybody would do in a clinch," he punned.

She groaned. "That's terrible, Jake. I think I'd prefer the black eye."

He grinned unrepentantly. "You're lucky I can still joke after a night like this one. For a while it was a draw whether the mob would kill you before I did."

"Oh, my God, I haven't thanked you!" she gasped, horrified. "You and Captain Benjamin probably saved my life, and I didn't even tell you how much I appreciate it."

"You were a little busy at the time," Jake said mockingly. "For that matter, so were Marc and I."

"And you were hurt," she cried remorsefully, her fingers gently touching the bruise on his cheekbone. Impulsively she reached up and pressed a fairy-light kiss on the bruised flesh. Then she drew back in a panic of shyness.

There was a curious flicker deep in Jake Dominic's eyes, but his voice was light. "Do you always kiss to make well? It's not a half-bad idea. Perhaps I'll try it."

His hands slowly reached up and cradled her face tenderly. She forgot to breathe as she stared wide-eyed up into the dark intentness of his eyes. "Shut your eyes, brat," he said huskily. "I'm about to conduct a medical experiment."

She obediently closed her eyes, and was immediately rewarded with a kiss on the lips that wooed and caressed like the first gentle breath of spring. It was followed by a butterfly kiss on the closed lid of her bruised eye and then another, just as light, on the other lid.

"That eye wasn't hurt," she protested dreamily, lifting her face like a flower to the sun.

"Stop complaining," Jake ordered. "I threw that one in for balance." His lips brushed the tip of her nose with infinite gentleness. "Now, is there anyplace that I've missed? I'm completely at your disposal."

Jane slowly opened her eyes, feeling almost drugged by the honey sweetness of the moment. She felt as if he had wrapped her in a silken protective cloak of warmth and affection and irresistible tenderness.

Jake's face was close, only a breath away, his black eyes laughing into her own. Then suddenly the laughter was gone and his eyes held something else in their flickering depths. Something that charged the atmosphere with electricity and caused the blood to race in her veins as if she'd been running a marathon race. She felt radiantly alive and at the same time languidly dreamy.

"Jane," Jake said huskily, his flickering eyes mesmerizing her with their dark flames.

"What's happening?" Jane whispered breathlessly, feeling suddenly as if she were captured in a melting pool of sensation whose nucleus was the intent face and virile body of the man before her. "What's happening to us, Jake?"

The words ripped the gossamer spell that surrounded them. Dominic drew a deep breath, and his eyes became shuttered and impenetrable. His hands dropped from her face, and his mouth twisted in familiar mockery.

"That, my innocent little nitwit, is what is known as *chemistry*. Or to put it more succinctly—sex. For a moment, there, you looked pretty good to me despite that black eye."

"You looked pretty good to me, too," she said quietly, her eyes shining serenely.

Jake shook his head wonderingly. "They shouldn't let you run around loose," he said flatly. "Didn't anyone ever tell you that you shouldn't say things like that to a man like me? God, you'd be a pushover for a man who was really on the make."

Jane's eyes filled with tears at the cynicism in his voice. "So I'm stupid," she said huskily. "I'm not like you. I can't hide what I'm feeling. I wouldn't want to."

She tried to slip off the vanity counter, but he stopped her with his hands on her shoulders. "I know," he said resignedly. "Like I said, clear as glass. It's time you learned to put up a few defenses, Jane."

She looked at him thoughtfully for a moment, then slowly shook her head. "You don't mean defenses, you mean armor," she said quietly. "I couldn't live like that. Hiding behind a shield because I was afraid to reach out and touch someone."

"There is a middle road, you know," Jake observed.

"Not for me."

Jake Dominic studied her determined face and clear, steady eyes for a long moment. He lifted her gently down from the vanity. "No, not for you," he agreed quietly. "And may God help you, redhead!"

He touched her cheek gently with one long finger, before he turned away and said briskly. "I believe a dose of remedial whiskey is in order. I'll call Marc and tell him to meet us in the lounge."

---

six

JANE WOKE UP TOO LATE TO HAVE BREAK-
fast the next morning, having opted to sleep for a precious thirty
minutes more, after her late night. As this was the first morning
of her training as cook's help for Sam Brockmeyer and she did
not want to be late, she was half running when she came up on
deck.

Simon Dominic hailed her cheerfully and fell into step with
her. He noted the black eye and cut lip with frank curiosity.
"What a shiner!"

Jane made a face at him. "You should have seen the other
guys," she loftily. "I should have known that our little adventure
would have been all over the ship by this time. And they say
women are gossips!"

Simon grinned. "Well, you can't show up with a fighting
cock in your arms, and the three of you looking as if you'd been
in a barroom brawl, without exciting a little curiosity."

"I can't tell you about it now," Jane said briskly. "I don't
want to start off on the wrong foot with Mr. Brockmeyer by being late."

Simon gave her an understanding look. "I'll see you at dinner and help you lick your wounds. There may be even more of
them by then. Brockmeyer is a terror to work for."

"Don't worry. I cut my teeth on top sergeants," Jane said flippantly. "You only have to remember to get in the first punch." Ignoring Simon's answering chuckle, she broke into a brisk sprint in the direction of the kitchen.

She had only a moment to appreciate the stainless-steel cleanliness of Brockmeyer's domain, before a voice bellowed menacingly from the planning desk in the far corner of the room. "You're late!"

This was patently untrue, as could be seen by the large clock on the wall. Jane moved forward serenely to stand before the cluttered desk and forbore apologizing, which the archdemon of the *Sea Breeze* obviously expected of her.

"Good morning, Mr. Brockmeyer," she said cheerfully. "I'm Jane Smith. I'm looking forward to working with you."

Sam Brockmeyer was a tall, lanky man in his late thirties, with a slightly receding hairline and the creased, jowly face of a mournful bloodhound. His soft brown eyes should have been appealing, but there was nothing endearing about the stony glare that the chef was directing at her.

"And I thought they had given me the dregs before," he said scathingly, his eyes running distastefully over her battered face and diminutive figure, in its oversized garments. "You must be Captain Benjamin's final revenge."

Jane smiled at him sunnily. "No, actually I'm your reward for being such a brilliant chef," she said sweetly. "My grandfather hated poor food, and since we often lived in less civilized corners of the world, he had me trained in Paris. Naturally, I'm not up to your standards, but I think you'll find I'm adequate." She paused. "I think you can teach me a good deal more, and I'm not about to be intimidated by your shouting or slave driving. Do we understand each other?"

Brockmeyer stared at her for a long moment, his face impassive, before saying slowly, "We understand each other, Miss Smith." He gave her a toothy grin.

In the next four days Brockmeyer appeared to be trying to make her eat those brave words. If Jane had not been absolutely sincere in what she had told the chef, he would have terrorized her, as he had her predecessors. Jane found herself working ceaselessly from six in the morning until nine at night in an atmosphere of turbulence that made a tropical hurricane appear as gentle as a summer breeze. The slightest clumsiness or mistake was met with a virulent diatribe from Brockmeyer's scourging tongue, and he obviously was taking malicious pleasure in singling out Jane for attention.

Jane accepted both the exhausting labor and verbal abuse with a cheerful serenity that frequently brought a look of baffled frustration to the chef's face. Though only allowed to do the donkey's work to begin with, Jane was gradually permitted minor cooking tasks. She made it her business to be in the general area when Brockmeyer was cooking, in order to observe the master at work.

Brockmeyer considered himself personally responsible for lunch and dinner for the crew and all of Jake Dominic's meals. The meals for the crew, since they were presented cafeteria-style, were less elaborate, but Brockmeyer still insisted that they be excellent. The meals prepared for Dominic were epicurean delights.

Jane gradually became aware that her hard work and uncomplaining attitude were earning Brockmeyer's grudging respect. This fact was brought home to her when a mistake by Ralph, the steward, who was entrusted with serving Dominic's lunch, threw Brockmeyer into a towering rage.

"What's the fool trying to do to me?" Brockmeyer howled, his spaniel eyes shooting fire. "I make Trout Almondine and the idiot serves red wine! I'll strangle him with my bare hands!"

As the guilty party had discreetly vanished at the first blistering words, this was not very likely to happen. However, Jane and the other kitchen minions busily went about their own tasks knowing that any word would immediately bring the chef's wrath down upon their own heads.

"How can I be expected to tolerate these blunderheads?" he raged, storming to the phone and dialing rapidly. Jane could not hear what he said and was quite surprised when a frowning Marcus Benjamin strode into the kitchen. Jane hid a smile. So even the captain was not immune to Brockmeyer's autocracy.

"I won't use that ass of a steward again!" Brockmeyer declared explosively as soon as Benjamin walked in the door.

Benjamin shrugged. "So I'll assign you another one," he said soothingly.

"And have the same thing happen again?" Brockmeyer asked caustically. "Your men are all ignorant philistines where fine cuisine is concerned."

"They're all good seamen," Benjamin said. "Ralph's mistake was surely minor."

"Minor!" Brockmeyer roared, "You call red wine with Trout Almondine minor?"

"Well, perhaps—"

"It will not happen again," Brockmeyer interrupted. "You'll assign her as Dominic's steward." He punched a finger in Jane's direction.

Jane almost dropped the potato she was peeling. She looked up, her eyes wide and startled.

Benjamin looked equally startled. "You want her out of your kitchen?" he asked slowly. "I suppose that I could change her duty assignment again."

"I didn't say that," Brockmeyer snapped. "She's adequate at her job."

Jane grinned happily at this grudging admission, which was the equivalent of the highest praise.

"She can be excused from her kitchen duties long enough to attend to Mr. Dominic. At least she can't be worse than those other idiots you sent me."

"Then it's done," Benjamin consented, relieved. He turned to go, obviously eager to escape.

"Just a moment," Brockmeyer said. "We're not finished." He waved a hand at Jane. "Look at her. Just the sight of her is enough to put anyone off his food. Even my food. You must get her out of those monstrosities she's wearing, before tomorrow. Do you understand?"

"We happen to be at sea," Benjamin reminded him dryly, "or didn't that occur to you?"

"That's your problem," Brockmeyer said tersely. "I won't have her serving my meals looking like a ragpicker."

"I'll speak to Mr. Dominic," Benjamin said, "but I can't promise anything." He turned and left the kitchen.

Whatever the tenor of Benjamin's conversation with Dominic, that evening the *Sea Breeze* anchored off the tiny port town of San Juárez. The next morning a launch was sent to pick up a number of packages that had been flown there, first by jet and then by helicopter, from Mexico City.

When Brockmeyer piled the packages into Jane's arms a few moments after they were delivered by launch to the *Sea Breeze*, he had a grimly triumphant smile on his face.

"You'd best check to see if they fit," he said gruffly. "You'll be serving lunch today."

Jane hurried happily to her cabin, more excited by the gift of these garments than she could ever remember being before. It wasn't surprising, she thought wryly, after tripping around in clothes that made her look like the second banana in a vaudeville show.

She hurriedly ripped off the heavy expensive wrapping paper on the packages and stared blissfully at her treasures. There was not only a handsome steward's uniform much like Simon's, but also several pairs of designer jeans, blouses, sweaters, a swimsuit, a nightgown, low-heeled shoes, and bras and panties. There was even a lavish makeup kit.

For the next twenty minutes Jane tried on everything that she had received, with a growing appreciation for the person who had ordered her new wardrobe. Everything fit perfectly. Someone had a very good eye, and she rather suspected that that someone was Jake Dominic. After all, he had probably had a lot of experience in buying clothing for his women.

When Jane finally donned the uniform, she was more than pleased with the result. The white polyester slacks were a perfect fit, as was the white turtle-neck blouse. The caramel-beige waist-length jacket gave her rather the appearance of a bellboy, but it also fit beautifully, and the color went well with her hair, she noticed, pleased. She added a touch of peach gloss to her lips and brushed her hair until it gleamed. It was amazing what a little lipstick could do for the morale. For the first time in nearly three weeks, she felt truly feminine.

No, not the first time, she thought, remembering that dizzying moment in Jake Dominic's cabin when she had felt more a woman than she had at any time in her life. She dismissed the thought firmly, and hurriedly put away her new things in the small teak chest before returning to the kitchen for her final instructions from Sam Brockmeyer.

Brockmeyer had informed her that unless Mr. Dominic had a large party of guests aboard, he preferred to have his meals served in the lounge. Though the surroundings were casual, Brockmeyer's table arrangements were not. It took Jane a full thirty minutes to set up the table in the elegant manner the chef felt his creations deserved, and then to transfer the meal in specially heated trays from the kitchen to the lounge. She then carefully chose a suitable bottle of wine from the wine rack behind the bar and moved briskly to stand beside the table.

Jake Dominic entered the lounge a few minutes later, and his brows shot up in amusement as he noted Jane's almost military stance. "For heaven's sake, relax! You make me feel like the prince in a comic opera."

Jane shot him an indignant glance but remained at attention. He looked like a prince, she thought with a little tingle of awareness. The dark prince Lucifer dressed in fitted black jeans and a black long-sleeve sport shirt. Jane had not seen him since she had started her duties with Brockmeyer, and she stifled the unreasoning surge of pleasure at the sight of that dark face.

"I have my instructions, sir," she said sedately, as he strolled to his chair. She was immediately behind it and ready to seat him.

He frowned threateningly. "You do that and I'll smack that pert little bottom, brat."

Jane's face drooped with disappointment, but she obediently moved back to her former position and poured the wine with a little flourish. His crooked eyebrow rose mockingly as she uncovered the soup and set it carefully before him.

"You're overplaying it, Jane," he said dryly, picking up his spoon. "Why don't you pull up a chair and join me?"

Her eyes widened. "Oh, I couldn't," she answered, shocked. "Mr. Brockmeyer would be positively furious."

"And I will be equally furious if I have an attack of indigestion from all this hovering," he said silkily. "Sit down!"

She reluctantly drew up a chair and perched on it gingerly, her face stormy. "You're not being fair. I'm only trying to do my duties properly," she said. "You wouldn't invite Ralph to sit down and have lunch with you."

"The same rules don't apply," he said coolly. "I wouldn't threaten to smack Ralph's bottom, either." Ignoring her sudden rush of color, he commented casually, "That uniform fits very well. I thought it would."

This confirmed her earlier suspicion, and she said gratefully, "Everything fits beautifully. Thank you."

Jake shrugged, his eyes gleaming wickedly. "Personally, I was growing rather fond of your Orphan Annie image," he drawled. "But it was either garb you decently or court ptomaine poisoning for the remainder of the cruise. How did you tame our Tiger of the Kitchen in just four days?"

"Mr. Brockmeyer is not a tiger," she protested stoutly. Then, meeting his skeptical look, she conceded, "Well, if he is, he has good reason to be. He's totally dedicated to his work and is a great artist. It's no wonder that he's so difficult. Just look at his background." She paused for effect. "He was born in Cleveland!"

Jake took a sip of his wine and said solemnly, "How very unfortunate." There was a suspicious twitch to his lips as he added, "I suppose that does have some significance, but I can't quite grasp it."

"Well, of course, it does," Jane said impatiently. "Whoever heard of a great chef from Cleveland, Ohio? The entire restaurant world is prejudiced in favor of French chefs. Even Italian chefs are given more opportunities than Americans." She leaned forward, warming to her subject, her cheeks flushed. "I read an article in *Gourmet* magazine a few years ago about Sam Brockmeyer. Do you know that, as great as he is, he wasn't able to get work in any four-star restaurant in the world until he assumed the name of Pierre LeClaire?" Her voice rose indignantly. "Why, he even had to fake a French accent to get his first prestigious job! Can you imagine what that would do to a man of his temperament?"

Jake was grinning unashamedly now, his ebony eyes dancing. "I can see that a delicate flower like Brockmeyer could suffer irreparable psychological damage."

Jane smiled reluctantly. "Well, he is a brilliant artist. He must be very sensitive under that gruff exterior."

Jake's smile was cynical. "It doesn't naturally follow. I'm considered rather brilliant myself in some circles, and I assure you that I'm as hard as nails."

She shook her head, her face troubled. "Don't say that. You couldn't be that tough and still be so kind to me. I'd probably be behind bars now if you were."

"Don't make the mistake of putting me on a pedestal, red-head," he corrected her wryly. "I'm a selfish bastard, and I always do exactly as I please. If I'd been in a different mood that night, I'd have turned you over to the authorities without a second thought."

"I don't believe that," Jane said quietly, her eyes steady on his.

"Then you're a fool," he replied softly, his dark eyes ruthless. "Ask Marc what kind of man I am."

Jane's gaze dropped. "I trust my own judgment," she insisted stubbornly.

"You'll forgive me if I fail to be impressed by your efforts in that area to date. Well, I've warned you, Jane, and that's more than I've done for any other woman. Just don't expect me to be better than I am."

"I don't think you know what you can be," she said daringly. "Or who you really are."

Jake's lips tightened, and his black eyes flickered. "And you do, I suppose," he remarked caustically.

Jane shook her head hesitantly. "Not yet," she said quietly, "but I'm beginning to think I may soon."

The look he bestowed on her was half angry, half amused, before the impenetrable shutter once more masked his expression. "You'd better pray that the final unveiling doesn't scare the hell out of you, redhead," he said lightly.

He reached for the bottle of wine and filled another glass and handed it to her. "Now, if you won't join me for lunch, at least have a glass of wine," he ordered, grinning mischievously. "I promise I won't tell Brockmeyer."

A few mornings later, they anchored at a small island off the southern coast of Mexico in answer to an urgent radio message from one Sheikh Ahmet Kahlid, a Middle Eastern oil potentate and apparently an old friend of Dominic's. Though Simon had apprised her of their passenger's arrival, Brockmeyer had kept Jane so busy in the kitchen that she didn't get a glimpse of the sheikh until it was time for her to go to the lounge to serve lunch.

She drew a deep breath before opening the door quietly and striding quickly across the lounge to the bar to choose the wine to accompany the meal. Kahlid and Dominic were sitting in the two large brown leather chairs in the center of the room, conversing lazily. Though Jake looked up when Jane came in the door, he didn't greet her, as he usually did, and she drew a breath of relief. It was clear that she was to be treated as just another steward, in the presence of Dominic's guest. She would have found it exceedingly uncomfortable to have to submit to Jake's teasing in front of this stranger.

Ahmet Kahlid's appearance was not exactly dashing, she noticed from the corner of her eye. His large, sturdy body was dressed in a gray business suit that screamed of Savile Row. He was well over six feet, with dark hair and beard and expressive dark eyes, which twinkled like bright buttons. He reminded her vaguely of a big, cozy teddy bear.

Jane pulled a bottle out of the wine rack and examined the label with satisfaction before placing it on the bar.

"No, not that one!" Jake called sharply, rising to his feet. "Excuse me, Ahmet, but there's a rather good wine I want you to try."

He strode across the room and behind the bar. Jane watched in surprise as he reached for a bottle of quite ordinary vintage. The one she had chosen was much better, she thought indignantly. She opened her lips to tell him this, then closed them quickly as she met Jake Dominic's dark, furious gaze.

"What the hell are you doing here?" he muttered in a harsh undertone. "I thought even Brockmeyer would have the sense to send a substitute, with Kahlid here."

"Why should he?" Jane hissed back indignantly. "I'm perfectly capable. Mr. Brockmeyer trusts me completely."

Jake Dominic muttered an imprecation beneath his breath and thrust the bottle at her. "I don't want to hear a word out of you, do you understand?" he asked, his eyes flashing. "And tell Brockmeyer I want a different steward by dinner."

He turned and walked back toward Kahlid, the smooth mask once more in place on his dark face. Jane stared after him, her face flushed with confusion and hurt at the sheer injustice of the attack. As she turned away, she intercepted Kahlid's curious, speculative gaze.

Jane was conscious of several such glances from Kahlid during lunch as she carefully obeyed Jake's orders. Not one word did she utter as she served each course and kept the wine-glasses full. When not needed, she stood at rigid attention behind Jake Dominic's chair, her blazing golden eyes staring straight before her.

It was a building fury that caused her to make the blunder that was to have such far-reaching consequences. Her hand was shaking slightly as she refilled Kahlid's glass for the third time, and she splashed a little on the white damask tablecloth.

Without thinking she murmured absently in Arabic, "Forgive me, effendi," and dabbed at the spreading stain with a linen napkin.

Kahlid broke off what he was saying to Dominic to stare in surprise at Jane. "But this is a wonderful surprise, Jake. Why did you not tell me your little servant spoke Arabic?"

Dominic shot her a furious look before smiling coolly at Kahlid. "I have to confess to ignorance, Ahmet. I wasn't aware that she did."

Kahlid smiled gently at Jane and said in Arabic. "It warms my heart to hear my language on your lips, little one." He sighed mournfully, reminding her once more of a cuddlesome teddy bear. "One gets homesick for the sound of one's own tongue."

Jane's golden eyes were glowing with sympathy at his words.

The sheikh was really quite nice, she thought warmly. She, too, knew the longing to hear one's own language in a foreign land.

"I spent two years in Kuwait as a young child," she replied gently in Arabic. "I am pleased that my small accomplishment brings you pleasure."

"You may go, Jane," Dominic interrupted abruptly. "Please give Mr. Brockmeyer our compliments."

"No! No!" Kahlid protested, his shining eyes running eagerly over her, from the bright red curls to the tip of her sensible brown leather shoes. "Do not send her away, my friend. It pleases me to have her here. She is a most unusual type, *n'est-ce pas?*"

"Oh, most unusual," Jake answered dryly. "You might say she's one of a kind." His hand tightened imperceptibly on the stem of his wineglass as he gazed expressionlessly at Jane. "However, the girl has duties to perform in the kitchen. I'm afraid that you'll have to do without her."

"The kitchen!" Kahlid scoffed. "It is criminal to send this one to the kitchen, when she could give such pleasure to me. You have any number of servants who can work in the kitchen. Send one of them!" He turned to his friend with the pleading look of a lonesome puppy. "Assign this little Jane to me as my personal steward," he asked impulsively.

Jane's eyes widened in surprise as they flew to Jake's impassive face.

"Impossible," he said coolly. "As I said, Jane has other duties. I assure you that you'll be quite content with the steward whom Captain Benjamin has assigned you."

Kahlid shook his head stubbornly. "Content, perhaps, but not happy," he argued, his eyes running almost caressingly over Jane's heart-shaped face. "I know this little Jane could make me very happy," he finished softly.

A flicker of annoyance passed over Jake's face at Kahlid's persistence, but his tone was still even. "I said no, Ahmet."

It appeared that Kahlid was a man who did not recognize the meaning of the word. He smiled jovially. "Then you must change your mind, my friend," he said persuasively. "You are not usually so inhospitable to your guests. What I have asked is not unreasonable. Did I not provide you with all that you could desire when you visited my home in Algiers last year?"

"You don't understand," Dominic said deliberately, "Jane is *my personal* servant."

The jovial smile faded from Kahlid's face, and he sighed despondently. "I suppose that I should have suspected. Never before have you had a female servant on your yacht." He turned back to Jane, his bright eyes regretful. "It is really too bad, little Jane; you would have brought me much pleasure." Without waiting for a reply from the bewildered girl, he asked Jake, "If you grow weary, you will send her to me?"

Dominic smiled mockingly. "Are you not my friend?" he asked evasively. He rose and threw his napkin on the table. "Now, if you will excuse me, I'd like a word with Jane before she returns to her duties. I'll join you in a moment."

He took Jane by the wrist and strode toward the door, forcing her almost to run to keep up with him. He did not stop until they were out of the room and on deck. When they'd reached a deserted area a little distance from the lounge, he released her wrist, but only to take her by the shoulders and swing her roughly around to face him.

His black eyes were blazing. "Was it too quiet for you?" he raged. "Was everything going so smoothly that you were compelled to raise a little hell just to make things interesting?"

"It's you who's raising a fuss over nothing," she said indignantly, trying futilely to pry those iron hands from her shoulders. "All I was trying to do was perform my duties as efficiently as I was able, and all you can do is yell at me and order me around. I didn't want to be there, you know!"

"It wasn't enough for you to come prancing into the lounge

wriggling that cute little bottom in front of Kahlid, but you had to coo sweet nothings in Arabic to him," Jake said furiously. "Have you no sense at all?"

"Prance? Wriggle?" she squeaked, outraged. "I do not wriggle, and I was merely being courteous to the man. What was I supposed to do, ignore it when I spilled the wine?"

"You were supposed to serve lunch, keep your mouth shut, and stay the hell out of Kahlid's way. Now look what you've done, with all that melting tenderness and cooing."

Cooing? It was the second time he had used that nauseating word. "I do not coo," she said between her teeth. "I was merely being sympathetic to the poor man. He was obviously homesick and a little lonely. What harm did it do to show a little concern and kindness? I only uttered a few words to your friend."

"They were evidently the wrong words," Dominic snapped. "Ahmet was most persistent about having you assigned to him. What would you have done if I'd let him have you?"

"It wouldn't have been so bad for a few days," she said defiantly. "The poor man just wanted to have someone to talk to."

He shook her again, his face dark with exasperation. "Don't you realize that you'd have been in Ahmet's bed tonight if I hadn't refused to hand you over to him?"

Her golden eyes were astonished, and her mouth dropped open. "That's crazy," Jane said faintly, when she could speak. "He couldn't have meant that when he asked for me. He wouldn't have assumed that you could snap your fingers and order me into someone's bed just because I happen to work for you. This is the twentieth century!"

"Not in Kahlid's country," Jake replied grimly. "It's a different culture and a different century. Oh, he's got a surface sophistication, thanks to his Western education, but the basic beliefs are still very much alive in him. Did you know that he had two wives, last time I counted?"

That cozy teddy bear of a man? She had known from her

stay in Kuwait that such arrangements existed in the East, but it appeared slightly incongruous in connection with Kahlid.

Dominic continued relentlessly. "It might interest you to know that he also keeps three or four pretty female servants at his home in Algiers in case his male guests want a woman."

"Is that what he meant when he said he provided you..." Jane's voice faltered.

"Why not?" he said, his voice hard. "As I said, it's a different culture. The women are more than willing, and they're free to leave Ahmet's house at any time." His dark eyes flickered. "I doubt if you would have proven so compliant."

Jane shook her head dazedly. "I still don't believe it," she protested. "I don't even have the looks Arabs admire. I'm much too thin."

"Kahlid has developed a variety of sexual appetites," Jake said meaningfully. "Believe me, you'd appeal to quite a few of them."

Her face was puzzled. "I don't understand."

"Forget it!" he snapped impatiently. "Just accept the fact that we have a problem, thanks to your blasted naïveté."

"But there's no problem now," she protested. "He accepted it very well when you convinced him you really meant your refusal."

"Heaven help me!" Jake swore. "He accepted it because I told him you were my personal servant. In other words, I've reserved you exclusively for my own bed."

Jane's face was now as scarlet as her hair. "Surely that wasn't necessary." She choked, her eyes not meeting his. "I could have just told him no. He seemed an understanding man when I spoke to him in the lounge."

"Kahlid is charming as long as he gets his own way, but in case you haven't noticed, he doesn't know how to accept a refusal. He just keeps plowing ahead like a bulldozer. Ahmet informs me he'll be with us at least until we reach Cozumel, and I assure you he'd be after you a large portion of that time. I have no desire to set a guard outside your door. Ahmet would consider it an insult."

"And I suppose that would be simply terrible," Jane said ironically. "We mustn't offend the man just because he may have the intention of raping me."

He shot her a quelling look. "As I've already explained to you, he wouldn't look at it the same way another man would. He would think your refusal was merely to tease him." He frowned. "I have no intention of antagonizing Kahlid if I can help it. He has enormous influence, and he was very useful to me last year when I was filming in Tunis."

"Charming!" Jane replied caustically, "Perhaps you should hand me over to him. After all, one must maintain one's contacts."

"Be quiet," Jake gritted, his black eyes flashing. "You've caused enough of a problem without adding your damn insolence to it." His lips thinned as he said ruthlessly, "I warned you I like things my own way, and that's exactly how I'm going to have it. I'm going to keep Kahlid resigned to the situation and moderately content. I'm going to keep my Middle East contact"—his eyes flickered cynically—"and if we're extremely lucky, I may keep you out of Kahlid's bed until he leaves the ship at Cozumel."

"And how do you intend to accomplish all this?" Jane challenged. "Move me into your bed instead?"

"That won't be necessary," Jake retorted coolly. "Ahmet won't expect you to sleep with me permanently or move into my cabin. That privilege is reserved for a mistress. A woman of your status would receive only an occasional invitation and a moderate amount of personal attention. Most of the time he would expect you to be treated exactly like any other servant."

"Then it will be quite easy to deceive him," Jane said, relieved. "We need only continue as we are now."

"Not entirely," Jake said dryly. "Kahlid is no fool. We must spend some time alone together to give an appearance of intimacy." His eyes narrowed thoughtfully. "I think perhaps you'd better meet me each morning for a swim and have breakfast with me on deck. That should be adequate."

"Are you sure this is really necessary?" Jane asked unhappily, biting her lip. "You know what the crew is going to think if you start paying attention to me."

"Exactly what Kahlid is going to think," Jake said indifferently, then his eyes hardened. "Who are you worried about, the crew or Simon?" he asked harshly. "Do you think it will turn him off to think he may be sharing you with me?"

There was a look of shock and hurt on Jane's face, and quick tears filled her eyes. "There's nothing like that between Simon and me," she said huskily. "We're just good friends."

"Just good friends," Jake echoed. "Then you won't mind if he thinks what the rest do about you."

"I mind very much what he thinks about me," she said quietly. "I wouldn't want anyone to believe I was anything more than a member of the crew. It will be very painful and embarrassing to know that they think I'm just another one of your playmates."

For a moment there was a curious flicker of regret in Jake Dominic's eyes. "You should have thought of that before you involved us both in a situation that presents no other solution," he said curtly. "I can't get you out of *this* mess just by knocking a few heads together, Jane."

"I suppose not." She sighed despondently. "I just wish—"

"Too late for that," he interrupted tersely. "Meet me on deck at seven tomorrow morning and we'll begin our little charade." He dropped his hands from her shoulders and stepped back. "I rather expect your attitude should be respectfully adoring in public," he continued mockingly. "Work on it, will you?"

"I'll try," she said wryly. "You may have to use all your directorial skill to wring a plausible performance from me. I'm no actress."

"I'm fully aware of that," Jake said resignedly. "Why do you think I picked early morning for our supposed romantic trysts? Ahmet will be up and about only occasionally, and it shouldn't be too much of a strain on that blasted transparency of yours."

"Shall I tell Mr. Brockmeyer that I'm to be replaced as your meal steward?" Jane asked.

He shook his head. "Kahlid will expect you to continue, under the circumstances. In my place he would display you with a certain discreet pride of possession."

"You seem to understand him very well," Jane said slowly.

"Perhaps I do," he said cynically. "Kahlid and I aren't so very far apart in our rather primitive reactions to certain situations. You'd be wise to remember that."

Jane's eyes were troubled as she asked hesitantly, "Is there no other way? Couldn't you just release me from our agreement and send me home? I promise that I'd send you payments every month until the panel was paid for."

Jake's dark eyes sparked dangerously. "No, damn it, you stay here!" he said harshly, his face suddenly satanic in intensity. "You belong to me for the rest of the cruise. We'll handle the problem exactly as I've indicated."

Before she could answer, he had turned and walked away.

seven

JANE SHOULD HAVE GUESSED THAT ANY PLAN that Jake Dominic had devised would be a total and unequivocal success. The morning rendezvous obviously thoroughly convinced Kahlid of Jane's supposed position in Dominic's life. After joining them two or three times during the next week for breakfast and a swim, Kahlid evidently decided his presence was an invasion of their privacy and subsequently ordered breakfast in his cabin.

Though his absence relieved Jane from the strain of acting the adoring paramour Jake had described, their meetings were still charged with the same burning restlessness that had characterized their association before Kahlid's arrival.

Jane looked back wistfully at those first uncomplicated evenings they had spent in the lounge, bent in amiable conflict over the chessboard. Now it seemed that everything she said to Jake was wrong. She seemed to have a talent for setting off that famous mercurial temperament without the least effort, and her own temper responded like a brushfire in a strong wind.

She had reluctantly come to the conclusion that Jake Dominic was entirely correct in his assessment of Kahlid's attitude toward her and the necessity for their charade. Though Ahmet was perfectly charming to her in their brief encounters when she acted as steward, a few times she had noticed an appraising glance that was totally foreign to the innocent teddy-bear image. Once, when he joined them for a swim, his frank approval of her in the tiny bikini verged on pure lechery.

It had struck her as positively ludicrous that a girl of her quite ordinary appearance should provoke passion in the breast of the sheikh, and she had tried to make Jake see how funny it was. She had finally faltered and fallen silent before the stormy anger in Jake's face. It appeared that she had blundered again, she thought morosely. It seemed everything she did these days was wrong.

During one of her periods of depression, she had asked Jake if it might not be safe now to stop their morning rendezvous, since Kahlid had ceased his visits with them. The answer she received was rude, explicit, and ended with Jake's telling her icily that he would decide when they would call a halt to their meetings, and would she please refrain from making stupid suggestions.

After this savage, unprovoked attack she did, indeed, refrain from making any suggestions at all, as well as much conversation. Their time together, before she could escape to the less demanding duties required by Brockmeyer, rapidly became a painful chore.

Jane had even taken to arriving on deck a few minutes early and diving into the sea before Jake Dominic arrived, so that she could have a few minutes by herself in the silken serenity of the cobalt water. She desperately needed that time alone before she faced the tension that his presence aroused.

Marc Benjamin was at the rail, staring absently at the swimmer whose slick red head bobbed in and out of the waves as she cleaved through the water with smooth, economical strokes, when Jake Dominic appeared on deck one morning. The captain had formed the habit of occasionally dropping by to have a cup of coffee and chat with the two of them before he went about his duties. He turned at the sound of the other man's footsteps and appraised the bronze, muscular figure in black swim trunks, a white terry-cloth robe slung carelessly over one shoulder. Marc Benjamin's calm eyes drifted up to Dominic's face, and he saw there the tense, restless frown he wore constantly of late.

"She's really very good," Benjamin commented casually, nodding toward the figure in the water.

Jake gave Jane a cursory glance before throwing his robe on the deck chair and turning to the captain. "A veritable water baby," he said caustically. "She tells me she learned to swim in Tahiti. One wonders how the island survived."

Ignoring the sarcasm, Benjamin continued to stare at Jane's distant figure. "It's strange that a girl who has knocked around the world as much as she has still retains that almost crystal simplicity."

Dominic did not reply, but his dark eyes turned to gaze at Jane's red, seallike head, his face taut. Benjamin glanced keenly at that face before asking softly, "Why don't you let her go, Jake? You're making her miserable."

Dominic's head jerked around, his eyes blazing. "Mind your own business, Marc. I won't tolerate your interference in this."

"She's just a kid. She doesn't understand," Benjamin continued calmly. "You've been ripping at her like a wounded tiger, and she doesn't know why."

Jake's mouth twisted. "And you think you do know?"

"I've known you for twelve years," Benjamin replied with a shrug. "I can make a pretty good guess about what's bothering you. Since you're not going to do anything about it, it's rather masochistic to keep her around, don't you think?"

Jake's eyes took on their familiar, shuttered look. "How do you know I have no intention of doing anything about it?" he said obliquely. "Perhaps I'm just biding my time."

Benjamin shook his head. "You haven't the patience for that

type of cat-and-mouse game. Let her go, Jake. You can't claim that she amuses you now."

Dominic laughed harshly. "No, by God, I can't claim that. But I'm not letting her go." His hand tightened on the rail. "Stay out of it, Marc."

Benjamin sighed and turned back to watch Jane's bikini-clad figure, now floating lazily on its back. "Well, I tried," he said philosophically. "She deserved that from me."

Jake Dominic turned moodily to follow his gaze, and suddenly his body stiffened. "Oh, my God!" he breathed, his face turning white.

Benjamin's keen eyes roamed the horizon searchingly, and then he too froze in horror. Not a hundred yards from that small, unaware figure was a triangular gray fin, lazily cleaving the water.

"We've got to warn her!" the captain said, and raised his hands to his mouth to make his shout more resonant.

"No!" Jake grabbed his friend's arm. "Don't startle her. I don't think he's seen her yet. She's safer if she makes no motion to attract his attention. Get two life preservers ready." He poised to dive at the open rail.

"Jake! For God's sake let me shout and warn her!" Marc urged. "What's the sense of your both being in danger?"

Jake ignored him and dived cleanly into the sea.

Jane could feel the warm sun on her wet face and see bits of blue sky through her half-closed lids as she let the sea cradle her floating body with its gentle rocking motion. It was divinely peaceful just to give yourself up to the elements and let them take you where they would, like a bit of flotsam, she thought dreamily. In the vastness of the great soothing sea, even the roar of Brockmeyer, or the biting sarcasm of Jake Dominic seemed unimportant and far away.

"Stay exactly as you are," Jake's voice ordered crisply. "Be very still and just listen to me."

Her eyes opened to see Jake's white, taut face above her, his dark eyes sharp. Oh, Lord, she thought unhappily, he was in his usual black mood. She instinctively started to swing her body upright, when he grabbed her by the chin and said, "Damn it, be still! I should have known you couldn't take a single order without messing it up."

She looked up to reply indignantly, when she noticed he wasn't looking at her at all but at something over her head, and that his bronze face was a shade paler than usual. "What is it?" she asked quietly, not moving.

He looked down at her, his dark eyes flickering, an exhilarated smile on his face, "We're going to play lifesaver," he said lightly. "You're going to be the victim and I'm the rescuer, and I don't want you to move a muscle. Understand?"

"I understand," she whispered, and turned her head slowly to where he had been gazing a few seconds ago.

"Oh, no!" Her cry was almost a whimper as she glimpsed that menacing fin. A surge of primal terror shot through her.

"Don't panic," he ordered quickly, starting to propel her through the water with a smooth, easy crawl. "He hasn't spotted us yet, and we just might get back to the ship before he does. The important thing to remember is not to make any wild splashing movements or rhythmic sounds. Either one will attract a shark's notice."

She smiled through teeth that had a tendency to chatter with terror. "You mean like the noise a swimmer would make as he splashed through the water?" she asked throatily. It seemed insane for them to be moving and talking so calmly, when close by a hungry monster with sharp teeth was searching the blue waters for his breakfast.

"Exactly!" Jake said with a trace of his mocking grin. "That's why you're playing victim. It lessens both the motion and the noise factor for me to do all the work." He looked over his shoulder. "We're almost halfway to the ship. We may make it yet." Dominic looked down into her strained face, and she was again conscious of the strange ghost of excitement deep in those dark eyes. "Marc will throw us two life preservers when we get within reach of the ship. Grab one, put it on, and hold on for dear life." He actually laughed at the irony of the unintentional pun. What kind of a man was he that he could laugh at a time like this, she wondered dazedly.

"Marc and some of the men will jerk you out of the water and onto the deck. We're almost two-thirds of the way home," he commented with another look over his shoulder. "If I tell you to swim for it, I want you to swim like blazes for the ship, but quietly, with a minimum of splashing. Okay?"

"Okay," she choked out, wondering what difference it would make at that terrifying point how much splashing she made.

But he didn't have to tell her, as it happened. Marc Benjamin's voice came over the water in a clarion call. "He's seen you! God! Hurry, damn it!"

"Go!" Jake ordered curtly, turning her over with lightning swiftness and giving her a mighty starting shove through the water.

Jane's arms moved under the water with a panic-driven urgency that propelled her through the water like a small torpedo. She could dimly hear Jake to the right of her and remembered with relief that he was an even stronger swimmer than she was. He would make the ship in a few more swift strokes.

She lifted her head, and there was the *Sea Breeze* before her, white and beautiful in the morning sunlight, with Marc Benjamin and several seamen standing tense and still at the rail. A life preserver floated a few feet in front of her, and she slipped it over her head and under her armpits.

"My God, pull her up! He's right behind her!" Benjamin's voice contained a chilling panic, and Jane could feel her breath stop in her lungs. There was a tremendous splashing in back of her. Was he so close, then? she thought. Was she to be ravaged by those razor-sharp teeth when she was within seconds of being rescued?

Then she was jerked out of the water with a mighty heave. She dangled awkwardly for a few seconds and then was pulled the rest of the way up to the deck. Several pairs of eager hands reached out to receive her, and she collapsed on the deck, her breast heaving with exertion and fear. A towel was thrown around her shaking shoulders, and she sat up, looking around quickly for Jake. He wasn't there!

Jane noticed for the first time that the captain and the men were still at the rail, the silence gripping them ominously tense. No, he couldn't still be in the water with that gray horror! Why hadn't they pulled him out? She was on her feet, elbowing her way through the men at the rail. She stared down at the water that had cradled her so lovingly such a short time ago and now seemed to hold all the horrors of hell. There was Jake's crisp black head, but he seemed so terribly far away from the white life-preserver in the water.

"He was right beside me," she whispered to Benjamin, her hand grabbing his arm in a panicky grip. "My God, what happened? He was right beside me!"

His eyes did not leave the triangular gray fin that seemed to be circling behind Dominic's powerful, still-moving figure. "The shark was headed right for you," he said tersely. "We would never have gotten you out in time. Jake cut through the water between you to divert him."

That loud splashing, she thought dazedly, it had been Jake, deliberately baiting the shark away from her.

"He's going to die," she moaned, as she watched the strong arms cleave through the water with boundless vitality. "He's going to die, and it's all my fault."

"No, I think he's going to make it." Benjamin's voice was tense. "His actions seemed to have confused the shark. He's been circling like that since we pulled you on board."

"Oh, God, please," she prayed, her eyes on that swimming figure that suddenly, wonderfully, seemed closer. "Please let him live. Please let him be all right."

Then the life preserver was over Jake's head and under his armpits. With a motion from the captain, he was jerked out of the water in the same graceless fashion that Jane had been. A cheer went up from the men as, hand over hand, they pulled him aboard like a fresh-caught marlin. They crowded around him, ridding him of the life preserver and slapping him on the back in congratulations, laughing and jesting in the sudden relief from tension.

Jane sank down on the deck, her legs suddenly too weak to hold her. She leaned against the rail, forgotten for the moment while the crew gathered around Jake. She was content to have it so. She only wanted to sit there and run her eyes over the vibrant aliveness that was Jake Dominic. It seemed a miracle that he should be there, sitting on the deck, the white towel draped over his bronze shoulders, his eyes gleaming with that familiar mocking deviltry that she had thought might be extinguished forever.

Jane felt that she was opening up like a flower as she sat looking at that dark face. The petals of her soul were blossoming and reaching forth to a sudden maturity that was as irreversible as it was beautiful. She knew with almost painful clarity that she loved Jake Dominic and would until the day she died. It was a fact so simple and undeniable that she had no defense against it. How many times had she pushed that knowledge away, afraid to admit to herself that no one else could cause her the joy and pain that he could with a word or a twitch of that crooked eyebrow? Not until that terrible moment when she thought she might lose him had the truth burst on her with the force of an exploding nova. She didn't want to live in a world without Jake Dominic. She'd want to die also if that vibrant, complex man was taken from her.

She closed her eyes. Oh, God, for once, couldn't she have

done something with less than her usual all-or-nothing style? He filled her whole life, making everything else seem unimportant in comparison.

She opened her eyes as she heard Benjamin's teasing voice across the deck. "Jake, you looked like a bloody bullfighter, cutting across in front of Jane like that. I was wishing I had a cape to throw you."

Jake Dominic pulled a face, then stood up and began to dry his hair with the towel that had been draped around his shoulders. "I would have appreciated a speargun more," he said dryly, his black eyes dancing.

Suddenly the captain reached back and touched a red stain on the white towel. "This is blood!" he said sharply. "Where are you hurt, Jake?"

Jane sat up as alert as if she'd been galvanized. Oh, no, let him not be hurt, she thought feverishly, not now!

Jake grinned lazily. "It's just a graze on my back—the shark caught me with a tooth as I swam past."

Benjamin was behind him looking at the wound with critical eyes. "It's not too bad," he decided. "But I'd better put something on it. It's a good thing it didn't bleed more; it would have driven the shark into a frenzy."

Jane could feel the blood draining from her face at the casual remark, and she pulled herself to her feet, clinging desperately to the rail. Jake had been so close to death, down there in the water. If the cut had been deeper . . . if the shark hadn't been confused . . . So close.

She saw with unbelieving eyes that both Jake and Marc were chuckling as if nothing had happened. Then she suddenly remembered Jake Dominic's expression as he pulled her along behind him—that flicker of excitement deep in the mocking eyes. He had even laughed, she thought incredulously. He had gotten some sort of queer kick out of playing with death. He had almost died, his life had almost ended, and he had laughed! She felt a burning anger start deep inside her. It was her life too that he was risking so carelessly—she wouldn't have wanted to live without him.

She moved forward slowly, pushing through the crowd that surrounded Jake Dominic, her legs shaking with a strange fatigue but charged with the force of her fury.

The laughter died in Jake's dark eyes as he caught sight of Jane's white face and blazing gold stare. His keen glance swiftly took in the violent trembling that was causing her limbs to shake, and there was a flash of concern in his face.

She stopped a few paces from the two men, her eyes fixed desperately on Jake's face. "You enjoyed it!" she accused hoarsely. "Damn you! You enjoyed it!"

Jake moved forward impulsively. "Jane—"

"You laughed!" she cried, the tears running down her face. "You got some kind of wild kick out of it all." Suddenly her fists started beating wildly at his bare, hair-roughened chest. "Damn you! Damn you!" The tears poured down her cheeks and great sobs shook her body, as her legs suddenly gave way and she felt herself falling.

Jake caught her and swung her up in his arms in one swift movement. She dimly heard Benjamin murmur, "Shock," as she clung desperately to Dominic's broad shoulders and buried her head in the wiry dark hair on his chest, while the sobs continued to rack her body.

"I'll take her," Benjamin offered quietly, and he took a step closer. Jane felt Jake's arms tighten around her, and she clung even more desperately at the threat of being separated from that vibrant strength that was now the center of her universe.

"No!" he said. "I'll take her to her cabin. Fetch her some hot tea with plenty of sugar," he said over his shoulder. "Maybe a sedative, too."

Jane could not seem to stop her tears as Dominic carried her swiftly to her cabin and deposited her on the narrow single bed.

He would have withdrawn his arms and stepped back, but she held on to him in a stranglehold, still sobbing piteously.

"Jane!" Dominic said with exasperation, trying to pry her arms from around his neck. "Jane, damn it, let me go! I've got to get this wet suit off of you."

She barely heard him, but he finally managed to unclamp her clinging arms. He sat down beside her on the bed and with swift, experienced hands stripped the wet bikini off her shaking body and wrapped her, like a papoose-child, in the warm gold blanket that he found at the foot of the bed. He went into the bathroom and came out with a thick white towel and proceeded to dry her hair, with more vigor than gentleness.

The sobs were subsiding now, but the tears still poured from a seemingly inexhaustible fount while she watched him with feverishly intent eyes. He cared for her as gently as if she were a beloved child. His face was set and stern, his dark mocking eyes strangely serious. When he'd finished these tasks, he threw the towel on the floor beside the bed and merely sat looking at her, his eyes filled with a helpless exasperation at the tears that wouldn't cease.

"Damn it, Jane, you'll make yourself sick," he said huskily. "Stop it!"

"Hold me," she whispered. "Just hold me, please." She fought to release her arms from the strictures of the gold blanket to pull him to her, but he stopped her with a swift movement.

"No, lie still, I'll come to you."

He stretched full length on the narrow bed beside her and pulled her blanket-wrapped body into his arms, fitting her head in the curve of his shoulder. "Now, will you stop that damn crying?" he said hoarsely, his hands running soothingly over her back through the wool blanket.

She knew a dreamy contentment as he continued to stroke and caress her while she lay curled against him. She even imagined she felt a light kiss pressed against her temple when she snuggled to get even closer to him.

"I can come back later," Benjamin said dryly from the door.

Jake muttered an imprecation and jerked away from Jane as if he'd been burned. "She's shaking," he said, running his hand through his hair as he swung off the bed and onto his feet. "And she can't stop crying."

"May I suggest that a heating pad and a large handkerchief might prove to be considerably safer for the girl?" Marc offered politely, coming forward with a glass of water and two tablets in his hands.

Jake shot him a quelling glance and took the water and tablets. He sat back down on the bed and cradled Jane's shoulders in one arm while he fed her the pills and water. She took them like an obedient child, and as he laid her carefully back on the pillow he observed with anxiety the dark circles beneath her eyes and the pale, pinched cheeks. "She's too damn docile," he said thickly. "Where's the tea?"

"She won't need it," Benjamin answered laconically. "She'll be out in a few minutes. That sedative is fairly strong."

Already Jane could feel the fuzziness that dulled the edges of their voices above her head and lessened the nameless urgency that drove her to keep Jake within constant reach of her hand. She could see Marc Benjamin's speculative gray gaze as if from far away.

"You know, I would never have thought that she would fall apart like this," she heard the captain say thoughtfully. "She's really a very strong personality."

Jake turned on him savagely. "She was almost eaten alive by a shark!" he said explosively. "How the hell do you expect her to react?"

Benjamin shook his head. "Take it easy. I'm not impugning the courage of your little lamb," he drawled. "We both know that she's got plenty of it. It was just a comment." He moved forward to put a hand on Jake's shoulder. "You'd better come along and let me tend to that graze."

"In a minute," Jake said absently, putting the glass on the bedside table and brushing the red ringlets away from Jane's forehead. "I don't want to leave her like this."

She could dimly see his concerned face hovering over her, before her lids closed unexpectedly and there was only the darkness.

Jane awoke several times that day, only to fall back into that cocoon of sleep. She was conscious of Jake's presence several times, and of the sound of voices reverberating as if from the bottom of a well, but she could make no sense of the words. Once Simon was there with a luncheon tray, a worried expression on his handsome young face, but she couldn't rouse herself from her lethargy enough to obey his plea to eat something. She only wanted to return to the healing darkness.

It was late afternoon when the sedative finally wore off. She was alone in the cabin when she opened her eyes and looked around sluggishly. Her mouth felt dry and sour, she had a dull, throbbing ache in her head. That sedative must have had the force of a blackjack, she thought blearily, as she struggled to her feet on legs made of rubber. She dropped the gold blanket on the bed and then snatched it up again as she remembered that she was naked and her tiny cabin had recently resembled a Cecil B. De Mille crowd scene.

She vaguely remembered Jake's removing her tiny bikini, but she felt no embarrassment at the thought. Holding the blanket around her, she stumbled to the chest of drawers and drew out the gauzy green polka-dot shorty pajamas. She put them on hurriedly and ducked into the bath to brush her teeth and wash her face.

She was feeling ridiculously weak as she tottered back to the bed and slipped between the sheets. On the bedside table she discovered a thermos of rich beef broth, but she had only a scant cup before she was overcome with the lethargy that she seemed unable to conquer. She barely managed to pull the cover up about her before she was asleep once again.

Probably because the principal effect of the drug had worn off, her sleep was much lighter and more restless. She was plagued by hideous nightmares in which she was being chased by a giant shark with horrible sharp teeth, and each time she was about to be savaged, Jake Dominic swam in front of the monster and was devoured in her place.

Over and over the dream replayed in her subconscious, until she awoke with a shrill scream of pure agony on her lips.

Jake's face was above her, his face drawn with anxiety. He was shaking her roughly. "Damn it, wake up," he said harshly. "For God's sake, it's only a dream. Come out of it, baby!"

She threw herself at him, wrapping her arms around him convulsively while the silent tears flowed down her face. "You're alive!" she whispered achingly, her ear pressed to his chest. She could feel the steady throbbing of his heart through the fine material of his shirt, and it was gloriously reassuring. "I thought you were dead. I thought he'd eaten you!"

"I'm fine. It's you we've been worried about." He pushed her away to look at her face. His hand brushed at her tear-stained cheek with a gesture of exasperation. "If you don't stop that crying, you'll drown us both."

Jane chuckled huskily and wiped her eyes childishly with the back of her hand. "I'm sorry. I can't seem to stop. Stupid, isn't it?"

"Very," he said succinctly, as he pulled a handkerchief from his pocket and handed it to her. "Just the sort of thing that I would expect from an annoying brat like you."

She smiled, thinking how handsome he looked in his navy-blue slacks and white sport coat.

"I'm all right now," she assured him, wiping her eyes

thoroughly. "I expect it was only the nightmare. Please go on to dinner."

"My dear girl, dinner was three hours ago. I was just stopping by to check on you before I called it a night." A startled glance at the bedside clock verified that it was after eleven. She had slept all day and half the evening! "Ahmet sends his regards and hopes that you'll be well enough to receive a call from him tomorrow."

"Oh, I'll be back to work tomorrow," Jane said, surprised. "I'm fine now."

"So fine that you wake up screaming," Jake said grimly, his eyes fixed on the delicacy of her heart-shaped face. "We'll see how you are in the morning."

"It was only the nightmares," she insisted, her eyes darkening with strain. "I keep having the same dream over and over." She shivered uncontrollably.

"I can guess what about," he said slowly. "An experience like that may give you nightmares for some time to come."

Jane swallowed anxiously at the thought of facing that horror every time she fell asleep. "I suppose so," she replied nervously, moistening her lips. "Well, I'll just have to contend with them, won't I?" She smiled shakily.

"The hell you will!" Jake said abruptly, his dark eyes flaming. "I'm not about to let you shake yourself to pieces in this clothes closet of a cabin."

"It's quite a nice cabin," she said defensively, looking up at him in bewilderment.

"Jane, for God's sake, don't argue with me. I do not intend to spend the rest of the night in this cracker box holding your hand, after already spending the best part of the day here. There's just not enough room!" He stooped and picked her up in his arms, blanket and all, and strode swiftly from the cabin.

She looked up into his grim face and asked quietly. "I hate to be overly curious, but may I ask where you're taking me?"

"Why, to my bed, of course." She stiffened in surprise, and he mistook her response for resistance. "Don't fight me, Jane. I'm not leaving you alone tonight. You can battle your own dragons some other night, when you're more fit." His mouth twisted cynically. "You can't claim that one night in my bed will ruin your reputation, when everyone on the ship assumes you're already very familiar with it."

When she merely continued to look at him with wide eyes, he went on aggressively. "Damn it, I'm not about to rape you, redhead, I just want to take care of you." His mouth twisted wryly, as he added, "In a bed where I won't develop a displaced sacroiliac."

She didn't answer, but her arms tightened around him nervously as he opened the door to his cabin and marched across the room to the king-sized bed and deposited her on the black velvet spread. He stepped back to look down at her still figure with wary dark eyes.

"What, no arguments?" he asked, arching an eyebrow inquiringly. "I expected you to fight me tooth and nail. You must be in worse shape than I thought."

She looked up at him serenely, her hair a brilliant flame on the black spread. "Why should I fight you?" she asked quietly. "You're quite right. I don't have any reputation to lose and I don't want to be alone tonight."

The wariness was still in his eyes. "That's very sensible of you," he said skeptically. "Not at all what one would expect from a frightened virgin."

"Really?" Jane sat up and threw off the gold blanket. "I'll try to act more in character next time."

His dark eyes were fixed compulsively on the bodice of the shorty nightgown. Her high firm breasts were clearly outlined beneath the gauzy material, even to the shadowy pink of her nipples.

"Not on my account," he drawled softly as he came toward

her. His hand reached out to stroke her cheek with a gentle hand. "You look like a baby fresh from its bath," he said lightly. His hand rubbed her cheekbone with the sensual pleasure of a man stroking his favorite kitten.

Her breath caught in her throat, and she looked up into his dark eyes and saw a flicker in the hidden depths that caused her heart to increase its tempo. Then the flicker was gone and he had turned and walked toward the bathroom.

The usual mockery was in his voice as he said over his shoulder. "If you want to spare me your girlish blushes, I'd turn out the light." He disappeared into the bathroom.

Jane dove into the black velvet bed as if a nude Jake Dominic were going to appear the next instant. Then she had to jump out again to flick out the light by the door, and scrambled back under the covers again. It seemed an incredibly short time until the light in the bathroom was off and the door opened. She stiffened involuntarily as the bed sank under Dominic's weight when he slipped beneath the covers. She could feel the mattress shift while he stretched out like a cat, then turned over to rest on his back.

There was a moment of strained silence that stretched on interminably before he suddenly spoke. "For God's sake, relax!" he said with exasperation. "I'm not going to pounce on you. I can feel you trembling clear over here."

"I'm sorry," she whispered shakily, "I guess I'm nervous. I've never done anything like this before."

"That makes two of us," he said wryly, turning his shadowy face to where she lay. "I think I can safely say that I've never occupied a bed with a woman without intending to reap the full benefit."

"It must be difficult for you," she said huskily. "I never meant to be such a bother."

"Be quiet," he said impatiently. "And for pity's sake stop that trembling."

There was a moment of tension that was as fine as a stretched violin string. "Jake." Her voice was a hesitant whisper. "Will you hold me?"

She heard him inhale sharply and felt the sudden tension that tautened his body. "You can't be that innocent," he said roughly. "Don't try to play games with me, Jane. I'm finding this situation difficult enough."

She too was finding it difficult enough, she thought wildly. It had taken all her courage to voice that whispered plea, and she had only impressed him as being a tease. She took a deep breath, and before she could change her mind, she scooted over suddenly to press against the warmth of his naked body with trembling urgency.

"Please, Jake," she said huskily, pressing her soft lips to the throbbing pulse in his throat. "I'm not playing any games."

His body stiffened as if electrified, and his arms automatically went around her. "My God," he said raggedly. His arms tightened ruthlessly. "Damn it, how much do you think I can take?"

His hands began a feverish sensual symphony over her shoulders and back while his lips touched hotly on her ears and throat. Then his lips found hers, and it was like no kiss she had ever known. It was as if he were famished for the taste and texture of her. His mouth rubbed and caressed her own with frantic hunger before parting her lips to probe intimately with his tongue, and his hands moved down to cup her bottom and lift her to his aroused loins with heated urgency. His lips ravished her with breathless need while he rubbed her softness against his muscular body with frenzied movements.

He buried his lips in her throat, his voice muffled as he said hoarsely, "God, I want you! I've been going insane for weeks. Open your mouth, love, I want every bit of you." His lips covered hers again, and she felt as if she were writhing in a flame of need. She moaned deep in her throat, and he chuckled huskily.

"What a lovely sound," he groaned, his chest heaving. "I'm going to enjoy making you cry out for me, sweetheart."

Her hands slipped around his neck to become entangled in the crisp darkness of his hair, while his hand slipped under the loose gauze top to cup her small breasts in his hands, his thumbs teasing the nipples while his tongue invaded her mouth in numerous maddening forays.

She arched against him helplessly and again made a sound more purr than moan. "Jake, please, I want . . ." She trailed off as he suddenly lifted the gauze top to bare her breasts to his ravaging lips and tongue.

He chuckled again. "I know what you want, little love," he said mischievously, nibbling teasingly at a rosy nipple. "And I have every intention of giving it to you." His tongue toyed with the other peak lazily. "In my own time. Damn, I knew you'd be this responsive!"

He rolled her over and with deft experienced hands pulled the gauze top over her head and threw it to the side. "How lovely you are," he said thickly, as his hands cupped her breasts. "All strength and silk and fire." His head bent slowly to take her lips in a long slow kiss. "I've got to have you, Jane," he said hoarsely. "If you don't want it, for God's sake tell me to stop." He nibbled at the lobe of her ear. "I'm going to take you if you don't tell me no."

Her hands caressed the light stubble on his cheek with loving hands. "I'll never tell you no, Jake Dominic," she said tenderly, "until the day that you tell me to leave you."

His body stiffened above her, and he was suddenly still. His lips lingered for a moment on her earlobe, and then he breathed incredulously. "My God, what am I doing?"

In one swift movement he rolled away from her, leaving her bewildered, and chilled without the warmth of his arms. He reached over and fumbled with the lamp on the bedside table. Suddenly the cabin was illuminated by a pool of light.

Jane sat up dazedly, her golden eyes smoky and clouded with desire, her bare breasts still swollen and rosy from his lips. What had happened? she wondered in bewilderment as she watched Jake swing out of bed and march angrily to the wardrobe. When he returned, he was shrugging into a wine velour robe, and he tossed her a man's white shirt.

"Cover up!"

She looked up pleadingly into his dark eyes, but there was relentless purpose in their ebony depths. She slipped on the white shirt and began to button it despondently. "What did I do wrong?" she asked quietly.

"Not a damn thing," he said harshly, his black eyes flashing. "It was as pretty a seduction as I've ever seen. You had me crazy for you."

She brushed the flaming ringlets from her forehead, her puzzled eyes on his dark angry face. He fumbled in the drawer of the nightstand and drew out a pack of cigarettes and an ashtray, which he placed on the table.

"I didn't know you smoked," she said, rolling up the sleeves of the shirt.

"I don't. I gave it up years ago," he answered harshly as he lit one and inhaled deeply. "I keep them around for moments of stress, and this, my dear Jane, is definitely a moment of stress!" He sat down on the bed and eyed her bare golden legs impatiently. She quickly straightened and tucked them under her tailor fashion.

His face was set and hard, and he spoke curtly. "I'm in no mood for evasion, Jane, so you'd be wise to be honest with me. You knew exactly what you were doing to me tonight. You also knew that I had no intention of taking you, before you staged your seduction scene." His lips twisted sardonically. "May I ask why I was chosen to initiate you into the carnal arts? It couldn't be, by any chance, that you'd taken it into that tiny little mind that you owe me something?"

Her golden eyes widened. "Owe you something?" she asked, puzzled. It had never occurred to her that he would interpret her action as anything but what it was.

"It's remarkably coincidental that the day I'm instrumental in saving you from a shark, you feel called upon to present me with your nubile young body."

"It's true I owe you my life," she said quietly. "But that isn't the reason that I want to belong to you."

"Then may I ask why I'm so honored?" he asked, looking down at his cigarette with narrowed eyes.

"I love you," she said simply, her golden eyes serene.

His dark gaze flew to meet hers, and he smiled cynically. "I might be touched if I thought you knew what you were talking about. If such an emotion exists, it's not the hodgepodge of gratitude and sex that you're feeling right now."

"You're wrong, gratitude has nothing to do with it," she said softly, her eyes lingering on the bold planes of his face. "As for sex, if this sample was anything to go by, it promises to be pretty terrific, but I made the first move before I knew that, Jake."

His gaze returned to the glowing end of his cigarette. "So when did you get this great revelation?" he asked mockingly. "I saw no sign of it before tonight."

"I only knew today," she said calmly. "I watched you sitting on that deck looking so blasted pleased with yourself that I wanted to murder you, and I knew that I'd love you forever." Her lips twisted wryly. "It came as quite a shock to me."

"And you say it's not gratitude," he scoffed. "Let's face it, Jane, you were in a highly emotional state and you convinced yourself that you were feeling something that just wouldn't exist under normal conditions."

She shook her head, her lips curving in a tender smile. "If you want to believe that, I can't stop you. I just know what I feel, Jake."

His eyes were diamond-hard as he looked up again. "Then

you'd better get over it damn quick. In case you hadn't noticed, I'm not a safe person to care about. You'd come out of any relationship with me covered with battle scars. I don't think you could survive the game the way I play it."

She smiled sadly. "Don't worry about me—I'll survive," she said gently. "You're not responsible in any way."

He muttered a curse beneath his breath and crushed the cigarette out in the ashtray. "Charming," he said savagely. "So I'm to take what you offer and when I tire of you, simply cast you aside?"

"I hope not," she replied tranquilly. "I'm going to work very hard to make sure that I always have a place in your life." Her expression was endearingly earnest as she continued. "I promise I won't make things uncomfortable for you."

"You're not going to get the chance," he said roughly. "I've never found the idea of seducing innocents particularly appealing, and I have no intention of assuming the responsibility of your brand of commitment." His lips tightened ruthlessly. "I admit that I have a yen for that alluring little body of yours, but I can satisfy that urge with any number of women." His eyes were merciless on her suddenly pale face. "Benjamin said I should have sent you home, and he was right. You leave tomorrow."

She had listened to him silently, pain gradually dulling the gold of her eyes. She shook her head. "I won't go," she told him quietly. "I won't be a bother to you, but I won't leave you either, Jake."

"God, what a little fool you are!" he said brutally. "Don't you know when you're fighting a losing cause? I use women, I don't love them. What makes you think that a fresh-faced college kid is going to change my mind?"

"I don't expect you to love me," she answered passionately. "I only know that I love you and want to be with you. I don't know what place I'll find in your life. But whether it's as your mistress or your friend or just a steward on the *Sea Breeze*, I won't stand any chance at all if I let you send me away. I'm not leaving you, Jake!"

"I think you will," he said coolly, "when you find what a mistake you're making."

She shook her head, her eyes bright with unshed tears. "I told you once that there is only one way for me. It's still the truth, Jake."

His dark eyes were burning fitfully as he stared into her woebegone face. "Damn it to hell." His tone was exasperated. "You know I'll hurt you if you stay. Why can't you be sensible and put a few thousand miles between us? You just might be safe then."

She shook her head again, and suddenly two tears brimmed over and ran silently down her cheeks.

"Oh God, not again!" he groaned, and pulled her into his arms, rocking her as if she were a child and pushing her face into the soft velour of his robe. He stroked her hair gently for a long peaceful moment before he pleaded huskily, "Won't you please go away, redhead? I don't want to hurt you."

Jane nestled closer to his strong, warm body, her hand tangled intimately in the wiry dark patch of hair on his chest. She pressed her lips lovingly to his shoulder. "I have a chance," she whispered. "You like me." She kissed him again. "You want me. That's quite a bit to start with."

His chuckle reverberated under her ear. "You're so blasted determined," he said softly, his fingers gently rubbing the sensitive cord behind her ear. "I'm going to get rid of you, you know. I won't stand by and watch you mess up your life for an infatuation."

"You can try to discourage me tomorrow," she whispered teasingly. "But will you hold me tonight?"

He laughed again and shook his head ruefully. "Not on your life, redhead," he told her firmly. "I'm not about to let you consolidate your position in that particular fashion. We both know that you'd be my mistress by morning."

"Exactly," she said, grinning.

He slapped her lightly on her bottom and then pushed her firmly away. Pulling back the covers, he motioned sternly. "Get in, brat, and stay on your own side from now on."

She scrambled happily under the covers and scooted obediently to the far side of the bed. Without removing his robe, he also slipped beneath the covers, and flipped out the lamp. Jane sighed with contentment as she curled up on her side and prepared to go to sleep, which she did in only a few minutes.

On the other side of the broad expanse of mattress, Jake Dominic listened to the girl's even breathing with a grim smile on his face and eyes that were alert and wide awake. It was several hours later before he too fell asleep.

eight

SIMON WAS WAITING FOR HER ON DECK A few mornings later, and, as he turned to watch her hurrying toward him, Jane felt a thrill of uneasiness as she noticed the troubled expression on his usually sunny face.

"What is it, Simon?" she asked, puzzled.

"Look, Jane, it's none of my business," he burst out abruptly, running a hand through his blond hair. "But I thought someone should tell you."

Jane felt a cold finger of fear run down her spine at Simon's words. Her mind jumped immediately to the subject that dominated her life these days. She turned away to stare sightlessly at the sparkling sapphire sea. If Jake insisted, how could she prevent him from physically ejecting her from the *Sea Breeze*? Was this why Simon was so embarrassed and hesitant this morning?

Simon drew a deep breath. "Jane, I don't know how deeply you're involved with Jake Dominic, and I won't ask you to confide in me," he said awkwardly. "But I think you should know that he sent a radio message yesterday morning."

She turned to look at him, her body tense. "Yes, Simon?" she whispered.

He frowned unhappily, his blue eyes warmly sympathetic. "Oh, damn!" he said desperately. "The message was to Lola

Torres. He invited her to join the cruise. He's sending a launch this afternoon to pick her up at Cozumel."

Lola Torres. For a moment Jane couldn't place the name, and then it clicked depressingly. Lola Torres was a very well known personality—though in some circles she was considered more notorious than famous. The gorgeous Spanish-American woman had clawed her way up from the barrios of Los Angeles to become one of the highest-priced call girls in the world, but this hadn't satisfied her. She had wanted to be her own woman, and at twenty-six had written an autobiographical novel entitled, *Kiss and Tell*, wherein she had not only revealed the bedroom secrets of her famous lovers but had had the gall to rate their sexual techniques from one to ten. The book had become a best-seller, and made Lola Torres not only rich but famous. Her warm beauty and razor-sharp wit had made her a favorite on the talk-show circuit.

Jake had definitely brought out the big guns, Jane thought with a pang. He not only intended to show her her own relative unimportance in his life by flaunting another woman before her, but he'd chosen one of the most desirable women in the world to accomplish his aim.

Jane's expression was miserable as she tried to smile at Simon's worried face. "Thank you for telling me, Simon," she said dully. "You're a good friend."

Simon's blue eyes were filled with sympathy as he continued reluctantly, "That's not all, Jane. Captain Benjamin posted a new duty roster last night. You've been replaced as Brockmeyer's helper. Besides acting as Jake Dominic's meal steward, Benjamin has given you duty as Miss Torres's personal maid."

So he not only intended for her to observe his affair with Lola at agonizingly close quarters; he'd placed her quite deliberately in a humiliatingly subservient position to his mistress. He had wanted to hurt her and drive her away, and he'd chosen a method worthy of the Borgias.

She patted Simon's arm comfortingly. "It's all right, Simon." She spoke quietly, with a little ghost of a smile. "Jake's really not being as ruthless as it appears. He probably believes he's being quite benevolent. I'll be fine."

That afternoon as she watched a launch speed across the water toward the *Sea Breeze*, Jane was not quite so confident. At lunch Jake had arrogantly ordered her to be on deck to meet Miss Torres and show her to her cabin. His dark eyes had been alert for any sign of rebellion or distress on her pale heart-shaped face. She would not allow him that victory. She had merely nodded gallantly and carefully assumed a smooth mask to hide the anger and misery this new taunt had caused.

Surprisingly, Kahlid had exhibited a warm sympathy in the brief moment before she had collected the dishes to return to the kitchen. His dark eyes glowing gently, he had leaned closer to whisper in an undertone, "Never mind, *ma petite*, his little flings with the lovely Lola never last more than a week or so. He will soon return to you."

Jane had smiled warmly at the sheikh, glad even for this meager comfort. She had murmured a shy farewell in Arabic and quickly left the lounge.

Jake Dominic strolled casually to the rail, his eyes on the approaching launch. He was dressed in close-fitting dark trousers and a gray jacket, a black-and-white ascot knotted around his strong brown throat.

Jake's eyes darted to where Jane waited, her face pale and tense, her body straight and stiff in the steward's uniform. He said in an undertone that only she could hear, "I could order that launch to take you into Cozumel, you know." He continued persuasively. "In two hours you could be on a plane to Miami."

She shook her head silently, her eyes fixed on the launch with strained pain-filled eyes.

There was a flicker of frustration in the dark eyes as he muttered impatiently under his breath, "Then it's on your head, red-head." His face resumed its usual cynical expression.

Lola Torres was even more ravishing than she was reputed to be, Jane thought wistfully as the launch drew close enough so that she could see the brunette woman standing upright in the boat, her eyes fixed eagerly on Jake Dominic's figure at the rail. Her tall voluptuous body was garbed with understated elegance in black slacks and a white silk blouse that bore the unmistakable cut of a famous French couturier. The long lovely line of her throat was exposed as she tilted her dark silky head back to look at Dominic. Her brilliant smile lit up the olive perfection of her face, and the great dark eyes sparkled eagerly as the launch came alongside.

"Jake, you consummate beast, how dare you summon me like some little harem girl?" she called merrily. "In case you haven't heard, I'm no longer in that business."

Dominic grinned mockingly as he lifted her onto the deck and kissed her lingeringly. "The thought has infinite possibilities, Lola," he said lightly. "You'd make a fantastic harem girl. In six months you'd not only be queen of the seraglio but in all probability you'd be running the country."

Dominic kissed her again on the forehead before turning her around in his arms to face Jane, his hands resting lightly on the woman's waist. "This is Jane Smith, Lola. Knowing what wardrobe you consider minimal, I took the precaution of arranging maid service for you."

There was a look of surprise in Lola Torres's eyes as they met Jane's tormented golden gaze, but her smile was warm. "*Buenas tardes*, Jane. I'm sure that we'll get along very well together."

"Jane will show you to your cabin," Jake went on smoothly as he released her. "I'll see you at dinner, Lola."

Again there was a flicker of puzzlement in Lola's face, but she nodded agreeably. "As you wish, *querido*. I am a bit tired."

Jake grinned wickedly, his eyes meeting Jane's over Lola's satin head. "Be sure you rectify that before you join me for dinner," he said caressingly. "I want you to be well rested before tonight, Lola."

Jane's eyes blazed with anger at the sheer cruelty of the taunt, her fists clenching with helpless fury. She dropped her gaze hurriedly as her eyes met the shrewd, speculative gaze of the other woman. "If you'll follow me, Miss Torres, I'll show you to your cabin." She spoke huskily, trying to blink back the tears of rage and pain.

"But of course," Lola Torres replied absently, her eyes still on Jane's unhappy face, and with a final flashing smile at Jake, she followed Jane's swiftly moving figure.

The cabin that Lola Torres had been allocated was only a short distance from Jake's, Jane noticed morosely. Though smaller than the master cabin, it was a good size, and the decor was clearly aimed at pleasing a woman's taste. The thick carpet was a dusty rose, and the white satin spread on the bed and the cream velvet Queen Anne occasional chairs were elegant.

Jane opened the adjoining door to show the older woman the pretty pink vanity and shower area, before crossing to the porthole and throwing it open to let in the fresh coolness of the ocean breeze.

"Your luggage will be brought down shortly, Miss Torres," Jane said with an effort, trying not to look at the warm beauty whom Jake had so recently held in his arms. "I'll unpack for you as soon as they arrive."

"Call me Lola," the other said casually, closing the door and crossing to the bed to stretch out on the white satin coverlet. "Sit down and talk to me, Jane." Her eyes were fixed searchingly on Jane's vulnerable face. "Now, I want to know what game Jake is playing. Will you tell me?"

Jane smiled ruefully. Those gorgeous black eyes evidently concealed a perceptiveness that was positively intimidating. "Jake knows that I love him," she confessed simply, surprising even herself with her frankness. Perhaps it was the gentle warmth that Lola exuded that made her so easy to confide in.

"Yes, he would realize that in short order," Lola said impatiently. "You're fairly transparent." She bit her lip in perplexity. "But Jake usually doesn't find it amusing to be cruel to those who develop an infatuation with him. He merely ignores them. He was really quite vicious to you up on deck."

"He wants to send me back to college," Jane explained quietly. "I don't intend to go."

Lola nodded, comprehension lighting her eyes. "So he sends for me to discourage you," she said wryly. "It's not the greatest compliment I have received."

Jane rushed to reassure her. "It's a very great compliment, Lola." Her tone was earnest. "Who else could show me, just by comparison, how inadequate I am. You're quite a woman."

Lola smiled gently. "You're a generous child, aren't you? I can see why Jake is going to so much trouble over you." Her face was serious as she continued. "He's quite right, you know. He's much too tough and ruthless for a nice infant like you."

Jane shrugged. "Sometimes you can't pick and choose the things that are good for you. Sometimes things just happen." She smiled sadly. "If Jake had to choose anyone to try to discourage me, I'm glad it was you, Lola." She stood up and walked to the door. "I'll go and see what's holding up your luggage."

Jake wouldn't have been pleased at the result of his Machiavellian machinations. Far from being aggravated, Jane's agony and jealousy were inexpressibly soothed by her forced association with Lola Torres. Though both women avoided any further conversation of a personal nature, they got along quite companionably in the hours preceding dinner.

As Jane had expected, this period of tranquillity was to be shattered that evening at dinner. In honor of Lola Torres's arrival, both Jake Dominic and Ahmet Kahlid wore white dinner jackets and black ties, while the lady herself was lushly alluring, in an orange chiffon gown that clung lovingly to each generous curve.

Brockmeyer had outdone himself to provide an epicurean delight fit for the gods. The table was set with Royal Doulton china and fine white damask linen, and lit by soft, romantic candlelight. These accoutrements formed an ironically civilized background for Jake's ruthless campaign to savage Jane's raw emotions.

He was nothing if not thorough in his tactics, Jane thought almost hysterically at the end of dinner. He was absolutely charming and unfailingly attentive to Lola and coldly impersonal and brisk with her. He spoke only once to Jane during dinner, giving her a curt order to refill Miss Torres's wineglass.

As the meal progressed, Jake's sexual innuendos as he lingeringly caressed the Spanish-American woman became almost too much for Jane to bear. It was with heartfelt relief that she finished serving the after-dinner coffee and prepared to leave the lounge. But it seemed that she wasn't to be allowed even that small mercy.

Jake looked up with the sharp eyes of a hawk as she was walking quietly toward the door. "Wait, Jane," he ordered peremptorily as the trio rose from the table. His eyes were fiercely mocking as he said softly, "I think you had better stay. We may need something."

Jane's golden eyes held the same dumb misery as an animal in pain when she returned his mocking look. She swallowed hard and turned back obediently.

Lola Torres cast a shrewd glance at Jane's shadowed face and then placed a caressing hand on Jake's sleeve. "Send her away, *querido*," she murmured, pouting seductively. "You know I'm not at all fond of sharing the attention of handsome men."

There was a flash of displeasure in Jake's eyes before he smiled down at Lola's entreating face. "She would hardly qualify as competition for you, Lola," he said silkily. "She's only here for your convenience."

Jane flinched as if she had been struck, and she grew even paler. How much more of this could she survive? she wondered desperately.

Unexpectedly, Ahmet Kahlid came to her rescue. "Send the little one away, Jake," he said gallantly, his teeth flashing white in his bearded face. "I wish to wait on this enchanting creature myself. Who knows? By the time the evening is over, she may discover that I'm far more irresistible than you."

Jake frowned and opened his mouth to protest, but Jane had taken advantage of Ahmet's first plea to slip quietly out the door.

She felt passionately grateful to Kahlid for his intervention. She didn't know how she would have been able to tolerate another thirty minutes of Jake Dominic's refined torture. She scurried swiftly away, putting a safe distance between herself and the lounge, almost as though she expected Jake to appear in pursuit.

Like an animal searching for a secluded place to tend its wounds, she hid on a deserted deck, curling up in a deck chair to gaze out at the serenity of the silver-streaked sea. She stayed there for a long time, trying to banish the memory of the evening and to regain the strength of will that Jake had almost destroyed. How was she to last through the days ahead? she wondered despairingly. She would. She must. But, fresh from the agony of Jake's rejection, it seemed a herculean task.

When she had finally composed herself somewhat, she reluctantly left her peaceful haven and made her way to her cabin. She would take a long hot shower and go to bed, she thought resolutely. Perhaps if she tried very determinedly, she would be able to forget the thought of Lola in Jake's bed and find the welcome oblivion of sleep.

Unfortunately, this was not to be the case. After the hot shower she was more wide awake than ever. She changed to her shorty pajamas and flicked off the light. She was about to slip beneath the covers when there was a knock at the door. She frowned in puzzlement and then relaxed. It must be Simon checking to see how she had weathered the evening.

"I'll be right there," she called, and grabbed the matching polka-dot robe. It offered very little protection, as it also came only to her thighs, but at least it covered the transparency of the gown. She turned the light back on and padded barefoot to the door.

It was not Simon. Ahmet Kahlid stood at the door, still dressed in his dazzling white dinner jacket. He held a bottle of champagne in one hand and two champagne glasses in the other. His dark eyes were sparkling brightly, and there was a genial smile on his face.

His gaze roamed frankly and appreciatively over her scantily clad body. "How very alluring you are in that, *ma petite*," he boomed cheerfully. "You look like a young dryad."

She peeked up at him warily. "I was just about to go to bed," she said carefully. "I'm afraid you'll have to excuse me."

He shook his head stubbornly, his smile not losing a bit of its conviviality. "I most certainly will not excuse you," he said breezily. "I couldn't bear to think of you alone and brooding in your cabin. You must have a glass of this most excellent champagne with me so that you will feel happier."

"I appreciate your concern, but I really couldn't—" The rest of her sentence was lost, as Jane was forced to move quickly aside to avoid being trampled by Kahlid when he stepped into the cabin and looked around the room appraisingly.

"How can you breathe in this cabin?" he asked wonderingly. "I can hardly turn around." He put the glasses on the night table and sat down casually on the bed. He patted it invitingly and said softly, "Come and have your champagne, *ma petite*, and soon all your pain will bubble gently away."

Jane closed the door and came forward to sit gingerly on the bed beside him. She didn't want to offend the sheikh by refusing the comfort he offered. He had been very sympathetic today, and she was grateful for the help he'd extended tonight in getting her out of the lounge.

"I'll just have one glass, then," she said quietly.

"Good," Kahlid answered approvingly, and he opened the champagne and poured the frothy liquid into the crystal glasses. "You will see that I am right," he continued gently. "It is never good to be alone when one is unhappy."

Jane sipped the champagne slowly, liking the tart taste tingling on the tip of her tongue. Perhaps Kahlid was right at that, she thought. She certainly felt better than she had earlier in the evening. There was something oddly soothing about the big friendly Arab.

"It's very good champagne," she offered, smiling shyly. "But shouldn't you return to Jake and Miss Torres?"

He shook his head ruefully. "I'm very much afraid I was *de trop*. Jake has no desire for a third party when he is with a beautiful woman."

Jane bit her lip and lowered her eyes unhappily.

Kahlid made an impatient gesture. "What a fool I am. Forgive me, little Jane, I did not think." He poured some more champagne into her glass and then set the bottle on the table. "He is an idiot, my friend Jake," he went on gently. "Lola is a very desirable woman, but you have something special, Jane."

Jane stared at him, mesmerized by the intentness in the liquid darkness of Kahlid's eyes. Kahlid, too, was so absorbed that he did not hear the quiet opening of the door.

"Cozy. Very cozy," Jake Dominic said with savage sarcasm. "I must compliment you on your progress, Ahmet, but did you notice that bed is a bit too narrow for a successful seduction?"

Kahlid and Jane both looked up, startled, at Jake standing in the open doorway. He was still dressed in the white dinner jacket, but he had removed the black tie, and his white shirt was left unbuttoned at the throat. His dark hair was slightly rumpled, giving him the look of a rakish pirate. His face, too, had the taut ruthlessness and the blazing fury of a buccaneer about to be deprived of his prize.

Ahmet took one look at that cool deadly anger and instinctively moved away from Jane.

His tone was jovial, but his dark eyes were wary as he said flippantly, "Jake, my friend, you are most unwelcome. I thought I left you very well occupied, and yet here you are interfering with my own pleasure." He shrugged. "I will, however, be magnanimous and offer you a glass of your own champagne before you leave."

Jake Dominic's eyes were molten coals as his gaze took in the two champagne glasses and the half-empty bottle. "You don't usually have to get your women drunk to make them willing, Ahmet."

"She's not drunk," Kahlid said indignantly. "She merely needed soothing after the most unnatural way you savaged the poor *petite* tonight."

Jane shook her head to clear it of both the champagne and the sudden shock of Jake's appearance. "Please, won't you both go away?" she said huskily. "I can't take much more of this."

"You see?" Kahlid charged unhappily. "You have completely spoiled the mood, Jake. Now, go away, and I'll try to repair the damage you have done."

"I'm afraid you'll have to be the one to leave, Ahmet." Jake spoke with deadly softness. "I thought I'd made it clear that Jane was out of bounds."

Kahlid smiled genially. "But that was before you imported the lovely Miss Torres for your pleasure. You made it quite obvious that you were finished with your little servant girl, so why should I not enjoy her?" he asked with utmost reasonableness.

"You're not one for a *ménage à trois*, Jake, so don't be like a dog in a manger."

Jake's lips tightened, and his eyes flashed dangerously. "You're wrong, Ahmet, I'm not finished with her. I've barely begun. You'd be wise to leave us before I forget that you're my guest."

Kahlid rose slowly to his feet, his face composed. "As you wish. I have no desire to insult my host by trespassing on what is his." His dark eyes were reproachful. "It was a natural mistake. How was I to know you were so possessive of the girl? You should have made your desires more clear."

"I assure you that from now on my desires will be crystal-clear," Dominic said between his teeth, his furious eyes on Jane's bewildered face and flimsily clad figure. "Now, get the hell out of here before I lose what control I still possess."

Kahlid gave Jane one last regretful glance and moved toward the door. As he passed Jake Dominic's taut, relentless figure, he paused and said calmly. "In order to avoid further confusion, may I ask if Miss Torres is also in the same category?"

Dominic shrugged, his burning eyes fixed on the small red-haired figure on the bed. "Lola may do as she wishes," he said disinterestedly. "Just make damn sure you stay away from Jane!"

The speculation in Ahmet Kahlid's eyes changed to satisfaction. "Well, that is something, at least," he said philosophically. His doleful face was brightening by the second as he went through the open door and closed it gently behind him.

Jane was suddenly conscious of the brevity of her gown and matching robe under the scorching black eyes, which seemed to strip her with insulting thoroughness. She tucked her legs beneath her on the bed and folded her arms around herself with an involuntary shiver as she met Jake's scathing glance across the room.

Then she raised her chin defiantly as the sheer gall of Jake's action came home to her. How dare he come bursting in here, expelling Kahlid without so much as a by your leave, after his own heartless behavior earlier in the evening! It didn't matter that she had been relieved and grateful to him a few minutes ago for ridding her of Kahlid and an extremely touchy situation. For all Jake knew, she may have wanted Ahmet to stay, she thought indignantly. Yet Jake had arrogantly sent him away and now was looking at her with all the possessive fury of a jealous husband. Dog in the manger indeed, she thought grimly.

"If I were you, I'd get that defiant expression off my face pretty damn quick, Jane." His soft voice was menacing. "In case you haven't noticed, I'm a little perturbed with you."

"How very unfortunate for you," Jane said nonchalantly. "There seems to be no pleasing you, Jake." She took a sip of champagne and looked up to meet his gaze with blazing golden eyes. "You may have been able to intimidate Ahmet Kahlid, but you'll find I'm not so easily impressed." She gestured toward the door. "Why don't you go back to the lounge? I'm sure your friend is even now 'poaching' on your preserves."

Dominic's eyes narrowed dangerously. "Champagne courage, Jane?" he asked harshly. "If so, I think you've had enough." He moved across the few feet separating them in a pantherish stride. He took the glass from her hand and set it on the night table.

He looked down at her mutinous face, his eyes glowing with rage. "How did you dare let him come to you?" he said thickly. "I came close to killing the bastard."

Jane caught her breath as a jolt of electricity charged through her at the intensity of his words, his voice. She lowered her eyes and answered evasively. "Ahmet was right. How could he know that it mattered to you? Wasn't the whole exercise today designed to get rid of me? What difference does it make if I leave the ship or get involved with some other man? The result would be the same."

He tangled his hand in her hair and jerked her head back so

that she was forced to meet the flaming possession in his eyes. "Believe me, it makes a difference," he said, his voice tight. "I didn't drive myself crazy trying to keep my hands off you, only to have you drop like a ripe plum into Ahmet's bed."

"You've probably seen to it that it won't be Kahlid," she said softly, some perversity tempting her to taunt him. "But what happens after I leave? What's to keep me from jumping into bed with the next likely prospect who crosses my path?" She met his eyes challengingly. "You gave me a taste of the fruit of knowledge. You can't expect me to stop at just a bite."

Dominic's hand tightened; she felt a flicker of fear at the wildness she'd unleashed in the man looking down at her.

"You damn red-haired witch!" he growled thickly, "you'll belong to no one but me!"

His mouth covered hers with the burning brutality of a brand, stamping his possession on the softness of her lips with the explosive passion of a man driven too far. His lips left hers only to press hot, hungry kisses on her throat, cheeks, and lids before returning to her mouth as if starved for the feel of it.

"God knows, I tried to send you away," he said raggedly, between the deliriously sensual kisses that made her feel as if she were slowly melting from the fire they built in her veins.

His arms went around her, lifting and straining her flimsily clad body to his warm hardness, while his lips continued their ruthless pillaging. "I knew damn well that if I kept you around I wouldn't be able to stop myself from having you. Why the hell didn't you leave when you had the chance?"

Her hands slid slowly around his neck, her lips opening and her tongue striving to return the fire he was lighting inside her. He made a sound deep in his throat that was primal in intensity, and she could feel his aroused body tremble against her own.

Suddenly he thrust her away and Jane stared in dazed bewilderment at his flushed face and dark eyes, which were glazed with desire.

"Kiss me, Jake. Please!" she whispered achingly, her body trying to nestle closer to him.

"God! Don't look at me like that or I'll take you right here on this blasted nun's bed." Closing his eyes against the invitation in hers, a great shudder shook his taut body. Suddenly his eyes flew open, and there was purpose in their dark depths.

"Come along!" he ordered curtly, swinging her off the bed and onto her feet. Grasping her by the wrist, he moved across the cabin and opened the door. He strode along the deck and down the stairs, pulling her along behind him.

"Jake, I'm not even dressed!" she cried.

He opened the door of his cabin and ushered her in ahead of him, then shut the door and locked it before turning to flick on the light. Jane gazed at him, her eyes wide, a curiously expectant expression on her heart-shaped face.

His dark eyes shuttered, Jake leaned against the door and regarded her mockingly. "Having second thoughts?" he asked. "It's too late for that, redhead. I'm not going to let you go again."

She felt a wave of shyness wash over her under that mocking gaze. She wished he'd take her in his arms again. She felt no shyness or discomfort when he was making love to her, only the throbbing need and the ecstasy of being close to him.

She lowered her eyes and whispered, "No second thoughts. I want you to make love to me, Jake."

Impulsively he took a step toward her, his hands reaching out to bring her into his arms. He stopped before he touched her, and shook his head ruefully. "Not yet. Once I begin, I'm not going to be able to stop. I don't want your first time to turn you off." His dark eyes gleamed mockingly. "I intend for there to be many more."

He moved away from the door, shrugged off his white jacket, and placed it on a hanger in the closet. He turned back to her, his hands slowly unbuttoning his white shirt while his eyes went over her in frank enjoyment. "Remind me to buy you something more sophisticated in nightwear," he said casually. "That outfit makes me feel like a child molester."

Jane turned away and gingerly sat down on the black-velvet-covered bed, feeling suddenly inadequate. What was she doing here? she wondered desperately. He was used to the most talented and versatile lovers in the world. Jake Dominic was bound to find her inexperience laughable.

She turned to look at him, her golden eyes troubled. "Jake, what do you want with me?"

He chuckled, his dark eyes dancing, as he pulled his shirt out of his trousers and stripped it off. "Trust a woman to ask a question whose answer is so blatantly self-evident." His expression turned thoughtful. "No, that isn't what you mean, is it?" He stepped out of his shiny black dress shoes. "How long did you think I could say no to you?" he asked quietly. "No one in his right mind would describe me as having a taste for self-sacrifice, and I'm quite obsessed with you. You obviously want to play at being in love with me and to taste what life as Jake Dominic's mistress is like." He smiled cynically. "This will probably be the quickest way of showing you what a mistake you're making." He padded over to where she sat on the bed, and his hand lightly caressed the curve of her cheek. "It will certainly be the most pleasurable way for me."

Her golden eyes clung to his as she rubbed her cheek against his hand like an affectionate kitten. "I do love you," she insisted quietly. She smiled tenderly into the dark intensity of his face. "It's only fair to warn you that you won't get rid of me easily."

For a moment there was an odd vulnerability in the depths of Jake's eyes, before it was replaced by the familiar mockery. "I think I have a fairly accurate idea of what makes you tick, redhead." His voice was tinged with bitterness. "I'll be willing to wager that in a month's time you'll be running for your life."

Jane's eyes met his with such glorious serenity that he caught his breath. "You'll lose," she whispered. "Believe me, you'll lose."

Her small hands reached out to caress the bronze, hair-roughened bareness of his chest. The wiry hair on her sensitive palms generated a deliciously sensual tingle. "You'll have to tell me what to do," she said huskily. "Am I supposed to be getting undressed or something?"

He looked down at her inquiring hands, which were now gently teasing his hard male nipples. "I'd say you're doing pretty well without instructions," he said dryly, his crooked eyebrow arching with humor. "As for the other, I've always had a fondness for opening my own surprise packages."

"I'll turn out the lights," she said with breathless shyness, and made a move to rise.

His hands curved around her shoulders and gently pushed her back on the bed. "No way!" His voice was hoarse. "I want to see every inch of you." He lowered his lips to plant a kiss on the tip of her nose. "One expects such privileges from one's mistress." His hands were gone from her shoulders, and he reached over and snapped on the bedside lamp before moving to the wall switch and turning out the overhead light. He returned to sit beside her on the bed, and with infinitely gentle hands he pulled her carefully into his arms.

He felt so good, so hard, so male, Jane thought as she nestled into his arms like a homing pigeon. Her arms encircled his shoulders to knead and caress the muscles of his back with a sensual pleasure in the feel of their tensile strength.

She became suddenly aware that Jake's body was oddly still and taut as his hands caressed her back slowly and carefully. "Be still a moment, love. I've been wanting this so long that I'm about to explode."

She tried to obey, but he was too close, and she loved him too much. Her eager hands fluttered eagerly over his neck. Her lips brushed teasingly at the hollow of his shoulder before she placed a hundred butterfly kisses on the warm hard flesh of his chest and shoulders.

"You little devil." He chuckled raggedly, his heart beating like a triphammer beneath her mouth. He lifted her quickly to cradle her on his knees. "So much for exercising restraint with my little virgin," he said thickly. "Oh, well, there's always the second time."

His lips once more covered hers, and all thought of restraint was a thing of the past. She felt that the hot obsessive pressure of his mouth was absorbing her into his every muscle and bone by the simple process of melting her own body with a flaming need for him. His tongue licked teasingly at her lips before entering to explore her inner sweetness, his hands curving around her to cup her breasts in his hands through the thin material of her gown. She trembled at the heat from his hands, which weighed and toyed erotically with her breasts while his tongue ruthlessly plundered her mouth.

Then, with his mouth still probing hers, his hands were working at her robe, slipping her arms out of the sleeves and letting it fall discarded across his knees. His hands moved under the top to caress the sensitive line of her satiny back with feverish hunger. His lips left hers to bury themselves in her throat, while his hands slid around to play with the naked bounty of her small pert breasts, his thumbs flicking the nipples till they were hard with arousal. "I've got to see you, sweetheart," he groaned, and with one swift movement he pulled the baby-doll top over her head and threw it carelessly on the floor. She was wearing only the bikini bottom as he swept her over to lie in the center of the ebony velvet counterpane.

He lay above her, his weight resting on one elbow while he stared raptly at the lovely silken flesh bared to his gaze. Bending to take one rosy nipple in his mouth, he teased it with maddening skill until her breath was coming in little pants, as though she had been running. Her hands went around his neck to bury themselves in his hair and bring him closer, but he pulled away.

His hands cupped her breasts, his eyes clouded with desire. "Your breasts were designed to fit into my hands," he said hoarsely. "After the night you spent in my cabin, I'd lie awake and think of you lying like this under me, your breasts warm and rosy from my kisses. It nearly drove me crazy." His heart was beating wildly as he bent and rubbed his chest sensually against her bare breasts. She shuddered beneath him, and her arms tightened convulsively around him.

Then he was gone for a minute while he stripped off the remainder of his clothes. When he returned, the warmth of his naked flesh was dizzily exciting against her own.

What followed was a breathtaking spiral of sensation that she embraced with incredulous joy. Jake brought her from peak to peak with touch and tongue and with wild words that were an aphrodisiac in themselves.

She followed blindly, while he moved her, aroused her, built in her a frantic need that she was sure could not be satisfied. Then he set about proving her wonderfully and ecstatically wrong. If there was pain, she was not aware of it, so involved was she in reaching that summit that beckoned like a pot of gold at the end of the rainbow's spectrum of sensual sensation. When she did reach it, she discovered, after the first explosion of wonder and delight, that it was not a glittering treasure after all, but the deeper, primitive satisfaction of coming home.

She wriggled contentedly in Jake's arms, her heartbeat steadying as she felt a delicious languor attack her limbs. Jake's arms tightened automatically around her, his breathing still coming in short gasps, his heartbeat thudding beneath her ear with the delicious proof of his own excitement at their union.

She kissed the smooth muscled shoulder lovingly. Then she

raised herself on one elbow to look down at him with frank enjoyment. He was so beautiful, she thought with a new pride of possession. The magnificent bone structure that was the basis of his good looks was generally overlooked, so exciting were the mobility and expressiveness of his face. Now, with his eyes closed and his face relaxed, Jane could see the beauty of line and contour that would make him devastatingly handsome even in old age.

His eyes flicked open and lit with mocking amusement as they met the serious expression in Jane's eyes. "What are you thinking, redhead?" he asked curiously as his hand reached up lazily to trace the line of her shoulder.

"I was thinking what a distinguished old man you'll make," she said dreamily.

He pulled her down to kiss her lingeringly. "I'd rather you concentrate on my present attractions and talents," he said, grinning wickedly. He settled her head back in the hollow of his shoulder, his hand stroking her red curls gently.

"Would you like for me to get you a cigarette?" she asked suddenly.

"A cigarette?" Jake asked blankly.

"I thought all men wanted a cigarette after..." She paused delicately.

"It's optional," he assured her solemnly.

She accepted that, and after another blissfully lazy moment, another thought occurred to her. "You said you only smoke in stressful situations," she said curiously. "You don't consider this a stressful situation?"

His lips brushed the top of her head tenderly before lifting her chin to meet his eyes with surprising seriousness. "I consider this situation a delight!" He kissed the tip of her nose. "I consider it sheer enchantment!" He kissed her forehead. "I consider it a miracle!" His lips tasted hers with a blinding sweetness.

"Oh, so do I," Jane said enthusiastically, when their lips finally parted. She impulsively pressed her lips to his once more, eager to experience once again that melting tenderness.

Jake's eyes were dancing with amusement when their lips parted for the second time. "I'm glad that your first experience met with your approval," he said, his lips twitching. "I gather you have no regrets about your fall from grace?"

She shook her head tranquilly, her eyes shining with tenderness. "I regard it as falling into grace. Love in itself must be the ultimate in grace." She kissed him gently. "I could never regret loving you, Jake Dominic."

His face was unreadable as he stared into her glowing, eager face. "No tears, no demands, no guilt trips," he said slowly. "You make it ridiculously easy to take advantage of you, redhead."

She giggled happily and put her head back into the spot in the hollow of his shoulder that was becoming endearingly familiar. "It is I who am taking advantage of you," she said teasingly. "You're the one with all the experience. I'm just a humble novice. It's only sensible to keep you sweet, so that you're inclined to continue the lessons."

"You'll have no problem on that score," he said dryly. "I'm having to remind myself right now that you're new at this game and mustn't be overworked."

She lifted her head to stare into his face. "Already?" she asked, startled.

"Already," he affirmed, his dark eyes twinkling mischievously. "I have an idea that you're a born voluptuary, Jane. I'm eager to test the theory."

Suddenly his eyes lost their mockery and began to burn with a flame that she had already known once tonight. The world seemed to narrow into dark velvet intimacy, and she felt her own heartbeat accelerate in response to that evocative memory.

"I'm not that sore," she whispered breathlessly.

It was all he needed to hear. He rolled her over on her back, his warm, virile body a powerful shadow above her. "I'm afraid the results would be the same even if you were," he muttered thickly. "I'll try to be gentle, sweetheart."

"It doesn't matter," she said softly, her hands moving yearningly over his shoulders.

"Yes, it does," he denied huskily as his lips hovered lingeringly over hers. "The first time was for me, redhead. This one is for you."

nine

SHE WAS LYING IN A FIELD OF FLOWERS, THE sun caressing her cheeks with its golden warmth. A gentle breeze blew the silken petals of the wild flowers in an occasional drifting kiss across her face. She smiled in childlike pleasure at the lovely sensual sensation and arched her throat to expose more of her flesh to that delicious touch.

"Open your eyes, redhead," Jake said softly. "I want to make damn sure that smile is for me."

Jane opened drowsy eyes to see Jake leaning over her, his dark eyes narrowed in amusement and, incredibly, a touch of jealousy. The early-morning sunlight streamed into the cabin, revealing the sharp lines of cynicism and weariness around his mouth.

Her hands reached up dreamily to trace the grooves with gentle fingers. "It's for you," she said simply. "Everything is for you."

"It had better be," Jake growled as he nuzzled at the hollow of her throat. "I'd best warn you that I'm feeling surprisingly possessive of you, woman. I doubt if I'd tolerate your straying while you belong to me."

He didn't see the sudden flicker of pain in her eyes at that last remark. She had forgotten, in the breathless pleasure of belonging to Jake, the transient nature of their relationship. It was obvious from his casual statement that he had not been so blinded. Well, what had she expected? she asked herself impatiently. Jake was not about to display the same love-struck idiocy as she. She must learn to accept what Jake had to offer and be satisfied, expecting no more.

He had raised his head at the involuntary stiffening of her body, and his eyes took on a ruthless hardness. "I'm sorry if you don't approve of the terms," he said coolly. "You'll just have to submit to them if you intend to remain my mistress."

She half closed her eyes to mask the misery they revealed. "You don't have a reputation for demanding such fidelity," she commented lightly.

He shrugged and rolled away from her. He rested on one elbow, his hand playing idly with her curls. "Perhaps it's because I was the first," he suggested mockingly. "I feel quite primitive at the thought of anyone else having you."

"And will you give me the same fidelity?" she asked clearly.

"For the present," he said lazily. "I imagine I'll find you more than satisfying for some time to come."

"And Lola Torres?" she asked quietly.

"I owe Lola nothing," he said with casual callousness. "She understood why she was here. She'll understand why she's no longer needed. I'll send her away today."

Jane sat upright in bed, her eyes blazing indignantly. "You can't do that," she protested. "How would she feel? You can't just snap your fingers one day and have her fly thousands of miles to join you and then just say you've changed your mind. She'd be terribly hurt."

Dominic's lips quirked with humor. "What do you suggest I do? I doubt if I'd have the stamina to satisfy another woman after you," he said mischievously. "My new mistress seems to require all my energy." He reached out to cup one enticing breast, which had been bared by her abrupt movement.

Jane brushed his hand away impatiently and pulled the covers up around her, tucking the material under her armpits to hold it in place. "Don't be ridiculous. I'd probably claw her eyes out if you so much as looked at her. I just think that you should let her make the move to go. It will let her keep her dignity."

Jake grinned, his eyes mocking. "You're very solicitous of Lola's feelings. She's tougher than you could ever be, my little crusader. It goes with the territory."

"I'm sure she was forced by circumstances into that kind of life," Jane replied in defense, her face flushing with the force of her conviction. "And whatever she did, I'm sure it was with dignity. She's more courtesan than call girl."

"A delicate distinction, I agree," he said solemnly, his dark eyes twinkling. "All right, redhead, I'll let Lola make the decision to leave." He chuckled, shaking his head ruefully. "And to think that I was trying to protect your feelings by ridding myself of a former mistress." He touched the tip of her nose with one finger. "Do me one favor. Don't try to mother Lola. She would find it most uncomfortable."

Jane gave him an indignant glance. Why did he insist on believing that she was some sort of Joan of Arc just because she displayed concern for someone's feelings? She hadn't really been in trouble since the incident at the cockfight. Well, there had been the shark, but even he couldn't blame her for that.

Pulling the cover around her, she began to scoot to the edge of the bed.

"Where do you think you're going, sweetheart?" Jake asked, watching her try to hold the sheet under her arm and still wrap the rest of it around her slight body.

"I've got to report to work."

Jake suddenly reached over and hauled her protesting body back to the center of the bed. "My dear idiot Jane, you have no work to go to. Didn't it occur to you that it would be a trifle awkward to be both my mistress and my steward?"

"I don't see why," Jane said, pouting mutinously. "Kahlid and the crew already have accepted the situation!"

"I don't give a damn about Kahlid or the crew," he said deliberately, annoyance flickering in his face. "I don't want to have to come looking for you every time I want you. It seems you need instructions in the nuances of being a mistress. Perhaps you should have a talk with Lola."

She flushed at the cruelty of the jibe but persisted nevertheless. "Perhaps we could arrange a schedule," she suggested seriously.

Dominic gave a derisive laugh. "No way!" he said emphatically. "Jane, I'll give you any damn thing you want. All I ask is that you make yourself available when I want to be with you. Is that too much to ask?"

Jane could see his viewpoint. In his eyes her reluctance to comply with his request must seem completely unreasonable. She wondered if he'd ever known a woman who preferred menial work to the sybaritic and sensual pleasures he offered.

Her golden eyes were troubled, as she pleaded hesitantly, "Couldn't we go on just as we have been?" Then, as he looked at her blankly, she blushed and rushed on hurriedly. "Except for this, of course." She made a vague gesture indicating themselves and the bed. "I don't really think I'd be happy without some work to do. I'm used to being independent."

For a moment she thought she could read understanding and sympathy in Jake's eyes before he glanced away. "I'm afraid I couldn't allow that," he said, his voice hard. "You should have realized there would be aspects of our relationship that you'd find distasteful before you committed yourself." His smile was bitter. "It's well known that I'm a selfish bastard."

"But won't you . . ." Jane was suddenly silenced by Jake's lips on hers.

"God save me from an argumentative woman," Jake said thickly. "The only sounds I want to hear from you in the next hour are the delicious little moans you made last night." His hands deliberately pulled the sheet down to her waist and began their magical play on her body. "You also may say 'yes, Jake,' he decreed with a chuckle.

Jane's breath caught in her throat, and she felt the familiar melting in her loins. Her arms slid lovingly around his neck.

"Yes, Jake," she whispered.

It was almost two hours later when Jake phoned and ordered breakfast. At the same time he gave instructions that Jane's belongings be packed and brought to his cabin. Jane did not comment on this embarrassing and arbitrary ordering of her life. However, she disappeared discreetly into the shower shortly before the steward was due to put in his appearance. When she returned to the bedroom draped inelegantly in Jake's wine velour robe, her clothes had been delivered and a portable table had been wheeled in with breakfast.

Jake was seated at the table as she walked into the room. He looked up, his dark eyes knowing. "You can't run away from it indefinitely, you know."

Jane did not pretend to misunderstand him. "I know," she replied, not looking at him as she seated herself opposite him at the table. "I just thought it would be easier to face after the first novelty had worn off. The fact that I've officially moved in with you will be old news by tomorrow."

His lips thinned with anger. "I won't have you made uncomfortable. I'll fire the first man who raises so much as an eyebrow."

Jane smiled wryly as she lifted the silver covers off the various dishes and helped herself to eggs, sausage, and toast. She was surprised that Jake didn't realize that speculation and rumors couldn't be stopped by merely ordering them to. Even though no overt mention or acknowledgment would be made of her new position, she would still be conscious that every man on the *Sea Breeze* knew that she was now Jake Dominic's latest toy. She could not deny even to herself that the thought chafed unbearably at her pride.

When they joined Kahlid and Lola for lunch in the lounge, it was even more awkward for her. Both Kahlid and Lola accepted her presence as a guest instead of an employee with casual aplomb. Jane wished she could rival their composure instead of feeling this agony of shyness and discomfort. She was almost silent through the long lunch, though some of her nervousness was abated by the fact that the attending steward was almost a stranger. She had been worried that Simon would be chosen as her replacement, and she didn't feel she could quite cope with that at the moment.

Jake seemed to feel no awkwardness, and he treated her with a curious blend of mocking indulgence and possessiveness. He ignored her shyness and saw to it that she was included in the conversation by simply changing the subject immediately whenever Lola or Kahlid made reference to something outside her experience.

Jane was touched by the arrogant protectiveness of his attitude, but it only added to her embarassment when she met Lola's amused eyes across the table. The older woman said nothing until Jake and Ahmet Kahlid excused themselves to wander over to the bar. Lola then quietly invited Jane to go for a walk on deck with her.

They were no sooner beyond the door than Lola started to chuckle. "I haven't enjoyed anything so much in years," she drawled, her dark eyes dancing. "The sight of Jake Dominic in the role of shepherd to his lamb was absolutely priceless. That alone was worth the trip from Los Angeles."

Jane gave her a sheepish grin and said wryly, "He did rather overdo it, didn't he? He wasn't exactly tactful to you and Kahlid in his support of me."

"Jake can be the soul of diplomacy if it's called for," Lola said shrewdly. "In this case it wasn't necessary. He knew that Ahmet and I would get the picture."

"Lola, you've been very kind to me," Jane said hesitantly. "I just wanted—"

Lola waved her imperiously to silence. "For God's sake, don't apologize," she said cheerfully. "I would have had to be blind not to realize there was something in the air last night at dinner. Jake has never been known for his kindness to women, but he was completely unreasonable with you. Then, when he discovered Ahmet had gone to your cabin, he was like a madman."

"How did he know that?" Jane asked curiously. It had not occurred to her to question Jake's sudden appearance in her cabin in the tumultuous events that had followed.

"I imagine he'd given orders that he be told if Ahmet was seen going anywhere near your cabin," Lola replied with a shrug. "A steward came with a message for Jake shortly after Ahmet left the lounge. The ungrateful wretch didn't so much as say good night to me before he was off to the rescue."

"I'm sure he didn't *mean* to be rude, Lola."

Lola's lips twisted. "He didn't give a damn what I felt, my dear innocent. The only thing he could think about was you." Her eyes were thoughtful as she studied Jane objectively. "I believe that's all he's been able to think of for quite some time, from his reaction last night. I've never seen Jake with his emotions as well as his hormones involved. Perhaps I should be warning *him* about getting involved, and not you."

Jane knew a surge of hope that lightened the burden of anxiety and doubt she'd been feeling this morning. Was it possible that Jake was beginning to feel something for her besides desire and the urge for possession?

"Is that what you're doing? Warning me? If so, I'm afraid that you're a little late."

"I rather suspected I might be, but I thought I'd give it a try," Lola said, smiling gently. "Now we'd better return you to your lord and master before he comes looking for you."

They turned and retraced their steps to the lounge.

The rest of the day was spent in swimming, lounging, and desultory conversation. Jane found herself restless and dissatisfied despite the happiness she felt in Jake's presence. She was too used to hard work and constant activity to embrace the leisurely life with any degree of contentment. She was conscious of Jake's watchful eyes on her throughout the afternoon though he engaged her in only casual conversation in the presence of the others.

Thus she was only mildly surprised when he strolled casually over to the deck chair where she was lying watching the scarlet-and-pink glory of a sunset at sea. Kahlid and Lola had gone into the water for a last dip before going to their cabins to change for dinner, and she and Jake were alone for the first time since they had left their cabin that morning.

"Poor Saturday's child," Jake said mockingly as he dropped into the chair next to her. "Are you finding it hard to adjust to the lazy life?"

Jane was startled by his perceptiveness. Had her restlessness been so obvious? "I suppose I'll get used to it," Jane said doubtfully. She looked at him, noting the vibrant energy and impatience that seemed to charge his body even in repose. "How do you tolerate it?" she asked ruefully. "I would think the inactivity would drive you crazy."

"I admit that my boredom threshold is very low these days," Jake said. "I probably would have scrapped the cruise after two weeks if I hadn't had a certain troublesome redhead to divert me." He took her hand from the arm of the lounge and, bringing it to his lips, kissed the palm lingeringly.

Jane shivered as his tongue mischievously stroked the sensitive hollow, and he looked up swiftly in concern. He reached over her head to the white beach coat draped on the back of her chair and tossed it on her lap. "Put it on. It's starting to cool."

"That isn't my problem," Jane said demurely, her golden eyes dancing. "I'm beginning to feel definitely hot."

Dominic's dark eyes were amused. "Have you no inhibitions, woman?"

She shook her head. "Where you're concerned, they seem to have been left out of my makeup," she admitted serenely.

"Thank God," Jake said emphatically. His hand held hers tightly as his eyes slowly kindled with desire. "Damn it, why did I let you talk me into letting Lola stay? If she was gone, I could persuade Ahmet that he'd be better off roaming in greener pastures." His thumb sensually rubbed the pulse point at her wrist. "I warn you, redhead, you'd better enjoy the fresh air now," he said thickly. "Once I find a way of getting ridding of them, you may not get out of that cabin for a week."

Jane wondered if he could feel her pulse wildly accelerate beneath his thumb at these words. She rather imagined he could, by the teasing gleam of triumph that glittered in his eyes before she looked away.

"I think I'll go down to the cabin and change now," she said quickly, a flush turning her cheeks carnation pink. She stood up hurriedly and slipped on her beach coat.

Jake arched an eyebrow mockingly at her embarrassed flight. "Inhibitions, no. Shyness, definitely yes." He also got to his feet. "I think I'll join you. I feel the sudden urge for a long nap," he said, his lips twitching. "Do you suppose our guests would understand if we were a little late for dinner?"

"Jake!" she exclaimed, shocked, her eyes widening. He broke into irrepressible laughter, his face suddenly as young and mischievous as a boy's.

Jane was about to take him to task when she suddenly became aware of the jerky throb of a distant engine. She forgot what she was about to say when she saw a gold and white helicopter approaching from the east and progressing unmistakably in their direction.

Jake's laughing eyes followed her startled gaze, and he muttered an impatient imprecation as he caught sight of the helicopter. "What abominably bad timing," he said grimly. The deck was suddenly filled with scurrying, bustling seamen.

"What is happening?" Jane asked blankly, as the helicopter hovered directly overhead, the rotors causing a small tornado of wind and noise.

"A little gift for you," he replied casually. The side doors of the helicopter slid open, and Jane caught a brief glimpse of an olive-uniformed Mexican and then an enormous box and several smaller ones were lowered by net to the surface of the deck below.

"What on earth is it, a refrigerator?" she asked faintly, while the seaman briskly closed in on the net to remove the packages.

Lola Torres joined them, towel-drying her sleek wet head, before slipping on her scarlet beach coat. Jane had been vaguely aware of Lola's return to the deck at the approach of the helicopter. The other woman's face was frankly curious as she eyed the bundles that had now been freed from the net.

In answer to Lola's inquiring look, Jane said with a grin, "Jake's bought me a present. I haven't yet decided whether it's a refrigerator or a washing machine."

Lola examined one of the smaller packages lying on the deck. "I imagine Dior would be most outraged by your flippancy," she said dryly. She picked up another box. "Ditto Balenciaga."

"Jane's luggage was unfortunately left ashore in Miami," Jake put in smoothly "I took the liberty of ordering a replacement wardrobe for her."

Lola gave a little gurgle of laughter. "How simply divine!" Turning to Jane, she said gaily, "A 'present' like this deserves a party. We'll have to arrange something really splendid to celebrate, and I know just the nightclub in Cozumel to do it in!" She turned to Jake and ordered imperiously, "Tell them to hold dinner at least an hour. Jane will need that long just to open the packages."

An hour later, Jane sat dazed on the edge of the bed, staring in amazement at the boxes surrounding her. When she'd opened the huge crate, she had found that it contained two enormous steamer trunks filled with designer clothes of every description along with a shoe wardrobe to match every outfit. The loose packages were principally accessories and lingerie, with the exception of two of the larger boxes. One of these contained a full-length sable coat, and the other an ermine wrap. It was impossible not to be a trifle overwhelmed by the extravagance of Jake's gift. It was every woman's dream to receive a wardrobe of such classic elegance.

Yet how could she accept it and still maintain her self-respect and independence while living with Jake?

"Well, redhead, have you discovered anything that I've missed?" Jake Dominic stood in the open doorway, dressed for dinner in a white tropical jacket and black tie.

Jane didn't answer, and Jake sauntered forward. "You'll notice that I omitted any little baubles from Tiffany's. I prefer Van Cleef and Arpels," he said lazily. "I'll let you choose your own jewelry on our first trip over."

"I won't accept any jewelry, Jake," Jane said slowly, her cheeks pale. "I'll take the clothes because I realize that it might cause you some embarrassment if I didn't maintain a certain appearance, but I won't accept anything else from you."

"I suppose I should have expected something like this from you," Jake answered, his expression darkening ominously. "For your information, I didn't arrange for this wardrobe because I was ashamed of you. I did it because I want to give you a present, and women generally like this sort of thing." His voice was hard: "If you don't want them, throw them into the sea! Throw everything you own into the sea, I prefer you without a stitch anyway!"

Jane stared into his hard, ruthless face and saw something in the dark flickering eyes that she'd never seen before. Why, she had hurt him! She had grown used to thinking of Jake as the hard, cynical sophisticate, but now he had the defiant air of a young boy who had surrendered a treasure to a comrade only to have it scorned. Suddenly she wanted to take him in her arms and soothe away all of the hurts he had ever known. Because she knew that she must never show that she had seen that vulnerability, she dropped her eyes to the amber scarf in her lap.

When she raised them a moment later, her golden eyes were dancing with fun. "I like you better without a stitch, too," she told him, grinning. "I love the clothes, Jake. I'll be very happy to accept them." What was a little pride when it was balanced against the hurt she'd inflicted on the man she loved?

Dominic relaxed, his face regaining its cool insouciance. "Brat," he drawled. "You can't even accept a present without causing a ballyhoo." He strolled over to where she was sitting on the bed and dropped a light kiss on her forehead. "And the jewels?" he probed.

She wasn't willing to give him total victory. "We'll see," she replied evasively. Then looking up quickly, her eyes troubled, she said, "There's one thing that I can't accept, Jake." His face darkened swiftly, and she went on hurriedly, "It's the furs. I could never wear the skin of an animal that had been killed so that I could flaunt its beauty as some kind of status symbol. I just couldn't do it."

Jake's frown faded slowly, to be replaced by resignation. "No, I suppose you couldn't," he said wryly. "Knowing you, I should have realized that would be one of your *bête noires*."

Her face was serious. "I helped circulate a petition last year to try to get legislation passed against the killing of baby seals. Do you know how they kill baby seals?"

Jake placed a hand over her mouth. "No," he said firmly, "and I don't want to know. At least not before dinner." He removed his hand and tilted her head up to place a swift kiss on her mutinous mouth. "Suppose we send the furs back and use the money as a contribution to your seal fund."

Jane's face lit up with the power of a solar explosion. "Oh, Jake, could we?" she breathed excitedly. "They do need the money so desperately."

"If you promise to send the check in your name and not mine," Jake said, making a face. "I have no desire to be put on the hit list of every wildlife-preservation society in the country."

Jane jumped up and hugged him impulsively. "Jake, you're super. Absolutely super," she bubbled.

Jake flinched, but his arms went around her with swift possessiveness. "Please. Not that word. You make me feel like a rock star." His hands were moving in lazy circles on her lower back and buttocks beneath the beach coat, and Jane felt her knees turn to butter. She pressed closer to him and felt the swift exciting hardening of him against her. He drew a deep ragged breath and pushed her reluctantly away. "Damn Lola and her party," he said thickly. "I'd like nothing better than to tell the whole world to go to hell and spend the evening in bed." He turned away. "Get dressed, redhead. I'll see you in the lounge."

A short time later Jane gazed with breathless delight in the mirror. Why, she looked pretty. The chocolate chiffon cocktail-length gown was a masterpiece of artistic drapery that left one golden shoulder bare, hugging her high firm breasts and tiny waist lovingly before flaring to an extravagant fullness at the scalloped hem. The matching satin high-heeled sandals made her legs look deliciously alluring. Her hair curled in shimmering flames about her face in dramatic contrast to the rich darkness of her gown. Her topaz eyes and the tender pink of her mouth exerted a sensual witchery that Jane had never realized she possessed. The swift kindling in Jake's eyes as she walked into the lounge was as exhilarating and heady as champagne. She barely noticed Kahlid's flattering and verbose compliments as she basked in that ebony glow.

When Jake swung Jane down into the launch, she was surprised to see Marcus Benjamin and Simon Dominic at the wheel in the front of the boat. Impulsively Jane made a sudden movement toward them, and Jake gripped her arm swiftly.

"Over here, darling," he said caressingly, and shepherded her to a seat near the rear of the boat. He settled her so gallantly, so solicitously, that he might just as well have stamped her with a brand of ownership. She could feel her face burn in the darkness as Jake slipped a casual arm about her waist.

Jane had an idea that Jake's actions were as deliberate and primitive as those of a jungle cat staking out its boundaries. Her move toward Simon had been only an innocent impulse, principally aimed at reassuring herself that she still had Simon's respect and friendship despite her position in his cousin's life. Jake had seized on the excuse to establish his public claim with no regard to the embarrassment such an action would bring her. She couldn't help but feel a burning resentment at the inconsiderateness of his action. "I didn't know that Simon and Captain Benjamin were going with us," she said tightly.

"Lola insisted," Jake answered curtly. "She's never happier than when she's surrounded by men—a common feminine characteristic I've noticed."

Jane maintained a cool silence during the forty-minute ride to the pier at Cozumel. Her own reserve went unremarked in the wake of Lola's vivacious gaiety and Kahlid's equally good spirits. Jake seemed maddeningly undisturbed by Jane's disapproval and displayed a lazy good humor that was a barbed irritant to her rapidly deteriorating mood. Her gaze went frequently to the front of the launch, where Captain Benjamin and Simon conversed casually in low voices. Both men wore sparkling white uniforms that compared very favorably with Jake's and Kahlid's white tropical dinner jackets and dark pants, Jane thought idly.

Suddenly Jake's grasp around her waist tightened sharply, and his voice in her ear was a silken murmur. "I've always heard that women were fond of men in uniform," he said caustically. "Don't you think you're being a little obvious in your admiration?"

Jane raised her chin defiantly. "Perhaps I feel an affinity with them," she said with sweet sarcasm. "If you remember, I was wearing a uniform myself until today. There's a certain kindred spirit among us menials, you know."

Dominic's rapier glance was as black as his muttered imprecation, and he was grimly silent for the rest of the trip.

El Invernardero was a thoroughly enchanting nightclub located in the heart of Cozumel. It was a converted greenhouse constructed entirely of paneled glass, and a multitude of exotic plants and flowers bordered the interior walls in colorful profusion. The highly polished dance floor was encircled by the usual damask-covered tables, but on each was a charmingly arranged bouquet of fresh flowers.

Their party was shown to a large ringside table by an obsequious waiter. Jake pulled out a chair beside his own for Jane, but Lola had other ideas.

"Don't be selfish, Jake," she said, her dark eyes sparkling with mischief. "You can have Jane to yourself anytime." She gave Jane an imperious nudge that placed her across the table, between Kahlid and Simon. She herself slid into the seat next to Jake and smiled dazzlingly into his frowning face. "Now, isn't this delightful?"

"Delightful," Jake echoed grimly, his watchful gaze fixed on Kahlid as the sheikh helped Jane solicitously with her chiffon wrap.

For Jane, as the evening wore on, what had promised to be

an exciting and romantic evening with the man she loved rapidly deteriorated into a miserable debacle. Jake's mood progressed from testy to utterly foul. Separated by the width of the table, Jane was still conscious of the black looks she was receiving as she quietly spoke to Kahlid or Simon. What had she done now to deserve his lordship's displeasure? she wondered defiantly. She turned to Kahlid with a sigh of relief. Ahmet's attitude was beautifully uncomplicated. He cared not a whit for morals, blame, and responsibility as long as he was in the presence of an attractive woman and champagne was flowing. He saw to it that champagne continued to flow throughout the evening, and that Jane's glass was constantly filled to the brim.

As Jane's unhappiness grew, she was grateful for Kahlid's attention. Jake had not asked her to dance once in the hours they had been at the nightclub, though he'd danced frequently with Lola. To add to her misery, a depressingly gorgeous blonde with a face that had graced hundreds of magazine covers and wearing a gown with a neckline even more decolleté than Lola's had suddenly appeared at Jake's elbow. She'd been introduced to everyone at the table. Cindy Lockwood, a model from New York, had attached herself to Jake like a seductive limpet. He had danced with the model even more than he had with Lola, Jane noticed unhappily.

The explosive combination of Cindy Lockwood, her own unhappiness and resentment, and Kahlid's champagne sparked a wildness in Jane. She proceeded to ignore Jake entirely, dividing her attention between Kahlid and Simon with feverish gaiety. She didn't know how many times she changed partners in the next two hours as she whirled from Simon's arms to Kahlid's and back.

At one point she found herself dancing with a handsome Latin who held her much too close and murmured romantic Spanish nothings in her ear. She vaguely remembered gaily accepting his invitation to dance when the young man presented himself at their table. His name was Ramon de ... something or other, and she found that his arms were just as comforting as Kahlid's or Simon's if she couldn't be with Jake.

Then an authorative hand tapped the man on the shoulder, and she looked up to see a grim-faced Jake beside them. "My dance, I believe," he said crisply, placing his hand at Jane's waist and whisking her firmly into his own embrace.

Ramon frowned crossly, but after a glance at Jake's face, he turned sulkily away.

"Your Latin lover gives up easily," Jake said with a savage grin. "I'm disappointed. I was looking forward to rearranging those classic features."

Jane only half heard him as she nestled closer into his arms, everything forgotten but the blissful fact that she was in Jake's embrace.

"This is the first time we've danced together," she said dreamily as her arms slipped around his neck. "I did so want to dance with you, Jake." Her face clouded. "Then somehow everything was spoiled." She shook her head bewilderedly. It was all too complicated to think about now.

"You seemed to keep yourself well occupied," he said harshly as they moved languidly around the floor. "It was quite fascinating watching you try out your wiles on every man in the room. Did you enjoy yourself, Delilah?"

"No," she said simply, her cheek rubbing gently back and forth on his white linen shoulder. "I only wanted you." She looked up into his face with pleading eyes. "Take me home, Jake."

He looked down at her, his face expressionless except for the flickering flame in his dark eyes. "Champagne appears to make you quite amorous, my little sex kitten. By all means, let's go back to the yacht. After all, it's my privilege to end the evening with you, regardless of how many men you require to keep you contented." He stopped dancing in the middle of the room and turned away abruptly. Grasping her by the wrist, he strode through the dancers toward the front door of the nightclub.

"Where are we going?" Jane gasped, trying to keep pace with his long-legged stride.

"We're going back to the yacht, where else?" he replied mockingly. "You want to be alone with me, remember?"

A nagging uneasiness pierced the golden haze induced by the champagne, like the first rays of sunlight through the morning fog. "But we can't just run off and leave the others without saying a word."

They had reached the street now, and at Jake's imperious motion, the red-liveried doorman summoned a taxi with his piercing silver whistle.

"I don't see why not," Jake said coolly. "We'll send the launch back for them."

He bundled her into the taxi and climbed in after her with a curt order in Spanish to the cab driver.

Jane shivered as her bare shoulder touched the cold vinyl of the upholstery. "My wrap," she said vaguely, "I left my wrap at the table."

"Someone will bring it," Jake said indifferently. His arm slid around her, and he pulled her closer to the heat of his own vibrant body.

Jane rested her head in the curve of his shoulder. She was conscious even in the intimacy of the embrace that his hold was strangely impersonal, and the knowledge would have troubled her if she hadn't suddenly been overcome with drowsiness.

Her next recollection was of being lifted into the launch and wrapped in Jake's white dinner jacket, which smelled deliciously of starch and shaving lotion. Then, after another brief period of sleep, she was aware of being carried in Jake's arms and placed on the unmistakable softness of a bed.

Jane opened her eyes drowsily to see Jake straightening

slowly, his dark face shuttered. She looked around the master cabin of the *Sea Breeze* with a sigh of contentment. How strange that this luxurious suite had so quickly become home to her, she thought dreamily. Even the grotesque graffiti on the wall opposite the bed brought forth only an affectionate smile.

"I'm glad you're back with me, sleeping beauty," Jake said teasingly, "and in such a good mood, too."

She turned and smiled happily at him, admiring the tough masculine grace of the rippling muscles in his chest and shoulders as he stripped off the white dress shirt and threw it carelessly on the gray velvet chair across the room.

She came into his arms like a nail to a magnet when he sat down beside her on the bed. Her lips brushed his throat in a multitude of soft, yearning kisses.

His arms held her quietly. "Such a loving, passionate nature," he said coolly, pushing her away to look down at her with narrowed eyes. "I wonder how much of it is for me alone." His forefinger idly traced the full curve of her lower lip. "Would you fly just as eagerly into young Simon's arms, now that I've shown you the way?"

She looked up at him, her golden eyes clouded with bewilderment. "I don't understand."

"That was more than obvious tonight," he said softly as his hands left her shoulders and moved down her back to deftly unzip the chiffon gown. "But I have every intention of making sure that everything is quite clear to you by morning."

He unfastened the strapless bra and pushed it, with her dress, to her waist. His dark head bent slowly, and his lips and tongue lazily caressed the pink nipples that soon were blossoming into hardness. "Quite clear," he repeated thickly.

In the long hours that followed, Jane wondered at one point if she could survive the physical and mental torment that seemed to be tearing her apart. Jake Dominic, the passionate lover who had brought her to the peak of ultimate ecstasy with skill and tenderness and then shuddered in her arms with his own fierce pleasure, was not this Jake Dominic.

This man also had incredible sexual expertise, but he used it with cool, calculated control. Time after time he used hands and lips that seemed to possess a devilish power to raise her to feverish need. There was no part of her body that was not caressed and probed and then caressed again, until she felt that there was not an inch of her flesh that was not exquisitely and painfully sensitized to his touch. He would toy with her like a large cat, his hot black eyes gleaming with savage satisfaction, until she was almost sobbing with frustrated desire. Then he would grant her completion in a burst of ruthless driving passion that would leave her shuddering like an exhausted and bruised swimmer cast upon the shore by a tidal wave.

Over and over the ritual of arousal and savage assuagement were repeated, until the silent tears were running down Jane's cheeks. Bewildered, she looked up at him as he crouched over her, his face a dark mask of brooding determination.

"Why?" she gasped desperately, her head moving back and forth on the pillow in an agony of response. "For God's sake, why, Jake?"

"Because you're mine," he said hoarsely as he drove forward between her thighs with explosive passion. "You may not be mine forever, but for now you belong to me." His words came out in a tormented rhythm caused by the force of his thrusting movements. "I won't have you smiling at, or touching, or even looking at, any other man. Do you understand?"

"Jake," she whimpered, striving desperately to marshal the words to explain, to entreat, but she was so lost in the heated haze of urgency that she could not speak.

"No one else, ever," he repeated relentlessly. "Do you understand?"

"Yes!" she almost screamed, digging her nails into his shoulders as the scarlet haze exploded into a thousand fiery tendrils of sensation.

It was almost dawn when Jake reached for her yet again, and suddenly her sobs no longer could be restrained. Jane found herself shaking and trembling in a reaction to the sensual assault that had no relation to love or affection.

Dominic froze, his body still for a long moment. Then, with a swift movement, he released her and reached out to flip on the bedside lamp. Turning once again to look at her, he started to curse violently as his eyes noted and comprehended his work.

Jane's eyes were dazed and shadowed with shock and misery, her lips swollen and bruised with the force of his lovemaking. She instinctively shrank away from him as his face darkened with a forbidding frown.

"God!" he said huskily, passing a trembling hand before his eyes, but not before she had seen the sick torment in their depths.

He reached out and plunged the room once more into darkness and pulled the sheet over both of them, tucking the cover carefully around her as if she were a small child. "Stop trembling," he growled, "I'm not going to touch you again."

He turned and lay on his back, his arms beneath his head. Even in the dimness of the darkened room Jane could see that his face was set and still as he stared sightlessly into the darkness. Her sobs were now reduced to mere ragged breaths. She was as bewildered by this reaction as she had been by his earlier savagery.

"I'll arrange to have Marc take you to the airport this morning," he said quietly.

She stared at him in alarm. Surely she hadn't made him this angry—not to the point of sending her away from him.

"Why?" she asked shakily, wiping her eyes on a corner of the sheet.

"Why!" he exclaimed bitterly. "My God, I've just used you

as if you were a prostitute. I wanted to hurt you, and I set out to do it in the most humiliating and painful way possible." He laughed harshly. "My damned ego was damaged, so I decided that I'd prove that I could make you beg for it. And you ask me why?"

Jane tried desperately to think. Her mind was a muddle of emotions and half-formed ideas. There was only one clear thought shining through the morass. She must not be forced to leave Jake. This was perhaps the most significant and potentially dangerous moment in their relationship to date. If she couldn't relieve him of his guilt and bitterness, he might well send her away, and she could survive anything but that.

"It wasn't entirely your fault," she said tentatively. "I behaved badly at the nightclub."

"You're damn right you did," he said grimly, his voice hard. "If I hadn't known what was driving you, I would have strangled you. Instead, I took a revenge that I thought I could enjoy."

He muttered a savage curse and fumbled in the drawer of the bedside table. Soon she heard the strike of a match, and the small flame briefly highlighted the planes of his face as he lit a cigarette. Then the flare was gone and there was only the orange-red tip of the cigarette glowing in the darkness.

"Did you think that I didn't know what was bothering you?" he asked bitterly. "I told you that you'd be running for the hills as soon as you got a taste of what living with me would be like." The tip of the cigarette flared bright as he inhaled deeply. "I admit that I didn't expect it to be after only one day."

"I'm not the one running away, Jake," Jane pointed out quietly. "You're the one who's rejecting me."

Jane could feel the sudden stillness of his body as he lay beside her. Then his voice came out of the darkness with savage deliberateness. "What are you, some kind of masochist? Do you like the idea of being abused? For God's sake, I can't even promise that it won't happen again." He turned to look at her, the glow of the cigarette casting a shadowy aureole over his features.

His lips were twisted cynically, and his eyes held all the weariness of the world. "I'm a selfish bastard, and I have the devil's own temper. I've made it a habit to get whatever I've wanted for my entire adult life. It's not likely that I'll reform at this late date."

"I haven't asked you to reform," Jane whispered. "I fell in love with the man you are, not some idealistic dream of what you could be."

"Very tolerant of you," he said mockingly. "I imagine you'd be less generous if I suddenly decided to savage you again."

A ghost of a smile curved her lips. "It would take a little getting used to, but who knows, I might get to like it," she said lightly. "Isn't forceful and repeated seduction by the man she loves supposed to be one of a woman's favorite fantasies?"

There was a blank silence, and then Jake chuckled. "You're really incredible, redhead." He shook his head in wonder. "Any minute now, you'll be thanking me for broadening your sexual experience and granting one of your fondest desires."

"I don't think I'd go that far," she said serenely. "But it's not as if I didn't enjoy some of it, Jake. It would have been physically impossible for me not to."

There was another long silence before Jake turned and crushed his cigarette in the ashtray on the table. He turned back to her and said abruptly. "I want to hold you." There was an oddly formal hesitancy in his voice. "Will you sleep in my arms, redhead?"

Jane felt an odd melting in the region of her heart. Would she ever understand this strange, complex man? Part devil, part little boy, and all tough, brilliant male.

"I'd like that," she answered softly.

She was immediately brought into the warm haven of his embrace, and her head nestled in the hollow of his shoulder. He held her as carefully and sexlessly as if she were a child.

"You won't send me away?" she asked sleepily, her body suddenly languid and exhausted in the warm security of his arms.

Jake kissed the top of her head. "No," he said thickly. "God, no!"

"Good," she said contentedly, rubbing her cheek like a kitten against the hard bone of his shoulder.

"Go to sleep, redhead." Jake spoke softly, his eyes alert in his dark face.

Jane relaxed obediently and was almost asleep when he spoke again, the words sounding oddly solemn and stiff, as if the sentiments were foreign to him, as indeed they were. "Jane," he whispered, his hand gently stroking her red curls, "I'm sorry."

She smiled drowsily and went peacefully to sleep.

---

ten

WHEN JANE OPENED HER EYES, BRIGHT SUN-
shine was streaming into the cabin and she was alone in the
king-sized bed. A startled look at the digital clock on the bedside
table told her why. It was almost one o'clock, and lunch was always served at one-thirty. Why hadn't Jake awakened her, for
God's sake?

She jumped out of bed and headed for the shower, stopping
only to pull a yellow terry-cloth robe from the closet. She stepped
beneath the shower's steaming spray and closed the frosted cubicle door behind her. The pounding of the water on the tiles was
so loud that she didn't hear Jake calling her name until he spoke
right outside the shower stall. She immediately turned off the
water and called back, "I didn't hear you, Jake. I'll be right out."

"No, stay where you are," Dominic said huskily. "I had to
muster all my willpower to get out of bed and leave you, and I
don't have much left. You walk out of that shower naked into my
arms and it will all have been for nothing. I just came down to
give you a message."

Jane's breath caught in her throat, and she could feel an electric jolt of desire at his words. There was something erotic about
standing here naked and vulnerable and watching that virile

shadow on the other side of the frosted door and knowing that he wanted her. "Message?" she asked, moistening her lips.

"Lola asked me to tell you that she'd like to say goodbye," Jake explained tersely. "She and Kahlid are taking the four o'clock plane to Las Vegas to do some gambling. She's in her cabin packing."

"Jake, you didn't—" Jane started to ask indignantly.

"No, I didn't suggest that they leave," Jake interrupted firmly. "Not that I wasn't planning on it, but Lola saved me the trouble. A very clever woman, our Lola."

After last night it was no more than Jane expected. "I'll go and see her as soon as I get out of the shower," she said softly.

"You do that." Jake's voice was oddly absent, and she could see the shadow move a step closer and his arm reach slowly for the handle of the door. Then the hand dropped and she heard a low curse and the shadow was suddenly gone.

It took her a moment to steady her breathing and the trembling of her hand before she could reach out and turn on the spray again. She let the soothing water pour over her and wash away all tension and soreness. Besides a slight stiffness and languidness, she felt no other signs of Jake's punishing lovemaking of last night. Her mind shied away instinctively from the thought of those savage passionate hours, but she firmly and deliberately focused her memory on the events both before and after.

She knew she must face and accept what had happened if she was to keep her love for Jake free from fear. She had been afraid for a little while last night, she admitted to herself. Yet she had known that Jake would never really hurt her physically, despite the cold anger that had prompted his actions. What had really frightened her was the terrifying sense of helplessness that she had experienced as she lay in his arms. He had manipulated her inexperienced body as if she were a puppet on a string, using his sexual expertise to dominate her until she'd felt as though she were being absorbed, her own spirit and personality melting away under the force of his greater experience.

She reached absently for the shampoo in the holder and began to shampoo her hair. It had really not been Jake's dominance she had feared, so much as her own inadequacy. Her hands paused in their scrubbing motion as the realization came home to her. Jane reviewed the evening with lightning swiftness. Yes, that was the underlying factor that had started all the tension and misery and almost caused Jake to send her away.

Even last night, when she had felt more glamorous than at any other time in her life, she'd been conscious of her pitiful inexperience in comparison to Jake's usual companions. She had felt miserably unsure when she had faced the sexy sophistication of blond Cindy Lockwood. Even Lola had been the focus of her subconscious envy.

Though Jake had seemed pleased with her responsiveness in bed and she couldn't help but be aware that he had derived an almost insatiable pleasure from their lovemaking, she was still besieged with doubts. Was it only the novelty of their association that held him enthralled? Would he become bored once the newness of their relationship wore off? She had none of the tricks and skills of the experienced women who had graced his bed. The only advantage she might have over possible rivals was her boundless love.

So the problem was clear. In order to retain Jake's interest and her own confidence, she must become more knowledgeable. The pertinent question was, how was she going to get that expertise? She doubted that such knowledge could be obtained from books, though she was sure thousands had been written on the subject. She had no desire to experiment with any other man. Her forehead creased as she considered one possibility after another. Then her face cleared when the solution occurred to her. Of course—it was so simple. Why hadn't she thought of it before?

Jane hurriedly rinsed the shampoo from her hair and stepped out of the shower, drying herself swiftly and slipping on the yellow terry-cloth robe and matching scuffs. There wouldn't be time to dry her hair, she decided. She wrapped a towel turban fashion around her head and swiftly left the steaming bathroom.

In a matter of seconds she had crossed the short distance from the master suite to Lola Torres's cabin at the end of the corridor. She paused and drew a deep breath. Then, squaring her chin determinedly, she knocked firmly on the door.

Jake Dominic scowled darkly as he checked his wristwatch impatiently. Lola was already fifteen minutes late. Kahlid had finished saying his lengthy and cheerful farewells and was waiting in the launch with the seaman who was to take them to the pier at Cozumel. Lola's luggage had been collected and placed in the launch some thirty minutes ago, yet there was still no sign of her.

Then at last she came into view, and Jake relaxed fractionally as the Latin woman strode hurriedly toward him. An amused smile curved her lips when she saw the impatient frown on Dominic's face.

"Don't scowl at me, *querido*," she said lightly. "I would have been on time if it hadn't been for your *chère amie*. We have been having a little discussion."

"Why couldn't you have written her a letter?" Jake asked caustically. "Women have no sense of time!"

"You're such a chauvinist, Jake," Lola drawled. "Don't you know better than to resort to generalizations? I knew very well I was running late, but I felt that under the circumstances even you would rather I took the time to straighten out Jane's thinking."

Jake's eyes narrowed with sudden alertness. "And how did you accomplish that?" he asked slowly. "I was under the impression that Jane was a remarkably clear-thinking individual."

"In most areas I couldn't agree with you more," she said lightly, "but it seems the child has taken it into her head that she needs a tutor."

"Go on," Jake urged.

"Jane came to see me and asked my help," Lola reported, trying to keep a straight face, her eyes dancing. "It appears that she feels that she must improve her performance, and she elected to come to a professional."

"Performance?" Jake frowned, puzzled.

Lola's lips were quirking as she supplied a highly obscene Anglo-Saxon noun.

"Oh, my God!" Jake groaned, and ran his hand through his hair.

Lola chuckled irrepressibly. "If only you could have seen her, Jake, sitting there like a prim and proper schoolgirl and trying to persuade me to give her lessons in the oldest profession in the world." Her dark eyes were gleaming with laughter. "All the while she was trying to phrase it with great delicacy, so as not to hurt my feelings! She was absolutely delicious."

"Very amusing," Jake said ironically, his expression far from amused. "I'm sure you were a great help to her."

"Oh, she had nothing so short term in mind," Lola said, her eyes twinkling. "She suggested that once you start your next picture, she'll join me in Los Angeles for some in-depth study. She seemed to think that, with work and concentration, it shouldn't take more than a few weeks."

"The hell she will!" Jake exploded, his face grim.

"I thought that would be your reaction," Lola said tranquilly. "I tried to explain that to our little friend."

"You take her up on that insanity and I'll take great pleasure in breaking that lovely neck of yours, Lola."

"Don't be absurd, Jake," Lola replied, affronted. "I like the child. I'm not about to get her into trouble with you," she added with a demure smile. "I even told her that you must be more than satisfied with her to reject my expert services. It's up to you to build up her confidence if you want her to forget this foolishness."

"Thanks for the advice," he remarked caustically. "I'll handle Jane in my own way, if you don't mind."

She shrugged. "I was only trying to help," she said, turning away to descend the ladder into the waiting launch. She turned back abruptly, her face serious. "The only reason I mentioned our conversation at all was that I don't think I convinced Jane. She seems remarkably single-minded."

"Remarkably," Dominic agreed dryly, his taut face echoing his exasperation. "I haven't the least doubt that she'll carry it through with all the subtlety of a steamroller. I'll have to watch her like a hawk or she'll be opportuning the madams of every bawdy house in L.A. for lessons."

Lola's dark eyes were gleaming. "There is another way, you know."

He looked at her inquiringly.

"You could tell her that you love her," she said.

Dominic's body stiffened as if she had struck him. His face was abruptly wiped free of expression, the dark eyes shuttered. "Could I?" he asked tonelessly. "It isn't usually your custom to meddle, Lola. I wouldn't advise you to start now." He gestured toward the waiting launch. "You have a plane to catch."

The music was as soft and sensuous as an intimate caress. They moved slowly around the dance floor, their arms wound around each other in the dimness of the crowded room. In the past few weeks Jane had noticed that in the wee hours of the morning the band at El Invernardero invariably discarded the lively disco numbers and played only mellow romantic tunes suited to lovers. This met with her complete approval, and she nestled closer to Jake with a sigh of contentment.

Jake looked down at her, his eyebrow cocked inquiringly. "Tired?" he asked softly. "Would you like to go back to the yacht?"

She shook her head. "Not yet," she said dreamily. "I love to dance with you. Let's stay a little longer."

His arms tightened around her, but his voice was light. "Oh, for the energy of the young," he said, pulling a face. "Do you realize that this is the third time this week we've been here until four in the morning? You're going to make a physical wreck out of me, woman."

She looked up swiftly, her smile impudent. "You look in remarkably good shape to me in spite of our nights of dissipation," she said teasingly. "I didn't hear you complain when I suggested we come tonight."

Jake always looked devastatingly attractive in evening clothes, she thought. Tonight he was wearing the more conventional black tuxedo, and he looked as dangerous and virile as a stalking panther.

His eyes were flickering with mischief. "I wasn't anticipating a night on the tiles so much as my reward at the end of it," he murmured outrageously. "Gratitude always makes you more passionate."

They were both aware that this was patently untrue. He had only to touch her and Jane responded with all the combustibility of a brushfire in a windstorm. She looked back in wonderment on the casual, almost sexless woman she had been before Jake Dominic. He had thrown open all the doors of physical pleasure for her curious and delighted exploration, and she was as addicted to his lovemaking now as if it were the fruit of the poppy.

She suddenly grinned in amusement at the memory of the scene in Jake's cabin after Lola and Kahlid had left the *Sea Breeze*. He had been as outraged as a Victorian husband. While she had sat wide-eyed and cowed by his strong reaction to what had seemed to her a reasonable and simple solution to her problem, he had strode back and forth, wildly condemning her "hare-brained" ideas with fluent and precise obscenities. He had then turned to face her with a forbidding frown.

"So help me God, I don't want to catch you so much as asking a question of *anyone*, other than the time of day! If you want to learn any little erotic variations, come to me, damn it. I believe I have sufficient experience to satisfy you!" He had stormed out of the cabin, slamming the door with explosive force behind him.

Jake's claim had proved a massive understatement, and she hadn't needed to ask. She found the variations mentioned no less exciting than the more conventional sex play, and she had embraced them with her usual enthusiasm. To her delight, Jake's passion for her had exhibited no signs of waning since Lola's departure, and in fact his hunger seemed to increase rather than diminish. At times he took her with an almost insatiable desperation that was as heady as strong wine and left her glowing with love and the faint stirrings of hope. He had never said he loved her even in the throes of the strongest passion, nor had he ever indicated that their relationship was anything more than temporary. But surely she must mean something to him if she could stir him to such heights of pleasure.

There were other moments, too, that promised much. Golden moments of shared laughter and more serious conversation, when the exploration of mind and emotion was as precious as that of their bodies. The man who spoke of his work with such single-minded passion was as far removed from the mocking playboy as night was from day. It was no wonder he was so successful at his craft, she had thought at one point, watching the eager flare in the usually jaded eyes. She felt a twinge of jealousy as she realized that here was a much more formidable rival than Cindy Lockwood or Lola Torres, and then dismissed the thought immediately as unworthy. She loved the total Jake Dominic, and the composite was created as much from the brilliance and drive of this other aspect of his personality as it was from the devilish charm and mercurial temperament that made her totally his.

Jane recognized that this was a halcyon period of jewel-bright days to be treasured and stored up against the time when she would no longer be Jake Dominic's sole interest. If she was to keep whatever affection he felt for her, she must release him to this other mistress. Her thoughts had been turning more and more frequently to that time when Jake would return to work, and she knew that she must be prepared to substitute another interest when it happened.

"You're very thoughtful, redhead," Dominic commented teasingly. "I think you're half asleep."

"I was wondering if I should begin thinking about a career," she said seriously.

The smile faded from Dominic's face as he pulled her possessively closer. "Plenty of time for that," he said impatiently. "It seems that I must redouble my efforts to keep you interested."

"No, really, Jake," she persisted. "Don't you think—"

"I think I want another glass of champagne," he interrupted abruptly, stopping in the middle of the dance floor. "And I think you're being much too serious." Keeping his arm firmly around her waist, he guided her swiftly among the dancers to their table.

As he pulled her chair out for her, he said lightly. "Did I tell you that you're completely captivating in that gown? You remind me of the cotton candy that I used to buy at the circus." He bent closer and bit gently on her left earlobe. "Pink, fluffy, and utterly delicious," he murmured.

The chiffon gown in question was a pink so pale it was almost white, and she knew it looked exceptionally good with her fiery curls. Since Jake had already commented on this curious phenomenon earlier in the evening, she recognized the compliment as an obvious ploy to distract her. She shot Jake an exasperated glance when he slipped into his own chair. She knew better than to try to pursue a subject when Jake wanted it dropped. He could be maddeningly elusive at times. She would just have to broach the subject when he was more amenable.

"I always thought of cotton candy as cloying, sticky-sweet stuff surrounding an empty cone," she said caustically, still annoyed with him.

He raised his glass to his lips, his black eyes amused. "No one could ever accuse you of being cloying and sticky-sweet, redhead," he said, his lips twitching. "And I assure you, I intend to make every effort to make sure that the cone is not empty tonight."

"Jake!" she said, color flooding her face. Would she never be able to control these damn blushes? she thought. Jake took a satanic delight in making these outrageous remarks just to see her light up like a Christmas tree. She looked across the table at his mocking devil's face and met his dark laughing eyes.

Suddenly Jake's face was no longer laughing, and his eyes were flickering with a different emotion entirely. Her breath caught as the world narrowed down to contain just the two of them, in the now-familiar pattern.

He put down his glass and said thickly, "It's time to go home, redhead."

She nodded dreamily and rose to her feet, gathering up her wispy pink wrap and the tiny brocade evening bag as he carelessly threw some bills on the table. She turned to precede him, and was startled by a sudden blinding light.

"Hold it, Mr. Dominic, just one more, please."

There was a muttered curse from behind her, and suddenly she was pushed aside. The plump, fortyish photographer in a gray business suit had time only to shout a frantic protest before Jake wrested the camera from him and dashed it to the floor with all his strength.

"My God, you've broken it!" the man yelped furiously. "That's an eight-hundred-dollar camera!"

"Send me the bill," Jake said icily. Grasping Jane by the elbow, he pushed her through the whispering, staring crowd, his face white and strained with anger.

He was grimly silent on the taxi ride to the pier, his demeanor forbidding. It was only as the launch was nearing the *Sea Breeze* that Jane ventured to ask a question.

"Who was he?"

"Probably one of the freelance reporters who hang around resort towns and peddle their garbage to any rag that will print it," Dominic spat out.

"Was it wise to have gotten so violent?" she asked quietly. "Surely that will only make him more determined."

"Would you rather have your face spread over some scandal sheet as Jake Dominic's latest playmate?" he asked savagely.

"It wouldn't be pleasant," she admitted. "But it would be better than having you sued for damages."

"Forget it!" he ordered harshly. "I'll buy the bastard a new camera, and that will be the end of it."

Jane obediently subsided, but it was obvious that Jake did not forget the incident. He was moody and uncommunicative during the rest of the trip back to the yacht, and they had no sooner reached their cabin than he brought her forcefully into his arms.

There was a curious tinge of urgency in the way he stripped off the pink gown and tumbled her onto the bed. Tonight there were no preliminaries as he took her with a driving force that contained a bewildering element of desperation. There was an excitement all its own in his raw thrusting need, and when his strong body lay shuddering helplessly in her arms in an agony of release, she knew a satisfaction that was as primal as that of the first woman.

eleven

THE PICTURE WAS REALLY QUITE GOOD OF both of them, Jane thought absently as she spread the newspaper out on her lap. It was a Spanish-language newspaper, but the message would have been clear if it had been written in Swahili. Jake's possessive hand on her arm and the expression of dreamy desire on her own face told their own story. Lord, had she really been so transparent? She might just as well have worn a placard around her neck.

She looked up into Jake's face with wary eyes. It had been four days since the incident at El Invernardero, and Jake had been more moody and restless than she had ever seen him. Jane had been sunbathing in a deck chair when she had seen Jake striding toward her, his face a mask of rage, the newspaper clutched in his hand.

He had thrown the newspaper in her lap with a curt, "Look at this. That damn reporter sent it with the bill for his camera."

"He must have managed to salvage the film from the wreckage," she replied calmly. Her eyes ran swiftly over the accompanying story, and she breathed a sigh of relief. "It's mostly speculation and innuendo. I was afraid they might have stumbled on how I came to be on board the *Sea Breeze*." She made a wry face. "That would have been quite a scoop. Can't you see the headline: 'From bomb to bed!'"

"Jane!" Jake said savagely. "Don't you realize what this means? The A.P. is bound to pick up the story—it's too juicy to miss. In two days this picture will be in every newspaper in the world."

"I rather thought it would," Jane said quietly, folding the paper and dropping it distastefully to the deck. Her face was a little paler, but she smiled valiantly. "Well, it had to come sometime."

"Is that all you've got to say?" Jake asked hoarsely, his fists clenched in an effort to control the emotions that were running through him like high tide. He stooped to pick up the newspaper and waved it at her. "You'll be the topic of conversation and smutty little remarks over breakfast tables everywhere, and all you have to say is, 'It had to come sometime.'" He crumpled the newspaper into a ball and threw it over the rail into the sea.

"Aren't you overreacting?" she asked. "There have been dozens of other stories printed about you before with one woman or another and you obviously haven't given a damn."

Jake flinched, his face looking strangely vulnerable for a brief moment before it hardened into an unreadable mask. "Perhaps I'm getting tired of having my affairs publicized to give the masses a cheap thrill."

Jane gave him a skeptical glance. She knew that Jake couldn't care less what people thought of him. This violent reaction was completely out of character.

"It's not as if I hadn't known what to expect. I didn't walk into our relationship with my eyes closed. I knew that if I became your mistress, a certain amount of notoriety was inevitable. I accepted and came to terms with that fact a long time ago."

"How very adult and civilized of you," Jake snapped, his nostrils flaring. "Well, you're not going to have to test your sophistication in this instance. It's all over."

Jane sat bolt upright, shock and sudden panic causing all color to ebb from her face. "I don't understand."

He turned and gazed unseeingly out at the sparkling sea, his hands tightly gripping the rail. His profile was frighteningly implacable. "I'm sending you home," he said ruthlessly. "I should have done it weeks ago."

"That's crazy," Jane protested dazedly, standing up and automatically slipping on her white beach coat. "Just because some little man takes our picture and manages to get it into a newspaper? It doesn't make sense."

"I'm finding the game not worth it," Jake replied harshly, still not looking at her. "You're just not worth the bother, Jane."

She felt as if he had driven his fist into her stomach, so blinding was the pain. "I don't believe you," she said numbly.

"Why not? You knew it had to end sometime. You've lasted longer than most."

She stepped closer and reached out to put a hand on his arm, instinctively trying to penetrate his hard facade by touch where words were proving useless. He flinched away from her as if she had burned him. "Don't touch me," he said through his teeth. "God, how I hate a woman who doesn't exit gracefully when shown the door." He turned to face her, his face granite-hard. "Do I have to say it? You're beginning to bore me. I don't want you."

Each word was like a whiplash on her raw emotions. Jane shook her head as if to clear it, feeling as though she were caught up in a nightmare. "It doesn't make sense," she repeated blankly. "Not like this. Not so suddenly."

He shrugged, his gaze once more on the horizon. "I want you on the plane this evening. You'd better pack."

As she stared at him, the certainty grew stronger that her instincts were correct. This reversal was entirely too abrupt to be genuine. He couldn't have made love to her with such wild passion only this morning and then decided that she bored him now.

"You're lying to me," she said huskily. "I don't know why you're acting this way; perhaps it's because of that photo in the paper. But I do know that you're not tired of me."

She could see his hands tighten on the rail until his knuckles whitened, but when he turned to look at her there was nothing but scorn in his dark eyes. "My God, have you no pride? I've just told you that I don't want you anymore."

Her eyes were shining with tears as she wrapped her arms around herself to still the trembling that threatened to destroy her fragile control. "Yes, I have pride," she said simply. "If there ever comes a time when I believe that you don't want me, you won't have any trouble getting rid of me." She took a deep, shaky breath. "Until that time, not all the scorn and rejection in the world are going to keep me from fighting for you. You can force me to leave the *Sea Breeze*. You can even force me to get on that plane, but as soon as I get off the plane, I'll be on my way to the Coast. If you won't let me into your private life, I'll work and I'll study and I'll make myself so invaluable to you that you won't stand a chance of shutting me out of your work."

The tears were running freely down her cheeks now. "Damn you, Jake! Can't you see that what we've got is worth fighting for?"

For a moment there was a flicker of agony in the depths of Jake's eyes, and then he turned away. "I'll send someone down for your bags in an hour," he said without expression. "Be ready!"

"The hell I will!" For the first time Jane realized that it was really happening, that no amount of persuasion was going to shake that iron determination. She was going to be sent away.

She whirled and walked blindly from him, so lost in a haze of pain and misery that she cannoned into Marc Benjamin. With a broken apology, her face a strained mask of agony, she pushed past him, stumbling dazedly in the direction of their cabin.

Benjamin gave a soundless whistle as he gazed after the vulnerable little figure, before he turned back and approached Jake Dominic with a grim smile on his face. He waved the folded newspaper in his hand. "I guess I don't have to ask if you saw this little item," he said, tossing the paper casually on the deck chair. "I see Jane is pretty upset by it all."

Jake turned to face him, and Benjamin inhaled sharply. Jake's face wore the expression of a man suffering the tortures of hell. The dark eyes, which usually mirrored only mockery and cynicism, were wells of pain and torment.

"Have the launch prepared, Marc," Jake said dully, "and arrange to have someone go down and pick up her luggage in about an hour. Jane will be taking the evening plane to Miami."

Benjamin's face reflected his surprise. "I never thought she'd be that upset by this trash," he said thoughtfully, gesturing contemptuously at the newspaper on the deck chair. "I'd have bet it would have taken considerably more than that to make her leave you."

Jake's mirthless laugh was like the snarl of an animal in pain. "Oh, God, yes," he said bitterly. "If I'd let her, the little fool would have stayed and let the world smear her with the same filth that they attribute to me." His fist struck the rail. "Damn it, she even said she expected it!"

"She's a sensible girl in spite of all that idealism," Benjamin said slowly. "Jane always knew what she'd be facing, but she didn't care."

"Well, I care, damn it!" Jake said passionately. "I'm not going to stand by and let them hurt her. God, do you realize what a year as my mistress could do to a girl like Jane?"

"She wouldn't change," Benjamin said confidently. "The girl is stronger than you think." He looked at Jake's face speculatively, and the torment he saw there prompted him to make a suggestion. "Of course, there's another way that you could protect her if you chose. You could marry her."

Jake looked at him scornfully. "Do you think that I haven't thought of that?" he asked bitterly. "Don't you think that I'd like to reach out and grab what I want, just as I have all my life?" He shook his head, his lips thinned in a line of pain. "My God, I'm seventeen years older than Jane and a hundred years older in experience. Even a dissipated bastard like me knows that she deserves better than that." He smiled bitterly. "I've done her enough damage by making her my mistress." His hand struck the rail again. "But damn it, I wanted something for myself!"

"You love her," Benjamin stated, with wonder coloring his voice.

"Of course I love her," he said impatiently. "Who the hell wouldn't?" His eyes narrowed to brooding darkness. "She's like a vase of the finest crystal, absolutely clear, with none of the distortions and impurities that plague most of the rest of us."

Benjamin's lips quirked. Dominic was not only completely crazy about Jane, he was waxing lyrical. "I can't see the problem," he said. "Lord knows, the girl is mad enough about you."

"She'll get over it," Jake said harshly. "You know as well as I do that she needs someone as fresh and wholesome as herself for a lasting relationship."

"I'm not at all sure of that," Benjamin said slowly, "I rather think that Jane might need someone older and more experienced to take care of her."

There was a brief flash of hope in Jake's face before he shook his head. "Thanks for trying, Marc," he said morosely, "but I know that I'm right about this. She'll be better off without me."

"I'm not giving you some bull to give you an excuse for doing what you want to do," Benjamin said bluntly, his voice rough with impatience. "For God's sake, shake off that martyr's air and look at the girl's record to date. She's gotten herself mixed up with a bunch of crackpots and almost blown up the *Sea Breeze*. She nearly got herself raped or killed at that cockfight in San Miguel. She came within an inch of being devoured by a shark. To top it all off, she's become the mistress of one of the most notorious men in the Western world. Now, this has all taken place in the space of less than two months. Heaven knows what other trouble she's gotten herself into that I'm not aware of." He smiled grimly. "Personally, I don't know any wholesome young man on the face of the earth who could have handled all of that!"

There was a stunned expression on Jake's face. "You're absolutely right, you don't have the complete list," he breathed softly. "God, Jane's a walking time bomb!"

Coolly Benjamin regarded the dawning uncertainty on Jake's face. "You should also consider that a girl like Jane isn't going to recover from any love affair very easily. She's not the type to bounce back and locate this paragon you've mentally linked her with any time soon. It's far more likely that she would look around for some kind of work to take her mind off you." Benjamin's eyes narrowed thoughtfully. "Yes, she'll probably revert to her original plan."

Jake looked up swiftly, alarmed. "What original plan?" he demanded.

"The Peace Corps," Benjamin answered blandly.

"The Peace Corps?" Dominic echoed blankly.

Benjamin nodded. "She confided to Simon that she'd been considering joining for some time. She seemed to think that they'd take her like a shot. She'd be a godsend to them, with all the languages she knows."

Jake's dark eyes were dazed. "Jane in the Peace Corps!"

Benjamin smiled gently. "It's more than likely they would assign her to the Middle East. Kahlid was very impressed with her command of Arabic, wasn't he?"

Burying his face in his hands, Jake groaned. "Good Lord, even the United States Government couldn't make that big a mistake!"

"They'd snap her up, and you know it," Benjamin said

bluntly. "Young, intelligent, charismatic, *and* fluent in several languages."

"No!" Dominic almost shouted, his hands dropping from his face as he whirled to confront Benjamin. His dark eyes were wild and blazing. "In six months' time she'd be in a Middle East bordello or decorating the post outside some head hunter's hut." He ran his hand through his crisp dark hair. "Do you think that I'm going to spend the rest of my life worried about what kind of trouble she's going to get herself into next? No, by God!" He turned and strode furiously away, every line of his tall muscular body breathing fiery determination.

Benjamin gazed after him with a curiously enigmatic smile on his face before turning and strolling back to the bridge.

Jane was still in the peach bikini and the white terry beach coat when Dominic stalked into the cabin. She looked up from throwing things haphazardly into an overnight case on the bed, her cheeks wet with tears. "My hour isn't up yet, but I'm almost finished packing," she said defiantly. She closed and snapped the lock on the suitcase. "This is all I'm taking. You can give all the rest of those Diors and St. Laurents and whatevers to someone else."

"I suppose camouflage denims and khaki jungle shorts would be more practical for what you have in mind," he spat out, glaring at her furiously. "Well, you can just forget about it. Do you hear me? I'm not going to stand for it!"

She looked at him, puzzlement mixed with indignation in her golden eyes. It wasn't enough that the man was destroying her life, rejecting her, tearing her emotions to shreds. Now he had the gall to march in here and shout at her!

"I have no idea what you're talking about," she said belligerently. "I wish you'd just get out of here so that I can finish dressing. I wouldn't want to be late for that plane you're so anxious for me to catch."

"To hell with the plane!" he muttered. "You're coming with me, damn it!" He grabbed her by the wrist and pulled her, struggling and protesting, from the cabin. He strode purposefully down the corridor and up on the deck.

"Jake, let me go!" Jane gasped furiously. "I'm tired of being carried and pulled and pushed around like some sort of glorified piece of luggage. Will you please treat me with a little dignity?"

"Be quiet," Jake said between his teeth, pushing her ahead of him into the lounge. "You're insane if you think I'm going to let you make my life hell on earth. You can just forget about that bloody Peace Corps. You're going to marry me, damn it!"

Jane shook her head dazedly. Peace Corps? Then his last statement sank in.

"Marry you?" she whispered, her eyes widening so that they were enormous in her pale face.

"Marc has full authority to marry us on the high seas," Dominic said, striding toward the phone at the bar and dragging her along behind him. "I'm giving orders for us to get underway. In thirty minutes we'll be out of Mexican territorial waters." He reached for the phone, but she suddenly put her hand on the receiver and stopped him.

"Why, Jake?" Jane asked quietly, her face pale and tense. "Why do you want to marry me?"

"Why do you think?" he replied bitterly. "Because I'm a selfish bastard who can't even do one decent, unselfish thing to ensure your well-being. I don't give a tinker's damn anymore if I'll be good for you or not. I'm grabbing you and holding on, come hell or high water."

Jane felt hope flower in her, its golden petals tentatively opening to a beautiful, unbelievable possibility. "But why?" she persisted, her eyes shining like jewels in her heart-shaped face.

"Because I love you!" he snapped, his face grim. "Because I don't care what's right or wrong, or even what's best for you, as long as I can keep you with me for the rest of our lives."

Jane closed her eyes and took a deep breath. It seemed too gloriously, wonderfully perfect to be real. When she opened her eyes, Jake caught his breath at the glowing, starlike radiance in their depths.

She moved forward slowly, her arms slipping around his waist and her cheek nestling against his chest with a touching childishness. "You're not joking?" she asked huskily. "You really love me?"

Jake's arms went around her, and his voice was suspiciously ragged when he said, "I love you, redhead." One hand left her waist to press her head closer to his heart. "And may God help you, because I can't let you go." His hand tangled in the silky curls and tilted back her head to look down into her glowing face. His features were curiously vulnerable, and the dark eyes held an uncertainty that was foreign to them. "Last chance, sweetheart," he said thickly. "Tell me no now, and I might be able to muster enough willpower to stop myself. Once you're committed, I'll be the only man in your bed and in your life for the rest of your days."

"I told you once that I'd never say no to you," Jane replied firmly. "That hasn't changed, and it never will."

Dominic lowered his head and covered her lips in a kiss that was as solemn and binding as an exchange of wedding bands. When their lips parted, they were both shaking and clinging to each other like two lost children.

"You don't have to marry me, you know," Jane whispered. "All I ever wanted was for you to love me. I can understand if you'd rather not be tied down."

Jake kissed her lightly on the tip of her nose. "You may not mind living in sin, you shameless woman, but I find my reactions are verging on the primitive and the puritanical where you're concerned," he said, only half joking. "I want to tie you to me with every bond I can lay my hands on." His crooked eyebrow arched mockingly. "I hope you're not having second thoughts, because I've shed my last scruples. You're mine now—forever."

"You don't think that you may regret it later?" Jane persisted, a worried frown on her face. "I don't think I could stand it if it didn't last."

Jake's face was unusually solemn as he said, "You're my first love, my last love, and my only love, Jane. I didn't even think the emotion existed, until you walked into my life and turned it upside down. I'll never be able to do without you now."

He released her hair and reached over her head to pick up the phone receiver. Holding her close with one arm, he gave the order to get underway.

After he hung up the receiver, he slid his other arm around her and lowered his head to kiss her with a honeyed sweetness. Pushing aside the beach coat, his hand slid inside to caress the bare satin flesh of her waist and back. Then suddenly his lips were no longer sweet but hot and hungry, parting her lips with his tongue to probe and explore with suffocating passion. Jane instinctively arched to meet his body's arousal, and his hand wandered down to cup her rounded buttocks in his palm and bring her up against his thrusting loins.

Suddenly she pressed both hands against his chest and pushed, wriggling out of his arms at the same time. "No," she gasped breathlessly, her face flushed and her golden eyes clouded with passion. "I want to talk."

Surprise at her sudden rejection was mirrored in Jake's eyes, and his face reflected the temptation to ignore her verbal plea and attend only to the message that was still emanating from her aroused body. Then his own body relaxed slightly, though his eyes were glazed and hungry as they fixed on her full, swollen breasts in the tiny peach bikini.

"There's distinct evidence that you have ambivalent emotions on that score," he teased. "But I'll let you get away with it for now, redhead. Talk!"

Jane closed the beach coat hurriedly and backed away from him, her cheeks pink. She walked over to the brown leather couch in the center of the room and sat down. Tucking her feet under her, she looked over the back of it at Jake, still standing by the bar. She patted the seat beside her invitingly, and he obediently strolled over and dropped down beside her.

His dark eyes were dancing with mischief as he said softly, "Now you really know that I love you, sweetheart. I've never stopped at a moment like that in my entire life."

"How long have you loved me?" she asked eagerly, folding her hands before her on her lap. An expression of warm tenderness lit up Jake's cynical face; it would have astounded those who thought they knew him.

"Forever," he said simply.

"No, really, Jake," she demanded.

"I suppose that I knew for sure that night in San Miguel when I ran out the door and saw you buried under that pile of men," he said, grinning. "I didn't know whether to beat you or pick you up and run away with you. I'd never felt like that before, and it scared the hell out of me." He reached out to rub a finger along the sensitive curve of her lower lip. "Before that I was aware that you affected me more than any person I'd ever met—man, woman, or child—but I wouldn't admit that it was anything more than liking and a strange sense of protectiveness."

"Why didn't you tell me?" Jane asked indignantly. "I told you the very day that I found out."

Jake shook his head, his mouth twisting. "For the first time in my life I decided to be noble. I knew damn well I didn't have any right to you. I'm seventeen years older and have forgotten more wickedness and deviltry than you could ever imagine. I knew I should have sent you away the minute I realized what had happened to me, but I convinced myself that I could keep you near me and at least have these two months for myself."

His fingers slid down to rest in the hollow of her throat, stroking the sensitive pulse point sensuously. "Then everything blew up in my face. Between that damn shark and Kahlid, my good intentions flew out the window. I couldn't keep my hands off you. I rationalized my taking you to bed by telling myself that the only way to discourage you was to show you that it was a losing proposition." His lips tightened grimly. "That was a bunch of bull. I was wild for you. I wanted you more than I'd ever wanted anything in my life, and I reached out and took what I wanted."

Jane smiled with gentle irony. "It's no wonder you felt guilty. Anyone could see how unwilling I was."

Dominic's eyes became even warmer as he said, "God, you're sweet. I can't get enough of you." He shook his head ruefully. "I'd never had anyone respond to me with such open passion and affection. You had me as dizzy as a schoolboy."

His fingers moved from the hollow of her throat to slip under the beach coat and clasp one bare shoulder. He bent to lay his lips on the soft hollow that his fingers had just abandoned. Jane could feel her pulse leap as his tongue gently, leisurely probed the silky hollow.

"Yet you would have sent me away," she charged breathlessly, her hand moving irresistibly to caress the crispness of his thick dark hair.

"I'm a masochist," he said mockingly as his lips moved to nibble enticingly at her earlobe. "I knew it would kill me, but I couldn't stand seeing you smeared over every yellow-journalism sheet in the world. I'd taken enough from you without that."

"Thank God you overcame your scruples," Jane said huskily. "I had visions of having to pursue you on every film set in Hollywood."

He gave her ear a sharp nip that was far from loverlike. "And

I had visions of having to rescue you from everything from white slavers to man-eating lions. I don't want to hear anything more about this passion for the Peace Corps."

Jane wondered dreamily what on earth he was talking about, but as his other hand reached under the beach coat to lightly cup one eager young breast, she promptly lost track of the conversation. What had he said? Oh, yes, something about the Peace Corps. "They do very good work," she said vaguely, while Jake's hands located the catch of the bikini top and released it.

"So do I," he said mischievously, and proceeded to prove his claim with deft erotic hands and tongue. "And I'm never letting you venture any farther from me than the next room," he said hoarsely after several wild, heated moments.

Suddenly he was rising and crossing the lounge with swift steps. He shot the lock on the door, and as he turned back to her, he was already starting to unbutton his cream shirt. He unbuttoned the rest while he walked slowly back to the couch. She stared at him with yearning and fascination as he stripped off the shirt and threw it on the chair.

There was a teasing smile on Jake's face despite the leaping flame in his dark eyes. He gently pushed the beach coat off Jane's shoulders, and let it drop in a white pool on the brown leather couch.

"It just occurred to me that we're missing a once-in-a-lifetime opportunity," he said thickly as his thumbs stroked her nipples teasingly. "In another hour, we'll be just another old, stodgy married couple. This is our last chance to taste the forbidden fruits of living in sin. I don't think we can afford to pass it up, do you?"

Her arms slid around his neck and slowly pulled him down into her eager embrace. "It would be quite a shocking waste," she agreed happily. "I think you're absolutely right."

"You're damn right I am, redhead," Jake said with mocking arrogance, and bore her back on the couch.

about the author

IRIS JOHANSEN, who has more than twenty-seven million copies of her books in print, has won many awards for her achievements in writing. The bestselling author of *Stalemate, Killer Dreams, Blind Alley, Firestorm, Fatal Tide, Dead Aim, Body of Lies,* and many other novels, she lives near Atlanta, Georgia, where she is currently at work on a new novel.